Michael Carson was born in Merseyside and after an education at Catholic schools, he became a novice in a religious order. Deciding the religious life was not for him, he went to university, then taught English as a foreign language in the Middle East, Brunei and Africa. He is the author of the Benson trilogy (*Sucking Sherbet Lemons*, *Stripping Penguins Bare* and *Yanking Up the Yo-Yo*), *Friends and Infidels*, *Coming Up Roses*, *Serving Suggestions* (short stories) and *Demolishing Babel*. He now lives in Wales.

Also by Michael Carson

COMING UP ROSES
SUCKING SHERBET LEMONS
STRIPPING PENGUINS BARE
YANKING UP THE YO-YO
DEMOLISHING BABEL

and published by Black Swan

The Knight
of the
Flaming Heart

Michael Carson

BLACK SWAN

THE KNIGHT OF THE FLAMING HEART
A BLACK SWAN BOOK : 0 552 99628 9

Originally published in Great Britain by Doubleday,
a division of Transworld Publishers Ltd

PRINTING HISTORY
Doubleday edition published 1995
Black Swan edition published 1996

Set in Galliard by Kestrel Data, Exeter, Devon.

Black Swan Books are published by Transworld Publishers Ltd,
61–63 Uxbridge Road, London W5 5SA,
in Australia by Transworld Publishers (Australia) Pty Ltd,
15–25 Helles Avenue, Moorebank, NSW 2170,
and in New Zealand by Transworld Publishers (NZ) Ltd,
3 William Pickering Drive, Albany, Auckland.

Reproduced, printed and bound in Great Britain by
Cox & Wyman Ltd, Reading, Berks.

For Christopher and Felicity Martin

*We are candles that only have meaning if we are burning,
for only then do we serve our purpose of being light. Free us
from the cowardly prudence that makes us avoid sacrifice
and look only for security. Losing one's life should not be
accompanied by pompous or dramatic gestures. Life is to be
given simply, without fanfare, like a waterfall, like a mother
nursing her child, like the humble sweat of the sower of seed.*

LUIS ESPINAL, SJ

O what has made that sudden noise?
What on the threshold stands?
It never crossed the sea because
John Bull and the sea are friends:
But this is not the old sea
Nor this the old seashore.
What gave that roar of mockery,
That roar in the sea's roar?
The ghost of Roger Casement
Is beating on the door.

W. B. YEATS

1

'CHRIST!'

Declan stood up, his whey-white back turned to her. He picked up the fallout of his clothes from the floor and, carrying them like they were everything he owned in the world, retreated to the bathroom.

Boma stared down at the swelling below her breasts. She pulled the duvet up. It exhaled Declan's smell. Boma waited for Declan to reappear; to say he was happy about the baby.

A month later, lost now, Declan having bombed the life out of her, she was standing at the crossroads. Fumes reached her, wafted on the wind from a brewery near by. But she did not think to identify the smell. A red-haired man on a bike passed her, ringing his bell. The hair and the sound brought Boma back. She stared at him. The man looked around, wobbling. Boma turned away, looking up the Tralee street. She wondered which way to go.

Two women were watching Boma through a rain-drenched shop-window.

'I am black but beautiful, O ye daughters of Jerusalem!' said Mary Coogan, the owner of the shop.

'She's black, all right. Black as your hat, I'll grant you,' replied the customer, Mrs Carty of the Padre Pio Guest House. 'Beautiful I have doubts about. What's the damage?'

'But she's not really what you'd call black,' continued Mary Coogan. She turned away from the window. Her eye caught the Medical Missionary box with the picture of smiling African children on the front. 'Now those lads,' she said, nodding to the box, 'are what you'd call black. That woman is more coffee with a good splash of milk.' She turned back to look at the woman waiting on the adjacent corner. Boma hitched her duffle-bag across her shoulder.

'The poor soul looks tired out,' said Mrs Carty.

'She's six months gone, I'd say,' said Mary Coogan. 'What sort of age do you think she is?'

'Thirty-five?' Mrs Carty opened her purse. 'She's a tiny wee slip of a thing.'

'Will that be all, so?'

Mrs Carty nodded – wondering why transactions in Mary Coogan's shop always made her feel so guilty – and continued gazing at the brown woman.

'That's four-sixty,' said Mary Coogan. She buttoned open her greasy till.

Mrs Carty fished for the money, thinking that her purchases didn't feel like four-pounds-sixty-pence worth. 'What's she doing in Tralee, do you think?'

Mary Coogan shrugged. The shop bell sounded and she looked towards it with a hopeful, automatic smile.

When Mrs Carty came out into the busy street she glanced over to the corner where the brown woman had been standing, but she was no longer there.

*   *   *

10

Half an hour later the driver of a beer lorry on its way out of Tralee to make deliveries to the bars of Ardfert and Ballyheige saw the woman at the side of the road. He wondered whether to stop. A peculiar fright took hold of him, similar to what happened when a wasp suddenly entered the cabin of the lorry through an open window. In a split second he was remembering the rap music that had pumped into him through the flimsy floor of a tower block during his exile in Hackney a few years before; the ensuing scenes. And these memories warred with missionary boxes, Mary Robinson, and his notion of the decent thing. His right foot dithered between brake and accelerator.

The driver stopped and watched the woman through his wing mirror as she strolled along the road towards him. He drummed his fingers on the steering-wheel, eyed the slowed-down traffic behind through the wing mirror. The woman was taking her own sweet time.

Boma opened the door and looked up at him. He noticed her turquoise-blue eyes, the choppy matt ocean of hair pulled harshly back, the swelling belly. He smiled. 'I'm going as far as Ballyheige. Is that any good to you?'

The woman did not say anything, hardly even nodded. She slid a grubby duffle-bag into the cab ahead of her, then climbed up into the passenger seat. The driver reached across to clear a *Daily Mirror* and a Tayto bag from it, then tried to catch another glimpse of the woman's startling eyes.

'Ballyheige will do for you?' he asked, signalling, looking anxiously around for a break in the traffic.

'I want the coast,' Boma said, watching the little statuette of St Christopher dancing on the dashboard in time to the engine.

'Well, you'll find a whole lot of coast at Ballyheige, if that's what you're after. I don't know why you would want the seaside just now, though. It's the wrong season altogether. A holiday, is it?'

She nodded. The driver's question had not penetrated. She watched the short suburbs of Tralee, then green fields, passing by.

Though it was usually the custom of the driver to lift people, he expected some sort of conversation from those he picked up. That was the point of it really; what the lifted had to offer. The lifted stood in for the broken radio or the lonely heart.

'Are you coming from Tralee?' he asked.

'I am,' she said.

'Where are you from?'

'Dublin,' Boma replied.

'Are you on holiday in Ireland?'

'I was born in Dublin.'

He did not know how to proceed. Remembering the few phrases the woman had spoken since entering his cab, he saw that her speech had not struck him as being in the least foreign. It was just that he could not reconcile the woman's colour with Irishness.

'Were you now?' he asked jocularly, hoping for more information.

But the driver, and many another who had lifted Boma in the week since she had embarked on her journey to the coast, was to be disappointed. Boma was past chat.

The driver's first delivery had been at Ardfert. There he told the woman to wait for him. He jumped down from the lorry, unloaded his padded sack, laid it down on the pavement and started heaving the barrels of beer onto it.

The metallic sound irritated her, set her teeth on edge. It reminded her of the screaming trains that ran close up against the room by Euston Station she had shared with Declan.

She opened the door for air, but found that she was getting out of the cab. The cold west wind needled her. She took a few paces – she thought to stretch her legs – but she was walking away from the lorry.

The driver saw, shouted to her not to wander off because he wouldn't be long. She heard him, but did not turn. He paused at his work, scratched his head at the retreating figure. Later, his work in Ardfert completed, he would tell the publican about it. Then he forgot her until the strange happenings in Ardfert brought the silent brown woman he had lifted back to his mind, and he wondered what had become of her.

The peninsulas of Kerry in the south-west of Ireland point like arthritic fingers into the Atlantic, as if trying to grasp something invisible.

The most northerly, mountainous and – to those without prejudice – beautiful of these peninsulas, the Dingle, is best seen on a clear day from the flat lands across the Bay of Tralee to the north. There a walk south along the seven-mile beach from Ballyheige to Fenit reveals the outline of the Dingle Peninsula with the band of mountains stretching along its length, peaking at Mount Brandon far to the west. And from a small cove cut into the hem of his mountain, it is said that St Brandon sailed away in a small boat to discover that new world to the west. New to St Brandon, anyway.

As the walker progresses north to south along the straight dune-backed beach, he may well – good luck accompanying him – be blessed with the light show that weather in this part of the world can lay on: a concoction of cloud, rain-shadow, water-sparkle, sun-ray, rainbow and mists. Minute by minute it all changes, in the time it takes to reach down for a camera or consult a guidebook.

Some three miles inland stands the village of Ardfert, the village through which a brown woman from Dublin, a woman called Boma Hephernan, is wandering, though she does not know its name; nor, if she knew, would she care. This village, unremarkable in many ways, has a population of a couple of thousand, six bars, remains from what Cromwell's men gnawed: an ancient cathedral and a Franciscan monastery, and what sticks in old people's memories of the Crosby family seat: a fine building by all accounts with three hundred and sixty-five windows. All gone now – the only visible reminder a gatehouse abutting the main street which, like the grand family that used to pass through it, also seems to be on the way out.

Out of one of Ardfert's less-frequented shops steps its owner, Mrs Brid McCarthy. The sign above the shop proclaims 'McCarthy's Groceries and B & B'. Brid is on her way to early-evening mass, and from there she will set out for a short walk through fuchsia- and broom-sided lanes to McKenna's Fort. She carries a shopping bag in her right hand which contains her old missal, a purse, a chamois-leather – damp and in polythene – and a spray bottle of Dettox. The Dettox is experimental, a new product left, more in hope than expectation, by a rep.

During the Prayers for the Dead she remembers her husband, Matt, her recently deceased sister, Mary, and her good-as-dead son, Tim, blown away to Britain and not seen or heard from much recently. And, even though the silence allowed by the priest has not been sufficient for her to pray for all the Departed she wants to remember, she stays in the cocoon of her private reverie to pray for the man for whom the chamois-leather and Dettox is carried. And, pricking the fragile bubble of her concentration, she worries whether the Dettox will work as well as the Vim she usually brings.

Brid McCarthy does not waste time with the gossiping congregation after mass. She gets enough of that over the counter. Too much gossip and too little coin. Neighbours do not seem to think it strange that they can use her small shop as a place for swapping news while they hoof off to Quinnsworth's in Tralee for their real shopping. Now, a few of them watch her; the women cradling prayer books, the men dragging on postponed cigarettes. They know where she is going, because they have either followed her in the past or given children a small sum of money to spy and report back.

Along the small road to Fenit walks Brid McCarthy; then she turns right towards the sea by a rusty signpost that has lost its sign. A car coming contrary to Brid passes her. The driver salutes her by raising a finger from the steering-wheel. This half-hearted greeting is not sufficient to merit a return from Brid McCarthy. She passes the house of Pat McDonough, who has lived with his dad for the last thirty years, and now cares for the ailing old man. His door is open, a wheelbarrow is sitting in the centre of the small patch of grass at the front. But there is no sign of Pat. She would like to have seen Pat, wonders whether she should worry: Pat was not in his usual place at mass.

For half a mile she walks at a steady two miles an hour. Then she turns right into a field, makes her way along the edge, careful to avoid the sprouting crop, towards a rectangle of raised ground on which small sycamores, blackthorns and nettles grow wild.

This is McKenna's Fort.

She negotiates the memory of moat, then the earth-covered ramparts of this ancient place, ramparts that can still be discerned through the rags of undergrowth. She is careful, mindful of her eighty-five years. Everyone says she looks and acts like a woman a decade or two younger – she feels the truth of it – but she knows what a knife-edge she treads, that falling might mean not getting up again or, if she gets up, never being quite the same.

Puffed, she pauses and looks around. A skylark on this early spring day rises from the flat land, warbling its heart out. She follows it until she cannot distinguish it from the spots before her eyes. Then a few more steps and Brid has reached the object of her pilgrimage.

A four-sided memorial made of cemented stones, modest enough for a man a bit bigger than the usual to band with a hug, is topped by a pyramid of polished black stone. Its highest point comes up as far as Brid's chest. It is, she notes with routine disapproval, stained with bird droppings. Then, submerging the skylark, rooks start a ruckus from the circus sky as if admitting their fault, glorying in it. She aims angry looks in their direction and wishes she had a gun to pop them into a respectful silence. Then, remembering, Brid reaches into her bag, takes out the chamois, unwraps it from the polythene and aims the Dettox at the besmirched memorial with the trigger finger of her right hand.

She rubs at the side with the Irish inscription, the German, the English, and finally the sign that tells the visitor that the memorial was erected by the Gaelic League of nearby Tralee to commemorate the arrest of Roger Casement at this place on Good Friday, 1916. And as she rubs away the week's grime, she says out loud, 'My dear, poor man, forgive us. We didn't know. Pray for us! Rest in peace!'

She repeats the prayer until the black pyramid is pristine. The Dettox does the job. If the rep is to be believed you could now eat off the monument if you had a mind. She offers up a prayer for the safety of the rep on the rough roads of Connacht, his next destination. Then she straightens up and looks around her, folding the chamois, reaching for the polythene.

A heavy bank of cloud is heading over from the south-west. It has already obscured the slipping sun. She knows that a heavy burst of rain will soak her in ten, fifteen minutes, at the most; but she cannot immediately draw away from the place. The young nettles, she notes with disapproval, will soon take over for the summer, sting her and try to bar her path. A side of her thinks it's a pity that McKenna's Fort isn't kept in better condition, but the owner is of the opinion that it should be left exactly as it has always been. And it cannot be denied that this small rathe of wild undergrowth and a dozen sycamores stands up for itself in an area of wind-bowed hedge, bog, dune and flat, treeless field.

She remembers a man – one of many – who came to stay at her b & b to investigate. He had accompanied Brid to the place and pronounced himself well pleased. It was, he said, reminiscent of so many of the locations in the dear dead man's life. McKenna's Fort, he said, suited Sir Roger down to the ground: it was jungle and privacy for the enactment of hidden acts of cruelty, indecency or meditation. It should be left.

Brid takes her leave, walks carefully back to the road. She thinks she can make it as far as Pat's house before the rain comes. In this she is mistaken and, before arriving at his open front door, large drops of rain have polka-dotted her coat and hat.

'Can I come inside, Pat?'

'Is it you, Brid?' Pat calls down and she hears a toilet flushing above the sound of pattering rain on the porch-slates.

'It is. I'm after going to the fort.'

'Come on in straight. The kettle's on the hob.'

Brid enters the cottage, saluting the living and the dead as she does so by crossing herself with water in a saucer drawn from a nearby holy well.

From within a cell of undergrowth Boma had watched Brid McCarthy scrubbing down the monument. She felt no curiosity as to what the old woman was doing. She had become used to observing people off about their own business. She watched things happen like a tourist drifting down a river, past the teeming bank, occasionally catching an eye, but always aware that her own real life was in some elsewhere.

For as long as she could remember, Boma had known that she was looking out. Her deep-set blue eyes saw everything surrounded by an intrusive halo of brow and cheek-bone; and this dark circle around her vision kept reminding her that she was peeping out from the strange den of self, out to a people who would not be granted admission unless they had the password. And the password Boma herself did not know.

The nuns at the orphanage had tried to come in. She repulsed them with sulks and scratchy skirmishes as if waging a guerrilla war in defence of a homeland under alien invasion. There had been hearing and reasoning tests that sought to explain her unusual detachment – everything had been shown to be normal. Later, foster families said the same, wondered if she was all there, as did the Hephernans, who had adopted Boma when she was five, done their level best for her until she was fourteen, scratched their heads and consulted priests and social workers and telephone help-lines about her until she was sixteen, then breathed a guilty sigh of relief when she had upped and exited.

Boma had been upset to find, on strolling through Ardfert's one main street, that the village was, in fact, not on the coast. At once, glancing to neither right nor left, she had started walking out of the village, on the small road marked 'Fenit'.

She had noticed the turning with the signpost from which the sign to McKenna's Fort had rusted off. She followed the small road to meet the dark clouds heading towards her. Quite why she had decided to take the hundred-yard detour in order to reach McKenna's Fort she did not know. Perhaps she was tired, wanted to rest in a quiet place, though tiredness had been so long her companion that she was easy with it and had dropped the name. Or perhaps it was the trees and undergrowth growing upon the up-thrust Celtic remains, lost and foreign as herself, in the middle of flat fields.

She watched Brid McCarthy from her hiding-place and did not wonder.

The rain that caught Brid on her way back to Ardfert fell on Boma Hephernan also. She walked uncaring through it and back onto the road. Then she continued on, towards the ocean.

Drenched and shivering now, she passed Rahoneen Castle – known locally as Collins' Castle – then caught sight of the dunes as the rain stopped, as suddenly as it had started, and sunshine lifted the place with light. She walked on across boggy ground. Stagnant pools eyed the sky. Wind eddied the surface of the pools like fleeing shoals of silver fish. A notice said 'POISON LAND', though it looked fit enough. A blight of bungalows skulked behind the high dunes ahead.

She passed another monument, a large obelisk approached by steps and surrounded by a wall of water-stained concrete, but she was not curious about it and did not veer from her path to investigate. She wanted a sight of the ocean; to achieve her destination.

This proved more difficult than it looked. Farmers had erected single-strand fences across the dunes and cattle grazed on the rough grass. When she tried to climb over one of the easy-looking wires a small electric shock went through her – aided and abetted by the wetness of her – making her cry out. Boma looked to right and left. There were only curious pool-eyed heifers to hear her. She followed the wire until it met a sandy track.

Between the dunes she walked, following the level track. She came to an empty car-park. Cans, bottles, a knotted condom lay on the ground. Ahead of her a steep sand hill. She stopped. The baby kicked. She called out to stop it, to forget it, and the sound came back to her like the crying of the gulls, which all about flew like lamenting souls on the wind. With difficulty she climbed the hill. Each step of the steep ascent caused her to drift half a step back. Sand filled her shoes. She took them off and left them there, continued on in her stockings.

Then she wondered where the duffle-bag had gone. It did not matter. She came to the top of the hill and the monstrous crying wind hit her and tugged at her hair. The ocean lay below her now, parallel bars of spuming white, spitting and raging, chased by the wind, breaking up on the beach.

Boma tumbled down the hill onto the pebble-backing of the beach. She hopped across them and then, making it to the sand, stopped to look at the object of her quest.

She thought of why she had come to the west. There was perfectly serviceable sea around Dublin – or Holyhead for that matter – sea that would do the job she wanted of it well enough. But that sea was called Irish. She did not want the Irish Sea. The Irish Sea was too small. It looked the wrong way, back the way she had come. She wanted the Atlantic Ocean. *Ocean*, she said out loud. She repeated the word as the breakers crashed against the sand. The word copied their sound. She looked out at it, mesmerized. *Ocean*, she repeated. Every drop of this ocean – the word went on and on, putting *sea* in its little place – was connected to places far to the north, the west, the south. This stretch of water without seam lapped warm African shores, great American cities, islands of ice and tropical heat.

When bored in classrooms, she had taken out her atlas and traced her finger around the world, using the blue as her free-wheeling road. The blue took her everywhere. If she could walk on water she could reach Rio, Bombay, New York. Of course, that was impossible but if you took the palm of your hand and splashed the surface of the ocean the splash would reverberate around the world just as surely as, she had heard, radio waves resounded off into the universe for ever and ever.

Boma took off her coat and dropped it behind her.

In an hour the sun would set and it would be over. Declan would be satisfied. Blown away and dispersed by his gift-wrapped bomb or by the ocean's bombast, it all amounted to the same thing. This way, that, or the other, he would be satisfied; all would be satisfied, even if too far away to hear the slap she made upon the water.

Boma walked into the ocean. The black-and-white waves, like angry nuns catching her smoking in cloakrooms, made to boss and bully her back to the sand. *What about the baby? Destroy yourself, if you want – you've always been a self-destructive devil, so you have – but think of the child!* She swore at them. She fought them and a row gave way.

But the next one pushed her back to the sighing sand. *No forgiveness for a baby-killer, Boma! Better a bomber in a good cause than a baby-killer!* Angry now, feeling a panic kick inside her, she launched herself again into the ocean, determined to make her way through it to the deep; to lie inside it as her loved-hated, half-baked baby lay in her warm fluids. She knew she was cold, but that only made her the more determined to put an end to sensation. It was right that it should be cold. Hearts, beds, even gifts – especially gifts – all had been cold. More than cold. Compared to them, the ocean – the *ocean* – was as warm as a hug.

'Will you do us a favour, Boma?'
  'I don't mind, Declan. What sort of favour?'
  'Will you take a present to a friend for me? Did I tell you about Joe? He's homeless – hopeless too – and . . . I shouldn't be telling you this . . . there go the jewels from my heavenly crown! I help him a bit, anyhow, you know. Today's his birthday. We're snowed under at the workshop. Would you take him a present?'
  'Where?'
  'You'll laugh!'
  'I won't laugh.'
  'Hungerford Bridge. He begs there. You can't miss him. He's a wee white dog with him. I said I'd be there at twelve . . .'
  'OK.'

OK. Boma laughed. Water entered her mouth and she was coughing. OK. But the neatly packed parcel, the sweetness of it and what it revealed about Declan, had turned out to be a bomb that, but for the thieving beggar, would have blown her to bits. She could still, in the middle of the water, feel the red, wet wind of it ripping away her clothes, planting despair, setting her on the road to the ocean.

OK, so. Coming to a calm place, up to her neck in water, Boma pushed herself off the sandy bottom, exhaled and slapped the surface of the ocean with the face, the reflection of which had always made her think she was a stranger on the cold earth.

'Will you get off of me? Haven't you the whole ocean to sport in without landing on top of me?'
  Boma heard the voice, felt the hands gripping her and, thinking

that this was drowning, struggled to bury herself deeper in the mattress of the ocean.

But something would not let her. A wave stuffed her mouth and, coughing, she was reeling round out of control, like clothes in a washer. But the grip on her shoulder: was that the devil coming to take possession of her soul; the last great explosion of imagination before death pulled down the shutter? She struggled against the sound, making her own, trying to inhale water to stopper herself.

'You haven't a chance. I'm a good deal stronger than you are, my girl. We mustn't fight, you and I. For aren't we on the same team? No, that isn't cricket. Not cricket at all.'

Another wave took her and she felt, through coughing and retching and great kicks in her stomach, those hands. Then the collision of her body against sandy bottom told her that she was failing. She opened her eyes and saw long white fingers. She was so close to them that she could not quite bring them into focus, so close that they confused, confounded, her circle of vision. The fingers moved to caress her eyes, to smooth back eyebrows, her ocean-saturated, sopping-wet hair. They pinched her nose.

'Such a pretty girl! But a silly one, too. Amn't I right? Who's a silly girl? You're a silly girl. That's what you are. As if there weren't enough trouble in the world without you adding to it. I'd have expected better from you, so I would. This isn't like you at all. This sort of nonsense isn't in your blood, young lady!'

Boma closed her eyes, felt the hands turning her, pulling her out of range of the hungriest wave, away from the water-drops that connected her to the other world. Back to Ireland.

'Upsy-daisy, Boma! Up you come! That's enough swimming for you for one day. Time for you to get warm. That's right. Just lie there a while and get your breath back. Then I'll walk you to a nice warm place.'

Boma panted, coughed and wept. She was aware of the man's warm hands caressing her forehead; then, back, combing his fingers through her wet hair. She looked up at his bearded face, panicked for a moment at the sight of it. Perhaps she had drowned and this was The Lord or The Devil. The pointed beard could betoken either. Was he going to lift her up or cast her downwards into the pit of her worst expectations?

'Don't you worry your head, my dear,' said the man. 'You're on terra firma.' He looked around, upwards. Then his face lit up and he pointed. 'See up there! A skylark. Will you listen to him? His voice could quicken the dead! Unstopper your pretty little ears and give him a good listen like he deserves! Did you ever . . . ? Listen!'

And Boma, returning to full consciousness, conscious too of a strange feeling akin to joy, listened to the bird of spring rising above the grey dunes.

When Brid McCarthy heard the knock, she was confused for a moment. The knock had broken into her train of thought. Standing in front of the Stanley boiler in her parlour, she had been working out the procedure that would lead her to the easy chair with a cup of tea on her lap. Her wet hat, like a curled black cat, sat on one of the hob-covers, and she had been about to put her coat on the hanging-dryer. A kettle needed filling.

But the knock sent all that flying. It came from the side door – the summer door she called it, the one for guests. Normally, visitors came through the shop. It was too late in the day, too early in the season, to be a stray tourist. Of course, it was not impossible. Automatically, she glanced up at the statue of Our Lady on the television, said a prayer that the knock might mean good company; the sort of little miracle that nobody notices, that gets dismissed as a stroke of luck.

She made her way through the shop to the side door and tried to open it. It was a struggle. She blamed the insulating tape she had let a tinker fit the previous November.

'Hold on, I won't be a tick,' she called through the letter-box. Taking a knife from the table permanently laid for guests, she sliced it down the door-jamb with vigour, cursing the tinker as, with might and main, she tried to unstick it.

The man smiled at Boma Hephernan. 'You'll be fine with Bridget,' he said. She turned to him for reassurance, to ask him his name, to thank him, but was only in time to catch sight of him striding away towards the Cromwell-ruined Ardfert Cathedral. She opened her mouth to call to him, but then the door cracked opened and Brid McCarthy was standing in the doorway, panting, with light behind her, a blunt knife in her right hand.

Boma saw the old woman, recognized her at once from McKenna's Fort. But she was covered in confusion now, and did not know what to do next. She looked out and waited.

Brid saw a wet, brown woman and wondered for a moment if her eyes were playing tricks on her. 'Hello,' she said. 'Sorry about the door. It's martyrdom to open the big stupid thing.' She noticed the knife in her own hand. 'This is for that,' she said, gesturing to the door. 'It's not meant for you. At least I don't think so anyhow.'

'Hello,' Boma replied. 'Are you Bridget? I've been told that you might have a room for the night.'

Brid thought of Our Lady on the television and her heart lifted. 'You've been told right,' she said, only then wondering that the woman had called her *Bridget*. Nobody called her that. 'You're my first customer of the year, I'll have you know. I don't know which of us is honoured more, now. Come in. Come in. Is it still raining?'

Boma had to lift her face towards the sky to find out. Yes, the drops were hitting her. She was drenched. Why had she not noticed during her walk with the man?

'It is. Lashing it down.'

Brid stood aside to let Boma enter. She took in the woman's wetness, at once saw the swollen belly, the wet, too-thin clothes emphasizing it. 'Have you no bag?' she asked.

'No bag. I lost it.'

Brid was left wondering. 'But look at you! You'll have to change. What are you going to wear?'

Seeing the state of the woman, Brid's suspicions were aroused. No pockets to speak of. No bag of any sort. Where, then, did she keep the money to pay her for a night's bed and breakfast?

Brid showed Boma the ground-floor bedroom and asked if it would be satisfactory. She bit her lip and remained silent when tempted to question Boma further. This was not characteristic of Brid. She had been long enough in the b & b business to have been taken for many a ride by sleep-and-runners. But this time, when she knew she should have been most suspicious, she kept quiet and did not enquire further. Later she was to think that it was the intervention of the Holy Spirit that had stayed her tongue.

'You'll be needing a bath. The problem is what are you going to wear while your poor clothes are drying?'

Boma stood in front of Brid waiting for everything to work out. The man had said everything would. She held the small linen-wrapped package in her palm, the package the man had told her to give to Bridget.

But there was no problem. Brid fussed about, ran a bath, placing a cube of her Christmas bath salts in the water. She made her way upstairs and located the towelling dressing-gown that Tim had left and which she kept on a hanger in the hope that he would blow back at some point.

When she returned to the bathroom, Boma – still in her wet coat – was standing beside the bath, looking into the steaming water, thinking with a peaceful detachment of what had happened. An hour ago she had been half-drowned in the Atlantic. The man had stopped her, led her back to Ardfert, told her to stay with Bridget, given her money, schooled her on what to say if Bridget questioned her. What was that? What did she have to say? She was to tell Bridget everything. Bridget could be relied upon. Boma waited to see what would happen next. She abandoned herself to her benefactor.

'Slip into this when you get out, then come through to the parlour – it's across the shop – and keep warm in front of Stanley. I'll go and put some turf into him.'

Brid was not questioning her. She seemed to accept her presence as the most natural thing in the world. Nevertheless, Boma felt she had to say something. 'He told me to tell you that you'd understand. He gave me something for you.'

'Who did, dear?'

'The man.'

Brid added some cold to the bath, ruffling up the water to melt the bath cube. 'They take their time in melting, those things. You mustn't get in until it's all dissolved away. It's gritty to sit on,' she said. 'I got them from Mary Coogan in Tralee last Christmas. I swear I gave them to her the Christmas before. Still, my memory's not what it was. Mary Coogan knows that, of course, and thought she'd chance it.'

The scent of pine filled Boma's nostrils. The bath was inviting. It would be nice enough to take a bath.

'You must be frozen.'

Boma thought about that. The ocean in April. But she wasn't frozen. The whole way back from the ocean with the man she had been light and warm. 'I'm fine. Fine,' she said.

Brid stood, regarding Boma. Then she thought she understood why the woman was looking at the steaming bath, not moving. 'I'll go outside and you can hand your clothes through to me,' she said, thinking of modesty. Modesty was, after all, the guardhouse of purity.

Boma nodded and started pulling off her clothes. These she handed through a small gap in the door, while Brid looked at a damp patch on the wall to the right. Then, when all the clothes were passed through, Brid saw a small, square, linen-wrapped package sitting in the centre of Boma's palm.

'This is what the man told me to give you,' Boma said from behind the door. Her voice echoed from the tiled room. 'He told me to thank you, too.'

'What do you mean, dear?' Brid asked.

'The man. The man who brought me here; he gave me this to give to you.'

'And he was the man who called me "Bridget", was he? I know it sounds odd, but Bridget doesn't seem like my name any more. I've been "Brid" to everyone all my life.'

Brid looked at the package but for a second did not take it, so interested was she in the contemplation of Boma's palm. White with the lines etched in brown, a tidemark of colour running along the side of her thumb and leaking up between the fingers.

'He said you'd understand.'

'Who, dear?' she asked.

'The man,' Boma replied, and the hand in the gap of the door moved forward.

'I can't think . . .' But Brid took the package. She looked at it. 'I'll see you in a while or so. Take your time. Have a good soak.'

She closed the door and, wondering, walked into the parlour. She placed the package on the table. Then she gave all her attention to the wet clothes. She hung everything carefully on hangers and hoisted them up onto the drier over Stanley. Then, knowing that she had something exciting to think about, but forgetting what, she looked around.

'Was it tea? I was making tea when the door went.' Then she saw the package Boma had given her. The covering was stiff and brittle. When she turned it over she saw that it had been sealed with wax at one time blood-red but now dark brown in colour.

Brid did not open the package at once. Instead, she sat down at the table and looked at it. 'Who could have given you to the woman to pass on to me?'

Then Brid wondered about the brown woman in her bath, her first customer of the year. It should be worrying her but it did not worry her. That should be worrying in itself. She tried to unruffle herself. 'Sure, I'm not surprised by surprises at my time of life,' she said out loud.

She looked at the package for a full minute. Recollection of where it had come from drifted in and out of her mind like waves to a cave at the back of the beach. She searched about for her scissors, aimed them towards the package and cut open the linen wrapping. The cloth fell away, threadbare and dry as old bone, as if it had been waiting for this moment to dissolve. Beneath it a layer of thin oilcloth. She felt it, rubbed it with her thumb. It reminded her of childhood but she did not know why. It unfolded and, as it opened, it seemed like the woman's palm in negative. White folds and black skin.

The silver medal slipped out of its covering. Brid looked at it hard, turned it over in her palm. For a moment it was a friend to whom she could not put a name. She cleaned her glasses on the hem of her skirt. Before her glasses were back on her nose, tears were streaming from her eyes.

Half an hour later, Boma knocked at the parlour door.

'Come in, dear,' said Brid. She watched Boma enter and a thousand questions fizzed in her brain. But all she said was, 'Sit down by the fire. Stanley's nice and hot.'

Boma wondered what Brid meant but followed her pointing finger to the easy chair next to the boiler.

'I've a cup of tea in the pot for you,' Brid said.

'Thanks.'

Brid poured out the tea, adding milk. 'The sugar's there if you want it.'

Boma didn't usually take sugar but Brid's mentioning it made her suddenly crave it. She heaped two spoonfuls into her mug while Brid sat back down at the table and looked at the medal.

'Who gave you this, can you tell me?'

'The man.'

'You don't know his name, do you?'

Boma shook her head.

Brid turned the medal over in her palm. 'The package you gave me. There was a little silver medal inside. The medal used to belong to me. It was a gift from my ma and da; it was hung around my neck at my christening. I haven't seen it for almost eighty years.'

'And you can still remember it?' Boma asked. And Brid for the first time heard Boma's Dublin accent.

'You're Irish, aren't you?' Brid said.

'Yes, I'm Irish.'

There was irritation, an ominous rumble of bored aggression, in Boma's voice which Brid was not sure how to interpret. 'I'm sorry,' Brid said. 'It's just . . .'

'My whole life,' said Boma. 'Every day, give or take a few, people ask me where I'm from. It gets to the point where you don't know yourself. I mean, you know and you don't know. My name's Boma Hephernan.'

'Boma Hephernan,' repeated Brid. 'My name's Brid. Brid McCarthy. But you know that. Stop me when I repeat myself. I do it a lot. "Boma". It's not a name I've heard before. Was it B.O.M.A., Boma?'

Boma nodded.

'No, I'm stumped,' Brid said. 'If you were Bona – with an "n" – then I'd have known. St Bona is the patron saint of air-stewardesses. Of course, that's unusual enough. There are not many people who would know that. But you're in the right place. I was the all-Ireland champion on patron saints. Me and Mags Devlin won a clock on *Saints Alive*. It used to be on the radio. Gone now, of course. The clock is with Mags. We take turns. It's her year for it.' Then Brid looked down at the medal. 'I don't know whether I'm coming or going,' she said.

'Did you lose the medal?'

'No, I didn't lose it.' She stopped. 'No, I didn't lose it. I gave it to someone.'

'And you can remember that far back?'

'There's lots I've forgotten. But not that. I could never forget that. I can remember that better than I can remember what happened a minute ago. What's your name again, dear?'

'Boma. Who did you give it to?'

'Bona. Air-stewardesses. But with an "m". I'll remember now. I wonder where you got that name from. Have you no idea, Boma?'

Boma shrugged. 'I was an orphan. It was the name I had,' she said. 'But who did you give the medal to?'

'A man. I gave the medal to a man.'

'You must have liked him to give him your christening present.'

'Yes, I remember liking him. But what I want to know is how you come to be giving it to me.'

'I've told you, the man gave it to me.'

'Where did you meet this man?'

Boma looked into her mug of tea. 'On the shore.'

'You were on Banna Strand?' Brid asked. 'I thought from your clothes you'd been somewhere sandy.'

'I don't know the name. Anyway that's where I met him.'

'What did he look like?'

'He was tall. A bit thin. Well over six foot, I'd say. He had a beard and he spoke in an English way.' Boma thought about that, trying to be accurate, wanting to be exact because of the intensity of the look Brid was giving her. 'But I'm not sure he was English. A bit like an Irish politician or a newsreader. Yes, that's how he spoke. Sort of posh. He was dressed in a really old-fashioned way. A suit. And . . .' Boma stopped.

'Yes?'

'He was kind and he had a lovely smile. I remember his smile most.'

Brid was racking her brains trying to think of people who would fit such a description. 'It wasn't Father Devenish, was it?' Then she answered her own question. 'No, it couldn't have been him. He's no beard. I can't think. What sort of age?'

'I don't know. He had a lot of grey in his beard. Fifty? Fifty-five?'

Brid shook her head.

'Can I see it?' Boma asked.

'What?'

'The medal. Can I have a look?'

Brid picked up the medal and handed it across to Boma, placing it in her palm.

Boma felt the medal warm against her skin. She looked at the heart on the face of the medal, the thorns wrapped around it and the flames rising out of it. In the middle of the flames stood a cross.

She turned the medal over and, around the central motif of a chalice surrounded by a crown of thorns, read:

To Bridget from Ma and Da, 4 February 1909

Brid watched Boma. The questions continued to bubble and she dreaded the answers, answers that might contradict, turn to lies, the central, private story of her life. That story had sustained her. She had placed candles and hopes, woven her private mythology and wonders, around the kernel of the narrative. And inside the kernel, like a seed, lay the medal.

Shaking, Brid went over to the dresser and brought out the bottle of Paddy. Pouring two generous measures into sherry glasses, she offered one to the brown stranger sitting in her son's white dressing-gown.

Boma took the glass with one hand, returning the medal with the other.

'We'll drink this and then eat something. I'll need something to help me keep sober. You look starved. A weekday's no time to be going on a tear,' Brid said. 'Are you all right?'

'I'm all right,' said Boma, marvelling still that this automatic lie, paraded for so long, was turning out to be true.

'I think we both have stories to tell,' Brid said. She drank a mouthful of Paddy and it went straight to her head. She had a sensation of wings flapping all around her. She stared over at Our Lady on the television and it seemed to her that the figure was shining. She sat back in the easy chair and began to tell her side of it.

'I was born in this house,' Brid said. 'Where we are now is just about the same as it was then. Stanley is new, only about ten years old. But the rest is the same. My da kept the shop and I keep it now because it's always been there. Not much in the way of customers. And I don't blame them at all. Can't they go off to Tralee and buy what they want at a much cheaper price than I can offer? Still, I keep it on. I eat for wholesale anyway.

'I'm one of two daughters. Mary, my big sister, never married. She lived with us; with Matt, my husband – long dead – and my son, Tim. Upped and left now. For all the Irish reasons I'm sure you're fed up to the hair with hearing. Mary and I soldiered on here until she died five years ago. I won't go into the whole thing but I must tell you about this medal, though I've not told anyone before. I'm eighty-five and people say I don't look it, just like they say that you don't look Irish, I expect. I wore that medal around my neck on a silver chain from my christening day until the twenty-first of April 1916. I expect you're wondering how I can remember the date so clearly. It must all be a big mystery to you. Well, to understand that you'll need to know where we are. This is Ardfert and the stretch of shore you were on is Banna Strand. Doesn't it ring any bells with you? You don't even know the song? *They took Sir Roger prisoner and sailed for London Town. And in the Tower they laid him as a traitor to The Crown. Said he, "I am no traitor!" but his trial he had to stand . . . for bringing German rifles to the lonely Banna Strand.* You don't know it? History wasn't your best subject. Well, on that day in 1916, Sir Roger Casement landed on the Strand. Do you know who he was? You know the name, do you? Well, that's something, I suppose. But I hope your teachers told you more than that. Sure, they've left it up to me. Sir Roger Casement was an Ulsterman. He spent most of his life abroad, in the African Congo and South America. Shocking hot places. He did an awful amount of good for the natives, wrote reports on the terrible treatment they were getting at the hands of the rubber companies. The King of England gave him a knighthood for his great work. But, while Sir Roger was working in these hot old places, he began to see that the wickedness being done to the natives was no different from what the English were doing to us Irish at home. His loyalties pulled away from England, and he took up the Republican cause.

'Just before the 1914 war Sir Roger went to America to get help for the Irish Volunteers. They were short of arms, while the Ulster Volunteers had guns coming out of their ears, bought from Kaiser Bill by those traitors to Ireland, Carson and Craig. War was declared and Redmond told the English that they could rely on the loyalty of the Irish in their hour of need, if you please! You must know all that. Anyway, Sir Roger saw that England's danger was Ireland's chance for freedom. He went to Germany and tried to recruit Irish prisoners of war to fight for Ireland against the English. He didn't have much luck. Anyway, after two years in Germany, he returned to Ireland so as to bring in arms for the Easter Rising. At least I think that's why he came. He may have come to stop the Easter Rising. I can never get it straight and I'm not sure Sir Roger knew himself. He and two other fellows made their way from Banna Strand to McKenna's Fort – it's just down the road from here. The two men left Sir Roger there – he was soaked through, tired out, and why wouldn't he be? – and went off into Tralee to get help. He stayed at the fort all morning. Then Constable Riley of the constabulary arrested him. They brought him into Ardfert on a pony and trap and put up at the police station.

'That was where Mary and I saw him. He was sitting taking the sun outside the constabulary station between two policemen. He smiled at me as we passed. His clothes were mucky and wet through. I think the constabulary men had let him sit in the sun to dry off. They'd have been better Christians if they'd given him a change of clothes. Do you know how long it was before he was able to change? Ten full days. It was a disgrace, and after all he'd done for the world. Anyhow, we hung around looking at him. People had been saying that he was a German and we had never seen Germans – though we've seen plenty since and will see plenty more, please God. They're wonderful guests. Always give the bathroom a good clean after use.

'I don't know why, but I went up to him – it may have been a dare and I can still remember Mary calling me back – and stood in front of him, basking like a cat in the sun at the smile he gave me. He asked me to say a prayer for him. It was Good Friday and we were on our way to church. Maybe I had my missal with me. I said I would. He reached over to me and touched my medal. He turned it over and said, "So you're Bridget." And I said I was, wondering how he knew. Of course, it's written on the medal. But even then nobody called me Bridget.

' "You won't forget to say a prayer, will you, Bridget? The prayers of little girls are worth a ton of mine, and I need them."

'And he started to cry. And when I saw him crying, it started me doing it too.

'One of the constabulary men said something to him and he stood up. It was only then that I saw how very tall he was. I did not think. I wanted him to be happy. I wanted him to stop crying. He had admired my medal. I took it from around my neck and gave it to him.

'When we got back from church he had been taken away to Tralee. Mary had been pestering me all along the way to get the medal back off of him, but I said I would not. It was mine to give if I wanted to. Of course, memory is deceiving. Perhaps I've invented it since; maybe I'd have asked for it back if he'd been there – which he wasn't – but I think I remember thinking that giving the medal to the man was the first good deed I'd ever done. Maybe I'm romancing. Anyhow, I've thought of it a lot since. That night Mary told Ma and Da, and I caught it from them. But later, when we found out, they saw everything differently.

'I haven't seen that medal from that day to this, anyhow. It makes me destroyed with worry. I had always hoped that the medal would have given poor Sir Roger consolation, perhaps have been buried with him. Now it looks as if it was taken off of him in Ardfert, kept for all these years and returned to me now. I don't understand it.

'But you don't know the story, do you? They took Sir Roger to London and tried him as a *traitor*. Traitor to what is what I'd like to know! How can you be a traitor to England when it had been grinding us down for all those centuries? How could they expect an ounce of loyalty? Anyhow, he was found guilty and, in spite of appeals from the Pope and all sorts of people, they hanged him and buried his body in a limepit. And not only did they kill him, they brought out some diaries that they said they had found in his rooms in London, forged all sorts of lies to blacken his character, and sent copies all around the world to silence the people who had wanted to save Sir Roger from the hangman's noose. Yes, they killed him and his reputation and he stayed in the limepit from 1916 until February 1965, when the English Prime Minister Wilson had the bones dug up and sent to Dublin for burial in Glasvevin.

'You're probably wondering how an old woman who keeps forgetting everything can remember all this. Well, all my life, every day of it, I've thought of him. Ardfert, too, has been full of Sir Roger's memory. Many people have been racked with the guilt of it because, though we had the opportunity to free him, we did nothing. Some people from here even gave evidence for the prosecution at Sir Roger's trial and they suffered for it later. They were accounted "Casement Killers" and had to leave the area. It was unfair in a way. No-one except the constabulary – maybe not even them – knew who he was. As I was saying, they thought he was a German spy and, I suppose, the times were confusing. But I was happy because of the medal I had given him. I can honestly say that not a day has passed by between then and now when I haven't thought of Sir Roger. That's why I'm upset that this man gave you the medal. All my life I've thought that it might have brought him comfort at the last. He became a Catholic on the night before he died, you know. But now it looks as if one of the policemen – somebody anyhow – took it from him, kept it. It's odd him returning it to you now, though I suppose it must be a descendant with a bad conscience. I wish he hadn't. I really do. I've always had a picture of him wearing it at his death. That thought's been a comfort to me, Boma.'

'It's a great story,' Boma said. 'You know, as you were telling it, I began remembering bits and pieces. But I was never much of a listener at school.'

'You're not unique in that at all, Boma. I could never get Tim – he's my son – to listen to my stories about Sir Roger. But to me it's as natural as breathing. He feels like part of the family. Does that sound daft?'

Boma shook her head. 'I saw you before,' she said.

'Where did you see me? In Ardfert?'

'I saw you cleaning that memorial stone.'

'At McKenna's Fort? I didn't see you.'

'I was hiding.'

'Why were you hiding?'

Boma thought about that. She could hardly remember herself why she had been hiding. She shrugged.

'I think it's your turn now,' Brid said.

'My turn?'

Brid got up and switched on another lamp. 'Yes, your turn! I've told you about myself – more than I've told people for ages, I can tell you. But you're a great mystery. You've got some *craic* in you, to be sure!'

'There isn't much to tell.'

'I don't believe that for a minute.'

'My name is Boma Hephernan. I'm thirty-four.' She stopped.

'You look younger.'

'I feel older. A lot older. I was born in Dublin. I was an orphan and was with the nuns out in Wicklow until I was two. Then I was fostered out around Dublin until I was adopted by an elderly couple. That's where the Hephernan comes in.'

'And where does the Boma come in?'

'Like I said, it was the name I had. I don't know if there's a St Boma. I doubt it.'

'Well, if there isn't, you'll just have to be the first,' Brid said. 'That's what I tell the kids who come into the shop, them with the oddest names. We've a Wayne O'Flynne down the road. I'm surprised at the nuns not calling you after a saint. Your patron saint's really useful in a crisis. I don't know what I'd have done without Bridget.'

Boma nodded, waiting. 'I lived with the Hephernans until I was sixteen, then I ran away. I went to England and worked in a pub.

Then I started training as a nurse but I didn't like it. I got married but it didn't work out. No kids. I thought it was my fault. Funny, it was his problem all the time, as you can see. I came back to Ireland when my dad died. I'd been back for my mam's funeral. Their house came to me. I was their only relative. I sold it and, like a fool, lived high on the hog for a few years. Didn't work at all. Just pleased myself. Then I moved in with a man called Declan in London. He's responsible for this and . . .' She stopped, though she did not want to. Then, having stopped she was back, puzzling out the conundrum that had filled her head since life had been blown to bits on Hungerford Bridge.

'Go on.'

'This is probably shocking you.'

Brid shook her head, even though it was. 'Not at all. But why did you come to Ardfert?'

'I didn't. I just ended up here this afternoon. To tell you the truth . . .' Boma stopped again, looked hard into Brid's eyes, thinking of what the man had told her. 'To tell you the truth, I came here to drown myself in the Atlantic – it had to be the Atlantic, don't ask me why – the Irish Sea just wouldn't do somehow. I walked to the ocean, past the church and that old fort, where I saw you. I threw myself into the ocean. But the man wouldn't let me go through with it.'

'God save us,' said Brid. 'And you with a baby on the way! You must have been desperate.' And behind her talk she was praying, thanking God for a task, for the mission-field coming to her.

'Yes, I must have been. There didn't seem to be any way forward. And there was no way back. I couldn't face the prospect of the baby. I couldn't . . . couldn't . . . get the energy together, you know,' Boma replied, wondering again why things seemed different now. 'I don't know why I'm telling you this. I usually keep everything dark.'

'The more we share stories the less strangers we'll be,' Brid said pedantically. She wanted to ask Boma if she had made an act of contrition, wondered whether she should ring the presbytery and get Father Devenish round – she could tell the priest it was an emergency – but the story, and her curiosity, won. 'But you said the man wouldn't let you. Did he jump in to save you?'

'I don't know. I had been having the devil's own job getting out to a deep place. The waves kept knocking me back.'

'They'll do that.'

'And when I did think I'd found a place and pushed myself under, he was just there.'

'Just there?'

'In the water. Well – and it's hard for me to think of exactly how it was – it seemed as if he was there waiting for me, under the water. I know that's impossible. But I can remember his hands on me, strong and warm even in the middle of the cold.'

'And how did he bring you back here? Did he have a car?'

Boma laughed, remembering. 'We walked. First he had to help me find my coat and shoes. I'd left them in the dunes. I didn't think I'd need them again, you see. It was starting to get dark.'

'Then?'

'Then we just walked. I don't remember much about it. He kept telling me not to worry; that he'd bring me to a warm place.' Boma smiled.

'And how were you feeling?'

'I was high. Happy. I can't explain it. Still am.'

'It's the Paddy. It'll do that.'

'No, it isn't the Paddy,' said Boma.

'And he brought you straight here, did he? You didn't try anywhere else along the way? Mrs Grogan at St Theresa's? She's closer to the fort and she's got a shamrock from the Board. As she'll tell you if you give her so much as a second. But I shouldn't be uncharitable . . .'

'No,' she replied, 'he brought me straight to you.'

'I can't think . . .' said Brid.

They sat in silence for some time. Then Boma said, 'Brid, you know you mentioned food? I've a real hunger on me.'

'And why wouldn't you? You've had a time of it. And aren't you eating for two?'

Brid put on her pinny and went into the kitchen. There, she tried to puzzle everything out. She came to Boma's story and started making acts of contrition on Boma's behalf. Then she planned to get her down on her knees to say the rosary before bed. She went in to tell Boma about times of mass in the morning. But when she looked in, she found her asleep in the easy chair.

Brid looked at her lodger for a long moment, then went back out into the kitchen to prayerfully heat up the fat for the chips.

* * *

An hour later they parted at the door of Boma's room. Before she left her, Brid, having thought about things, and holding the rosary beads she was going to tell when she got into bed, said, 'You must stay here with me as long as you like. There's no question of money. You mustn't bother your head about it. This is your home now for as long as you need it.'

Boma smiled her thanks, and went into her room. Inside she found the curtains drawn and both bars of the electric-fire on. *A Simple Prayer Book*, open at 'Penitence', lay on the bedside table. She wondered about it, closed it and set it down next to a pair of rosary beads. Then she turned off the fire and got into bed. Her bare feet touched a hot-water bottle moulded in the shape of a rabbit. Boma held it against her breast and fell immediately asleep.

The following morning, two hundred miles north of Ardfert, a young man parked his motor bike in a car-park a few hundred yards outside Enniskillen's security zone. He locked the front wheel, anchoring his crash-helmet to the saddle with a chain, then lifted the double-panniers from their position across the back seat. He walked away from the motor bike, towards the busy centre of the town.

The young man passed the town's Craft Centre, where a distant cousin of his had set up in business making and selling reproduction Celtic crosses. He was tempted to go inside to have a look. But that would have to wait for another day.

Reaching the main street, he hitched the panniers onto his other shoulder. He crossed himself for luck as he walked past a Catholic church. He thought of his mother. He thought of his friends, waiting at the cottage within sight of lower Lough Erne, a few miles down a track off the Belleek Road. He looked at his watch.

There was plenty of time, too much time almost. To kill some he went into the church, crossed himself with his free hand and, genuflecting, sat down in a pew near the back, placing the panniers on the seat behind him.

A few old people were saying their prayers. At the side of the nave a woman sat at a bare table, waiting behind a book of condolence for people to come in and sign it, to protest against one of the more spectacular atrocities by the IRA. A middle-aged couple had just signed the book, exchanged a few words of support with the woman, and were now walking up the side aisle.

The young man bowed his head. *I'll sign it*, he thought. *Why not?* But for a few more minutes he sat in the pew, his head bowed. He could feel his heart beating too fast, the looseness in his bowels which told him that, were he to relax for a second, he would shit himself.

His tummy rumbled noisily and the sound made one old woman turn. They exchanged glances, then the old woman smiled at him. He smiled back as he had been taught. She understood such rumbles. Sad to see it afflicting one so young. Still, if the young man were anything like her, it was probably the beer that did it. Or crisps.

The old woman turned back to telling her beads, thinking as she prayed about what she needed in Wellworths – the shop opposite Woolworths – down the street. Then she castigated herself for letting her mind wander, saw Mrs O'Neill behind her table, remembered the explosion in Enniskillen when the young nurse had been killed at the war memorial, and prayed harder.

She saw the young man pass her, holding the panniers. He was approaching Mrs O'Neill. It was good to see a young man signing the petition. Not that the black-leather get-up was in any way suitable attire for a church . . . then she was castigating herself again. In a godless age it was encouraging to see any young person – no matter how dressed – coming into church. And he was the young man with the rumblings afflicting him. Well, perhaps he had his reasons; perhaps he was in poor health. It happened. Jimmy Regan's youngest was in Belfast having a new bone marrow put in. It's true, we never know the time. In the midst of life . . . Reining herself in, the old woman returned her thoughts to the front.

'We're sending the book to the relatives of the bereaved in the Harrogate bomb,' Mrs O'Neill told the young man in a whisper.

'OK, so,' he said.

'We're sending it off tomorrow. It must be there for the memorial service.'

The young man bent forward, signed a name. He wondered what his friends would think if they could see him. He wondered what his mother would think. Standing up straight he saw the flicker of the sanctuary lamp.

Mrs O'Neill looked at the name, but in the subdued lighting of the church could not read the writing. 'Thank you,' she said.

'It's nothing,' he replied, handing back the Bic. 'I must be off. Bye.'

'God bless you,' she said.

He nodded, his back already turned to her.

Outside, the young man looked at his watch and set off towards the town centre. He entered the busy shopping street, walking into the crowds. Nobody looked at him twice. Nobody knew him.

He passed the shops, his bowels rumbling, heart beating enough to break his ribs. At last, almost running, he reached the new public conveniences which adjoin the Old Customs House on Gaol Square. He smiled at the notice: *Partly Funded By A Grant From The European Economic Community's Development Fund*. He went inside. It was empty. He checked all the stalls. All empty. He went into one, locked the door and took his pants down . . .

He exploded. He flushed straight away, before even thinking of cleaning himself up. Then, while doing so, he looked up at the partitions. This would be the difficult part. The place had to be empty.

Just as he had thought he was clean, he felt a tickling down there and another rush. Still, he thought. This always happened. The boys all said as much. He flushed, repeated the tiresome procedure with the hard paper. He flushed again, stood up and pulled up his pants.

He listened but could not hear anything. He left the panniers, one section on each side of the outflow pipe. Listened again. Nothing. He stood up on the toilet pedestal and then, giving a great push, lifted himself up against the face of the partition. He scrambled up it; hung at the top for a second, then dropped into the next stall, coming down on his right foot, while the left was immersed in the water at the bottom of the toilet bowl. He sloshed as he walked out of the stall; jumped when he saw a tall man standing sideways on to him at one of the urinals. The man turned to look at him. Smiled.

'Lock fuckin' stuck,' said the young man.

The man nodded, still smiling.

Back on his motor bike the young man did not need to return through the security zone. Being careful to keep under thirty, he drove the vehicle along Brook Street and out to the A48, the Belleek Road. When safely out of the town, he increased his speed to fifty.

At Drumcose, he turned off to the left on the narrow road to Shankill, then right after a mile and onto a rutted track where the spring grass grew like a median line. Right again, then left. Another mile and he was in sight of the cottage.

The young man's friends, hearing the roar of the bike skating across the mud, came to the door of the cottage and cheered. One held out a bottle. The young man parked the bike and pushed past them. They laughed the more, knowing exactly where he was going.

They went inside and closed the door.

'Get that down you!' said Sean, the older man, the head of the household, when the young man reappeared, buckling his belt.

He took the bottle and slugged some down. 'It was no trouble. No trouble!' he said. 'I even had time to pray for you heathens at the church!'

'Any problems?'

The young man thought of the tall man at the urinal. He decided not to mention it. He did not want to destroy the aura of victory that surrounded him. 'None,' he said. 'Has the warning been done?'

Sean looked at his watch. 'Five minutes to go. She'll be doing it now.'

And as the older man spoke, a pretty young woman in South Boston picked up a Micky Mouse telephone and punched out the number of the RUC in Belfast. She gave the code-word resentfully, hating the anonymous voice on the other end. She told it flatly about a bomb in Gaol Square, Enniskillen. She hung up and wondered about the accessories to wear for her sister's wedding the following Saturday.

'Just think what it's like in Enniskillen town centre now! People running about all over the shop! Police sirens!' said a freckle-faced youth.

Sean reproved him. 'It won't be pretty, Kevin. No reason to take any pleasure in it. It's the price we pay.'

'Sorry,' Kevin said.

'One minute to go.'

'If the timer's working.'

'Watch it, you! Pat's timers always work. You can rely on them. Like Big Ben.'

There was a knock on the door. The four men froze. The older man put his finger to his lips. After five seconds the knock was repeated. Three in quick succession. A pause. A single knock. Four slow, evenly spaced . . . one for each of Ireland's green fields.

'Who is it?' the older man asked.

'A friend of Maeve's,' came the reply.

Reassured by the knock and the coded reply to the question – but still on edge – the men went to the window and looked through.

The older man saw a tall, bearded man standing at the door. The man saw him looking, smiled. *I know you*. The smile melted him. 'Open the door,' the older man said to the young man. 'It's a comrade.'

The young man put down his drink, unlatched the door and opened it.

'This is yours, I believe,' said the tall, bearded man.

The young man stared at his panniers at the man's feet, and wet his pants.

'Who is it?' called Sean. Receiving no reply, he went to the door.

'Come out of the house,' the man said. 'All of you. Be quick! Your bomb is only not exploding through the power of grace. It's draining me, lads! If this goes on much longer, I doubt I'll be able to put myself together again!'

The men edged past him. 'I could have blown up the lot of you. That's what I'd planned originally, to tell you the truth. It's a fitting end for a merciless bomber to be blown up by his own handiwork. We upstairs can't help giggling, though we know it's a mite uncharitable. But on the way over from the Enniskillen jakes I thought I'd give you another chance. We all need them, so we do. A second, third and fourth.' He approached each man in turn, giving them a gentle slap on the cheek, like a bishop at confirmation. 'Don't do it again! Do you hear? We're fed up with it. Fed up! Now be off before this blows up. And tell your bosses what's happened.'

The men, stunned to immobility, watched the man as he walked into the cottage. He turned, smiled, gestured them to be off. The door closed. The men looked at one another, came to themselves and ran.

For a minute all was pastoral peace around the cottage. New lambs called to their mothers over in the adjoining field; a blackbird gabbled a warning or a mating-call. Then a massive explosion demolished the cottage, in which had been raised eleven generations of tenant farmers. A fireball rose into the sky. The sheep stampeded across a pasture. Terrorized rooks beat about the sky, a sky they shared with burning shards.

But in the chaos of Enniskillen's town centre nobody heard the explosion. A leaking cistern dripped in the empty public convenience. In the Catholic church, Mrs O'Neill had long since snapped her Book of Condolence shut and run for safety. That night she would spend five minutes Tippexing out the bogus name – IRA Fury – written in the book earlier in the day by the young man. The same young man who now lay on the floor of a friend's lounge in Buldoran, weeping and telling himself the story of his first job; seeing the bearded face of the man he had seen in the toilet, the man who had knocked at the door and returned the bomb; the man whose picture, placed between Pearse and Connolly, was staring down at him – wearing that same smile – from the lounge wall.

> *Come speak your bit in public*
> *That some amends be made*
> *To this most gallant gentleman*
> *That is in quicklime laid.*
>
> W. B. YEATS

2

BOMA'S FIRST DAY AT BRID MCCARTHY'S WAS THE MOST SERENE SHE could remember. Woken by a gentle tap on her bedroom door at eleven, she saw Brid walking towards her with a breakfast tray. Brid did not stay to chat, saying that the shop needed looking after. Boma thanked her and tucked into the breakfast. Then she fell back into deep sleep.

It was dusk when she finally got up. She washed herself in the bathroom; then wrapped Tim's left-behind dressing-gown around her. In the hall she could hear Brid talking to a customer and did not dare cross the shop to get to the parlour. She went back into her bedroom and waited to see what would happen.

Brid came in and told her Stanley had been waiting for her, cooking scones in his stomach, making the kettle raise its hat. Boma joined her there, watched television, listened as Brid ruminated on who could have given her the medal . . . talked over the television . . . told her she could stay as long as she liked.

On the news Boma learnt about the blowing up of a bomb-making factory in the North. A film clip showed the smoking ruin, closed in on a tattered pullover hanging from the branch of a scorched tree. A mangled motor bike. She thought of Declan; his morose silence when he had found out about the baby, silences that had lengthened to boycott. Then the sudden change of heart that had remelted her hungry heart; a blissful weekend of smiles and tenderness; the gift for delivery to Declan's homeless friend who hung about Hungerford Bridge. What a sweet secret between the two of them that gift had been – a confirmation from Declan that he was secretly a quiet philanthropist who sprang birthday surprises on the unfortunate. The wrapping paper on the parcel had *Shoplifted just for you* written all over it.

Boma closed her eyes against the pictures of carnage in front of her.

At eleven, Brid asked her to say the rosary with her. Boma consented but said she had no beads.

'Didn't I put a pair by your bed, Boma?' Brid asked. 'Next to the prayer book?'

'Sorry. I didn't know they were for me.'

'And who else would they be for? I always keep them in the room for guests. I'd say you need them as much as anyone.'

Boma went to her bedroom to collect them. She did not like the dark few steps through the shop. When she saw the rosary and prayer book, she remembered the page she had seen the night before. 'Penitence.' She gathered the beads into her palm and went back to the parlour.

Brid was switching off the television. They knelt against their easy chairs and Brid set off at a cracking pace. She had to help Boma with naming the mysteries. 'The Visitation,' she said. 'The Presentation in the Temple,' she said. And Boma recited the well-known formulas. She wondered what her friends would say if they could see her now. They would split their sides.

At the end, Brid prayed: 'Grant that Boma will stay here in Ardfert and brighten up the life of a poor sinner. Grant that she will be able

to sort everything out – with You especially.' She stood up, put the
light back on and sent Boma to bed with the rabbit hot-water bottle
and a cup of chocolate. And Boma, wondering about the prayer, slept
again, her fears still unaccountably defused.

The following day Brid took Boma to Tralee. She left the shop door
unlocked, saying that her customers knew where everything was and
would note down their purchases in a book. They crossed the road
and Brid waited to be lifted.

After a few minutes a car came along from the Ballyheige direction.
Brid waved to the driver.

'Would you be going to Tralee, Matthew?'

'I'm aimed that way, Brid. What part of Tralee?' Matthew asked. 'I
only ask because I'm picking up some sisters and taking them off to
Dublin. They're having a big shindig there. Time's getting on . . .'
he smiled and winked at Boma, '. . . as it will, you know.'

'We're going to the museum. But anywhere will do,' said Brid.

Boma stepped into the back.

'To the very door I'll take you.' Matthew looked at Boma through
the mirror. 'You've got a friend, Brid McCarthy.'

'I have,' replied Brid. 'A good Irish girl. She's come to the west for
a bit of fresh air. Her name's Boma. She's a Hephernan.'

'Boma. That's an unusual name,' Pat said. 'Excuse the shocking
smell of fish, will you, Brid? You too, Boma?'

Both women inhaled.

'I can't smell any fish, Matthew,' Brid said.

Boma could, but said nothing.

'I've two big salmon at the back. I promised it to the sisters for
their party. Wild salmon. None of your farmed nonsense. I'm surprised
you can't smell it. My last customer nearly got out because of them.
I've them wrapped in three plastic bags but it still leaks out.'

Brid sniffed the air again. 'No, there's nothing there to smell as far
as I can see, Matthew.'

'I can,' said Boma. 'But it's not strong.'

'It's youth you've got,' said Brid.

Matthew left them outside the Tralee Museum. 'See you again, Boma,'
he said.

'Drive carefully on those old roads,' said Brid.

'The sisters'll see to that. For women who have offered up their lives they're awful keen to hang on to them and not meet their Maker before the timetable says,' said Matthew.

Matthew drove around the corner, where four nuns were waiting for him outside the front gate of the Hospital of the Flaming Heart.

'Four, is it?' he asked them. 'I thought it was only three. It's going to be a tight squeeze, Sisters. Are you sure you're able for it?'

'There'll be plenty of room,' said Sister Aquinas, the Prioress. 'In the back, Sisters.'

On the journey Matthew told Sister Aquinas about his lifting of Brid McCarthy and Boma. 'Boma Hephernan her name is.'

Sister Aquinas turned to the nuns in the back. 'It's an odd name, isn't it, Sisters? Boma.'

'It's no saint that I know,' said Sister Benedict.

'No, I've never heard of it either,' said Sister Louise.

'She's coloured, this Boma, like I said. She's lovely blue eyes. Blue as Mary's mantle. I don't know where Brid found her.'

'What sort of age was she, this Boma?' Sister de Porres asked from the back.

Matthew scratched his head. 'Thirty. Thirty-five? But they're as hard to place as you sisters.'

'And you're sure her name was Boma, are you? Boma Hephernan?'

'Yes, Sister. Boma Hephernan.'

Sister de Porres filed the name away, thinking of Sister Paula, whose golden jubilee as a member of the Order of the Flaming Heart they were going to Dublin to celebrate.

As they approached Limerick, Sister Louise asked Sister de Porres, 'You were with Sister Paula in Africa, were you not, Sister?'

'Yes, Sister,' replied Sister de Porres. 'I was. Indeed I was.'

'This used to be the council offices,' Brid said, as they went up the steps of the museum. 'They've been knocking it about recently. I read it in the papers. It's a grand building, so it is. I tell you, Boma, Tralee's got everything a body could ask for!'

Inside they had to pay £3.75.

Brid searched in her bag, muttering.

Boma acted distracted while Brid paid. It was dawning on her why Brid had insisted on bringing her to the museum. She had been saying what a grand town Tralee was. The museum was her way of convincing Boma of that, and convincing her to stay.

'What'll we do first?' Brid asked.

'Most clients like the trip through Geraldine Tralee – that's what we call the Tralee of the old days,' said the receptionist. 'It's in the basement. There's a grand film about Kerry upstairs; then there's a Living History exhibit to spice up the permanent collection. You've got all the time in the world. Don't forget the Living History. There haven't been too many customers and the characters are getting restless.'

Brid nodded but, not understanding, didn't enquire further. 'It's down to the basement, so,' she said.

'Irish, English, Japanese, German or French?' the man asked them, tearing a section from their tickets.

'I don't get you,' Brid said. 'And what's this?'

'It's a car that will pull you through Tralee of the fourteenth century. You won't have to walk at all. And you'll get a commentary as you go.'

'What's that smell?' Boma asked.

'That's atmosphere,' the man said. 'We've used the latest chemical technology to simulate smells of the time. See if you can recognize them. If you do, come and tell me. I haven't the foggiest.'

They got in. 'Was it English you wanted, by the way?'

'Oh, yes. English, I think,' Boma replied, as Brid was distracted, looking round.

The car lurched off along its track. The commentary started up – a man and woman taking it in turns to be breezy about Irish history, told them about old Tralee as they passed animated tableaux. A sentry at the wall demanded tribute but the woman reassured them that he would let the car through. In the first shop a butcher was pulling a calf to slaughter; a great iron hook was gripped around the animal's neck. It called out noisily against its fate. The car turned a corner on to the main street of the town. Boma turned back to watch the calf.

They passed a pub. 'I wish they'd shut up in there,' said Brid. 'They stop me concentrating on the talking. It's interesting, though, isn't it? It fills you up. Like having the radio and the vision on together. Will you look at this street? It could do with a good clean. A pool of water in the middle! Ducks quacking. What's that old biddy doing in the upstairs room? She's going to empty her pot all over that poor man, that's what.'

Boma was silent as the car passed a beggar with one leg. His face was hidden by a hood and only when the car passed him could they see the diseased skin, the satanic expression. A mother stood in a kitchen, holding a ladle out, as if to hit her daughter with it. The girl stood looking defiantly up at her mother. Daring her. Then they turned off the main street and left the raucous town behind. Ahead lay a straight cloister. The sounds from other parts of the exhibit still leaked through the stone-rendered plasterboard. Boma could hear the frightened sound of the calf with a hook around its neck, spending its whole day – its every day – being pulled towards the knife; the cries and fiddling from the pub; the angry admonitions of the mother.

Now a monk came into view. He sang plainchant, reading from an illuminated manuscript. His lips opened and shut like a fish deprived of oxygen. Neither here was there any peace, for the cries from all around the mad town, the bland English commentary, determined to be joky, and not to terrify the trippers, to pour linguistic neon over the darkness, impinged.

Boma hated the ride, wanted it all to stop – the tape loops to cease turning; the animated manikins to shudder and die; the cacophony from the pub to sweep down to base, like a record stopped in its track; the car to jolt to a standstill. Were that to happen, she fancied, she would know the feeling that she had so wanted to have as she negotiated the road across Ireland: the delicious absence of sensation; the buzzing silence of annihilation; life as a fading twang of pointless sound.

And as the thought came and she nuzzled it, pushing herself up against Brid who noticed and was happy, the car stopped with a jerk, the sounds decreased in volume and died like a buzzing fly in the last second of life.

'Lord, Boma! What's happened?' Brid asked.

'I don't know, Brid.'

But the actuality following so fast on the thought panicked Boma. She gazed into the dark, shaking, fancying that she could see shapes – shapes so black they turned the surroundings to grey – about to envelop her, place a black hood over her head, carry her away. Brid pressed her arm and the unexpected feel of it made her jump. She waited for the stealthy shadows to approach, place the tips of their guns against her head, pull the triggers.

'Please!' she cried.

Brid put her arm around Boma. 'Don't be frightened, dear. They'll fix it. It's the electricity's gone. If it's gone in Ardfert too, I'll have to get Colm Devlin in to fiddle with the clock. They'd better fix it. Wait until I get out of here. I'll give them a flea. And you a visitor too.'

'Brid . . .'

'No, you're more than a visitor,' Brid said. She felt Boma's fear. 'You will stay, won't you?'

'I can't understand why you want . . . why they can't . . .' On the bridge a homeless man with a small dog was asking her if there was anything in the parcel for him. But he was not the beggar that Declan had described. He was middle-aged, tall, bearded, dishevelled. She gave him fifty pence to buy him off. But he followed her. *A little something for a poor old man!* Then, in the middle of the bridge, he grabbed the parcel, tore it out of her hands. She watched, helpless, the man running away with her gift – dragging the dog – across the bridge . . .

The lights went on. The car jolted, the tape loops jerked up octaves, the manikins clicked back to life, the monk prayed joylessly. The raucous town gathered itself together and hubbubed as before, quite forgetting its recent stroke.

Brid found herself watching the look of terror on Boma's face. She did not know what to do, what to think; so she prayed.

'That was an experience!' Brid told the man as he helped her from the car. 'A pity it had to let itself down like that.'

'Sorry about that. But you liked it apart from that, did you? What did you think of the smells?' the attendant asked, anxious to please.

'I could smell something the whole time,' Brid said, 'but it didn't change much. Probably just as well.'

'A lot of people say that. I don't think they've got the technology quite up to the minute as yet,' said the man. 'Some clients say there's too much coming at you all at once.'

'What did you think, Boma?'

'Can we go now, Brid?'

'It's a great tourist attraction. Great,' said Brid.

'The season hasn't started yet,' said the man.

'Well, try and iron out the bumps before it does,' said Brid. She took Boma's arm. Brid could feel her shaking. She said goodbye to the man and they went upstairs.

'Are you all right, Boma?' Brid asked, on the stairs.

'I'm all right,' Boma replied. 'The breakdown gave me a fright, that's all.'

'We don't have to stay, you know,' said Brid.

'It seems a shame after spending all that money.'

'Let's do it quickly, so,' Brid said.

In the dark they watched the colourful film about the delights of Kerry. After that, the permanent exhibit was a great change. Shards of pottery, ancient tools and models of beehive hermits' huts snoozed in their glass cases. They wandered through it while the custodian sat in a chair and snoozed too, the better to fit in with the things he guarded.

Boma lost Brid for a while among the partitions and cases. She caught up with her near the exit, gazing at an old concertina camera, its single eye staring out at her from a glass case.

'It's Sir Roger's,' Brid said. 'It says he used it in South America. That's where he saved the poor people who were being ground down by the English rubber company.'

Boma approached the object until her nose collided with the glass. She pulled back, stung.

'Are you all right there?' Brid asked. 'They should put tape across it, like they do on the one at the Eight 'til Late. Mrs Heenan collided with the door. She's had headaches ever since.'

'I'm all right,' Boma said, the sting pulling her back from the edge. She caught sight of her face mirrored in the lens of the camera.

'Ah, I see you have found my camera! I gathered much damning evidence with that. Indeed I did,' said a voice.

Boma turned. A bearded man, dressed in an Edwardian suit, was standing behind her. A piece of moustache on his left upper lip was coming away. 'Who are you?'

'I, madam, am Sir Roger Casement. I am here to answer any questions you may have about my eventful life.'

'You're going to lose your moustache.'

'I'm not, am I?' said the man, feeling his lip, slipping out of role.

He made to stick it back to his lip but as soon as it was pressed down it curled up again. 'I've had a shocking time with it.'

'Who's this when he's at home?' Brid asked.

'He says he's Sir Roger Casement.'

Brid looked at the man with some hostility.

'Living History, Irish heritage,' whispered Sir Roger, stepping once again into role and pukka English accent.

But Brid was unconvinced. 'How old are you?' she asked Sir Roger.

'Forty-three . . .' he said, '. . . and a half.'

'You're too young to be Sir Roger!' she said. 'You're playing a cruel trick on an old woman, that's what you're doing!'

'Brid . . .' said Boma, aware of how Brid's voice was filling the silent hall.

'And will you look at his shoes? Can you imagine Sir Roger Casement turning up in pumps? He would never have allowed himself to slip into such slovenliness.'

'They're black,' said Sir Roger defensively. 'They go with the suit, don't they? I didn't think anyone would notice – not that we've had many in. It's been dead as I don't know what. Anyhow, Oliver Cromwell took my shoes. He said St Brandon took his, but I'm certain he left them at home.'

Brid looked at the young man, unmollified. 'It's not good enough, is it?'

Sir Roger hung his head. 'No. Sorry,' he said.

Mick, the dozing custodian, woke up and walked over. Sir Roger whispered into the man's ear: 'Will you tell them what it's about? Jesus, Mick, if they'd only read the brochure they'd know. Why doesn't Philomena warn them? It's not as if she's rushed off her feet.'

Mick nodded with gravity and turned to Brid and Boma. 'Now, I think there's a bit of confusion,' he said. 'Your man here is playing the part of Sir Roger Casement. We have characters from history patrolling the gallery, waiting to accost innocent visitors like yourselves. I'm surprised you haven't come upon any.' He looked at his watch. 'They're on their tea-break, I expect. They're here to answer your questions, anyhow.'

'I see,' said Brid. 'You mean he isn't Roger Casement but he's pretending he is?'

'You're right. He's really Eamonn McCann from Dingle Street.'

'Not the son of Mary and Joe McCann?'

'The very same.'

Brid appraised Eamonn McCann. 'And what are you doing impostering as Sir Roger Casement? I thought you were a White Father?'

'It's true, I was. I was testing my vocation but . . .' He shrugged.

'But it broke, did it?' Brid asked. 'There's too many backing out of the religious life. There's going to come a time when we're not the land of saints and scholars that we were.'

'I know what you mean,' said Eamonn McCann, 'but I didn't have the calling. It's better to find out sooner than later, isn't it now? That was a long time ago, anyhow. I've been to training college since. I'm a qualified teacher.'

'So why aren't you teaching? Teaching's a vocation too, you know.'

'I did my share, but I couldn't manage in the classroom after a while. Burnt out, so I was. Pearls and swine, if you get me. Still, I'm teaching in this job. Ask me anything. Go on. I'm the expert on Sir Roger Casement.'

Brid was thinking what a whole flight of steps down it was from being a White Father to impersonating Sir Roger Casement. She smelled the stale whiff of blasphemy. 'I don't know . . .' she said.

'You know about Casement, do you?' he asked.

'Of course I do. I'm from Ardfert,' Brid replied. 'I'm Brid McCarthy.'

'I thought I knew you,' Eamonn said. 'You're Tim McCarthy's mother.'

'I was.'

Eamonn stepped back a pace. ' "Was"?'

'No, nothing like that. At least I don't think so. Mind you, Eamonn, he might as well be dead as far as his old mammy's concerned.'

'How is he?'

'Blown out. Blown away. He's a teacher too. Well, he was when I last had word. Apart from cards and a bit of conscience money, I haven't clapped eyes on him for five years.'

'That's a long time.'

'It is a long time, Eamonn. I always thought he was a good son, just like I thought you were a White Father. It's getting to the point where you just change right with wrong and you'll be right.'

Brid looked round, wondering where Boma was. She saw her standing by a large black-and-white photograph of the Dublin Post Office.

'Ask me anything,' pleaded Eamonn, now back in role.

'All right. Seeing you're Mary's boy. Still, I'm not sure I approve of this.'

'A man's got to have a job. Go on, ask! I'm full of it. Exploding with it, I am!'

'Where were you born, Sir Roger?'

'I was born, madam, at Doyle's Cottage, Lawson Terrace, Sandycove, Co. Dublin on September the first, 1864,' Sir Roger replied.

'Are you sure about that? I thought you were an Ulsterman.'

'I am. An Ulsterman and proud of it. But I am, first and foremost, a man of all Ireland. And didn't Eamon de Valera say that Ulster is the most precious of Ireland's four fields?'

Brid nodded piously. 'He did. God rest him. What else can you tell us?'

'I can tell you how I came to go to Africa, if you like. I know it backwards.'

'How's your mammy, Eamonn?'

Eamonn, in some confusion, said she had died in childbirth when Sir Roger was nine. Brid looked hard at him. 'Mammy's fine, Mrs McCarthy,' he replied.

'You'll be sure to give her my regards. Tell her to come and see me. We can talk about the heartaches of motherhood.'

Eamonn as Sir Roger had been bursting to tell his first customers of the week more of what he had learnt about his workday self. He had mastered the dates and places that hung Casement's life to the wall of history. But Brid did not want to know anything of that. She wandered off to study the glass cases.

'Are you visiting Tralee?' he asked Boma.

'I suppose you could say that. I'm staying at Brid's.'

'You're from Dublin, aren't you?'

'I am.'

'It's a grand city, so it is,' he said.

'Is that Eamonn talking, or Sir Roger?' Boma asked.

Reminded, Eamonn stood up straight, lowered his register, changed his accent. 'It could be either. Wouldn't you like to know how I got to Africa?' he asked, a different, more confident, man.

'I would.'

'In 1880 I crossed the Irish Sea and took a job in Liverpool. I worked for the Elder-Dempster Shipping Line and stayed with some relations of mine, the Bannister family. But I didn't take to the stuffy office life and prevailed upon Sir Alfred Jones, the owner of the shipping company, to allow me to become a purser on the West Africa run. I sailed away on the SS *Bonny* in 1882, made three round trips and then – my heart full of Africa – joined the Congo International Association, set up by Leopold the Second of Belgium.'

Brid wandered back. 'It's cold in here. You'd think they'd heat it better.'

'You would, Mrs McCarthy . . . er . . . later I returned to the Congo, exposing the horrors of King Leopold. I was a one-man Abraham Lincoln at a time when the rest of the western world thought colonialism would be the making of everything. But it was seeing the horrors inflicted on the Africans that made me realize that what the English were doing in Ireland was part and parcel of the same thing.'

'What same thing?' Brid asked.

'National self-interest. I perceived it to be a cancer,' Eamonn replied. 'Er . . . later on, after my arrest at McKenna's Fort, and at my trial in London, the British tried to make out that I was a johnny-come-lately to the Irish Cause. But you only have to look at letters I wrote home to my cousin Gertrude Bannister to know that Ireland had always been in my thoughts.' Sir Roger sought about in the pocket of his jacket and produced a notebook. 'I quote,' he said, turning the pages. ' "There is so much to do here in Ireland that sometimes my heart faints when I think of the Congo and all its claims upon me, but I cannot, even for the sake of my own dear country, forget the poor people over there. And that is the way, I am sure, the claim of the Congo people must appeal to every sincere and genuine Irish native; the more we love our land and wish to help our people the more keenly we feel we cannot turn a deaf ear to suffering and injustice in any part of the world. I am quite sure that if I had not been an Irishman and an ardent believer in the nationality and rights of Ireland I should have passed through those Congo scenes of suffering humanity with a cold or at any rate so reserved a heart that I should never have committed myself as I did to assume an attitude of insistence so uncompromising that the doubts of my chiefs were swept away." ' Eamonn put the notebook away. 'No, the English could not blacken my character by asserting that I had suddenly changed allegiances, so they found other ways . . .' He looked hard at Brid and Boma. His face contorted as though he were a ham actor retelling Poe. 'You've heard of The Black Diaries, I presume. They are supposed to show that, while I was gathering information on atrocities in the Putumayo I was indulging in the grossest of unnatural practices with the natives. But I want to tell you, ladies, that those diaries were a complete and utter forgery, despite anything you may have heard to the contrary. And, if you read that contrary, remember the letter used to blacken Parnell's name; the forged medals that the British minted in Birmingham and then said had been given to the U-boat crew who sunk the *Lusitania*. The Black Diaries, so called—'

'I don't want to hear any more,' said Brid. 'We all know about the wicked forgeries. I think, Eamonn, that your account of Sir Roger's life would be much better without a word about the diaries. Still, I have to give you credit; you know a lot about Sir Roger. But what a White Father you'd have made, son!' She turned to Boma. 'Come on, Boma. We'd better be off to the shops. We've great shops in Tralee.'

Brid made off, while Boma hung back. She went up to Sir Roger. 'Thank you for that,' she said.

'You're welcome. If you want to know anything else, just come in. Will you do that?' Eamonn caught himself talking like he imagined Sir Roger would. He slumped back to himself, his back bowed, his voice rising half an octave. 'I mean, if you'd like,' he said.

She smiled at him.

'Only if you like, you know.'

'Thanks,' she said. 'I will. Goodbye, Sir Roger!'

Boma left, catching up with Brid. Mick watched from his chair. 'You'd be all right there, Eamonn,' he said.

'Get away, will you!' Eamonn replied, thinking of those blue eyes.

'Will you come to mass with me?' Brid asked Boma after breakfast the following morning.

'I haven't been much of a one for mass.'

'All the more reason to get back in His good books,' said Brid.

'Couldn't I mind the shop? I'd like to do something useful,' Boma tried.

'You could not!' Brid replied. 'Much more useful to accompany an old woman to mass. At my age I open and shut the shop when I want, anyhow. You saw what I did yesterday. I just close the door and forget it. The regular customers will come in and get what they need. And the blow-ins can just go on to the Eight 'til Late. They usually do.'

Boma was thinking of last night's rosary, the force-feeding of grace before and after meals. She knew she was being pulled back, just as she had been pulled back at Banna Strand. It was something that people had always done. *What is it about me? When they look at me, do they think, 'poor, benighted heathen'?* She didn't know whether to protest or not.

Brid was giving Boma a straight up-and-down look. 'I've another coat should fit you all right. It's just right for mass. I'll go and fish it out.'

After mass Brid introduced Boma to Pat McDonough. He was chatting to the curate, Father Devenish, at the church porch.

'So this is your friend, Brid McCarthy. I've been waiting for a view,' said Pat. He was a tall, slightly stooped man with a full head of snow-white hair and a tanned, lined, face. 'We've been hearing a lot of things about her.'

He looked at Boma. She returned his stare, then dropped her eyes self-consciously. 'Every last thing as good as gold,' he said, hoping Boma would look at him again, show him those wonderful eyes.

'She didn't go to Communion,' Brid said.

'No?' asked Pat. He twinkled at Boma.

'Of course, it's none of my business,' continued Brid. 'Still, there's Novena tonight; Boma could go to confession and then she'll be shipshape.'

Boma remembered how she had stopped going to mass partly because she hated to be seen not taking Communion with all the good people. It made her feel doubly a sinner. She resented the way a sinner could be so publicly spotted. It all seemed to be part of the plot. But she had never been subjected to such public castigation before. She was silent.

Brid looked around, waiting for a reaction.

'I'd better be off. I've the schools to visit,' said Father Devenish.

'Goodbye, Father,' Brid said. She turned back to Boma. 'No, it's none of my business. What time's confession, Pat? Eight, is it?'

'Leave it, Brid,' Pat said.

Boma looked at him in surprise. He winked.

'I was only trying—'

'Brid,' said Pat, 'if you want to keep your new friend you'd better try a bit of tactfulness.' He bent down, approached close to Brid and tapped the side of his nose with his index finger.

Brid stepped back a pace. 'We were thinking of going for a walk, Pat.'

'And I know where,' said Pat. 'You'll wear out Sir Roger's monument at the rate you're going, Brid McCarthy.'

They walked with Pat as far as his house on the road to the coast. He left them there. 'You know where I am, Boma. Daddy and me love a visit.'

As they were walking along the road, Brid said, 'Take no mind of Pat.'

'I liked him.'

'He gets bees in his belfry sometimes. Still, he's a good man. Great with his old dad, great; and he never misses mass. But he is a bit crazy sometimes.'

'I didn't notice.'

'Didn't you, Boma? You didn't notice the way he started fussing when I mentioned confession?'

Boma stopped in the road, marvelling how Brid could be so opaque.

'Are you tired, dear?' Brid asked.

'Yes, I think I am. I just don't understand you, Brid. What you said outside the church. It made me feel really small. If it hadn't been for Pat I'd have walked away then and there, so I would.'

'I only—'

'You only painted me in all the colours of a sinner. You humiliated me in front of the priest. Why did you do it, Brid?'

'Well, I'm sorry you feel like that, Boma.'

'I do feel like that. I feel very much like that. There I was thinking that you weren't judging me; that you had accepted me as a friend. But all the time you had me down as a magdalen and a suicidal one as well.'

'Well, that's what you are, Boma. Sure, I'd hate to think of you dying without going to confession. It could happen at any moment, you know. Just like that. The papers are full of it. It's for your own good. It's my duty, my Christian duty. What sort of friend would I be if I didn't care about your soul and its eternal destiny?'

Boma turned her back on Brid and started walking briskly back the way they had come. She pretended to ignore Brid's cries, but they echoed down all her years; so many people who wanted to love and reform her, who had taken her as their own little spiritual garden. *Now what?* she thought. *Now what? I should be walking back to the ocean.*

Then she heard a man's voice, calling her name.

She stopped, wondering if it was Pat. She turned, saw Brid standing, looking lost, where she had left her.

'Boma! It's me!' the voice called. 'I'm at the fort! Come over here and pay me a visit, will you?'

Boma did not move.

'Don't you owe me that?'

Briskly, Boma turned round and walked back towards the gap in the hedge that led to McKenna's Fort. She passed Brid but averted her eyes, turned onto the track and walked quickly towards the elevated clump of undergrowth.

She could see him there, waiting. His hands were pushed deep into the pockets of his jacket and he jittered his legs against the cold.

'Thanks for stopping,' he said as she approached him, passing the monument without a glance.

'It's you,' she said.

'Yes. You've been having a barney with Bridget, I see. You're not the first, I can tell you that. You've come up against Bridget's drystone wall. What can I tell you? She means well. But, Lord, I know it doesn't always come over like that.'

'All my life . . .' Boma said.

'You don't need to tell me, Boma. I know. I know how people get when they think they've sorted out the world to their satisfaction and God smiles down on them and all their works.'

'I didn't mind until just now,' Boma said, feeling a weight lifting from her chest. 'I've put up with her pushing me down for the rosary without a by your leave. God, I've been surrounded by people like her all my life but no-one has ever gone so far as telling everyone what a wicked woman I am in front of other people.'

'Stick with it, Boma. I think you've probably taught her a lesson.'

'I don't know.'

'Look, she's coming,' the man said. 'I warn you, don't expect a climb-down. If I know Bridget – and I do – she'll go on as if nothing has happened. She won't forget it, though.'

Brid soldiered up the last rise into the fort. 'Why did you go rushing on like that?' she asked.

The man smiled. 'What did I tell you?'

'You're here now, Brid,' Boma said.

'No thanks to you.' She looked around and the feeling the fort always gave her returned, making her meditative. 'Here he waited, Boma. For me it's the saddest time of all. Sir Roger's agony in the garden. Think about it, Boma. Sir Roger was into his fifties and he had led a life that would have killed most men. Twenty years in the White Man's Grave of Africa. Another few in the jungles of South America. He was never still. He never owned a house. Then two years in Germany, not speaking the language, not having any success with the Irish soldiers. Then a wretched two weeks in the submarine. A soaking. Can you imagine how he must have felt here? He waited here from seven in the morning until he was arrested at one in the afternoon. April. Soaked to the skin. Imagine it.'

Brid laid her hand on the plinth, leaned forward and started panting. 'The poor, dear man,' she said. 'Forgive us! Forgive us! We didn't know!'

Boma looked at the man.

'Leave her be. She's always like this,' he said.

'We've been trying to puzzle out who you are. Thanks for what you did. But I didn't think I'd see you again,' she said.

'I wouldn't leave you after what we went through, would I? When people save one another, how can they help but be friends?'

'You certainly saved me,' Boma said. 'I've been trying to work out how you managed it.'

'You'd be surprised,' he said. 'Still, touching what Bridget was saying about me, she's wrong to think I was in agony here. I danced and skipped in this place. Partly to keep warm, I'll grant you. But not only that. No, not only that.'

'I'm sorry . . .' Boma began.

The man pointed and on cue a skylark arose twittering from the field beyond the undergrowth of the fort. They followed its ascent until it collided with the sun.

Boma looked over at Brid. She was standing straight, looking at Boma hard.

'Are you all right, Brid?' Boma asked. 'This is the man who—'

'Are *you* all right?' Brid asked. 'You've been chuntering on to yourself like a lunatic.'

'This is the man who saved me,' Boma said, 'who gave me the medal.'

'Who is?' Brid asked.

Boma frowned at Brid, wondering whether she was holding a grudge, being deliberately opaque. She smiled at the man. 'I'm sorry,' she said.

'Don't be. It's not Bridget's fault,' he said.

Then Brid stepped between Boma and the man, staring hard into Boma's face. 'What's the matter?' she asked.

'I'm looking at the man who saved me.' She took hold of Brid and gently turned her around so that she was looking straight at the man. 'Now tell me you can't see him,' she said.

'I can't see anything, Boma.'

'Brid's speaking the truth, I'm afraid,' said the man. 'She can't see me.'

'But . . .' blurted Boma. She looked for Brid, locating her below her, on her knees.

'Is he there? Can you see him? It's Sir Roger, isn't it?'

The man winced. 'Will you tell Bridget to call me Roddie? That's what my friends call me.'

'He says you must call him Roddie,' Boma said automatically. 'Can't you see him, Brid? See him, please! I'm not cut out for this.'

'I can't. No, I can't. Jesus and Mary, I wish I could!'

Boma turned back to the man. She approached him, put out her hand to touch him, expecting that he would melt away or that her hand would go through him. But, when she touched the man's hand with the tip of her fingers, she met warm flesh. 'Jesus!' she said.

'Did you say "Jesus" prayerfully or vainly, Boma?'

'A bit of both, Brid.'

'Did you return Bridget her medal?' he asked.

'I did.'

'Thank her again for me.'

'He says thank you for the loan of the medal.'

'I'm sorry it took me a lifetime to return it to her. Tell her that.'

Boma did so.

'Even that day she gave it to me, as soon as the two children had gone off to the church, I regretted accepting Bridget's gift. It didn't seem fair. But tell her it gave me great consolation in the gaol in those difficult months before my execution.'

Boma told Brid.

'Tell her it was instrumental in bringing me back to the Catholic Faith. She'll like that.'

Boma told Brid.

Brid told Boma to tell Sir Roger to show himself to her.

The apparition bristled. 'There'll be no *Sir Rogering* me here. They stripped me of the knighthood after my execution. And I'd stripped myself of it years before. Nobody ever took from me anything that I surrendered more readily. I'm Roddie to the two of you.' He gazed at Brid. 'As for showing myself to Brid. I can't. I'm most awfully sorry but that's one of the conditions. Making myself visible eats up the supply of grace I've brought with me most dreadfully.'

Boma told Brid.

'Tell him I don't believe that for a minute,' said Brid vehemently. 'Our Lady appeared to three youngsters at Fatima; to I don't know how many boys and girls at Medjugorje; to all sorts in Madrid; to Fiona Bowen in Inchigeelagh and to that girl in Mayo.'

'Bridget was always a great one for the apparitions,' Roddie said. 'Don't tell her that.'

Something suddenly clicked in Boma's head, though she was not sure whether the switch was now on 'open' or 'closed'. 'I know,' she told Brid. 'The two of you are joshing me. I don't know why you would. Maybe you want to get me on my knees to the priest like a good unmarried mother. Is that it? It's a joke, isn't it? You can see him, can't you, Brid?'

'How could you say that, Boma? Do you really think I would make fun of the sacred?'

'You really can't see him?'

'No, I can't. I wish I could. Oh, I wish I could.'

'Tell Bridget she really doesn't need to see me. All these years she and I have been fast friends.'

Boma told Brid.

'So why have you come to me?'

'You forced me into it. I left much undone in my life. I don't suppose I was unique in that at all. But I've been watching you, Boma. Your whole life I've been watching you. Not in a threatening way, I trust. Not at all. But in the way a man may watch over the descendant of a good friend. Of course, we have many calls on us. We watch constantly. I've had more to do of that than most,' Roddie sighed. 'The price one pays for an eventful life, I suppose.'

'What's he saying?' Brid asked. She had taken out her rosary and was passing the beads through her fingers.

'He says he's been watching me,' Boma said.

'The dear, poor man,' Brid said.

'You might tell Bridget to stop saying that, too.'

Boma made to do so. 'Not now. Give me a chance to cut out. Tell her later. Tell her with tact. Of course, I know why she's saying it. She thinks I came to a bad end. She does not know I ascended the scaffold like a bride to her beloved . . . well, you get the idea.'

He looked around the fort. 'I spent the happiest hours of my life here, dear Boma. Strange but true. I was back in Ireland. I had jumped into trouble with both feet, shouting, "We can throw off the yoke! It is possible! It is worth dying for!" Of course, when Constable Riley and Sergeant Hearn appeared, coming along that track at the side of the field, trembling behind their carbines, I thought to myself that it was a rather unpromising start. I might have been a poacher. Still, life's full of unpromising starts. Death too, if you want the truth.'

'Ask Roddie what he wants us to do,' Brid commanded.

'I can hear her,' Roddie replied. 'Brid can tell the priests in Ardfert if she likes. I doubt they'll believe you but, Boma, you and I will convince them soon enough. Tell them Roddie is not best pleased with the way things are going. Tell them that.'

Boma told Brid.

Brid was not sure. 'Not best pleased? I don't think I could tell Canon Dawson that.'

Roddie sighed. 'It doesn't matter. They'll find out soon enough. Just tell them I'm here. You and Brid go together. It doesn't have to be today. There's no hurry. I'll tell you what you can do for me, Boma. Read one of the books Brid has about my life. She's got several tucked away. I'd recommend the one by Brian Inglis. A good man. I know him well. Anyway, things may become clearer to you.'

'I will,' said Boma. 'Thank you again. For what you did.'

'Dear Boma, it was the very least I could do.' He reached out, touched her. 'God, you're a beauty,' he said. 'Still, I'd have expected that. You're from grand stock, so you are.'

'How do you mean?' she asked.

'Your mother was a fine woman. But your father . . . now there was a man!'

'I didn't know either of them. Can you tell me about them?'

He placed the index finger of his right hand upon her lips and drew the tip down the generous 3-shape. 'Later,' he said. 'I must go. Now, watch carefully. It will help you believe if you're not convinced. I may not do this again. It really drinks up the juice.'

She saw him turn, peering out through the hedgerows towards the ocean. 'Be good to Bridget. I know she's got her rough side, but she's been a good friend to me. I'd still be in purgatory if it wasn't for her. Tell her that, but do me a favour: wait until I've cut out.'

The apparition waved his hand, then parted the branch of a tree, walked off down the ramparts of McKenna's Fort, and disappeared.

Brid saw the branch move in the still air. 'He's going, isn't he?'

'Yes,' Boma replied. 'He's going.'

'Did he say when he'd come back?'

'No, but I think he will.'

'Did he tell you anything else?'

'He said that he wouldn't be here if it hadn't been for you. You got him out of purgatory.'

'That's wonderful news,' Brid replied. 'Mind you, it would have been a poor do if I hadn't got him out. And what was he doing in purgatory anyway? The dear, poor man. What else?'

'He told me to tell you to shut up about confession.'

And Boma set off back to the road, leaving Brid to make her own way.

*Poor Indians! You had life – your white destroyers only
possess things. That is the vital distinction. I take it,
between the 'savage' and the civilised man. The savage is,
the white man has. The one lives and moves to be; the
other toils and dies to have.*

SIR ROGER CASEMENT

3

THE REFECTORY OF ST CLARE'S CONVENT, DUNDRUM, THE MOTHER-
house of the Sisters of the Flaming Heart, was completely filled up
by the voices of African singers. Sister Paul of the Cross, in charge of
the proceedings, had turned the volume of the old Black Box
record-player to maximum.

The nuns had gathered from all over Ireland and Britain for the
Feast Day. They sat around the rectangular oak refectory table at
the head of which, behind a white cake, sat an elderly nun wearing
thick pebble spectacles. The cake had iced on the top in green Celtic
script, 'SISTER PAULA: FIFTY YEARS WITH THE SISTERS OF
THE FLAMING HEART'.

The cutting of the cake was to be almost the last act of the feast-day celebration. Soup and a main course of Matthew's salmon accompanied by jacket potatoes and salad had been eaten. White wine contributed by the bishop had flowed in quantities modest enough, though with a liberality seldom to be seen at St Clare's.

To Sister Paula's right sat Sister de Porres, who had arrived for the festivities from Tralee the previous day. It was Sister de Porres who was the first to see the tears trickling from behind the thick lenses of Sister Paula's spectacles.

Thinking that the music was to blame, Sister de Porres tried to signal to Sister Paul of the Cross to fade it out and allow her to make her speech and presentation before things got worse. But she could not catch the nun's eye. Anyway, she thought, perhaps it was no bad thing to weep. There was plenty to weep about. She might do it herself before the evening was out.

'I hope you're having a good time, Sister,' she said.

'Grand,' replied Sister Paula. 'I know you don't expect blubbering from me, but I haven't heard those lads for years. I've got the EP in my room. I had nothing to play it on there. And, to tell you the truth, it hasn't been given much of an airing since. In spite of the passing of years, it hurts.'

'*Agnus Dei, qui tollis peccata mundi, dona nobis pacem!*' sang the voices of men and boys of the Luba tribe of Lualaba Basin in the south-east Congo.

The music stopped and this was followed by a few seconds of silence. Then conversation slowly, bashfully, started, the nuns conscious that talking was a rare event in the refectory.

Sister de Porres fiddled with her fish-knife. 'I'm not going to embarrass you when I make my speech, Sister. But I have to tell you how grateful Sister Mary and I are to you. If it hadn't been for you I doubt we would be sitting here together now.'

'I'm glad you won't be saying that, Sister. I'm not sure it's true, anyway. Still, thank you.' Then she heard Sister Dennis from the Liverpool convent say, 'That music was on *Desert Island Discs*, Sister. Can you pick it up in Dublin?'

'We can, Sister. On long wave,' replied Sister Mary.

'Ken Livingstone – he's a politician – chose it. After they played a little piece he said that he thought the singers were probably all dead.

He stopped me in my tracks when he said that. You don't think it's true, do you?'

'Who knows? There was such chaos, then and now. They could well be.'

'When was it recorded, do you know?'

'Some time in the Fifties.'

'When you were there.'

Sister Mary glanced towards the head of the table. Sister Paula looked at her plate. 'Yes, Sister. They were called The Singers of King Baudouin. It was an unfortunate name to give them when you think of what happened.'

Sister de Porres rang a little bell. Silence descended at once in the practised way of St Clare's.

'Sisters, we are here to celebrate Sister Paula's fifty years as a nursing sister in our dear Order of the Flaming Heart. I don't want to make Sister Paula blush by talking about all her good works over the years. I wouldn't want to rob her of the smallest jewel from her heavenly crown. But as someone who was with Sister Paula in the Congo – now Zaïre – all those years ago, I think it was very appropriate that Sister Paul of the Cross chose to play the mass of the Luba people. For it is those people whom Sister Paula served for the first ten years of her African apostolate when she was based at the Nyangwe Mission. I firmly believe that there are many people in that region – perhaps with a few grey hairs by now – who still remember our sisters fondly; and young – I repeat – young Sister Paula. For to the Luba people Sister Paula will be forever young. Those people were singing to you, Sister.

'I, as I'm sure you can see, am years younger than Sister Paula. We did not meet until I was sent out to Boma in 1952. By then Sister Paula was an old Africa hand. It was a great blessing for me to have Sister there. She taught me so much and, when the Congo troubles came, she was like a lioness protecting her cubs. Some thirty-five years have passed since we left Africa, and all of you round this table don't need me to tell you anything of that. Anyway, Sister is going to have to walk her head back to her cell in a wheelbarrow if I go on. So I won't. But I will make the presentation.'

And Sister de Porres produced the framed illuminated scroll of commemoration and gave it to the elderly nun. Sister Paul of the Cross made them do it again so that she could take a snap of the exact moment.

'Let's have a speech!' called out Sister Mary.

Sister Paula stood up. 'You'll get no speech from me, Sisters. Just a thank-you. A big thank-you. God bless you. Pray for me.' And she cut the cake.

Half an hour later Sister Paula was sitting alone with Sister de Porres in the small parlour adjoining the refectory. A perfunctory turf fire was burning in the grate. From the refectory came sounds of the other nuns clearing away and doing the wash-up.

'Not too much of an ordeal, Sister?' asked Sister de Porres.

'Not at all!' replied Sister Paula. 'It was grand. Worth staying around for.'

'It's not quite over yet.'

'It isn't? Oh dear. I don't think I'm up for any more jollifications. If the Pope himself rang the doorbell I'd shout down to him to come back in the morning.'

'It's better than that, Sister.'

'Well, that's not difficult. A lot has to be better than that.'

'You're still a straight talker, I see.'

'I am.'

Suddenly, Sister de Porres saw Sister Paula, the years stripped away, standing on the veranda of the hospital, telling the armed men to leave at once, telling them straight in their own language that they were behaving disgracefully. 'I don't know . . .' she said.

'Don't know what, Sister?'

'I'm not certain that what I'm going to tell you is reliable. I'm not even sure I should be telling you. The taxi-driver from Tralee mentioned a couple of women he'd lifted from Ardfert – you know Matthew, the driver, comes from Ballyheige, near Tralee? Anyway, he mentioned, just dropped it in conversation – you can't get him to shut up – that one of the women was African-looking and was called Boma.'

Sister Paula looked at Sister de Porres questioningly. At that moment, in the refectory, Sister Paul of the Cross turned over the record of the singers of Luba and their voices filled the room.

' "Boma", are you sure he called her that?'

'Yes, it's at least a coincidence, isn't it?'

'It certainly is, Sister.'

'Of course, it may not be her. I asked Matthew about her age.'

'And what did he say?'

'He said it was hard to tell but he thought thirty-five or there-abouts.'

'Did he say what she was doing in Ardfert?'

'No, just staying at this old woman's bed and breakfast.'

'I see.'

'I thought you should know.'

Sister Paula stood up. 'You did the right thing, Sister,' she said. 'Lord knows what I'm going to do about it, but you were right to tell me.' She listened to the Singers of King Baudouin for a moment. 'Did you hear what Sister Dennis said? About the singers being dead?'

'I did, Sister. Yes, I did.'

'You don't think it's true, do you? I can see them so clearly. Every one of them. If I thought they were dead, it would break my heart.'

'No, I'm sure it isn't true,' replied Sister de Porres. 'It was a politician who said it. And you know what they're like.'

The following morning Brid was up early. She washed herself quickly and then went upstairs to the attic, where Tim's belongings were stored. There she started rummaging through boxes of his books and papers.

She found a biography of Roger Casement and searched through it, looking for photographs. Finding nothing, she put it back in the box and started shifting the others around. At last she came upon a box that had been at the very back. She opened it, smelled the damp coming off it. Inside were piled all sorts of books; textbooks from Tim's school, old paperbacks. Then she found what she was after. She lifted the Brian Inglis biography out and was about to go back downstairs to make Boma's breakfast when her eyes were caught by a bright paperback. She took it out, read the title, *Song of the Loon*, and looked hard at the picture on the cover. It showed a young bearded man dressed in a long gown. He was sitting next to a near-naked, dark-skinned man – perhaps an American Indian – who was playing a flute. The hand of the bearded man was on the Indian's shoulder.

Thinking that the book must be about the missions, Brid took it and went back downstairs.

When she had seated Boma at the table, she said grace, brought her cereal, following it up with the full Irish breakfast. She sat down to share tea with her and, while Boma was drinking, produced the biography.

'Do you recognize this photograph, Boma?' Brid asked.

Boma put her cup back into the saucer. 'I think so. Are there any others? He's terrible young there.'

Brid fanned the pages until she found a photograph of Roger Casement taken shortly before his execution. He was leaving the law courts, on his way to a waiting car after his appeal against his death sentence had been dismissed. He wore a suit – perhaps made of tweed – and a white handkerchief peeped out of his breast pocket. His hands were joined in front. He was holding his hat. There was no sign of handcuffs. He was staring ahead of him at the ground. A passer-by was looking at him with a smile on his face.

'Yes,' Boma said. 'That's the man who saved me, the same man I saw at the fort.'

Brid was not surprised. Even before the incident at the fort, there had been something in the air, signs and portents and a heightened awareness. A buzz of excitement. Life had taken on drama. So, at long last, after a lifetime of prayer, Sir Roger had returned. He would help out, perhaps warn, rail against the heathen influences spreading into Ireland. It was what he had done his whole life long, wasn't it? He had deprived himself of a settled family life in order to wander the planet alleviating suffering. Then, when he returned to his own land, he had not been blind to the travails of his own people. And his devotion and commitment, which had cost him his life, had also caused him to come back from the after-life.

Our Lady had come back to warn, to strengthen faith. Knock, Ballinspittle and who knew where else. So why not another saint? Why not Sir Roger Casement?

Brid had long since made the transition from praying for Roger's soul – something she recalled doing immediately she heard of his execution at the hands of the English – to praying to him, through him, to put a word in for her with the Lord. While other women of her acquaintance patronized St Theresa or Padre Pio, Brid had chosen Casement. She did not ask anyone's authority to do so. It was a secret of her heart.

'I think I ought to go,' Boma told Brid after breakfast.

They had washed up the breakfast things. Brid had opened the shop though no-one except a man delivering cream had come in. Brid bought one carton of double cream while the huge lorry idled outside. Then they chatted, leaning against the counter while the fridge purred and cars passed by outside in the main street.

'And where do you plan on going? Have you cloth ears? Have I not been telling you till I'm blue in the face that your home is here? I know Ardfert isn't the bright lights but it's a good enough place. There's a church near by. Only a hop and a skip to Tralee too – you liked Tralee, didn't you, Boma? – and you with a baby on the way.'

There really was nowhere to go. She had a few friends in Dublin, but none of them would welcome her. Most were in touch with Declan in one way or another, would think her dead. The news would spread. And it was better that she remained dead. More than better, perhaps staying dead would save her life. 'Do you really mean it? I haven't a bean, you know.'

'I'm saying it, aren't I? I'm tired of saying it. You're company for me. You need company yourself. Especially now. And Roddie's sent you to me. He wouldn't want you to up and leave now, would he?'

Boma didn't say anything, just looked out.

'You think I'm a daft old woman, don't you?' Brid asked.

'No, I do not. It's just . . .'

'You'll stay, so. We'll get you signed on at the baby clinic. You're no spring chicken to be having your first baby.'

'Thanks very much.'

'Think nothing of it. Have you finished your breakfast, Boma? While I take out the dishes you say grace. Then you can start reading about Roddie.'

For the sake of peace Boma crossed herself, but instead of praying, she wondered what was going to become of her. Then she remembered the apparition and what he had said. Roddie had come to save her and would not let anything bad happen to her. He was there. She had seen him, though now she could see him no longer.

Later in the day, Father Devenish, the young curate of Brid McCarthy's church, watched Brid and Boma walking side by side down the path between the church and the presbytery. He wished that the parish priest had been in to hear what they had had to confide.

He did not know what to think; had told Brid and Boma that. It was, he said, completely beyond his experience, indeed beyond the experience of Holy Mother Church who had, he said, seen everything. Our Lady came back, the odd saint, too, with a gripe or a helpful hint, but not Anglo-Irish rebels who had died on the scaffold and whose reputation was in limbo. Dead rebels stayed quiet, except for the odd memorial, a mention at meetings of the Old Hibernians, an occasional outpouring of fusty national piety. It might be dismissed as a bit of nonsense except for the fact that Brid McCarthy was no fool.

Luckily for Father Devenish, he did not have time to think too much about the alleged apparitions. There were visits to be made, the Sacrament to be delivered to the sick of the parish. He bent down to put on his cycle-clips, got out his bike and wheeled it out of the presbytery grounds.

Standing in front of the monument to victims of the Black and Tans stood a bearded man whom the priest could not remember seeing before. He was in his shirtsleeves, over which were slung a pair of old-fashioned braces attached to buttons on his too-large trousers. Father Devenish saluted the man as he mounted his bike.

'Good-evening!' called the man. 'Might I have a word, Father?'

'It'll have to be a quick one. I'm off on my rounds.'

'I won't detain you long.'

Father Devenish got off his bike and wheeled it over to the man. 'Hello there,' he said. 'I haven't seen you around here before.'

'No, I haven't been here in years. I've only come back because I have some business to take care of.'

'What's your name?'

'Roger Casement, but my friends call me Roddie.'

Father Devenish wasted no time. 'So you're the one who's been putting ideas in the heads of Brid McCarthy and her friend. Aren't you ashamed, man?'

Roddie gazed back at the priest steadily, the priest's words widening his smile.

'You realize it could be very dangerous for a woman Brid's age to have all the upset? She doesn't know whether she's coming or going! And impersonating a great Irish hero too! That beats everything!'

'You're wrong, Father. It'll be the making of Bridget.'

'What do you want from her? Money, is it?'

Roddie shook his head, still smiling. 'They all told me getting people to believe was going to take up all my time. They spoke the truth. I'll tell you what,' he said, looking up the road, 'signal that car to stop.'

Father Devenish looked back along the road to Fenit where an old eleven-hundred was heading their way at a steady twenty-five miles per hour.

'I will not. I don't have time for such nonsense,' said Father Devenish.

But the car stopped without bidding.

'Evening, Father!' called the driver, Colm Devlin, a farmer who lived with his mother, Mags Devlin, on the road to Ballyheige. 'Will you be coming to bring Communion to Mammy tonight?'

'I will. I'm on my way, Colm.'

'That's grand,' said Colm.

'Ask him if he can see me,' said Roddie.

'I'll do no such thing. Will you listen to this man, Colm? Will you listen to him?'

'Sorry, Father?'

'Your man here says he's Roger Casement come back to visit us!'

'God rest him!' said Colm Devlin, worrying that the Paddy with Guinness, taken on the hoof in Tralee, was affecting him. He looked around, trying to find the imposter.

'You can see him, can't you?' pleaded Father Devenish. 'He's there. Right next to me.'

'I can't see anything, Father.'

Roddie was smiling. 'Some people see me and some people do not. Isn't it always the way, Father? I'm sure you've experienced that yourself many a time. Some people get what you're saying and some don't. Life's like that.'

'Shut up, you!' commanded Father Devenish. 'Colm, describe the man I'm talking to!'

Colm blinked up at the priest.

Father Devenish let go of his bike, though he was not aware that he had been holding it. It fell with a crash onto the verge. The priest pulled the car door open and grabbed Colm Devlin by the arm, lifting him out of the car.

'Father, will you—'

'Just stand there,' said Father Devenish. Colm stood, from Father Devenish's point of view, eyeball to eyeball with Roger Casement. 'Now tell me you don't see him, if you dare.'

'I don't see a thing, Father. Honest to God!'

Another car was passing. The driver, seeing Colm pulled out of his car by an angry priest, stopped a few yards past the monument and got out. 'Are you having a problem, Father?' he asked.

Father Devenish let go of Colm Devlin and strode over to the new witness. He pulled him over, standing him up beside Colm. 'What can you see?' he asked him.

'I can see the memorial to brave Irish men and women killed by the beasts of the Black and Tans,' said the driver piously.

'What else? What else can you see?'

'Fields, sky, grass.'

'Not over there. Here.'

The man shrugged. Then he brightened, a eureka expression coming to his face. 'An empty Surf packet. It's a disgrace what people leave behind. "Take your rubbish home", that's my motto.'

'You're supposed to be seeing Sir Roger Casement!' Colm told him.

'The fuck I am!' said the driver. 'Sorry, Father!'

Father Devenish went behind Roddie, seized him by his shirtsleeves, and pushed him forward. Roddie smiled. 'O ye of little faith!' he said.

'Now can you see him?'

The men saw the young curate, arms grasping, hands half-clenched, embracing the air in front of him. They looked at one another.

'Will you let me go, Father? Look, they can't see me. Just as Brid can't see me. How can I make you believe me, Father Doubting Thomas? Your man, Colm Devlin, has been in Murphy's Tavern in Tralee. He's had a Guinness and a whiskey. Go on, tell him that.'

'You've been at Murphy's and you drank a Guinness and a whiskey,' said Father Devenish.

'How did you know that? Is there no such thing as a piece of privateness any longer in the world?'

'He told me.'

'And I'll tell you something else,' continued Roddie. 'The other man is from Ballyheige. He owns a bar across the road from my statue and he's been to Tralee to buy tumblers. I won't tell you what else he was doing there.'

Father Devenish repeated what Roddie had told him.

'Ten on ten,' said the driver. 'How in God's name did you—' But he stopped speaking as Father Devenish sank to his knees, finally realizing that he was in the middle of a miracle.

'None of that, Father,' said Roddie. 'None of that. This isn't one of those. This is a different thing altogether.'

Roddie lifted the priest up, saluted him and walked back along the road towards Fenit.

In Harrogate the following day the memorial service for seven victims of an IRA bomb was taking place. The book compiled by Mrs O'Neill in Enniskillen was, along with many others, lying on a table in the nave, waiting to be blessed and presented to the Lord Mayor. Security men were making one last sweep of the church before allowing the congregation, welling up in huge numbers behind the barricades outside, to enter.

A few hours earlier, in Leeds, a Ford Transit van had been stolen by two men. They drove the van to a lock-up garage behind a block of Fifties flats in the south of the city and loaded the back with a deadly cargo. They then waited until an hour and a half before the service was due to start and began driving through the afternoon traffic, traffic building up to rush hour, towards York.

Neither man spoke. They listened to the radio and went through the plans they had made. The Transit was to be driven to the centre of York and left close to the Minster. They were not going to leave the van until five minutes before zero at five, exactly the time of the commencement of the memorial service in nearby Harrogate. No warning was to be given.

Though Sean and Declan, sitting in silence in front of their bomb, were unaware of it, the IRA had been panicked by the misplaced bomb in Enniskillen. Despite the silence imposed on those involved, news was leaking out. This bomb in York was to be the answer to talk of supernatural intervention.

Declan, in the passenger seat, looked at his watch.

'OK?' asked Sean.

'Great.'

'And at the back?'

Declan glanced round to look at the concoction of Semtex, fertilizer explosives, broken glass, ball-bearings and nails. 'Happy as Larry,' he said. He turned back to the front but he could still see the lethal parcel in his head. It was about the size of half a dozen shoe-boxes. Neat, old-fashioned looking, it was; wrapped in brown paper and string. In an hour less two minutes it would explode and hit the headlines. But

Declan could hardly believe it. It did not seem possible to him, even though he had been a part of many such bomb-delivering expeditions stretching back over a decade; he could never believe *at this moment* that the deadly cargo he carried was, in fact, deadly. He knew it was a foolish thought but he could not rid himself of it. It was, despite devastating evidence to the contrary, unbelievable, and he could not get his mind round the reality.

At the start of it, he had wanted to tell people. Once he had almost let it slip to Boma. When his mother clucked ambiguous disapproval of the sight of one of his bombings – she was for the bombs but against the carnage – he had wanted to say, 'I did that, Mam. All me own work.' He hadn't. Now she thought he was fully employed as a garage mechanic in West London. And he was, though his boss was understanding about time off. But his attitude had changed. He no longer half-wanted to be known. He kept himself aloof, even within the cell of the IRA that had swallowed him. The IRA sent money in his name back to his mother; had even opened a pension scheme for him. Bombs had become a second job, more a job of work than a political cause, the jam on his bread and butter. Bombings and political posturing were their – and his – stock-in-trade. The organization which had in his youth seemed like the only guardians of poor Catholics in Northern Ireland, now seemed like the main cancer in those same communities. The fine sentiments rang hollow. They had, like any mafia anywhere, gained power but lost love. They were Robin Hoods who, starting out robbing the rich, now went for the easier option of the poor. They had slipped into it a step at a time. While still reciting the old slogans of change, they did not, in their heart of hearts, want that change – for change would reduce coin and privilege.

'Slow down a bit, Sean. We're getting ahead of schedule.'

'Right,' replied Sean, easing the van down to fifty-five. He decided to move to the slow lane. He checked his windscreen mirror, saw Roddie smiling at him, and accelerated in panic, hoping to leave the smiling figure behind him. He looked again, but the face was still there, smiling.

'Jesus!' said Sean. 'There's a man in the back, Declan!'

Declan looked across at Sean, saw him gazing into his mirror and looked behind him.

Roddie was sitting on the bomb holding two wires apart. He smiled serenely at the sight of Declan. 'Did I give the two of you a fright?'

he asked. 'Your poor hearts must have missed a beat when you saw me. It isn't a nice feeling, is it? It's a tiny moment that mimics death, lads. I can tell you that. There's nothing worse. Except the real thing.'

'Stop the car, Sean! Pull over!' shouted Declan.

'What would happen if I join these wires?' Roddie asked. 'Would your bomb explode? I know very little about such things but I have received some coaching from some late bombers of late. They assure me that these two wires will do the trick.'

'What . . . ?' asked Sean.

'Just keep driving, lads. Face the front and listen.' The men did so. 'I know what you're planning. We've been watching you over the years and they sent me to stop this nonsense. You know me, though you've never met me before. When I tell you who I am you will probably not believe me. *There must be some logical explanation*, you'll think. *This can't be happening to me*. Well, I advise you to put all those questions aside. My name is Roger Casement and I am here to knock heads together. Yes, that's the gist of it, boys. I'm back from the limepit to settle things once and for all. You're in the middle of a miracle, me buckos. And this miracle will either kill or cure you.'

'You were hiding in the back,' said Declan helplessly.

'I was, was I, Declan O'Hare of Seventeen Kidderminster Road, Camden, who abused himself – I use the Catholic parlance – three times last night, thinking of Princess Anne and a lady who will remain nameless, the while? Nerves, no doubt. I'm the last one to stand in judgement. But I know you, Declan. Through and through I know you. All your doings: your every bomb and bullet. And you don't believe in me either, do you, Sean McMahon of Flat Four, Highbury Lodge, Islington, who took a pill early this morning to calm the nerves, washing it down with Nescafé and powdered milk; who left his ladyfriend sleeping in the put-me-up bed? It's a small flat, but nicely furnished with Irish scenes. Your Irish Writers calendar in the kitchen is still on February. You keep meaning to turn it over but you're too idle. Believe it now? Well, I can't be bothered going on trying to convince you maggots any more. The whole time allotted to apparitions is spent in getting heathens to believe it. It really doesn't matter. In my hands I have your death. That's clear enough, isn't it? A few days ago I returned a package left in a public convenience in Enniskillen by a young man. He and his companions were given another chance. You two I abhor even more but I'll think about letting you off the hook if you do the right thing.

'The right thing. That's what I'm after. What you have been doing is not the right thing. You've been slaughtering innocents for far too long. Yes. Innocents. Massacres of the innocents through the land. And when you do that you send a cry to heaven for vengeance. You maggots are busy making sure that the history of the future will be miserable for our people. I'm here to tell you that none of your forefathers who fought for Ireland's freedom wanted this. You are bringing shame on our memory and we're fed up with it. What are we?'

Neither Sean nor Declan replied. Roddie seized hold of the short hairs on Declan's temple and pulled. 'What are we?' he repeated.

'Get the fuck—'

'What are we?'

'Fed up.'

Roddie released his grip.

'That's right. Now I haven't yet decided what to do with the two of you. I may blow us all to blazes – though I must tell you that for me explosions are really rather exhilarating – but not for you, I think. For me, they're like coming to the top of the dunes and feeling the wind from the west buffeting my face. Well, it was the last couple of times. Yes, I could set off the bomb here and now and we get another bomb exploding before its time. There've been a lot of those and all the while you thought it was "human error". *Au contraire*, my friends, it was "divine truth" speaking, but you were too blinkered to understand. I really don't know why I'm telling you this. You should know it perfectly well already. Look around you – not just Ireland, but everywhere – and you see people living and dying by the sword. You're all so busy being manly and strutting and arrogant. It's past Green and Orange, English and Irish now. It's in that wretched ram-headed territory of pride.'

Sean reached into his inside pocket for his gun. He took it out and, using the mirror to guide him, placed it on his right shoulder. He fired a shot.

'Goodness, what a noise!' said Roddie. 'It went quite through me. Shoot me as much as you like, lads. Give the gun to your man and let him have a good go. Maybe that'll convince you I'm past killing.'

Declan grabbed the gun from Sean and fired repeatedly at Roddie's head. The bullets buried themselves in the coachwork of the Transit.

'What a smell! Open the window, there's a good lad. Now the alternative to a big bang is for you to turn off the road to York and listen to what I have to tell you.'

Sean glanced over at Declan. Declan nodded and Sean looked for a turn-off.

They reached a parking-place and Roddie told the men to stop.

'I'll say this once, and once only. Either I'll blow the two of you to Kingdom Come. Pearse and Connolly and Clarke and Davitt and Parnell and I don't know who else – not to mention the innocents you've done to death in the past – are itching to give you a jolly good rollicking. It isn't a prospect I'd fancy myself. Still, perhaps you feel you're both man enough for it. Being real men is very important to you, isn't it? You don't like being thought of as sissies. No, you've spent your whole lives running away from cries of sissy. The other way may be more difficult. It's hard – really rather courageous – to be a sissy around hard-cases. You can be my messengers. Go back to your chums in the IRA and tell them what's happened today. Tell them that Roger Casement told you to stop it. Of course, they won't believe you, and when they don't believe you, tell them that signs will follow. I'll see to that.'

Neither man spoke. Neither could.

'Come on,' said Roddie. 'We haven't got all day. I've got a tight schedule.'

'What'll we do with the bomb?' Sean asked.

'Take it back to the garage where you got it from. I'd say it won't explode unless the two wires are connected. Tell that devil, Paddy, to come and take it to bits. When you've done that, it wouldn't be a bad idea to go to confession. If the priest shouts at you, take it on the chin. Now which is it to be?'

'We'll do as you say,' said Sean.

'And what about you, Declan?'

'OK,' said Declan.

'Right you are,' said Roddie. 'And don't forget, I'm watching you. If you ask me it was the lot of you starting to think that no-one was watching you that got us into this jakes of a situation in the first place. Anyway, now you know. If you look like you're forgetting again, or thinking that this was just a dream, I'll be back. And next time it'll be the worse for you.'

'What about you? Are you coming back to Leeds with us?'

'No. I'll get out here, thank you very much.'

And Roddie yanked the wires, bending them apart. The two men saw them vibrate, felt a warm wind for a moment as Roddie disappeared.

Sean started the van and drove off, back towards Leeds. He looked in his wing-mirror and a tall bearded figure was waggling his finger at him in warning. He looked across to Declan, who was weeping, his hands covering his face, thinking of his sins, wishing Boma Hephernan would come back and open her blouse, let him rest himself between her breasts and tell her his troubles. But she could not do that. Boma and her half-made baby had flown upwards from the bomb blast on Hungerford Bridge. Now they sat on their high cloud and pointed accusing fingers at Declan.

Brennan, the owner of the tavern in Ballyheige, was telling a bar-full of customers about the strange apparition he had witnessed being witnessed on the Fenit Road the day before.

'Father Devenish was beside himself, so beside himself that he was coming out his other side. Kept saying again and again, "Can you see him?" Of course, me and the other fellow – don't ask me his name, farms near Ardfert – couldn't see a fucking thing. Father was chatting away to himself, swearing blind he was talking to this fellow. And this fellow was masquerading as Roger Casement.'

'Same again,' said a customer. 'And a packet of Tayto – doesn't matter which flavour; she'll eat anything – for the missis.'

Brennan pulled the pints and fetched the packet of crisps. The customer took the crisps out into the vestibule, where his wife sat alone. Then he returned to the bar and collected his Guinness. 'So what happened?' he asked.

'Father said the man walked away towards Fenit. He was a bit wobbly and we took him back to his presbytery and gave him a drink.'

'They've got a fine stock at the presbytery,' said the customer.

'How would you know that, Pat?' asked an old man, Peter Coughlin, sitting on his stool at the corner of the bar. 'You haven't darkened the doors of a church since I don't know when.' Then he motioned to Brennan. 'Get out of me light, will you? The television pictures come all that exorbitant way from Argentina by a great expensive bugger of a satellite and then to be stopped at the very last split of a second by your big bum!'

'I don't know what to make of it,' said Brennan.

'Forget it,' Pat said, pulling on his pint. 'Father'd probably had one too many.'

'He was sober. I may not know much but I know a sober man when I see one.'

'Which is seldom,' said Peter Coughlin.

'What do you think, Peter?' Brennan asked.

'I think it's old Ireland's fate to be visited by every member of the Holy Family and their hangers-on. They probably get a free trip to Holy Ireland as a prize in the tombola.'

'Ye old blasphemer, ye!' mocked Brennan.

'And Peter's missis you'd think was carved into the communion rails,' said Pat.

'Look it,' rejoined Peter Coughlin, '– and I'll thank you to keep my Eileen out of this – we're not required to believe in visitations by the Blessed Virgin or whoever else. Show me where it's an article of faith? Show me that!'

Pat mumbled into his drink.

'And what difference has it ever made, them coming down and perching on a rock in front of kids? I'll tell you, it's made the shop-keepers rich, that's what it's done. A good apparition and the town's made! It beats a German factory by a mile, so it does.'

'Ballyheige could benefit from an apparition, and that's a fact,' said Brennan.

'You see?' said Peter. 'He's licking his fat chops already! Bums on his old bar stools, statues of all the holy saints behind the bar. He'd love it. A couple of years and he'd be up and off to Marbella.' Peter laughed at the thought and turned his attention back to the silent football match.

'But this time it isn't the Blessed Virgin, it's Roger Casement,' said Brennan.

A young man sitting with his girlfriend, who had not spoken before, just watched the proceedings with a wry smile, said, 'And he was queer as a goose.'

'Who said that?' Peter Coughlin said in a loud voice, addressing the whole bar. 'Go on, who said it?' He stood up.

'Said what?' asked Brennan.

'I can't bring myself to repeat it. Who said it?'

The young man said, 'About Roger Casement being queer as a goose? I said it.'

'Take it back!'

'I will not,' said the man. 'It's well known. It's a proven fact.'

Peter picked up his walking-stick and made to cross the room to the young man's table. Pat held him by the arm. 'Let go of me, I tell you! Let me at that maggot!' Peter shouted, though he did not pull hard against Pat's restraining arm.

'There'll be nothing like that in here,' said Brennan.

'I never thought I'd live to see the day that an Irishman would dare to blacken the memory of a great Irish patriot,' said Peter.

'Who's blackening it?' rejoined the man. 'All I'm saying is that he was queer and that, being queer, it's unlikely he's going to come back from heaven above now, is it?'

'Shut it, Tommy,' said the young man's girlfriend, seeing the bar hardening against her companion's opinions.

'He's English,' said Peter, trying to regain some composure while at the same time hurling the greatest insult in his stock. 'If he was an Irishman he would never say that. Not in a month of Sundays.'

'I am fuck English. I'm a Limerick man,' said the young man. 'I read a book about Roger Casement, which is more than any of you have, I'm thinking.'

'The wrong book. Some damned English book,' said Peter Coughlin, sitting back down.

Tommy made to respond but Peter went on. 'I don't want to hear ye. Pin your lugholes back and I'll tell you how it was. The British had up Roger Casement as a traitor to England for trying to bring guns in for the Irish Volunteers. The case for the prosecution was handled by the Unionist F.E. Smith who three years before had, along with that bastard Carson, run more guns to the Ulster Volunteers than Casement ever planned to do. Just before the war Carson had said that he would turn his back on England, get in the help of a foreign king, just like the Orangemen did with King Billy, to stop the Home Rule Bill from going through.'

'He was still queer.'

Peter ignored Tommy, just held up his arm both to calm him and keep him out of his sight. 'I'm getting to that piece of filthy calumny. I want you to see the context of Sir Roger's actions. You know what a context is, do you? It's what young know-alls like yourself don't have. Anyhow, the whole trial was a disgrace and many English people knew it was a disgrace. The English government were scared that the appeal against the sentence would bring great support for Casement. He still had a place in people's hearts for his work in foreign places; so they showed pages from what was supposed to be his diaries to people who mattered. This shut them up. And the appeal failed. Now the English had had their hands on Casement's papers for two years before he was arrested. Plenty of time for them to forge them, like they forged the Parnell letter. End of story.' And Peter signalled for another drink.

Pat nodded his agreement over to the young man. 'There you are. You're speaking to Ballyheige's resident expert on Roger Casement, me lad. There's nothing Peter doesn't know.' He called across the bar. 'Isn't that right, Peter?'

'And another thing,' Peter continued, 'if the so-called diaries of Roger Casement are true then why did it take them so long to release them? I'll tell you why, they're frightened to be caught out in a damned lie. They needed lots of time to make sure they looked like the genuine article. They're still up to their necks in Ulster and didn't have the guts to admit what they did to Casement. Because they're still doing it now to lots of Irishmen. You think it's over? It isn't over.'

Tommy, treading carefully, said, 'In the book I read, it said Michael Collins had read the diaries and said they were in Casement's handwriting.'

'If I get near you I'll give you a thick ear.'

'You and whose army?' said Tommy, while his girlfriend tried to pull him up.

'Let's be going, Tommy.'

The couple, Tommy eyeballing Peter Coughlin as he allowed himself to be led by his girlfriend, left the bar.

'Good riddance,' said Peter Coughlin.

'Well,' said Brennan. 'Maybe Sir Roger needs to come back to sort everything out. Myself, I don't understand what all the fuss is about. We're in the Common Market, it's all legal and above board now.'

Peter Coughlin said nothing.

'What was your mum's maiden name, Peter?' Brennan asked.

' "Gorman". What of it?' Peter replied.

'It's just I heard talk that she had some part in Casement's arrest.'

Peter looked hard at Pat. He put his half-finished Guinness down on the bar, picked up his stick and walked out.

'You shouldn't have said that, Pat,' said Brennan. 'Peter's very sore about it.'

'Sure, none of them knew who he was. They just thought he was some big German fella. Mary Gorman did no more than her duty.'

'Duty to who? To the British? She shouldn't have ratted on him, even if she thought he was German.'

Brennan shook his head. 'You can say that now. It's easy enough. But people were mixed up then. Many an Irish family had sons fighting in the War.'

Pat nodded sardonically. 'None of those buggers in Ardfert lifted a finger to save Casement. None of the boys in Tralee neither. They could have got him away, but they didn't.'

'They didn't want to blow the whistle on the Easter Rising. Orders came from Dublin that there were to be no disturbances to arouse suspicion,' said Brennan.

'And poor Sir Roger paid the price?'

'He knew what he was getting himself into.'

'And now he's back.'

Brennan laughed. 'Don't give me that!' he said.

The following morning Brid McCarthy opened her shop. Waiting for her first customer of the day, she sorted through plastic-covered packets of bacon, cheese and cooked ham, looking for any whose sell-by date had passed into memory. These she took to the kitchen, wondering what meals she could come up with from the random combination.

As she was gazing into the icy grotto of her fridge she heard the shop-door open. Mrs Brennan from the bar in Ballyheige came in, looked around, then called Brid's name.

'I'm on my way,' Brid called.

The two women greeted one another and asked about family. Brid was wondering why Mrs Brennan had come in, and Mrs Brennan tried to think of ways of broaching the topic.

'I'll have a half-pound of butter, Brid,' Mrs Brennan said as a softener.

'Irish or New Zealand?'

'Irish. Salted, if you have it. Best to support Irish farmers, isn't it?'

'It is, but I saw on the television that New Zealand is having a bad time of it,' countered Brid.

'It's a problem, so. Still, which one is salted?'

'They're both salted.'

'That doesn't help me then. I'll stick to the Irish.'

Brid looked at the packet. 'Will you be eating it quickly? I ask because its time was up yesterday.'

'I never take any notice of that,' said Mrs Brennan. 'Good Irish butter never did anyone any harm.'

'You're right,' said Brid. She popped the butter in a bag. 'Anything else for you today, Mrs Brennan?'

Mrs Brennan thought. She was a fat woman, but publicans' wives, in Brid's experience, often were. 'I've been hearing things,' Mrs Brennan said.

'Hearing things?' Brid asked, all innocence.

'About you having a coloured girl to stay.'

Brid looked around, hoping that Boma – reading by Stanley – would be out of earshot.

'I have. A good Irish girl.'

'And I heard something else too. Not about you but about Ardfert.'

'And what was that?'

'Father Devenish was granted an apparition on the Fenit Road.'

'An apparition! Lord save us, I hadn't heard that. Still, he's a fine man. It wouldn't surprise me. Not at all.'

'And it was no ordinary apparition. My husband saw the whole thing. Well, he didn't see the apparition, of course, but he saw Father Devenish seeing it. He was on his way back from the Cash and Carry in Tralee.'

'Anything else?' repeated Brid.

'What's that book you're reading, Brid?'

Brid picked up the book she had discovered among Tim's things. 'It's a book of Tim's,' she said. 'It's about the missions, I think. I haven't read it yet. To tell you the truth I thought I might have a go at it this morning. There aren't many customers in the shop these days.'

Mrs Brennan felt guilty, though she had enough small shops to feel guilty about in Ballyheige. She played for time. 'A tin of your tongue,' she said, pointing to the shelf behind Brid.

Brid got out her steps from under the counter and climbed up towards the tin.

'Roger Casement, who'd have thought it!' Mrs Brennan said, just as Brid was reaching the last foot upwards towards the tin.

Brid stopped reaching, tried to think. *I mustn't let on. I mustn't. I must keep my stopper on.* She caught the tin of tongue and negotiated the steps down, dusting off the tin on her pinny as she did so.

'There you are, Maeve,' she said. 'A good tin of tongue for you. It's great with a plate of salad.'

'Do you hear what I'm telling you, Brid?'

Brid decided to play for time. 'What was that?'

'Father Devenish says it was Sir Roger Casement who appeared to him.'

'Does he? Well, I don't know . . .'

Brid's thoughts were racing. Humility warred with pride, with loyalty to the clergy. A side of her was extremely put out that Roddie had deigned to visit Father Devenish after remaining invisible to her. She also felt unhappy that the news was out, had reached the five miles down the road to Ballyheige. 'Anything else?'

Mrs Brennan looked about her, stuck.

The door opened and Eileen Coughlin, Peter's wife, came in with her unmarried daughter.

'Sure, Ardfert's being invaded by Ballyheige!' Brid said. 'How are you, Eileen? How's Peter?'

'You've heard?' asked Eileen Coughlin, eyeing Maeve Brennan.

'I have,' said Brid.

'I haven't been able to sleep since I heard. Peter came back from the pub' – she smiled tightly over at Maeve – 'and told me all about it. I've been moithering my mind ever since.'

'What galls me,' said Maeve Brennan, 'is why Sir Roger chose Ardfert to appear in and not Ballyheige. He got nothing but grief in Ardfert, as you well know, Eileen Coughlin.'

'Peter's mammy didn't know who he was. She thought she was doing the right thing. He'd have got the same treatment if he'd come in at Ballyheige, of that you can be sure.'

'So why did the Government choose to place a statue to the man at Ballyheige? Answer me that?' asked Maeve Brennan.

'Who can understand the reasoning of the politicians?' asked Eileen.

Maeve decided to answer her own question, as it was clear that no-one else would. 'Because Ardfert sent Sir Roger packing, that's why. Despised and rejected. In Ardfert, anyhow.'

'Everyone thought he was a German spy,' Brid said, having a mind to Eileen. 'It was no-one's fault. What can I do for you, Eileen?'

Eileen thought about that. 'A loaf of bread. Brown, if you've got it.'

'We only keep bread to order,' replied Brid.

'I'll have a box of tissues off you,' said Maeve.

Brid reached for the tissues and gave the box a bang to dust it off.

'I don't understand,' said Maeve Brennan to Eileen Coughlin, 'how you can talk about Ardfert deserving an apparition after what your own mother-in-law did to poor Sir Roger!' As she was speaking she looked pointedly at Brid. Brid looked back with icy eyes.

'Mammy was but a young slip of a girl,' replied Eileen.

'Old enough to have a job of work to do. Old enough to keep her big trap shut!' countered Maeve Brennan.

'Anything else?' Brid asked.

'Anyway, she wasn't the only one,' said Eileen. 'The lad who took Sir Roger to Ardfert in his pony and trap, and showed the constabulary the codes Sir Roger had thrown away. Nobody did anything.'

'When he was in Tralee,' said Maeve, 'my Uncle John ran a message for him. Sir Roger was waiting at the railway station with the policemen and one of them beckoned my Uncle John to come up to them. Sir Roger gave him a florin and asked him to go and buy chocolate for him. He bought him twelve bars. Sir Roger laughed when he saw all the chocolate and gave all but one back to Uncle John. Then, when Sir Roger was shipped off on the Dublin train, Uncle John waved him goodbye. He remembered that until his dying day.'

Brid had never heard that story before. 'Somebody would have done better to give Sir Roger some warm clothes, if you ask me,' she said. 'As it was he was taken to London in the suit wet through from the ocean. They put him in a draughty dungeon in the Tower of London and he didn't get a change for two weeks!'

'Still chocolate was what he fancied. A widow's mite it might have been, but it was something anyhow.'

'And what's that supposed to prove?' Eileen asked.

'Only that not everyone rejected him. Only the people of Ardfert.'

'I . . .' began Brid, but she bit her lip.

The two women looked at Brid.

'Will that be all, Maeve?'

Maeve Brennan nodded and Brid added up the total on the top of the pile. 'That'll be £3.05.' She took the money and handed Maeve back her change. Then she looked at her customer pointedly.

'I'll wish you good-morning,' said Maeve Brennan.

'I know I shouldn't be uncharitable . . .' began Eileen Coughlin.

'No. Will there be anything else?' asked Brid, suddenly hopelessly tired of shop-work, wanting to start on Tim's book about the missions and to consider her own private miracle.

Think of a long road in a valley low
Think of a wanderer in the distance far
Lost like a voice among the scattered hills
And when the moon is gone and ocean spills
Its waters backward from the trysting bar.
And in the dark furrows of the night there tills
A jewelled plough, and many a falling star
Moves you to prayer, then will you think of me
On the long road that will not ever end?

SIR ROGER CASEMENT, 14 JULY 1916

4

'NOW WHERE SHOULD I START, TIM? I'LL READ YOU THIS BIT, I THINK. It should get us in the mood for Ireland.'

'Chris,' Tim said, irritated that Chris had burrowed himself down in the back seat. He was missing historic Cork, and Tim's learned commentary on its delights. He could, Tim reckoned, have been helping him map read now that he had put on his reading-glasses, consigning his distance specs to the case. Instead, he had raided Tim's box of books. 'I won't be able to concentrate. You'd be better keeping an eye out for the Blarney turning.'

Chris began, oblivious. ' "Cold awfully bad. Took lots of quinine and stayed in bed. Sending Ricardo to Putumayo today by *Beatrice*.

Young pilot came at 9 a.m. Very well dressed. Sat down and I stroked his knee and gave 10 shillings and cigarettes and photos. Would like it I am sure. Caressed hand too. His is a big one I know. To come on Saturday to pass some time with me and get his photo taken. He is beautiful. Tells me Ignacio Torres is on SS *Ucayali* as steward. She is now 'on voyage'. Will tell Ignacio to come to me on return. Cold much worse so go to bed. Saw some splendid ones too again today and such lovely faces. Very heavy rain – began at 8.30 p.m. and till 11 in deluge, then stopped and then began again at 5 or 6 a.m."
What do you think of that?'

'Ah, there's the turn-off,' Tim said and took it faster than he would have liked. 'Are you sure you want to see Blarney, Chris? It's a bit on the touristy side. I can show you the *real* Ireland.'

'Oh, yes, I think so, don't you? It's one of the musts,' Chris replied. 'Tim, listen to this—'

'I've already read them, Chris.'

'Quite a bit by the look of it.'

'It was second-hand when I got it.'

'Story of your life,' Chris said. ' "Thursday, 26 October. Up at six-thirty. Heavy rain all night. Took quinine. Soldiers out and 'palm' of yesterday in his knickers and other one embracing young thick-set soldier of 18 – a beauty. The lovely boy of 20 came to Reuss' store at seven this morning and two carters to shift whisky, etc. He smiled and bowed. I love him. Also one of the carters, a big Inca (white) peon with blue shirt and pants and a perfect monster. It swings and shows a head about 3 inches in diameter! He has enormous shoulders and curved strong back, about 27, and is as strong as a stallion. Saw it at 9 a.m. swinging and I'll swear it is 3 inches across. Lovely boy looked up and smiled and his is a big long soft one, or his pants are loose and yet it and his bags hang down a lot. He has a lovely gentle face, about 19½. I expect Jose some time today. River 63 foot 8 inches." . . . Ahh!'

'What's going on at the back?' Tim said.

'I should have stayed in Africa, Tim. Sir Roger's making me realize.'

'Africa has enough problems without you adding to them,' Tim said, then he wanted to take back his words, even though he had felt slighted by the remark. Chris didn't say anything. There was a silence between them. Trying to breathe balm to the back, Tim added, 'Anyway, you're quoting from the South American diary, not the African. You all right? Reading in a car always makes me feel sick.'

'I'm cold. I have the feeling I'm going to be cold all the way across Ireland.'

'The heater's on full blast. The fan only works on "1" so it'll take some time to get to the back. If you were sitting in the front like a Christian—'

'But I'm not.'

'Have you got the sleeping-bag over you?'

'Yes,' Chris said sulkily. 'How far to Blarney?'

'Only three or four miles.'

'Do you think kissing the Blarney Stone will make me better?'

Tim looked in the driving-mirror for a clue of how Chris meant that, but he'd scrunched down out of sight. 'Course. And if Blarney doesn't do it, Knock will.'

'That's all right then.'

'You know Knock's mentioned in the Bible, don't you? "Seek and ye shall find Knock and it shall be opened to you." '

Chris didn't react to that. His remark about wishing he was in Africa was still niggling Tim. He wasn't sure whether he had been meant to take it personally or not. It was, after all, Chris who had wanted to be shown Ireland. It was the first time Chris had suggested a trip which Tim had dared agree to. In the past Chris had written to ask him to go across Africa with him; another time to India. But such far-flung places had seemed too much like hard travelling, too much like work, to Tim. He imagined beggars and bandits pulling him apart. But with the disease weakening Chris, putting a leash of caution around his neck, India had gone west. Tim had thought Chris would be happy to be with him in a country he knew and loved and hated, a place that seemed more like home, with all the mixture of positive and negative implicit – to him – in the word.

Tim could hear Chris flicking over the pages of the diary.

'Your Sir Roger Casement didn't let the grass grow under his feet. Never a dull moment,' Chris said. 'Pity he didn't fill us in a bit more on what happened. A bit of a tease, your Sir Roger.'

'Chris, I do wish you'd stop saying that.'

'What?'

' "Your Sir Roger". He isn't mine. He only has a couple of walk-on parts in my article. I'm writing about Sir Alfred Jones.'

'Oh, yes, I forgot. It's your mammy who thinks the world of Sir Roger. You, as in so much else, have gone the other way.'

'What's that supposed to mean?'

Chris didn't reply.

'Anyway,' Tim said, 'to answer your question, I expect that the diary was just a memory aid. He was probably perfectly well able to fill in the details himself. If they're his diaries. It's not proven that he wrote them, you know. A lot of people still think they were forged.'

'Well, if they are, somebody's done a damned good job with the sensibility of a size-queen. And it goes on page after page.'

'It's funny, that's what I think too, but it's hard to build a logical argument around that sort of intuition. "I submit, your Honour, that Sir Roger Casement's diaries are genuine because his erotic landscape exactly coincides with my own." They could have got a tame size-queen to forge them. Plenty in the Foreign Office, then as now,' Tim said. 'Blarney's coming up. I'm not saying that they *aren't* genuine, only that there's still a debate going on. And that's what's so interesting.'

'What do the Irish make of Casement?'

Tim thought about that, as he often had before. He thought about his mammy and her lifelong devotion to Sir Roger. But Mammy wasn't typical, was she? Surely, he thought, the whole Irish nation wouldn't want him canonized. He decided to keep to the straight and narrow, as if Chris were one of his students. 'Most of the Irish biographers of Casement – we can park here – tend to back the view that the British forged the diaries to make sure that public support for his reprieve dwindled. It worked like a charm. Many of Casement's friends went very silent after the English government distributed them. Not all ran a mile, mind. Conan Doyle and Bernard Shaw stayed loyal. The Quaker, William Cadbury, too. Casement's cousin, Gertrude Bannister, moved heaven and earth on his behalf; lost her teaching job over it. What I don't know is whether the Irish would change their minds if the diaries were analysed and found to be genuine. I know someone who wouldn't believe a word of it. And most, I suspect, would still say it was a wicked plot by the English. We don't have any reason to have much faith in British forensic tests, you know.'

'Here's a good bit. Listen to this,' Chris said.

'Too late!' Tim said. 'We're here.' He drove into the castle car-park.

It was much larger than he remembered it. 'Bloody hell! The castle isn't open.'

'It's still early. I don't know why those fuckers on the ferry couldn't have let us sleep a bit longer. They said we'd be landing in fifteen minutes and it took at least another hour.'

'They have to clean up the boat. Anyway, it doesn't feel early.'

They shambled out of the car, looking round at the bleak grey day. Chris, wrapped up in his heavy top-coat and scarf, shivered.

'Is it always like this?' he asked.

A man in a café opened up early especially for them, and this seemed to lift Chris's mood. They chatted with the man while he cooked them breakfast. Hearing Chris's American accent, he confided that he had relations in Connecticut, and Chris had been to college in Springfield. Tim was greatly relieved to see Chris lifting. He had begun to think that they would have to phone up the ferry company to see if they would change the ticket and take them back to Britain two weeks ahead of time.

Tim had been anxious as they waited in the car deep in the bowels of the ship. A whooshing fan spinning to their right, a terrible grating sound that turned into a shudder, jogged memories of *The Herald of Free Enterprise*. Ahead of them, past a jam of cars that would have made escape impossible, the mouth of the ferry would either open to disgorge them like insects to spread over Ireland or to reveal a wall of water that would sweep down and wipe them away, like Pharaoh and his hordes.

After Chris had gone to bed in their cabin, Tim went to the duty-free shop but didn't buy anything. There had not seemed to be much of a saving and the way the thousands of bottles jiggled to the motion of the ship, making an ominous, pre-earthquake, warning tinkling, had unnerved him. He had thrown his basket onto the pile and made for the bar.

There, he got talking to a man on his way back home from his job in London. Tim, sounding English enough to pass, decided to play the chameleon. He was on holiday in Ireland, he said. The man confided that Beamish was a better stout than Guinness and that you could draw a line down Ireland. To the west of the line, the people were Catholic, decent, Irish. To the east, pagan consumers, supporters of abortion and deviant sexual practices. And the line followed the fading of the signal from British television.

Tim had argued the toss with the man, saying that he had seen satellite dishes in the far west on previous visits. English papers, too. But his heart wasn't in it. He could see his point.

'Are you married?' the man asked.

'No, I'm single.' A pause and a quick change of colour, an automatic darkening of the vocal chords. 'The right girl hasn't come along. You know. Old story.' And as he spoke Tim was thanking his lucky stars that Chris wasn't about to hear his lies. Chris would have made short work of him. Chris was completely without shame.

'Do we have to pay extra, do you think?' Tim asked Chris, eyeing the man who was waiting for his first stone-kisser of the day.

'Don't worry about it, tight-wad. We're probably expected to tip him. I'll do it.'

'I'm not a tight-wad. It's just I like to know where I am.'

Chris took off his coat, handed Tim his passport, wallet and traveller's cheques. With his spare hand Tim held the umbrella over him. Old men clouds were spitting at them. The man instructed Chris to sit on the rug and then helped him backwards. He held him by the hips and Chris stretched back, grasping his hands correctly to grip the metal bar, then reaching back to kiss the stone, set in the sill of one of the keep's protruding battlements. Chris's shirt rode up and his pitifully thin waist and ribcage were exposed. Tim reached down and covered him up.

The man recited a litany of American celebrities he had dealt with. Tim started thinking uncharitable thoughts about the man whom he felt was a bit like Barry Fitzgerald, and knew it, had studied the actor in order to help perfect his role as professional Irishman. Then he caught himself, realizing that some would say he had turned himself into a professional Englishman.

'Barry Fitzgerald' had, he said, a book chock-full of autographs, including President and Mrs Kennedy's.

Chris struggled back. 'That must be worth something,' and he gave the man a pound coin. Tim passed him his things.

Back Tim stretched. He felt his shirt ride up. He sucked in his paunch. The stone was close to his face, too close for his eyes to focus upon. He puckered his lips and thought of germs. Then he was praying not for the gift of the gab but for Chris. He might have been kissing a relic. The Stone, like the foot of a bronze statue, had been worn by all the kissing.

'How much did you give him?' Chris asked.

'One pound fifty.'

'May the road ride up to meet you, begorra.'

'Are you warming up?'

'I'm fine. The breakfast is repeating on me.'

'Me too. I haven't had black pudding for ages. You should go easy on those breakfasts.'

Chris didn't say anything. They stopped at a sign with several branches. 'Shall we go to the caves?' Chris asked, already following the sign.

'It's raining.'

'Come on.'

They viewed everything on offer in the castle grounds; at Chris's insistence they followed all the signs one by one. Tim found the Fairy Glen particularly depressing. He sensed that the whole place had been set up to graft phoney fantasy on a piece of ground that could have shone if left to itself. He ached to show Chris real things.

In the souvenir shop Tim bought a St Bridget cross, made of reeds.

'Who's that for?' Chris asked. He had bought four postcards and the stamps to go with them.

'Me.'

'You and your knick-knacks,' Chris said.

'I like my knick-knacks.'

'I know you do. I've got the wounds to prove it.'

'Let's get on. We've the Ring of Kerry to do,' Tim said. Chris nodded and they got back into the car.

'So you're joining me in the front?' Tim said, glad that Chris would get the benefit of the heater.

'Why not give you a thrill?'

They headed towards Skibbereen, the wipers on full. The rain was settling in.

Chris reached behind for maps and the AA book. He consulted these for a few minutes then, still studying the map, said, 'What do you say if we go straight to Ardfert – maybe make a detour to see the Rock of Cashel – and do the Ring of Kerry on another day?'

'It'll mean doubling back on ourselves,' Tim said.

'Better double back than do all that mountain driving through Kerry not seeing a thing.'

Tim kept on driving towards Skibbereen.

Chris looked up. Tim glanced over at him and saw he was peering through the windscreen at the black road ahead. The light, extruded through rain, further cut by the glancing blows of the wipers, caught his face badly, made him look haggard. And lost. Tim said a prayer. 'What do you say?'

'OK. I'm looking for a good place to turn round. It's a bit of a long way round the houses to Cashel. I'm not sure about Ardfert,' Tim said.

'You're not sure about anything.'

Tim ignored him. 'OK. Let's go to Cashel and think about it then.'

'This is the sort of day we should look at ruins,' Chris said.

Tim almost replied that he was already looking at one. He parked his tongue against his soft palate.

They came upon the Rock of Cashel after an hour's drive. It rose, steep and unexpected, from the surrounding plain. Grey rock against a slate and sunbeam sky.

Close to, there was some scaffolding shrouding parts of the complex of Bishop's Palace, ruined cathedral, Cormac's Chapel and round tower.

Tim parked the car at the foot of the rock and pointed out the ruins of a monastery a field away to the south.

'Now here's something worth a detour,' Chris said, looking up. 'How old is it?'

'There've been forts on the site since pre-history. St Patrick is said to have visited it. The only story I can remember is about that.'

'Out with it.'

'Well, during some ceremony St Patrick accidentally impaled the King of Munster's foot with his bishop's crozier. The king, thinking his impalement to be part of the ceremony, bore the pain in silence.'

'Odd to have a crozier with a point. I assume it had a point. What did St Patrick say when he found out what he had done?'

'I don't think it's recorded. He probably would have told the king to offer it up for the Holy Souls.'

'You Catholics are quaint. What's a Holy Soul?'

'Someone who dies with venial sin on his soul. He has to go to purgatory to have the sins burnt off.'

'Like hell?'

'No, not like hell,' Tim replied. 'Hell is for ever. Purgatory is temporary. Souls have hope in purgatory. It may be as painful as hell, but hope of freedom makes it bearable.'

Chris was silent. Then, but not fast enough, he smiled. 'It sounds like a holiday in Ireland.'

'Chris, it was you . . .'

He ignored Tim's pique. 'And your pain can help these Holy Souls, can it?'

'Yes. Prayer, sacrifice, indulgences can be offered up for them.'

'You still believe it, don't you?'

'A bit. Let's go and see the rock.'

Tim realized halfway that it was a long walk for Chris through the streets of Cashel. Before they had found a way up the rock to the entrance, Chris told him to slow down. When they were halfway up the hill they passed a souvenir shop. Tim told him to wait while he brought the car round. It would save them on the way back, he said.

Chris seemed relieved. He sat down on the wall and Tim trotted back to the car.

He drove the car all the way up the hill, almost to the entrance of the site. As he passed he waved, but Chris didn't see him. He was still sitting on the wall, looking down at his feet. Tim looked for something to offer up and hit on his visit to his mammy.

'Where's the car?' Chris asked.

Tim pointed up the hill to where he had parked it. 'I passed you. You were miles away. Completely out of it.'

There was a tour at twelve. They paid the entrance money, bought a guidebook and looked around the Hall of the Vicars Choral, which had been restored since Tim's last visit.

A group of young Italians was waiting for the tour. They were well dressed, noisy, good-looking. One of the boys, around seventeen, was spectacularly beautiful. The girls were vying for his attention. He had thick curly hair, brown eyes haloed by lashes that brought the flicks of Arabic calligraphy to mind.

Chris looked over at Tim and raised his eyebrows. 'Your Sir Roger would have written something about that one,' he said.

When the guide arrived they trailed out onto the windy rock. The sky had closed up again. Rain lashed them. The guide took them to the door of Cormac's Chapel and started her off-by-heart monologue: built by King Cormac McCarthaigh; begun in 1127 and consecrated in 1134; the earliest Romanesque church in Ireland. Tympana, the carved work above both north and south doors, very rare in Ireland. The centaur over the door about to be shot by a soldier wearing what is thought to be a Norman helmet . . .

The beautiful Italian was laughing and passing remarks with one of the girls. The guide stopped what she was saying. 'The tour isn't obligatory, you know. You can go around on your own if you want.' The Italians did not, Tim thought, understand what she had said but they got the implications, exchanged glances and stopped talking. The chastened group went inside.

A small chapel with a barrel ceiling. Along the walls strange Celtic symbols. The guide said they showed the Irish making the Romanesque their own. Around the arch at the sanctuary were twenty-five heads. They might have been gargoyles, but were in no way fanciful or exaggerated; rather the sort of heads you see lying on deep pillows in long hospital wards.

Chris stayed at the back of the chapel, examining a broken sarcophagus, consulting the guidebook. 'It's supposed to be Cormac's sarcophagus,' Tim said.

'It says here that it predates the chapel. I wonder who bashed it about,' Chris said.

'Cromwell, shouldn't wonder. It was Cromwell that made the Irish landscape so sad.'

'You'll have to explain that . . .'

The guide came over, followed by the Italians. She was clearly not enjoying her duties that day. 'I don't know why they bother if they're not going to listen,' she said.

'They're young,' Chris said, surprising Tim with his unusual indulgence.

They listened attentively to the guide as she repeated what Chris had already gleaned from the guidebook about the sarcophagus. Then they let the group pass on into the ruins of the cathedral. Chris held back. 'Stay here a minute. Don't say a word.'

Tim usually obeyed Chris in such matters. They stood still. Tim felt cold, the sort of cold that takes a quarter of an hour in a hot shower to melt down. He worried about Chris. To distract himself he recounted the gargoyles and the bands of brickwork on the barrelled ceiling. The sounds of the guide and her quiet-chirping listeners receded and disappeared.

Then Chris said something. Tim was far away and had to ask him to repeat what he had said.

'Promise me that when I die you won't pray for me.'

'You're not going to die.'

Chris sighed audibly and for a moment it seemed as if light had ebbed from Cormac's Chapel. Tim was thinking, *I shall never forget this*. 'Have it your way. But, in the unlikely event of my death, promise me you won't pray for me.'

'I don't—'

'Promise!'

'No, I won't promise any such thing.'

Chris gave Tim a killing look and walked out of the chapel, following the group.

For the rest of the tour he stayed close to the guide as she pointed out the features of the archbishop's palace and the ruined cathedral. Tim stayed on the fringes for a while. The guide pointed to slit-windows high in the wall of the cathedral, where lepers were permitted to stand and hear mass out of sight of the decent, clean people. Chris was looking at Tim angrily.

Unable to stand the atmosphere, Tim wandered off by himself. He walked back through Cormac's Chapel but didn't stop, as a young couple were embracing by the altar. He came upon the round tower in the middle of the graveyard, reputed to have been built in a night by Cormac to protect the rock from surprise attack.

Some said the round towers were much older. They were invariably built with an unencumbered view to the east and the rising sun. Similar constructions were to be found through India and Iran, across the Mediterranean and up through Spain and France – the route of the Celt – and may have been fire-temples. Remains of ash and half-burned logs littered the bottom of many of them. Still, in this climate perhaps a more prosaic purpose for fire could be inferred.

They resembled space ships. Tim, remembering, imagined monks cowering in them as marauding Vikings torched their monasteries. He wondered if they had ever prayed for the miracle of lift-off.

*   *   *

They ate lunch at a pub in Cashel town. The rain was still pounding outside. Umbrellas that looked as if they had spent the whole winter outdoors were impaled into wooden tables.

Tim said, 'I'm not ready for Ardfert just yet, Chris.'

'Have you told your mother you're coming?'

'What do you think?'

'You've been putting it off. Well, I'm not going to enter it. It's much too complicated for a poor hick like me to get. But she *is* your mother. And you're a big boy now.'

'I'll be OK in a couple of days. Let's go to Bantry. Perhaps the weather will change.'

As they crossed back into County Cork, having taken a small road from Mallow to Macroon, they picked up a hitch-hiker, heading for Dunmanway. Chris climbed into the back, letting the lad have the front.

Name of Liam. Studying electronics in Dublin. Tim told Liam that they were on holiday. He asked if Tim was English and did not seem to believe him when he said he was Irish. He didn't seem to know quite what to make of him and spent most of his time talking to Chris about the States.

They dropped him outside his house in Dunmanway.

'Imagine coming from here,' said Chris. 'And, after leaving, imagine coming back.'

'Chris,' Tim said, as they followed the signs to Bantry.

'What?'

'If you die before me, I won't pray for you, if that's what you want.'

'Thank you.'

'My prayers would probably do you more harm than good, anyway.'

'Tim, I believe in neither carrot nor stick. You should know that by now.'

'Yes. That's fine. Neither do I.'

Chris laughed. He knew Tim of old. 'Do you want to pick up this hitcher?' he asked. 'I thought hitch-hikers were an extinct species. Better grab them while we can before it all changes.'

Tim slowed down, passed the man by the road. He had his raincoat drawn up to shelter his head. 'He looks a bit down at heel.'

'He's your countryman,' Chris said. 'And I expect I look a bit down at heel, too.'

They had already passed the man but Tim stopped and, putting the car into reverse, drove back to meet the man as he shambled forward to meet them.

Father Devenish was momentarily startled when the figure of a man walked past the presbytery window, blocking for a second his view of a lapis evening sky. Below the window, sitting in an easy chair with his back to it, was Canon Dawson, his parish priest. A large glass, that had until moments before contained an inch of whiskey, stood on a table at his elbow, along with a litre bottle of soda water.

'I don't know,' said Father Devenish.

'I'm going to break the habit of a lifetime,' Canon Dawson said, something he said most nights. He stood up and took his glass over to the drinks cabinet. There he poured himself another measure of whiskey. 'Don't tell Miss O'Shea, will you, Terence?'

Father Devenish didn't reply. He glanced down at a picture of Roger Casement. It was the man he had seen the night before. Casement was shown sitting on steps with five other people at the Gaelic League Irish College in Cloghaneely, Co. Donegal, in 1904. His stance was hunched, his arms crossed on his lap, only part of the right hand showing. While everyone else in the picture stared into the camera, Casement was gazing away to the right. He wore a suit and tie but there was something sad about him. He was too thin, his shoes seemed down at heel, their soles to have seen too many lonely roads. He looked cold.

Canon Dawson settled back down. 'So what do we do about it?' he asked, and quaffed a mouthful of the neat whiskey back before adding an equal amount of soda.

'I think you're right, Canon. We must just hope and pray it was a one-time occurrence. I know Brid McCarthy won't say a word. At the moment it's only me who people think had the apparition. And I'll say nothing. I can hardly believe it happened myself now.'

The canon nodded at the wisdom of that. He watched while Father Devenish fanned the pages of the old biography of Casement, stopping at pictures of the man. 'I do know that all the pictures immediately bring the man who appeared to me to life. I can see him in all of them.'

'Sure, he's probably been making himself a tidy living for years impersonating Sir Roger Casement!' replied Canon Dawson. 'Somebody once told the fellow that he had a startling resemblance to Casement, and he's never looked back.'

'But how do you explain the fact that no-one else could see him except me?' Father Devenish asked. 'And he said some strange things, Canon . . . some wise things. When I got to my knees he lifted me up and said I wasn't to do anything like that; that this was different. That had a ring of truth about it.'

'Rogues and fools are not past a piece of sageness.'

'No, but then there's the fact that he knew exactly where the two men had been.'

'Well, it doesn't take a saint from heaven to know where those two had been, does it, Terence?'

'No, but he knew exactly. And about Brennan going to the Cash and Carry.'

'Did you notice if Brennan had anything in the back of his car with a Cash and Carry bag?'

Again the splinter of doubt. 'No.'

'You know what I've been thinking?' asked Canon Dawson. 'I've been thinking that Brennan and Devlin could easily have set this whole thing up.'

'But, Canon—'

'Think about it, Terence. A man comes into Brennan's pub in Ballyheige looking the spitting image of Roger Casement. Brennan knows what Casement looks like because they've got a huge, great statue of the man right opposite the pub. A thought – a temptation – forms in Brennan's head. Maybe business hasn't been great. Maybe there are bills to pay. Maybe he sees the weather and thinks of the last wicked summer that kept the trippers away. And he thinks of places like Knock that do very nicely out of apparitions. And, doubtless under the influence, he hatches up this game of charades. I know I'm being uncharitable, Terence, but that's how it seems to an old whiskey-sodden priest.'

'But what about Brid McCarthy?' asked Father Devenish. 'She's as honest as the day is long. And she's as sane as anyone.'

'Yes, but she's had what you might call "a devotion" to Roger Casement her whole life. I've got the mass book going back to the 1920s and every third of August as regular as regular there's the name of Roger Casement and Brid McCarthy. He's been her life's work, Terence.'

'But Brid said she couldn't see Casement. It was the coloured girl . . .' he sought about, '. . . Boma who had the apparitions.'

'And where does she come from? She turns up out of nowhere.

Nobody knows her. Blows in from Dublin by all accounts. But could this Boma not have blown in from Brennan's Bar in Ballyheige? Might not Brennan have got her to set the ball rolling? She's the one that says she got the apparition and convinces Brid they're true, after all. I'd have thought that Casement would have appeared to Brid before anyone else. It's a matter of good manners really.' Canon Dawson laughed into his glass. 'But you know, Terence, it's funny how you get swept along in the details. Here we are wondering whether you've had an apparition and coming up with theories why you haven't and we've forgotten the most ludicrous of all.'

'What's that, Canon?'

'I'll tell you. Casement himself. Old Roger had a fair bit of burning to do before he'd scrape into even the lowest mansion of heaven. Brennan's picked a loser, if you ask me. Of course, you can see his reasoning. Casement's a local in a way. Still, he'd have been better to stick to someone dependable like the Blessed Virgin. A much simpler matter entirely. The coloured girl could have knelt prayerfully in some convenient spot not too far from Brennan's pub, nodded and smiled – perhaps even thrown herself about a bit in ecstasy like those African girls did on Miss O'Shea's video – and it would have attracted quite a few punters to the area to share in the Divine mysteries. Then, to put the cherry on top, the girl could tell everyone that the Virgin Mary is displeased – have you noticed, she always seems to be? – and wants repentance and a ban on pornography and abortion; possibly a return to the old liturgy. The Blessed Virgin seems to share the obsessions of the types who write to the papers. Haven't you noticed that? But Roger Casement! It's ludicrous! Not that I've anything against the man. He was a decent soul by all accounts. Heart in the right place, at least while he was abroad. But muddle-headed. He was no great asset to the Irish Cause. Everything he touched went wrong. We don't really know whether he came back to Ireland to start or stop the Easter Rising. And what did he do when he landed? He didn't take off to Tralee with the other two boyos; he just hung about McKenna's Fort like a great girl, waiting for arrest. I don't call that the action of a wise man. He was a cock-eyed, cack-handed idealist. Irish history is full of them, I'll grant you. And he was as bent as a corkscrew, by all accounts. Think about it, Terence. Do you really think Them Upstairs would let him loose on Holy Ireland?' The canon laughed again.

'I don't know what to think,' said Father Devenish.

'Well, let me do it for you, so,' replied Canon Dawson. 'I believe my own explanation entirely. I wish I could get that Brennan into my confessional. I'd soon get the truth out of the maggot.'

Father Devenish could see the whiskey working on the canon. In some ways, he knew, it was making him saner. All spiritual considerations were fading as the alcohol popped the idealistic helium of his brain-cells, pulling him down to earth. But Father Devenish was sober and kept thinking of the man who had met him outside the presbytery. He could remember the very solid feel of him but he could also see the alarm in the eyes of Brennan and Colm Devlin. Still, there was no point in tackling the canon further.

'Did you notice how many came to mass this morning?' Canon Dawson asked. 'News is out. My advice to you is to say nothing. I'll go and see Brid McCarthy in the morning. Brid'll do as I say.'

Father Devenish nodded. The telephone rang in the hall. He heard Miss O'Shea answer it. She came in. 'It's the Tralee newspaper, Father. They want to speak to you. Don't be long. Your supper's five minutes away from the table and I won't put up with any tardiness.' She disappeared.

Father Devenish picked up the receiver. The grip was greasy from Miss O'Shea's soda-breaded hands. 'Yes?'

He listened to the reporter – a woman – on the other end of the line. 'No comment,' he said.

'Have you tried St Theresa's?' Brid told the woman with the suitcase.

A few seconds earlier, behind the counter of the empty shop, reading the book she had found among Tim's things, Brid had not wanted to answer the knock on the summer door. She had not liked the direction the book was taking. Not at all.

The first few pages had seemed to reinforce her theory that it was about the missions but then the Indian stripped off and the bearded man with the canoe . . .

The knocking continued. Boma was taking her afternoon nap. There was nothing else for it. She looked at the book, snapped it shut.

'Are you Brid?' the woman asked her.

'I am.'

'I was told you'd be bound to have a room. I've come all the way from Dublin.'

In fact, the guest-room upstairs was still vacant but Brid did not want to take in anyone else. Didn't she have enough going on with Boma? And what if Roddie came back – as he surely would? 'I'm sorry,' she said. 'I can't help you.'

'Don't worry, so,' said the woman.

'I'm really sorry,' Brid said, feeling ill at ease about her unusual coldness, needing to make atonement. 'I'm up to my eyes. Still, come in and have a cup of tea with me. It's a raw old day. Then I'll point you to St Theresa's. You can phone from here if you like.'

'Thank you.'

The woman stepped inside. She followed Brid through the shop to the parlour where the table was, she noticed, set for two.

'Sit down by Stanley. I'll put the kettle on the stove in the kitchen. Stanley's a bit slow,' Brid said.

'It's very kind of you.'

While the kettle was heating up Brid joined the woman in the living-room. She looked at her, trying to decide how many years she was behind herself. Quite a few. Nice complexion. She took care of herself. Still, the pebble spectacles betokened eyesight far worse than her own. Sixty-five? 'It's a cold old day. What brings you to Ardfert?'

'I'm on holiday,' said the woman. 'My name's Lyons. Mary Lyons.'

'I'm Brid McCarthy – still, you probably know that. Did you come by car, Mrs . . . ?'

'Miss. Call me Mary.'

'You've come a bit on the early side to Ardfert, Mary. The tourist season doesn't start for a couple of weeks still.'

'I just wanted to get away for a while. A bit of a rest.'

'I feel terrible about not having any room for you.' She looked at Mary Lyons, feeling doubly mean to be lying to her. 'To tell you the truth, Mary Lyons, I do have a spare room but I'm not opening it. Life's a bit full at the moment to take anything else on.'

'Do you have any guests?'

'Yes, I do. Just the one,' said Brid. 'Boma's from Dublin too. But she's . . . well . . . she's sort of special.'

'You mean she's staying for a while?'

'Yes, I think so. I hope so.'

'Brid, you mustn't worry about me. I'll take your advice and go to St Theresa's.'

'You'll find it nice enough. It's just a step from here.'

'Isn't that the kettle?'

While Brid made the tea, Mary Lyons looked around the room. She picked up the copy of the Brian Inglis biography of Casement, left on the side-table by Boma. She did not open it, contenting herself with looking at Casement's photograph on the front cover. Then she laid it aside, glancing about her. The luminous Our Lady on the television, a framed picture of the Sacred Heart, an angel with huge corralling wings guiding two children over a rushing stream, a statue of St Brandon carved out of turf. This room could have been anywhere in Ireland. Three easy chairs ranged round a Stanley, a rag-rug.

Brid returned with the tea. She had raided the shop for a ginger cake. As she cut it she said, 'Shop-bought, I'm afraid,' as she always did.

'Don't you worry,' Mary replied.

They settled down to drink the tea.

'You've a book about Sir Roger Casement,' Mary said, for something to say.

Brid was at once put on the defensive. 'And why wouldn't I? Everyone around here has one, I wouldn't be surprised. He's our local hero.'

'Is he?'

'He landed at Banna Strand. It's just down the road. Ardfert is full of Sir Roger. You mean, you've not heard of him?'

'I've *heard* of him. Of course I have. I just hadn't realized he had connections here,' Mary said.

'More cake?'

Mary didn't have the heart to say she hadn't been offered her first piece yet. 'Thank you,' she said. 'I'll explore these places while I'm here.'

A door slammed in the distance. Brid started and looked towards the door to the shop. 'That'll be Boma,' she said. 'I make her have a nap in the afternoon.'

' "Boma" – that's an unusual name.'

'It is. When Boma came here *she* didn't know what it meant. It's a town in the Congo. Sir Roger was there.'

'It's a Swahili word,' said Mary. 'It means "enclosure".'

'Does it? I must write that down. Boma'll be pleased to know. She's been finding out all sorts of things since she came here,' replied Brid and, as she spoke, she wondered how the woman had known that.

'It's amazing what you learn from newspapers, isn't it?' said Mary Lyons. 'I'm full of that sort of thing. I remember things that don't matter while the important things go out the window. Odd, isn't it?'

'It is.'

'Well, I mustn't take up any more of your time, Brid. If you could give me directions to St Theresa's, I'll see if they have a place for me.'

'How long are you planning to stay in Ardfert?'

'I haven't really thought about it. A few days, I expect.'

'Mrs Grogan will be glad of the custom. Tell her Brid McCarthy sent you.'

The door opened and Boma, rubbing the sleep from her eyes, came into the room. She stopped when she saw the stranger sitting in her chair.

'Boma! Come in, dear. This is Mary Lyons. She's just blown in from Dublin. I'll get a cup for you. There's still life in the tea.'

Boma nodded to Mary Lyons. 'Hi,' she said, and sat down across Stanley from her.

Mary Lyons was unable to reply at once. Boma took the hesitation for the frisson of shock that often went through people upon first meeting her. It made her tired each time she confronted it but she was used to thinking fast, deciding whether it was worth breaking the ice for the other person, or if she would just let the atmosphere remain frozen. Now, she was not sure. 'I'm from Dublin too,' she said.

'What part of Dublin?'

'Swords.'

'Are you on holiday?' Mary Lyons asked.

'You could say that.'

'And when's your baby due?'

Boma looked down at her swelling belly. 'A couple of months. It's really obvious, isn't it? It's only in the last week or two that people have noticed.'

'You look great. I bet he'll be a lovely baby,' Mary said.

Boma wondered about that. 'Why did you say *he*?' she asked Mary.

'Why did I? Lord, I don't know. It's just horse sense. I was a nurse. We used to take bets on the sex of babies. I was right more often than not. Don't ask me why, though.'

'Did you hear that, Brid?' Boma asked, as Brid came back into the room carrying the extra cup.

'What?'

104

'This lady . . . er . . .'

'Mary.'

'Mary thinks my baby will be a boy.'

Brid seemed doubtful. 'Girls are easier.'

'It's only a feeling,' said Mary. She looked at her watch. 'I think I'd better be off. You've been so kind.'

'If you think you should . . .' said Brid.

'Come and see us again. We could go for a walk,' said Boma.

Mary smiled. 'That would be nice. Not too far, though. I'm not what I was for walking. And you've got to take care too.'

'I'll let you out through the shop,' said Brid.

Mary walked behind Brid, said goodbye to Boma and went out by the shop-door. She was glad there was a shop. It would give her an excuse for dropping in.

'Just go right here. Straight to the end and turn right again by the Eight 'til Late. St Theresa's is about fifty yards on the right. Don't forget to tell Mrs Grogan I sent you,' said Brid.

'You've been very kind,' Mary said. She walked away from McCarthy's.

Brid watched her go. She did not feel that she had been kind.

'Who's that?' Brid asked.

'A biddy from Dublin. She's here on holiday. She wanted a room but I told her I was full up.'

'Why did you do that? You've got that room upstairs. And I liked the look of her.'

Brid couldn't remember herself for a moment then, when she did, she knew that she could not pass on her reasons to Boma. 'It's too much fuss and bother for my liking. Another cup of tea, Boma?'

'What's wrong, Brid? You seem all upset.'

'Do I, dear?' She searched about for what might be upsetting her. True, she had never before refused a paying guest, but she could get out of that by reasoning that she was sending the person to St Theresa's. But, and this had happened before, Boma knew exactly when something was wrong. The problem was that she could not remember herself.

'Nothing that I know of, dear. I'd better get back to the shop.'

And, when back behind the counter she picked up *Song of the Loon* and looked at the cover of the bearded man with his arm on the bare shoulder of the Indian, she knew what was bothering her. She opened the book at random. She read a paragraph. Then she shut it tight and put it in the drawer.

She had hidden the book just in time, for no sooner had it disappeared from her sight than she saw the black car of Canon Dawson mount the pavement outside the shop. The Canon got out, waved to someone Brid could not see, and came into the shop.

Brid greeted Canon Dawson, offered to take him through to the parlour.

'No, Brid. Thank you. I mustn't stay. I've several stops to make still.'

'It's not often I see you at the shop, Canon,' said Brid. 'I think I know why you've come.'

'There isn't much you don't know, Brid,' said Canon Dawson.

'I wouldn't say that at all. I'm just a foolish old woman.'

'With twice your foolishness you could teach a good many round here a deal of wisdom.'

'Father Devenish told you, did he?'

'He did. But he also said that you had seen nothing,' said the canon.

'No, but I saw what I saw. I saw Boma seeing it.'

'How long have you known Boma?'

'Not long,' Brid said. She was beginning to discern the canon's scepticism. 'But there's more to it than that. I have proof.'

Brid reached under her jumper and brought out the medal. 'Read what it says, Canon,' she said.

'I haven't got my glasses.'

'Well, you'll just have to take it on faith, Canon. It's my baptismal medal, given me by Ma and Da. I've never told you this, Canon. I've never told anyone. But this medal I gave to Sir Roger Casement when he was in Ardfert. On the twenty-first of April 1916. I did not see it again until just a few days ago – when Boma arrived.'

'Could it not have been taken from Sir Roger? Could that not be the explanation of it?'

'You don't believe me, do you?'

'I'm hedging my bets, Brid. We can't be too careful.'

'Well, Sir Roger said that signs would follow.'

'We'll wait, so,' said the canon, scratching his nose.

Brid nodded. 'Maeve Brennan from Ballyheige was in my shop yesterday. She told me about what Father Devenish had seen.'

The canon frowned. 'Brid, promise me you won't say a word about all this. Will you promise me that?'

'But, Canon—'

'Let's just wait and see. I must be sceptical, Brid. It is required of me. Especially in this case. I won't burden you with it all, Brid. But if it got too far abroad that Roger Casement was appearing, well it might attract all kinds of undesirables to Ardfert.'

'He was a great man, Canon. A holy man!'

Canon Dawson nodded. 'I know what you think, Brid. If he's promised signs we must just wait and see. Until then . . .' He placed his finger over his lips, and winked. 'Will you do that for me?'

'I will, Canon,' Brid replied obediently.

'Will it be just for the one night?' Mrs Grogan at St Theresa's asked Mary.

'It could be longer. I'm not sure yet,' Mary replied, as she followed the owner of St Theresa's up the narrow stairs. She could not help watching the movement of the woman's large hips, like a giant's apple in a candystripe bag, filling the space above her.

'Will this do?' Mrs Grogan asked, holding open the door of the bedroom at the top of the stairs. 'The bathroom's down there on the left. Plenty of hot water. There's a sink in your room,' Mary peeped in, 'as you can see.'

'It's very nice.'

'I like to keep things nice. We rely on recommendations,' said Mrs Grogan. 'Who did you say sent you?'

'I don't think I did. It was Brid McCarthy.'

'Oh, it was? She's full up, is she? Now that surprises me. And so early in the year too. It's nice of Brid to send me custom.' Mrs Grogan paused, nudging to straighten the picture of St Theresa on the landing wall. 'It makes me feel a bit guilty because, between you and me, Miss Lyons, I don't return the favour. I don't think I can in good conscience. Did you see her rooms?'

'I didn't. No.'

'They're not – and I mustn't be uncharitable – quite up to the mark. She hasn't got a seal of approval from the Board.' Mrs Grogan nodded, submerging the coastal shelf of her chin beneath a sea of flesh. 'I have. You can tell by the shamrock on the sign.'

'She seemed a lovely, warm person.'

'*She's* warm, all right. I'm not sure you can say the same thing about her rooms. What reason did she give you for not giving you one?'

'She already has a guest.'

Mrs Grogan nodded. 'A guest and a half. Coloured, isn't she? Six months gone or more? No sign of a husband that I know of.'

Mary wanted Mrs Grogan to leave her in peace. She had her thoughts to collect, the immediate future to think about. But the woman showed no sign of leaving.

'We've been hearing things,' she said.

'Things?' asked Mary Lyons.

'Rumours.'

'I see.'

'There's been an apparition.'

'Indeed?'

'It's lucky you came when you did. If you'd put it off much longer – until the news spreads – there wouldn't be a place to be having anywhere between Tralee and Limerick,' said Mrs Grogan, matter-of-factly.

'Is that so? I hadn't heard about any apparitions.'

'You will. You will. I only heard this morning. When I saw you at the door so early I thought you must have got wind of it.'

'Who's the apparition of?' Mary asked.

'Roger Casement,' said Mrs Grogan.

'Roger Casement? I don't understand.'

'There's no understanding the workings of the Divine Plan.'

'Yes, but—'

'And between you and me, Miss Lyons, it could be the Singing Nun for all I care. The important thing is that it's an apparition. It makes all the difference to a place. It's exactly what Ardfert needs.'

'Yes, but—'

'I know what you're going to say. You're going to say that it's just the imagination of simple people running away with them. But, and it's early days yet, this apparition was seen by a priest.'

'When?'

'Yesterday or the day before. There were witnesses.'

'Yes, well, I suppose that does make a difference . . .'

'It has definite advantages, all right. It cuts down the time between the viewing and the acceptance of it as genuine. We don't want our apparition to be a flash in the pan like Ballinspittle. We want something that will stand the test of time. A Knock or a Lourdes.'

'Mrs Grogan, I . . .'

But it took a few minutes more before Mrs Grogan was ready to leave her guest to herself. When that time came, Mary Lyons closed and locked her door and lay down on the soft bed to think it all through. But, after a restless fifteen minutes, she got up again, deciding to take a walk while there was still light enough.

Like Boma and many another before her, Mary Lyons found herself, seeing the signpost with the sign missing, turning right at the intersection that led past McKenna's Fort to the ocean.

En route she had stopped at a telephone box to call Sister de Porres at the Tralee convent.

'Have you seen her?' Sister de Porres asked.

'I have.'

Sister de Porres waited. 'What do you think?'

'I don't know. I have to give it more time. Look, Sister, I'm staying at the St Theresa Guest House. I'm using my secular name. Mary Lyons. If there are calls from Dublin, tell them I'll be back as soon as I can.'

'Haven't you told them where you are?'

'Not exactly. No.'

'They'll think you've jumped over the wall.'

'Maybe I have, Sister.'

'Sister Paula!'

'I'm joking. Look, Sister, maybe you'd better ring the Provincial. If she gets angry – I know I should be working on the General Convocation – tell her they owe me this.'

'Will we be seeing anything of you, Sister?'

'I might need some money. I had forgotten how much you need out in the world. I've almost gone through everything I brought with me from Dublin. And the first day isn't finished yet! Twenty pounds goes nowhere, does it?'

'Are you all right, Sister?'

'I'm fine. Look I'd better go. My money is running out. Don't forget, if you have to call St Theresa's, I'm Mary Lyons. I don't want them knowing anything.'

Ten minutes later she was standing looking at the memorial to

Casement in the centre of the fort. A magnificent sunset – the weather making restitution for a wicked day – was taking place beyond the ocean and she stood watching it for a moment, her mind emptying of all the vexful thoughts of the last few hours.

Roddie watched her, as he had watched her before.

He wanted to break through to her. He called out her name, fought to connect, to penetrate the invisible wall of time, coincidence and unknowing that divided them.

He watched her and his sympathy was perfect. Her thoughts filled his head and buzzed, confused and tired him. She sat down and he wanted to. She let the sadness of a wasted life enter her; she entertained the thought, called herself hopeless, and he knew why. But the thought melded with his own thoughts. Two rivers, her consciousness and his own, like the converging of the Blue and White Nile, flowed together, their sediments dancing around, tumbling over and over like cream in coffee, like mixed races and backgrounds. He wondered whether he understood her because he had been granted insight or because he was like her, had reason to question his own life, to weigh it, find it wanting, ache to have done things differently.

She sat down on a stone, looking around her at the ebbing light. He crouched down beside her. *You shouldn't be sitting on such cold stone, Sister. You'll catch a chill. You, like me, will never be right for Ireland's weather after your years in the sun. You just don't get the knack back. Like the barrels of sherry they used to sling against the sides of ships to take on a sunny, sweaty trip to the tropics and then back to Europe for quaffing, you are sweeter, stronger, but you've taken on board a foreign spore that ill suits these climes. Still, sit there for a while. Sit and experience the place. It's not the best view in Ireland, to be sure. Not the most momentous place to choose for one's own. If I'd been a wise man I'd have landed by some monk's cell, by a Celtic tower, a great grand mountain old in myth. But I was fated to land here just as I was fated, having placed myself at a river's mouth, to head out to Africa. All Ireland was bred for export, I sometimes think. And it was abroad that our genius so often flowered. You and I, Sister Paula, have little to be ashamed of. Perhaps of me it could be said that I was at the phalanx of the colonization – the cruel colonization – of a continent which had managed itself quite decently before Europe started salivating over maps. Of you that you were spreading a narrow doctrine, a doctrine that doesn't suit everyone, too thinly. But we took the world as we found it and tried* to do something. Not enough, doubtless, but a great deal more than most. Do I sound arrogant to you? I know that you would never articulate such sentiments. It is an article of faith with you to deny your virtues. So let me do it for you. After all, I'm a man who took your religion when a wise man should. It's a fine firm hammock to die in, but I wonder about sleeping on it every night while life waxes and cavorts outside the porthole.

So here we are. And isn't it a fine state of affairs? I've been watching Boma for you. I wish I could have helped out a little earlier but they had me detained above and below with so much paperwork. Every year another man or woman who had a part in my life would pass away, and there would at once be missives from this or that recording angel and statements to be made and court-case and judgements to be arrived at. I suppose you think that heaven starts right off. Hell too. No, we're all in limbo until the whole thing is finished. And when will that be? When will The End come? Well, I can't tell you that. Everything is finished only when the last creature comes from the earth, when everything has been evened out. Only then can final judgements be made.

We, lost and saved and neither-up-nor-downs, ache for that time. We look for signs of final collapse. We would prise those ozone layers apart, tinker with vital safety equipment on your nuclear reactors, slip the plans for the making of hydrogen bombs to the most arrant ruffian, assist with vim the poisoners of rivers and oceans, applaud whale-killing lances on their way, add overdoses of food additives . . . if we dared. You see, it gets to be so very wearing to have to deal with the minutiae of our actions, the unknowing as to how our stories will work out. It is almost like a second Vale of Tears, but everyone is in such a terrible mood, teetering on tenterhooks, all the time. It is such a relief to be back here for a respite. To tell you the truth, I had started to complain rather.

While I have little sympathy for such as Vlad the Impaler and Leopold the Second, it would move the hardest of hearts to see them now. You see, those whose lives were writ large on the earth have the longest time to wait, the most miles to walk, papers to wade through, before their cases are settled. You can really guess the ones who are having the worst time. Then, when everything is settled all one has to do is wait for the Last Day. That wait, they tell me, is bearable, but only just. It's like pre-dinner drinks and an indefinitely postponed dinner. We know that something nice is being prepared beyond the door but our stomachs groan and our brains ache with the waiting. We can watch those who still have to get *everything sorted out carrying one more paper to one more angel to be added to one more scale. Don't ask me what's behind the door. I haven't yet experienced it, though I live in hope that this little trip will hasten the time.*

So I haven't come back to tell you about heaven – though I can speak fairly well on the subject of limbo. This, as far as I am concerned, can stand for heaven: an Irish coastal plain crowded with layer upon layer of memory as twilight pulses down to night and cold deepens; a landscape alive with spirit, and folk who, on the whole, mean well.

Our deeds ripple down the centuries for good or ill, dear Paula. I tell you that with great certainty. Vlad, Leopold and many another would tell you that also. And it is not a very profound notion when you think about it. The stone dropped in a field in one century can trip up a labourer a hundred years hence. A cruel word, a piece of cruelty, be mythologized and passed on down the generations like a language or a creed.

Why am I here? It isn't going to change anything much, is it? I was, after all, a minor player in my world. Not as great a reformer as a Wilberforce; as committed a patriot as Pearse or Connolly. No, I, Roger Casement, if I am remembered for anything, it is for causing people to be uncertain about me. Mention my name and a room goes quiet. Traitor or patriot? Noble idealist or debaucher? Protestant or Catholic? People don't know what to make of me and, to tell you the truth, I wasn't quite sure about what to make of myself. I was, I suppose, flawed. But what human being isn't? I learnt not to let that worry me too much. I learnt to accept the mixture in myself. The living was all.

But back to you. I will speak to you, my dear. Speak to you so you will hear. I'll prepare the meeting between yourself and Boma. Matchmaker, I'll be. You and I both know the matchmakers in the Congo, their power and power to charm.

Though you can't see me, I am with you for old and new times' sake. Be at ease, Paula. You have done well. Your office work up there will not take long. Many people will run to help you, as they helped me. We are of the same tribe, you and I. Irish and other.

You should think of going now, Sister Paula. God bless.

Mary Lyons – Sister Paula – sat through the twilight until she could barely see the memorial in front of her. When she roused herself to walk back to Ardfert and the first evening of her new, unregulated life, she felt light and untroubled and did not even stop to wonder why.

311643/146   3 August 1916
Sir,
    In reply to your letter of today's date, I am directed by the
Secretary of State to refer you to Section 6 of the Capital
Punishment Amendment Act, 1868, which provides that
the body of every offender executed shall be buried within the
walls of the prison within which judgement of death is
executed on him.
I am, Sir,
Your obedient servant,
E. Blackwell

5

'NOW THE PROBLEM IS,' SAID MRS GROGAN OF ST THERESA'S TO MRS
Taggart of the Ardfert Fancy Goods Emporium, 'how are we going
to put the halo on without the point of the compass making a hole
in Sir Roger's nose?'

'You could put a book or something – how about a chopping-
board? – underneath the picture and do the circle.'

'But the problem with that is the same! You'll still get a hole in
his nose.' Mrs Grogan thought for a moment. 'I know what. It's
been staring us in the face all this time. Put something hard on top.

A little piece of mirror. Something like that. That'll solve the problem.'

'You'll have to be careful to make sure that the point doesn't slip,' said Mrs Taggart.

'Never mind that. I'll get a bit of mirror.'

Mrs Grogan made off at speed for the kitchen. She found a mirror from her dead husband's brush-and-comb set. Seeing that the mirror was too big for her purposes, she took a meat mallet and broke it on the draining-board; then, picking up a large shard, made back to the dining-room where the picture of Roger Casement lay, on a doily.

'Here, this is just right,' she told Mrs Taggart.

'You didn't break the mirror, did you? You know what they say?'

'I know what they say but I'm not one to be believing such heathen nonsense, am I? Now, what I think is that we've got to be really careful to get it right first time. There aren't any second chances. If we make a mess of it we'll have to choose another picture and that lot at the Tralee library will be sure to notice.'

'I feel guilty about that. It was my ticket and—'

Mrs Grogan stood up to her full height and regarded Mrs Taggart. 'Don't we pay our taxes? A good deal more and more regularly than most folk, I'm thinking. And we never darken the door of the library from one year's end to the next. Sure, they owe us a couple of photos from the odd book. And look it, the book hasn't been taken out since June the eighteenth, 1987! It was mouldering away on the shelf till you got it out. And don't forget, it's the Lord's work we're about.'

'But do you think a simple line around his head is enough?' asked Mrs Taggart. 'Perhaps we should think about it a bit before we go ahead. It's an art putting in a halo, same as anything else. He's a good-looking man, so he is.'

'He is a good-looking man. He wouldn't have made a bad model for the Sacred Heart. A good deal better than some I could mention. Half of them look real sissies, so they do. Still, I understand what you're getting at. Maybe we should think about the sort of halo that would show up best.'

Mrs Taggart pointed to the picture of the Sacred Heart on the wall to the left of the television. 'You see the rays coming out in three directions behind His head? That looks impressive.'

'I wish our photo was coloured.' Mrs Grogan looked from the

photograph of the young Casement up to the Sacred Heart. 'No, it's no good. To be effective it would need to be in yellow-gold and that's no good with a black-and-white snap. Anyway, the rays from the Sacred Heart look like part of a cross. I don't think it'd be right for Sir Roger.'

'Have you got any other holy pictures? They might give us inspiration.'

'I'll get my missal.'

Mrs Grogan returned in a moment with her missal, swollen like a filofax but with holy pictures, *memento mori* cards and prayers written in calligraphy.

'Now that's good,' said Mrs Taggart, holding up a picture of the Little Flower. 'It's just a plain circle around St Theresa's head but they've added little gold stars. That's really lovely.'

'I was given it by Kitty O'Toole when she came back from Lisieux in 1967. Little good the trip did her.' She studied the halo. 'But I don't think it would suit. Look at this one of St Rita. I think that's what we should be aiming at. Just a simple circle around the head. If this one sells we can go in for something more complicated. We could engage our own painter to do a likeness with a built-in halo. But we're taking a risk at the present. I don't think we should be too ambitious. Not with the first batch.'

'Perhaps you're right,' said Mrs Taggart. 'And there is something impressive about that single line around the head. It says quietly, "I'm a saint", but it doesn't scream it. It's tasteful.'

'OK, so,' said Mrs Grogan. 'Let's get on with it.'

She placed the shard of mirror down in the centre of Roger Casement's face. Then she pulled the compass apart to a radius of about an inch and a half and set the point down on the mirror.

'A little to the left. Just a tiny bit, mind. There. That's it. Don't put the pencil down yet. Go around once or twice so's I can see it. Put the point a bit up. Not that far. Yes. Start a half inch from his neck and . . .'

Mrs Grogan glared at her friend. The point slipped on the mirror. The pencil made a mark on the forehead of Casement.

'Jesus! Fetch me a rubber, will you? It's you standing over me and giving orders like I don't know what! You were right in my light too, so you were!'

'I haven't brought a rubber,' said Mrs Taggart.

'Well, sure you'll just have to go and fetch one. You must have a ton in that shop of yours.' Mrs Taggart made to go. 'And hurry on back. I don't want Miss Lyons coming back and finding us at it. Complete security is required. You can trust the printer, I suppose?'

'He's my cousin,' said Mrs Taggart, putting on her coat.

'And not a word to anyone,' said Mrs Grogan.

When Mrs Taggart had gone off in search of a rubber, Mrs Grogan jittered about for a moment. Her thoughts returned to Miss Lyons and she decided to do what she usually did when her guests were out. Partly out of security, partly curiosity.

She tiptoed into her guest's room and made straight for the suitcase. The locks clicked open and Mrs Grogan saw the crucifix, the cap over which Sister Paula wore the prescribed headscarf, the grey skirt and the blouse with the Flaming Heart embroidered on the front.

Back downstairs she waited for Mrs Taggart's return, her heart high with incident and news to impart.

'This was all I had!' said Mrs Taggart, holding up a rubber cut in the shape of Ireland.

'It'll do,' said Mrs Grogan. She rubbed carefully at the line on Casement's forehead, blew, leaned back to see the results. 'There. Now let's get that halo drawn.' She repeated the procedure, her tongue sticking out between her lips in concentration. First time, she managed a perfect circle around Roger Casement's head. 'What do you think?'

'Just right,' said Mrs Taggart. 'How many should I get him to do?'

Mrs Grogan looked at the price list. 'Five thousand postcards and two thousand holy picture size.'

'That's a lot. It's risky.'

'Mrs Taggart, as a businesswoman you should know that risk is the name of the game. If you don't take risks you don't gain. I took a risk when I got basins in all the bedrooms but I got my shamrock from the Board and I've never looked back. You mark my words, we'll be reordering in no time at all.'

Mrs Taggart, thinking of all the unsold merchandise in her Fancy Goods Emporium, was not so sure.

'Can you keep a secret?' asked Mrs Grogan.

Mrs Taggart nodded, despite the fact that she couldn't. 'My guest, Miss Lyons, is a nun. Can you credit it? She's put her habit away. In mufti. It wouldn't surprise me in the least if she'd been sent here because of the apparition. I tell you, Mrs Taggart, it's taking off!'

Mrs Taggart nodded. It made her feel better about the expense to know that interest had already been aroused.

'Look it,' said Mrs Grogan, picking up the picture. 'Let's get this to Maguire so that he can print it in the morning. He said he'd rush it through if we got it to him by this evening. Tell him to do his best work. And don't say a word, do you hear?'

Mrs Taggart said that she would be as quiet as the grave, though she knew herself well enough to know that she probably wouldn't be.

The place they stayed at in Bantry was like no bed & breakfast Tim had ever experienced. So intimidated had he been by the grand house overlooking Bantry Bay that he stopped the car on the drive and asked Chris to think again.

'You're only young once,' Chris replied, and he sent Tim in to see if they had a room.

The woman at reception echoed the house. She was civil enough, but intimidating, and, Tim thought, far too grand to be asked the price. All through the evening he kept wondering what the damage would be, but he knew Chris well enough not to mention it. When Chris asked he just shrugged and said, 'Lie back and enjoy it.'

Hotels had always been Chris's one extravagance. Tim had letters from Chris in his flat in London written on the stationery of very flashy hotels indeed. It was one more thing Tim could not fathom about him. In every other area he was positively anchoritic. He had no home and now would never have one. He eschewed all touristy purchases. He even disposed of his books as soon as he had read them. But he liked a good hotel.

'It looks to me like when you've done one peninsula you've done the lot,' Chris said in the overheated room looking out over a half-refurbished Italian formal garden.

'I don't think that's necessarily the case,' Tim said, standing up for his homeland. Then he assumed his Irish self, perhaps to practise. 'A lifetime you could spend exploring them! A lifetime!'

Chris looked at Tim quizzically through his thick lenses. 'Well, let's pretend it's true. I vote we make for the Dingle Peninsula. That's the handiest for your mammy.'

Tim accepted that and asked Chris what he'd like for his dinner.

They ate at a fish restaurant in Bantry. Tim had scampi but when he saw the big portion of plaice that Chris was given, he wished he had chosen that. Chris had a side-order of green salad and found a bug sitting in the lettuce. 'See that?' he asked, holding up the green leaf.

'Don't tell; they'll all want one,' Tim said.

'I've never understood why people say that,' Chris said, laying the leaf back in the salad, then pushing the bowl out of his sight. 'Well, all I can say is that people can't come to Ireland for the food; they definitely don't come for the weather. What's the fascination, do you think?'

'The people are warm. Look at me, for instance.'

Chris raised his left eyebrow.

Tim continued, 'The landscape is wonderful—'

'When the mists lift.'

'There's a spirit about the place. An atmosphere. I don't know how to explain it. It has to do with religion and myth and history.'

'You should write for the Tourist Board.'

'I've thought about it,' Tim said.

Chris looked at his plate. 'I think I've finished.'

'Hand it over. Waste not, want not.'

'I must write that down.'

'You're feeling all right, are you?'

'As right as I'll ever be,' Chris said.

They slept well. In the morning breakfast was served by the owners. Tim heard the waiter addressed humorously as 'My Lord' by some people at the next table. Knowing a lord had served him his cornflakes made the parting with eighty pounds for the two of them a little easier, as in all probability it was meant to.

They stopped off to tour the gardens of Glengarriff. Chris wanted to see Garinish Island, where Shaw had written St Joan. The weather had improved. It was windless and a hazy sun shone.

Mid-afternoon they crossed into Kerry on the Kenmare road. Tim had plotted to skirt Kenmare and make for Killarney, perhaps stay there the night, but just outside Glengarriff Chris told him to stop for a man hitching.

Tim did as instructed. The hitcher opened the door of the car. He was a man in his early twenties. Pale complexion with freckles round the nose, carrot-red hair. His smile split his face wide open.

'Where are you making for?' Tim asked him.

'Kenmare.'

Tim was about to tell the man they were not going to Kenmare but Chris was out of the car and getting into the back, something that was becoming a habit with him. 'I'll take your bag. You get in the front,' he told the man.

'Mind it, mind,' the man said. 'It's got some good stuff in it.'

'I'll guard it with my life,' Chris said.

They started off, Tim smelling the whiskey on the young man's breath. The man seemed to sense that he would know.

'I'm a Power's man,' he said.

'A Power's man? What's that?' Chris asked.

It was obvious to Tim what a Power's man was.

'Whiskey,' he said.

'You like it, do you?' asked Chris.

'What do you think?'

'I think you do. How much do you drink?'

'In a day?'

'In a day.'

'A bottle; a bit more if I can get it,' the man said.

'That's going some,' Chris said.

'It can't do you any good,' Tim said.

'It doesn't do me any harm.'

He was a handsome young man and whatever harm Power's might be doing him hadn't yet showed. Tim wondered how he could afford it.

'Are you from Kenmare?' Chris asked, leaning forward to talk.

Tim listened. He had seldom seen Chris so interested in anyone. Certainly not in the last few weeks.

'No, sir, I'm not. I'm from Castlebar. My visit to Kenmare is by the way of being, as you might say, a courtesy call,' he said.

'Oh, yes?'

'That's correct. It's a matter of doing my duty, sir. I was in Kenmare a few months ago. I was sitting on a cliff drinking and I don't know what happened but I sort of fell off the cliff. Well, sort of didn't come into it. I fell all right. I landed on a ledge and came to myself straight away. I called for help. I couldn't get fuckin' up or fuckin' down. I was stuck completely and the bottle of Power's dead on the rocks below me. I had a good weep for her, and I'm not ashamed to be telling you. Anyhow, along comes a woman walking the cliffs with her dog. It was the dog saw me first. She barked and brought me back and I started shouting like a banshee. The woman used the lead of the dog and joined it up with her scarf and pulled me up the cliff. She could see I was in mourning for the Power's. She took me to her house and gave me a shower and some food and as much drink as I wanted. I stayed the night there. Got a great breakfast in the morning and a bottle of Power's to see me on my way.' He stopped.

'So . . . ?' Chris asked.

'So I'm going back to thank her.'

'She'll get a surprise when she sees you,' Tim said.

'Could be you're right, sir. Some people would just have gone off and not thought of it again. But I'm not that sort of fellow at all.'

They let the Power's man off in the centre of Kenmare; they never learnt his name. Tim was starting up the car again when Chris told him to park it.

'Why?' Tim asked. 'There's nothing here.'

'I want to follow him.'

'Why?'

'Isn't it obvious? Christ, Tim, isn't it obvious?'

'No.'

'I want to see that woman's face when he turns up. I want to see what happens. I want to see the end of the story!'

'He was probably spinning a yarn,' Tim said. He didn't understand, but he parked the car.

'Come on, Tim! Get going!'

Tim locked the car and followed him. Chris was running. Tim wanted to tell him to stop but it was all he could do to keep up with him.

The Power's man was shambling up a straight road with terraced houses on each side. He seemed uncertain about which one he wanted.

Chris crossed over, not looking back at Tim to see if he was following. He then stalked the Power's man, staying only slightly behind, out of his sight.

It occurred to Tim that perhaps Chris wanted to catch the Power's man out in a lie; to prove that he had somehow been spinning them a yarn. It would have been quite like Chris to do that, he thought.

The Power's man stopped at a house. He still seemed uncertain. He looked up into the top window. An Infant of Prague statue stood there, looking inwards at a lace curtain. This seemed to convince the

Power's man that he had reached his destination and he knocked at the door.

Tim was standing beside Chris then, but if he noticed him there he didn't let on. He was standing stock-still, watching. A man passed them, giving both a sideways glance. Tim nodded to him and he smiled, saluting him.

'Been a grand day,' the man said.

'Indeed it has,' Tim replied.

Then the door opened. A stout woman of around fifty was standing at the door. A dog beside her jumped up at the Power's man. He held out his arm to be play-bitten, hugged the dog to him. Then the Power's man was speaking to the woman. She laughed, swung the door open wide and fussed him into the house. The door closed.

'Right,' Chris said. 'Back to the car.'

'What's the verdict?' Tim asked him.

He didn't reply at once. Tim looked over and he was panting.

'You OK?'

'No, not really. Still, it was worth it. I think the Power's man is all right for tonight, don't you?'

'Yes, I'd say so.'

'I think we'd better see if we have as much luck,' he said.

'There's a good hotel by the lake in Killarney,' Tim said, still playing for time.

Back in the car, Chris took off his glasses, polished them with a cloth and laid them on his lap. He then took out the antibiotic eyedrops he used to clear up the last of the shingles and asked Tim to put three drops into the milky iris.

Tim did so, wondering why Chris had not asked him to do the chore before.

Boma snapped the biography shut. Then she held it out, feeling its bulk, gazing at its thickness. She had kept it by her since first opening it. When she left it somewhere she knew exactly where it was, and the thought of it had tugged her back. The page numbers of her reading advanced at a speed that seemed magical and now that it was finished she felt a tinge of regret, wondered whether she should start it over again, or find another book to tell her more.

The clock on the wall said three. Brid was in the shop dusting off the stock. Boma got up and went in to her.

'Brid,' she said, 'I think I'll take a ride into Tralee. I need a bit of fresh air.'

'Do you want me to come with you, dear?' Brid asked.

Boma pretended to consider. 'No. I'd like to be alone for a while.'

'Everything's all right, is it?' Brid asked, wanting to add, *You're not going to leave, are you?* but not daring further repetition.

'Everything's fine.'

'You know how happy I am you're here? You know that, don't you, Boma? In spite of everything.'

'Of course I do, Brid.'

Brid nodded and got on with her work.

Boma found herself a lift into Tralee easily enough. When she arrived at the centre of the town she walked around the shops for a while. She tried not to be conspicuous, not to stand out. She did this by avoiding people's eyes. She knew that the strategy did not work but it had always been her way, was second nature and now, when she was certain she did not want to meet anyone who might know her from her past life, was not the time to ween herself away from her ostrich strategy and face the world full-square.

The crowds oppressed her. She saw a park and walked into it, noticing the museum standing a hundred yards away through the mist.

'Off on your own, are we?' he said.

She turned and smiled at him, not in the least surprised. 'It's you. Brid's going to be angry she missed you.'

'You could save her disappointment by not telling her. Another secret between us will do no harm.'

'We went and told the priest,' Boma said.

'I know you did. I showed myself to him but he's busy trying not to believe it. For a man who lives by faith – and gets a decent living out of it at the same time – he's terribly anxious not to believe that I've come back.'

'But what do you want us to do?' Boma asked. 'That's the thought that's been going round and round. I just don't understand. You're a real tease, so you are.'

He took her hand. 'I don't mean to tease you, Boma. I'm sorry if you think that. I don't mean to tease you at all. It's just that there are so many things to be done. I've got a devil of a tight schedule. A lot to cram in.'

'Like what?' Boma asked.

'Did you read the Inglis book? I know he'll ask me when I get back.'

'I have,' she said.

'So you know most of it.'

'Just before the execution, you wrote that it was a terrible thing to die with all men misunderstanding. What were you thinking of?'

'Did I write that? I suppose I was worried about how I would be remembered. People do, you know. It didn't look too promising, Boma, to tell you the truth. A man about to die may be excused a passing piece of vanity, I suppose. Reputation is something that people value highly, isn't it? But none of it bothers me in the least now. What bothers me rather are the same things that bothered me in life, that boil and bubble in my head and will give me no rest. You see, Boma, when I was writing my reports and trying for the independence of Ireland I was viewing everything from the perspective of a new century. I fancied that it was all going to come round right. Expose the mischief of a Leopold or an English rubber company and I had played my part in the great upward heave of mankind. If I had to die the death I died it was a small thing. The people remaining would be there to make sure that progress marched on. For just as the engines of the twentieth century seemed unstoppable and offered a life of endless improvement, so in human affairs the slave would continue his dash for freedom, the oppressors' hearts inexorably melt. All that had to be done was place the declarations of freedom and improvement into the little barque and let them float down the hopeful, widening, crystal stream of the twentieth century. I would name those future years: 1939 . . . 1968 . . . 1979 . . . 1995 . . . and they seemed full of progress, of advancement. Perhaps you can do the same thing with the twenty-first century. Perhaps you see the future as brighter than the past. But for me this century has been a great disappointment, Boma. The evils that I saw then, the tortures visited upon the weak and powerless, have expanded in direct proportion to the power of the machine. Instead of mankind using its new powers for the betterment of all, inequalities and betrayals and corruptions and exploitation, the like of which the world has never seen in its history, have become the norm, so much the norm that it hardly rates a mention.'

Boma did not speak at once. Roddie waited, smiling. 'But why me? Why come to me?' she asked at last.

'Ah, Boma. You are *the* most important thing. I have no other function here other than to warn, to knock heads together, to try and make folk see sense, maybe bring a bit of comfort. But with you, it's a little bit different. I could not allow you to make away with yourself that day. The circle of my life was almost closed but, had you managed to do what you were planning, a tiny chink would have remained. A failure that could never have been righted. I had to go swimming with you.'

Boma shook her head. 'I don't understand.'

'You will, Boma. Look, I can't stay. But I'll be back for a good session. While I'm away will you take in that woman who came asking for a room? You know her as Mary, I believe. She's miserable with that Mrs Grogan at St Theresa's. Will you do that for me?'

Boma nodded.

'Do you promise?'

'I promise.'

'There's a good girl. Look, I must be off now.'

'When will you come back?'

'Quite soon. I promise that back to you. I don't like the idea of you walking about in the cold. Why not go back to the museum? It's warm there and you could talk to "Sir Roger".'

'It's true, I could.'

Roddie doffed his hat. 'He seems like a decent sort of chap,' he said, and he walked away into the mist.

'You're the first customer we've had for ages,' said Eamonn McCann. He saw Boma taking in his silver helmet, his uniform. 'I'm bleeding Oliver Cromwell today,' he said. 'I hate it when his day comes round. If we had any customers – which we don't, as you can see – they wouldn't want to hear a word from Oliver Cromwell. They know it already. They just give me looks that'd turn a fellow to stone.'

'So why do you do it?' Boma asked. 'Brid says you were going to be a priest, and you're a trained teacher.'

'A failed teacher is what I am. My life is a long, miserable book of failure.' He looked down at himself. 'As you can see.'

'At least you've got a job.'

'I went for an interview to be an air-steward once but they said that, though I had a pleasing personality, my hips were too big for the cabin.' He lifted his jacket to show Boma. 'They're not, are they – what's your name again?'

She shook her head, wondering about him. 'Boma,' she said.

He considered the name, seemed to be sucking on it like a sweet. 'Are you still with Brid?'

'I am.'

'How is she?'

'Fine.'

'But, apart from Brid, you're all by yourself?'

She knew what he meant. 'That too,' she said.

'How long before the big day?'

'About two months, I think.'

'Are you courting?'

'No, I'm not.'

He shuffled about, stood up, sat down again, contemplated his nails. 'Would you consider stepping out with me?' he said, as much to his nails as to her.

Boma had not expected that. She laughed a laugh that exploded round the displays of Irish heroes and Celtic remains.

'I see,' he said, unsurprised.

She saw again how he was. He had probably never had a girl-friend, had always been in a chaste twilight, wondering if God was after him. 'I wasn't laughing at you. I was laughing at myself. Do you think you're man enough to be seen with me in Tralee?' she said.

'I don't mind if you don't. Would you? A walk – a gentle walk – a drink?'

'I would,' she said. 'I really would.'

Oliver Cromwell smiled. 'You don't want to know about bleeding Oliver Cromwell, do you?'

'Not much.'

'You wouldn't be interested in the fact that I was only in Ireland for nine months but managed to permanently change the whole of the Irish landscape, both architectural and human?'

Boma shook her head.

'Or that I managed to ruin all the great treasure-houses kept safe for Europe through all the Dark Ages? That I murdered more Irishmen than the Potato Famine? You wouldn't like to know that?'

Boma shook her head again.

'That Irish people take me for the devil incarnate and can-not understand why my statue is standing outside the Houses of

Parliament in London? That they see me as akin to Hitler or Idi Amin? You wouldn't like to hear all that?'

She shook her head a third time. 'Forget it,' she said. 'Tell me about Eamonn McCann.'

Eamonn took off his helmet, dropped it on the floor of the gallery, sat down next to Boma. 'I'm no expert on him. Still as it's you, I'll do my best. What do you want to know about him?' he asked.

He could tell you things! Things I've tried to forget; things I never did know. He has had as many years of Africa as I have months – almost.

JOSEPH CONRAD WRITING ABOUT CASEMENT

6

OKONDO HEARD THE SIRENS, THE SHOUTING OF THE PEOPLE. HE FELT the dust thrown up by running bare feet, the burning pungency of freshly poured Tarmac. He coughed in his darkness under the hot midday sun.

It happened then. In the midst of mayhem he lost the hand he had been holding, the hand of Mbunza, his youngest son. Okondo stopped shock-still and described panicky urgent arcs with his cane. It caught the hip of a woman who was craning around heads to see the approaching cavalcade pass. She noticed the touch, though all around people were jostling against her. She saw Okondo's badly scarred face, his blank eyes, heard him repeating his son's name, but could not understand what he was saying above the sirens and the cacophony of the crowd. The woman watched Okondo's white stick and something about it terrified her; the white stick arcing this way and that, its search centred upon her as if divining that she was the one it was seeking. Already in awe of the events about to slide along the steaming Tarmac she moved away, oblivious to the loud protests of the ever-compressing crowd around her.

The stick caught others and they too looked and, not understanding the white code of the stick, moved out of harm's way. Life was hard enough without the touch of Okondo adding further to their trials. The flies that made straight for their eyes reminded them of the blindness that some could carry on their wheedling tentacles. They saw themselves in a week or a month lost and last like Okondo in a similar crowd.

'Mbunza! Mbunza!' Okondo called out, but his mouth was dry from the dust, his tongue and vocal cords thick and furred. 'Son, I am over here!' He turned on the spot, raised his cane in the air, waving it above his head.

A member of the crowd, a hidden policeman, saw the waving cane and pushed through the throng, fearing an incident. He grabbed it and, without hesitation, broke it in two over his knee. He then swore at Okondo, dropped the two pieces furiously in front of him, pushed himself away through the knowing crowd.

Okondo had heard the tiny sound of the cane dropping and he bent down to find it, Brailling the footprint-on-footprinted dust with his fingertips. He found a piece and picked it up. The other section of the folding white cane, still attached to the section Okondo held by a piece of elastic that had been once the mystery of its ability to fold, followed it up. The cane was precious, on loan from the School for the Blind. Okondo fingered the break; it chafed his sensitive thumb-end and had him racing ahead to explain the happening to the impatient man in the Blind School office. He saw. He saw himself hangdog and abject in front of the faceless man – for Okondo knew only the faces of those he had been allowed to touch – being refused foreign sponsorship money for Mbunza's education.

But then the motor-cycle outriders passed. The crowd surged forward and he was suddenly knocked over on to his side. A foot stood on his thigh. He smelled poor clothes and bodies, but could not recognize them. He cried out.

Then a pair of hands was lifting him, setting him on his feet. And, when he was on his feet, the hands did not leave him.

'Thank you, brother,' Okondo said.

The hands squeezed his thin shoulders. 'Stay still. Don't move until the President has passed,' said the man who had lifted Okondo.

'Thank you, brother,' Okondo replied, surprised to hear a Lualaba-speaker in Boma, but relieved to have found help. 'My son was leading me to the clinic. I have lost him.'

'Don't worry, Okondo,' said the man. 'The crowd is very great. I will make sure no danger comes to you.'

Just at that moment six outrider motor cycles, their sirens blaring, were heading down the single-lane strip of black Tarmac, laid two days before in preparation for President Mobutu Sese Seko's opening of a Civic Centre.

'Do I know you, brother?' Okondo asked the stranger.

'Maybe you do, Okondo. We'll see,' said the man. 'Now stay right where you are. I've a little errand to run. I won't be long.'

Okondo stood very still, resting his hopes on the man. He could sense the excitement in the crowd increasing. Bodies barged against him and he heard cheering from a distance away that increased in volume, approaching, like a wave, as Mobutu Sese Seko's limousine made its way along the road. The car passed and Okondo felt himself in the centre of the wave. He fought to keep his place, to stand on the speck of ground, to hold on to it for the man's return. But he could not. Bodies barged him and he almost lost his step. He fought not to fall, grasping at the bodies to hold him up. Strangers pulled his hands away, cursing him.

But Okondo was still standing and the noise was subsiding. In the distance a band struck up. A microphone shrieked.

Then he heard it. A dark cry from the crowd set between shock and fear. Then the silence returned and Okondo was left wondering if he had indeed heard the strange sound at all. He felt fearful and did not dare to ask what the sound betokened. He let time pass, hoping for the return of the man.

Then the close-packed bodies that suffocated him pulled back. Okondo waited, still as a statue, terrified by the silence and the sudden absence of people. He felt hopelessly vulnerable, as if he were in the middle of a huge sports stadium waiting for the bullets to scythe him down; for the crowds to roar.

Roddie, leading Mobutu Sese Seko by the arm, saw the crowds parting for them. He came upon Okondo standing bewildered in the dust by the streak of road. 'Here,' he said to Mobutu Sese Seko, 'guide this man. He's going our way.'

Mobutu Sese Seko looked at the blind man. His guards had been powerless against the bearded man. Resentfully, he took Okondo's hand and they continued on to the clinic, while the crowd and the cameras moved with them.

Okondo let himself be guided. 'A man broke my cane,' he said to Mobutu Sese Seko. 'I cannot find my son. I am going to the clinic.'

'I want to break your heart. I want to break your heart, Joe Mobutu,' Roddie said. 'Save yourself. While this nonsense goes on you are lost.'

Away from the black road the strange procession came to the rusting gates of the clinic. Women sat in the shade by the wall, exhausted after walking the many miles from their villages.

Inside the building Roddie forced Mobutu Sese Seko through each of the primitive wards. He lifted up infants to show Mobutu the filth of weeks. He showed him patients shaking with malarial fevers; skeletal people in the last stages of AIDS. 'Is your heart breaking? Is it?'

Mobutu Sese Seko stared down at his countrymen, the countrymen he had forced to change their names, saying everything was going to be better with the wicked colonialists gone. And he saw himself but for the safety net of several palatial properties abroad, billions in yeasty-bullion bubbling in the temperature-controlled stillness of Swiss cathedral safes.

'Nothing. Not a dicky-bird,' Roddie said. 'Well, I'll leave you to it now, Joe.'

Shaking his head he left Mobutu Sese Seko to his people and, invisible to everyone now, went to find Okondo. He was standing alone in the lobby of the chaotic clinic. Roddie led him to where he wanted to go.

'Who are you, my brother?' Okondo asked him when they had left the clinic.

'I am just what you say, Okondo. Your brother.'

'But I do not know you? Are you from Lualaba?'

'No, I am not,' Roddie replied, 'but I have been there.'

'May I touch your face? I want to know what you look like,' Okondo asked.

'Of course. Of course.'

Okondo reached out his hands and touched Roddie's beard, drew back in shock at the touch; then, holding both hands out in front of him gently followed the sharp contours of Roddie's face: his forehead, his nose, cheeks, chin. 'You are not an African. I think you are a white man. I think I know you.'

'Could I not be an Ethiopian or a Somali?'

'No, your hair is very straight. It is like the hair of Father Pierre.'

'You are right. I am an Irishman.'

Okondo lowered his hands from Roddie's face. 'Thank you,' he said. 'You are handsome.'

'It is good of you to say so,' Roddie replied. 'Now let us see if your picture of me is correct.'

Roddie kissed Okondo lightly on each eye and the touch burnt Okondo and he cried out and, as light flooded in, he hid his eyes in his hands.

'Take your time,' Roddie said. 'Not too fast now. Your eyes have had a long sleep. Take it slowly. That's it.'

Okondo, as the light pierced his eyes, wanted to plead for the darkness to return. He sat down with his hands covering his face for several minutes.

'Try again.' And Roddie gently pulled Okondo's hands from his eyes. 'Is that better?'

Okondo stared into the face that he had imagined.

'Was I as you imagined?'

But before Okondo could reply, Roddie had disappeared.

Okondo looked around. The ribbon of road leading to the Civic Centre lay at his feet. He had to close his eyes to reorient himself towards home by wind and smell and sense. Sight was distracting. But, when he found himself on the way to his part of the shanty town, he opened his eyes, saw the imagined geography of his poor life and began to run.

That evening Okondo, sitting outside his hut, surrounded by curious people, looked at his wife and children in the light of the tilly-lamp. They were much as he had always felt they were. But though he had known their features, the joy of their colour, their shine, the light and shade of their expressions mesmerized him. He asked Mbunza to fetch him his pipe and tobacco from inside the shack. His youngest son shyly presented the pipe to his father, afraid to look him in the eye. Okondo took it and turned the bowl in his right hand.

Okondo closed his good eyes, the better to Braille the carved surface of the pipe-bowl. He hardly needed to. He knew the carved face like he knew his own. He felt the forehead, the nose, the cheek-bones and the beard.

He opened his eyes and lifted his hands to silence the group of people about him. 'I have a story to tell you,' Okondo said.

The people sat down and were quiet. The men made an eager grunting sound in their throats, waiting for what Okondo would tell them.

'My grandfather made this pipe. He also made the four-legged stool on which I sit and the headrest inside my home. His name was Lulua and he was a great worker of wood. White men came long distances to buy the carvings he made. But my grandfather would never have become a carver if he had not lost his feet. He had come from the region of Luba Kasai as a youth because there was news that wealth could be earned here. But when he arrived he was caught by bad people who made him tap rubber in the forest. They then took the rubber but paid him nothing. When Lulua protested a guard struck him and then hacked off his feet with a machete.

'Of course, brothers and sisters, you know about this. We will not forget this time as long as our tongues can shape tales. Lulua had been left in the forest to die, and he used to sit on this stool where now I sit and tell us how much he had wanted to die, how he hit his head against the trunks of trees in order to stop the pain. He called on the Ancestors to witness what had been done to him, to destroy the white men who had come to our land in order to turn us into slaves. For Zaïre was then the private property of King Leopold of the Belgians. But you know all that. Lulua lay down, trying to die. But then he felt cold water on his face, looked up and saw a bearded white man above him, cleaning his head wounds. He was afraid, for the white man with his beard looked like the cruel men of Leopold. But this man gave him medicine which took the pain away and sent him sweet dreams. He woke up in a high room. That was the mission station. There the man who had saved him came to see him, brought him gifts of fruit and meal. He caressed Lulua's face, whispered gentle sounds to him that he could not understand.

'Time passed and Lulua began to recover. He was able to hobble around on his stumps with the help of a crutch. The man often came back to visit him. He brought other white men with him and they were angry when they saw his stumps and the mutilations of the other people. He gave Lulua money and Lulua bought this home and began to carve. And as the years passed by many people came to buy his carvings. But the man who had helped him did not return. Lulua carved many images of the man. He would ask people if the images of him they saw were recognizable to them. But no-one knew the man. He sold the images he made. But this pipe he did not sell. He smoked tobacco from this pipe every day of his life. You elders will remember him with it. I too remember Lulua with this pipe between his teeth, smoke rising blue, blue, in the air, carving heads and pillow-stalks and chests and chairs. And he would tell me about the man whose head he had carved on the bowl of the pipe.

'When my father, fighting for our independence from Belgium, was away from home, deep in the forest, I, his eldest son, was left to protect the family. We heard that mercenaries were coming to our village and all fled before them. But my grandfather, an old man by then and crippled, could not flee. I stayed with him and was there when the white men came and set fire to our home. My grandfather died in those flames. I was blinded and my body was scarred. My father, when he heard, became possessed by a terrible rage and exacted a great revenge. He killed many white people before he himself was shot. He torched their homes, offices, factories, schools and hospitals to avenge his poor father's death, the blindness of his eldest son.

'Brothers and sisters, all that I have spoken you know. I can hear your heads thinking, *But what is new? Where is his story? All this we have known since we learnt what our bodies were for.* Today has been a strange one. Some of what has happened I cannot speak of but already I hear voices whispering of the world being turned upside down. You yourselves, however, can see the strangest part of this day – or so you think. Okondo, the blind man, can see again. Okondo, whose face was covered in scars, is now healed. I lost my son on the way to the clinic and I was frightened because there were no neighbours around. A man helped me. He took me with the man

133

whose name we do not speak to the clinic. He helped me obtain my salve. Then he walked me towards home. He kissed my eyes and now I can see. But before he healed me he let me touch his face so that I would know the face of the man who helped me. And when I touched the face I knew that I knew it. I saw the face after he had cured me and again I knew I knew him. And now, holding this pipe, I know that the man who helped me today is the man who helped Lulua so many years ago.'

The people grunted satisfaction at the story.

'And there is my story,' said Okondo.

He reached for the tobacco box, took a pinch, filled the old pipe and lit it with a brand from the fire. He closed his eyes as the flames rose and fell, rose and fell from the bowl of the pipe. His palm clenched round the bowl and he felt it warming. And his palm, this night like any other night, saw the face of his benefactor.

The hotel in Killarney had been fine for them, would have been marvellous, had not a great dome of fog enveloped it. They could see from postcards for sale at reception what a beautiful view of the lake and its backdrop of mountains lay beyond the encircling gloom. But from the window of their room they looked out over a few monochrome trees still clutching winter, and a jetty that ended before it reached the water.

They drank too much at the bar and ate a long dinner. They did not talk much and Tim was tempted to say that they could go back to England if Chris wanted. But he kept his mouth shut, waited for Chris to make the first move, pronounce the trip a failure.

'What's on the cards for tomorrow?' Chris asked towards the end of the meal.

'I'll leave it to you.'

'Dingle,' Chris said.

The following afternoon they found a place to stay in Dingle; but they only lasted there half an hour. Tim had asked about the availability of showers and the man said, 'There's a bath.'

Chris, though they had just passed another blank day, seemed happy enough. He took off his clothes, put on a towelling dressing-gown and disappeared to the bathroom for a long soak. He came back in a minute. 'Come and look at this,' he said.

Tim followed Chris to the bathroom. He pointed to the hot tap. 'Do you see what I see?' he asked.

'What?'

'Try turning the tap.'

Tim tried but it wouldn't turn even slightly. 'It's stiff all right.'

'Yes,' he said. 'It's stiff, and I'll tell you why it's stiff. It's stiff because it's been soldered shut.'

'It hasn't!'

But, on looking closer, Tim saw that Chris was right.

'I'll go and complain.'

'No you won't,' Chris said. 'We're checking out. Now.'

'Who's the masterful one?' Tim said.

Fifteen minutes later they walked down the stairs with their bags. The man must have spotted them. He came out, cocked his head in enquiry.

'We're leaving,' Chris said.

'Why? You've only just come.'

He told the man about the bath. 'You recall us asking you whether you had one?'

'I recall saying we have one.'

'With the hot tap soldered shut.'

'It doesn't make any difference,' said the man. 'There isn't any hot water anyway, as I recall.'

'There you are then.'

The man shrugged and they left, putting the cases back into the car.

'What now?' Tim asked.

'I need a drink,' Chris said.

They went into O'Keeffe's Bar, down the street. Chris ordered a double whiskey and Tim a half of Guinness.

'Come far?' the barman asked Chris.

'That's difficult,' Chris replied. 'Not far in the immediate past but many too many miles before that.' He lifted the drink to his lips and swallowed it down.

'Go easy . . .' Tim said. 'We've been overdoing it.'

Chris glared at him.

'I see,' said the barman.

'We're over from England,' Tim said. 'We've just checked out of Brannigan's B & B.'

The barman turned and fiddled with the Jameson optic. He was tall, about Tim's height. His thin face had an arrogant cast to it, as if, like the camel, it might know but never confide the thousandth name of God. But the face was moody too, difficult to read. He looked very solemn in his mirror as he said, 'It's a funny time of the day to be checking out.'

'They had no hot water,' Chris said.

The face there in the mirror hung on to gravity.

'He solders the hot tap shut,' Tim said.

'I know that,' said the barman. 'Brannigan's famous for it. We often get people coming in after a few minutes' stay at Brannigan's. It's amazing what Brannigan's stuck tap has brought to us over the years.'

'You don't know a better place, do you?' Tim asked.

He turned back to face them and brought out a smile. 'You're sitting in one,' he said. 'Plenty of hot water. Twelve pounds a night, inclusive of full Irish breakfast. Two singles, is it?'

'It is,' Tim said.

'Do you want to see the rooms?'

'We'll trust you. Same again,' said Chris.

'Oh, you'll trust me, will you? You've just trusted Patrick Brannigan and you haven't learnt anything. I'm Jimmy O'Keeffe, the owner of this establishment.'

They introduced themselves back and were soon deep in conversation. At least, Chris was. Tim felt excluded after a while and took the dregs of his Guinness to the jukebox. He surveyed the tunes on offer, felt old. Then he fetched the luggage from the car.

He took the keys and went to see his room. Chris said he'd follow him up. The first thing Tim noticed in his was the framed print on the wall across from the washbasin of St Patrick expelling the snakes from Ireland. It commemorated a eucharistic conference held in Dublin in 1932. Tim had grown up with that picture. It was one of those stories that had eaten its way deep into his soul. Patrick at the summit of Croagh Patrick orders all the snakes to be gone from Holy Ireland. They dutifully depart over the precipice and drown in the sea. A popular print, it had been on the wall of his classroom. A statue of the same scene had stood in Ardfert church; Patrick in his bishop's vestments and mitre, looking like he meant business. The serpents departing.

It occurred to Tim for the first time that the snakes could well stand for the invader: Norse, Norman, English . . .

Tim had never doubted that the reason there were no snakes in Ireland was because St Patrick had expelled them. It didn't seem strange then at all. St Patrick was his saint and had worked this miracle fifteen hundred years ago and therefore no snakes existed in the land. For the majority of the Irish it was a piece of the skeleton that went into the body of faith, one more sign that justified that faith. Naturally, when Tim was growing away from the Church he had pushed all that stuff away too. There had to be some logical explanation. He had not researched the matter, however. He still did not know whether, were one to enquire from an archeologist, evidence of reptile life would be found perfectly preserved in bogland or sandwiched in stone. He had not looked into it. It was not his speciality. There were snakes in mainland Britain, and Ireland and Britain had once been connected; the east coast snuggling into the west coast of Wales; a land-bridge from The Giants' Causeway to Scotland.

Tim brushed his teeth at the basin, looking past himself in the mirror to the reflected image of the print. If there had been a land-route then why had no snakes managed to make the journey? Was the connection severed before reptiles embarked upon their evolutionary journey? What about the predecessors of snakes? Had they not inhabited what was to become Ireland? Did the Ice Age do for them? He didn't know. Those remote periods were a mishmash in his head. The time-scale too long and long ago to be taken in.

He spat, turned away from the basin and looked at the picture. He wanted, more than he had ever wanted anything, to believe in such a miracle, to be allowed to deconstruct the tough webbing that surrounded him; to cut the strings that held his nose in the air; his hands in affected gestures of cynicism; to bin the going-nowhere knee-jerk dogmas without a chance of after-light.

No sign of Chris. Tim unpacked, checked the hot water – it gushed like a miracle – and returned to the bar.

Chris was still deep in conversation with Jimmy O'Keeffe. Tim joined them for a while but, still feeling himself surplus to requirements, knowing the while that the problem lay only at his door, said he thought he would take a stroll while there was still light enough. The slight pique he had felt at his exclusion from the conversation

Chris had struck up with Jimmy O'Keeffe faded. It was nice to be off by himself, to have another stand in for him.

When Tim got back to O'Keeffe's, Chris and Jimmy were still deep in conversation. They stopped when they saw him. Jimmy went over to take drinks to a traditional music group setting up their stuff in the corner.

'You all right?' Tim asked Chris.

'Never better.'

'That's good. How many've you had?'

'Not quite enough, but I'm working on it.'

He saw Tim about to lecture. 'Don't,' he said. 'I need it. Like the Power's man needs it. You can understand that, can't you?'

Tim wanted to tell Chris what the doctors had told him; what the health workers in Bloomsbury kept emphasizing. Do nothing that strains you. And a peculiar, mean part of him – the flicking serpent-tail of his bad mood – wanted to put Chris in his place for getting on so well with Jimmy O'Keeffe. 'Yes, of course I can,' he said.

'What's your poison?' Chris asked.

Canon Dawson's confession queue had dwindled to Mrs O'Hara. After receiving absolution, Mrs O'Hara, asked by the canon if she was the last, opened the door, took a look, and whispered back that she was.

But Mrs O'Hara was in error. Roddie knelt down on the prie-dieu in the box, causing a switch to activate a red bulb on Canon Dawson's side. The canon had been in the act of standing up to leave but, seeing the light, sat down again unhappily, placing his elbow next to the grille, sighing into his knuckles.

'I have come to make my confession, Father,' Roddie said.

'Make it, so,' said Canon Dawson.

'I confess that I am Roger Casement, come back from the grave. I confess that I have made myself known to Boma Hephernan and Father Devenish. I confess to feelings of frustration that I am not believed.'

'What are you saying, man?' Canon Dawson asked. 'To fool simple believers, to try to fox my curate! That isn't enough, I suppose, without making a mockery of the confessional!'

'I am not making a mockery, Canon,' Roddie replied. 'I know what you have been thinking. I heard you and Father Devenish talking it over. Lord, it's the devil's own job making believers believe! How am I going to manage with the others?'

'All right. What was I doing while I was talking to Father Devenish?'

'You were drinking whiskey. A Paddy as I recall. You had a second and made out that it wasn't like you. But, of course, it was rather.'

'Oh, was it *rather*? You were spying on us through the window!'

'You told Father Devenish that you thought my character precluded my return. I had a fair amount of burning to do; my reputation was in limbo, you said.'

'Spying! Have you no shame at all, man? Laying sin on top of sin!'

Roddie sighed. 'Amn't I in confession?' he asked.

'You are.'

'And it is a great sin to tell a lie in confession?'

'A great sin; a sin of which you are in grave danger of being guilty—'

'I am trying to think how I can convince you that I am speaking the truth. It's an uphill task, you must admit. Do you want a spring to bubble up outside the church? I can give you that if you want. But you'd probably call the Water Board. How about if I turn Miss O'Shea's kettle water to Paddy? Any good? No, you'd just say I'd got in while her back was turned. A phial of blood to bubble away? That might do the trick, eh? Or maybe not. You see, what I don't understand is how you, who make your living from believing every last jot and tittle of Faith, who believe that this confession is being listened to upstairs, that the Good Lord has the time or inclination to hear past the screams from the poor planet, find it so hard to believe a tiny piece of divine intervention on your own doorstep.'

'All right,' said Canon Dawson, 'let's say I do believe you. What then?'

'I have my own reasons for being here. But I'd have thought that the fact of my being here would be immensely consoling for any poor sheep who are having trouble with their shepherds.'

'Not you. You'd be a scandal.'

'For why?'

'If you don't know I can't tell you.'

'You mean the diaries? It's amazing how they come to be the only thing that some people remember. Did I or didn't I write them? Was I or wasn't I? Father, believe me, though I had my fair share of original sin and a few scarlet letters on my front when I dropped, my jottings were the least of it.'

139

'Oh, you think so, do you?'

'You're not the first to think it, of course. The British government thought so. My prison guards too. I kept hearing that their distribution among friend and foe would do for me. Cardinal Bourne, when I asked to be received into the Church in the weeks before my execution, made it a condition that I wrote a letter apologizing for the scandals I had caused. I refused. Why should I apologize for something that was God-given? It would be like throwing a gift back in the Good Lord's face. Even if you might never have chosen it for yourself – and don't you find gifts are often like that? – manners are *de rigueur*. For I had caused no scandals. The British government it was who caused the scandal, distributing my private papers around the world like tongue sandwiches at a wake. And it worked too. You've swallowed it. I was made by my writing, then just as surely unmade by it.'

'But you died a Catholic?' said Canon Dawson, then, having asked the question, seeing that he was appearing to accept the invisible penitent's viewpoint, frowned to himself, invisible in his dark box.

'I did, but only *in articulo mortis* on the eve of the execution. They kept me on tenterhooks to the very end all right.'

'You know a lot about your subject, I'll grant you that,' said Canon Dawson.

'O ye of little faith,' Roddie replied. 'I'm not going to stay here any longer to beat my head against a brick wall. It will all come out anyway. I had hoped you might like to be the ones who passed on some good news for a change. I thought that was what you were about.'

Canon Dawson saw the light go off, heard the door whoosh closed. He got up quickly and threw open the door on his side of the confessional. He looked about him, but the church was empty.

There was no-one in Brid's shop when Mary Lyons entered. She coughed and looked around her, wondering what she should buy when Brid put in an appearance.

Boma came in from the kitchen. She had not heard the door, was passing through the shop to her room and was startled to see Mary standing there.

'Remember me?' Mary asked her.

'Sure, I do. Come on in,' Boma said. 'Brid's out visiting a friend.'

'Thank you . . . I really only came to . . .' And Mary let herself be led through into the kitchen.

'I've some tea on the go. Will you take a mug?'

'I will. If it's no trouble. Thank you. It's a raw old day.'

They sat down, and Mary watched Boma as she reached for the teapot. Then she saw that Boma had noticed the close inspection she was being given. 'When's the baby due?' she asked.

'In June, they tell me. Of course, whether he shows up then is another matter.'

'Your husband must be pleased.'

'I'm not married, Mary.'

'But you're pleased, aren't you?' Mary asked.

'You know, I am. If you'd asked me that a week ago you'd have got a different answer entirely. But, yes, I'm pleased. I'm trying to see a bright future for him now.'

'You've decided he's a "him", have you?'

'I have. It must be what you said. I trust your judgement.'

'Any names in mind?'

'Roger David,' Boma said.

'Lord, you're so definite. I'm worried now. I have been known to make a mistake, you know.'

'Join the club,' said Boma.

Mary did not know how to proceed. She drank her tea, looking at the river-like cracks in the mug.

Boma stepped into the silence. 'What about you? Are you getting on well at St Theresa's?'

'It's all right, you know. I shouldn't be uncharitable but I could do without the ear-bending I get from Mrs Grogan, to tell you the truth. I'd much rather be here.'

'And to toss the truth back to you, Brid has been feeling guilty that she threw you on the mercy of Mrs Grogan. She's never refused anyone before, she said. At least not when she had room. It broke a rule she's kept to all her life. I think you should come and stay with us.'

Mary wondered why Boma had said that. 'She seems a grand woman, Brid McCarthy. Is she family?'

Boma laughed. 'I've only known her a short while.' Then she thought about what she had said, hated the tossed-off feel of it. 'Yes,' she added, 'she's family.'

Mary nodded, wondering. *Now*, she thought. *Now I should wade in and get myself wet. Now I should tell Boma a bit about myself.*

She had practised, both in her room and on the walks she had taken that day. But now, faced with the reality of it, she thought it might be better to tiptoe silently out of Boma's life before entering too far, just as she tiptoed out of the convent chapel when called out by some errand. What possible use would be served, she now felt, by bringing up the whole wretched story? The damage that had been done. It would not be in any way undone by wading in, would it? What could she, an old woman, offer Boma? They both had their own lives, were two kites on separate strings dancing to their own airs. To try to guide them together now would only cause a tangle.

'More tea?' Boma asked.

Mary asked her to repeat the question. She held out her mug. Boma felt the pot.

'I'll freshen this. There's hot water in the kitchen. Stanley isn't hot enough.'

By the time Boma got back from the kitchen, Mary had felt her courage failing. She had made up her mind to drink her tea, exchange a few pleasantries and leave.

'That's great,' she said, watching Boma pour the tea.

Boma sat down. 'Who are you?' she asked, staring at Mary steadily.

'Who am I?' Mary asked, startled by the sudden frontal attack.

'Yes, who are you and what do you do?'

'This is very sudden . . .'

'It isn't a hard question, is it? You know who I am: a mixed-race, unmarried mother. It's pretty much written all over me.'

'I'm a nun, Boma,' replied Mary. *Yes*, she thought. *That came out easily enough. Perhaps that will satisfy her.*

'Which order?'

'The Sisters of the Flaming Heart. We're a nursing order. You know I was a nurse, though.'

'Yes, I knew that. Where did you nurse?'

Mary hesitated. 'Africa and South America mostly. Now I'm a bit long in the tooth for all that and these days I try to make myself useful around the mother-house in Dublin.'

Mary sipped her tea and Boma stared at her steadily. 'And what brings you here to Ardfert?'

She knows! Mary thought. *God knows how, but she knows. Perhaps Matthew the taxi-driver had said something; or Sister de Porres.*

By way of reply Mary stuttered; she rambled; she took every by-road that she knew would just miss her destination. And as she spoke she wondered at the stranger who was engaging in such prevarications. If the sisters at the convent could see her, the nun whom they had always thought honest to the point of harshness, what would they think? She had not been so indecisive since . . .

'I'd heard it was a nice little place. I needed a break after all the fuss over my golden jubilee – I'm fifty years a nun. And some space to think.' Mary took a sip from the hot tea. 'Also, I'd heard your name mentioned. Matthew, the taxi-driver, mentioned you to the sisters. I was intrigued because Boma is the name of one of the places I was stationed during my time in Africa. Of course, there are probably several places so named in Africa. Anyway, I just took it into my head to see you, and have a holiday too.'

'But why? Because of a word? You were curious about me because of my name?'

No, there was no way around it. 'Boma,' said Mary, 'can you tell me about yourself?'

'I was born in Dublin. I think. Some nuns kept me and they said my mother had christened me Boma. They fostered . . .' Then Boma was staring at Mary, wide-eyed. 'I know!' she said. 'I know! You were one of the nuns. You took care of me in the orphanage!'

Mary shook her head. Indeed there had been nuns who had taken care of Boma. But she had not been one of them. She could not even claim a shard of credit for that. Boma was still not near to nudging the truth of it.

'But you were there, weren't you? You were around when I was in the convent orphanage?'

Mary, unable to look at Boma, nodded.

'So you know who my mother was? My father? Who were they? Tell me, please.'

Too late Mary saw that she had been mistaken. Boma had gone straight for the heart of the matter.

'You must know! I bet you do! Tell me! Please!'

'I think I'd better—'

'Don't you move! You're not going anywhere until I know everything.'

Mary Lyons made to stand up. Boma gently but firmly pushed her back into her seat. 'Have some more tea. I'll get some cake.

I'll get Brid to make up your room. You can move in from St Theresa's. Anything, but you must tell me.' And as she spoke Boma remembered the times she had made the same pleas to the Hephernans, had felt angry and lost when they shrugged and shook their heads.

'Are you sure you want to know?'

'Am I sure? Of course I'm sure. When I was a child I'd see Shirley Bassey on the television and tell my friends that she was my mother. Then I switched to Diana Ross. I'd fiddle like mad with the geography, make up grand lies to convince my friends that I was a secret child of someone wonderful. I didn't fool them; they all knew I was a bastard. But don't you think it was cruel not telling me? Doesn't a child have a right to know?'

Mary nodded. She saw Boma making up her life year in and year out while she fulfilled her celibate vocation. Then, she had tried to convince herself that her daughter would be better off without her, would have found a secure home and be skating through life happily. Everyone had encouraged her in that opinion. Anyone could be a mother, they said. She, Sister Paula, had been called to a higher vocation. She should not give it up.

Her confessor had been adamant. A vocation to the religious life was, he asserted, given to those too weak to survive in the world. And she had believed him, despite the fact that in the late Sixties, when everything had shifted, windows in the Church been opened to cool, refreshing winds of change, the priest had become laicized himself and now wrote learned essays in *The Tablet* gainsaying many of the dogmas he had whispered to her.

But by then it had been too late. She had tried to find out what had happened to Boma. The social workers – those new dogmatists – had told her that it was their policy not to divulge such information. It was better all round, for both parent and child.

But in the recesses of her brain, the part she had been taught to call temptation, a voice kept repeating that things were not as they should be.

Now that the moment had arrived, it did not seem as difficult, as impossible, as it had before. Her admission would be like confessing to something embarrassing. Confession was not a problem for her. She was a past master at taking her punishment on the chin. She looked hard at Boma, remembered at once where the problem lay, established herself in that face once again, then closed her eyes, waiting for the explosion. 'I'm your mother, Boma.'

'Come off it!' Boma replied, without a pause. 'It's no joking matter, you know! I've had it up to here with jokes!'

There would have been relief in Boma's reaction, except Mary did not know how to proceed. She waited.

'You are joking, aren't you?' And getting no response, 'You *are*, aren't you?'

Boma looked at the old woman sitting by Stanley, her teacup on her knee. She wanted to shake the truth out of her. She saw the tears leaking out from behind the thick, protective lenses. 'Christ, you're not joking, are you?'

'No, I'm not joking,' Mary replied. 'I'm not. I wish I were. No, I don't mean that in the way it sounds. I'm no Shirley Bassey, though, am I?'

'No, you're not,' said Boma. She was now looking at Mary in a different way, trying to see herself in her. But when she thought she detected an angle, a cast in common, it faded before the knowledge that she was talking to an elderly nun. 'Are you sure?'

Mary nodded.

Boma pushed both hands through her long, combed-out black hair. 'I'm sorry. It's all too much. I can't seem to take it in. I—'

The shop-door banged shut. 'Boma!' Brid called. 'Boma, switch on the vision!'

'What is it, Brid?' Boma asked, unable to take her eyes off Mary.

Brid appeared at the door, stabbing her hatpin into her hat, looking agitatedly towards the television in the corner. 'Switch it on! Quickly!'

Boma flicked the television switch. Being a twenty-year-old black-and-white, it took its own time in warming-up. Mary watched the tabernacle of the blank screen while Boma stared into her face.

'I was passing Mrs Taggart's and she had her "vision" on in the living-room. I think I saw Roddie!' said Brid. She looked at the blank screen and saw Mary reflected in it. She turned. 'Oh, hello! You're still with us! I didn't know you were here.' Then she turned round to the television. The picture flapped open, but it showed a floozie out of her depth in *Gold Blend*. 'Try the other station. Quick!'

Roddie was manhandling Mobutu Sese Seko into the front entrance of the clinic, while holding tight to the shoulder of a blind man. The blind man turned as though startled and his scarred face was in the centre of the screen. Then all was confusion: a shaking sight of flip-flopped black feet and stone steps and littered dust, as the cameraman fled away with his whirring story.

Then the newscaster was speaking. 'The authorities have no idea what could have caused such an occurrence. Neither does anyone know who the strange white man seen in the film is. However, the incident has, it is thought, been the cause of the civil unrest that has convulsed the little town of Boma and which has spread inland to engulf the capital of Zaïre, Kinshasa. A curfew is in effect. The whereabouts of President Mobutu are not known.'

The news proceeded to other matters. Brid switched off the television and looked at Boma. 'It was Roddie, wasn't it, Boma?'

Boma nodded.

'How did he get out there, do you think? I know you've not seen him in days but . . .'

'The same way he got here, I expect,' Boma replied. Then she gestured towards Mary. 'Don't forget our visitor.'

'We'll have to catch it again at nine,' said Brid, oblivious. 'We've missed a whole chunk.'

Twilight had come to the room. Mary watched a little dot on the television screen. Though the current was off it refused to die. She stared at it and it seemed to wrap up all the strangeness that life had taken on. Then it wandered off, like a shooting star in slow motion, towards the bottom of the screen. She looked up and spoke to Brid, to Boma, to the shadows all around. 'The blind man in the picture. I think I knew him,' she said.

'Knew him? How could you know him?' Boma asked.

'I was midwife at his birth,' Mary said. 'Just before I left Africa, I nursed him after a fire. He was burnt down the right side of his face, like the man I saw. I knew his whole family.'

'What's this all about?' Brid asked.

'Brid,' Boma said, 'remember the night I came to stay with you? We sat down and we told one another our stories.'

'I do. Of course I do.'

'Well, tonight is Mary's turn.'

'Oh, it is?' Brid was looking at Mary – the opposition – with suspicion.

'And, Brid? You know the spare room upstairs? Could you get it ready for Mary?' She turned to her mother. 'I'll help you move out of St Theresa's. We can be back in plenty of time for the news.'

'I don't know . . .' Brid said.

Mrs Grogan at St Theresa's was unpacking cartons of pictures of Roger Casement delivered from the printer's that day. Several solid stacks of them stood on the oil-clothed table in her kitchen, each set banded by a paper circle.

She was pleased with the reproduction of the picture. A small segment of the home-made halo had failed to come out, but that made the hint of sanctity surrounding Casement seem tastefully tentative, mysterious. She found herself concocting a story. *We went to the printers with a picture of Sir Roger and it didn't have a halo then, did it, Mrs Taggart? But when we picked it up, there it was as clear as anything. The printer swears he didn't know how the halo appeared. We questioned him. But he's a good Catholic man with a family and would never have broken his printer's credo by adding anything to what he was given to print. No, something must have happened. Don't ask me what but something must have.* It would not be necessary to state categorically that one more miraculous event had occurred; simply to hint it would be enough; would do nicely.

There was also the matter of a change of name for St Theresa's Guest House. That day she had approached a sign-painter who lived in one of the bungalows behind Banna Strand to paint a new sign. Mrs Grogan had sketched out exactly what she wanted. At the top, *The Roger Casement Hotel*, in the centre a picture of a bearded man in the conning tower of a submarine looking out at the green hills of the Dingle Peninsula and below this, the shamrock of the Irish Tourist Board and *propr: Mrs Grogan*. The sign would be ready in a day or two. She would not put it up yet. She would wait for her moment.

Mrs Grogan heard the key in the front door, footsteps going upstairs and Mary Lyons opening the door of her room. She thought of the nun in plain clothes and this thought added to the mystery all about. Then there was a knock at the outside door.

'Mrs Taggart, what can I do for you?' Mrs Grogan asked. 'Did your cousin tell you he'd finished the . . .' she looked up and down the empty night street, '. . . items?'

'Let me in, Mrs Grogan,' said Mrs Taggart.

Mrs Grogan stepped back to let Mrs Taggart come in. 'You look puffed.'

'And why wouldn't I be puffed? I've just hoofed it from home, running all the while. Have you seen the television tonight? They're saying that Sir Roger has appeared in Africa! There's film of him!'

'Jesus and Mary! When did you see this?'

'About half an hour ago. It was a film from one of those African places and then the fellow on the news interrupted himself to say that people had been ringing in to say they thought the man they had seen was Sir Roger. He treated it as a bit of a joke, your man, but knowing what we know . . .'

'Sit yourself down, Mrs Taggart,' said Mrs Grogan. 'I don't know what to make of what you're saying. I can't decide if it's good news or bad.' She gestured to the stacks of cards on the table. 'Those have arrived, by the way. It's worrying, Mrs Taggart.'

'Why worrying? Doesn't it add to your faith in what's happening?'

'Of course it does, Mrs Taggart, but it takes away the centre of everything from Ardfert. It's here that he should be. Pilgrims hoofing it off to Africa or Belfast aren't going to do a thing for us here in Ardfert, now are they?'

'I suppose you're right. Still, if people get interested in him they're bound to come to see where he landed.'

'Some will. But it's all small beer entirely, Mrs Taggart. If we're not careful Ardfert will just get the fag-end of everything, same as we do now. Look it, with the whole of the Dingle Peninsula spread out in front of the tourist in one direction, Killarney in the other, how many of the maggots are going to make a detour to Ardfert? No, Mrs Taggart, what we need is a definite apparition. And the more the better.'

Mrs Taggart, who had also, unbeknown to Mrs Grogan, visited the sign-painter that day to have *The Sir Roger Casement Fancy Goods Emporium* painted on a piece of pine for overlaying *Ardfert Fancy Goods Emporium*, felt her heart sinking.

'What should we do?' asked Mrs Grogan portentously.

'I don't know. We can't force Sir Roger to come back, can we?'

'We can *pray*, Mrs Taggart. We can do that.' She gestured towards the cards. 'We've an investment there and we can pray for a return on the investment. We can certainly do that. Down on your knees, Mrs Taggart.'

Mrs Taggart got down on her knees automatically. She had been used to obeying that command her whole life long. Someone, either her mother or her late husband, had got her down on her knees with a short gruff command at the end of most of her days.

Down she went.

'O Sir Roger,' began Mrs Grogan. 'We, two poor women of Ardfert, know you have come back to bear witness to how great is the power of the Lord. Visit, we beseech thee, this habitation and the devout village of Ardfert. Show to the poor sinners of this village that the favour of the Most High shines upon us wicked sinners—'

Mary, accompanied by Boma, knocked on Mrs Grogan's door. Both could hear the murmurings from within.

Mrs Grogan and Mrs Taggart turned in alarm towards the door. The knock was repeated. They looked at one another. Mrs Grogan smoothed the front of her dress.

Again the knock.

'Come in!' called Mrs Grogan tremulously.

Mary opened the door and saw the two women down on their knees looking anxiously towards her. 'Er . . . Mrs Grogan, may I speak with you for a second?'

Mrs Grogan and Mrs Taggart picked themselves up.

'What is it you want?' asked Mrs Grogan.

'I've decided to leave this evening. Thank you very much for your hospitality. I've brought you the money I owe.'

Mrs Grogan regarded Boma.

'And this is Boma. I'm not sure you've met.'

Mrs Grogan nodded to Boma and took the money.

'I've included the money for tonight. I think you'll find it's all correct.'

Mary watched Mrs Grogan with the money in her hand. She was making no effort to count it. 'Well, we'll be off. Thank you again.'

Boma picked up her bag, smiled at the two blank-faced women and left, closing the door of Mrs Grogan's parlour.

Outside it was raining. The snake-sounds of a car going through Ardfert in the Ballyheige direction underlined the silence. They walked along the road back towards Brid's.

'Did you see what that woman had on her table?' Boma asked.

'No, I didn't.'

'Stacks of postcards. Pictures of Roger Casement.'

'That isn't surprising,' said Mary. 'This place is obsessed by him. He seems to be everywhere.'

'We must talk,' Boma said.

'Yes, we must,' agreed Mary.

But talk was postponed until after the main news. The film from Africa had become the first item on the bulletin.

An historian was interviewed after the film. He had his doubts, he said. He could not explain it other than by clever cutting but it was too absurd to be taken at face value. One more hoax, he said. Like the Hitler Diaries.

But, said the newscaster, how could the expert explain the events in Zaïre since the happenings? The curfews, the shootings, the news blackout? The expert couldn't. He expressed surprise that an uprising hadn't occurred in Zaïre long before.

The newscaster spoke of other sightings of Sir Roger Casement. Separate and unconnected. 'Well,' he said piously, in a tone designed to suit all his audience, 'there are more things in heaven and earth . . .' shuffled his papers and went on to the next item.

'He never mentioned Ardfert!' Brid said.

'And why would he have done that?' Mary asked, excited, amazed, feeling herself to be mounting steep steps of strangeness leading into the sky.

Boma looked at Brid. 'I think it's time to explain,' Boma said. 'Have you anything in to drink, Brid?'

Brid fetched a bottle of sherry and three glasses, wondering why Mary should be entitled to explanations.

'Right,' said Boma. 'You first, Mary.'

Mary wanted to protest, to postpone the inevitable. It was not so much Boma she was worried about as Brid. She was eyeing her strangely, her expression close to antagonism.

'Mary Lyons is my secular name. I'm really Sister Paula. I'm a member of the Sisters of the Flaming Heart—'

'That's a nursing order, Boma. You do grand work on the missions,' said Brid. 'Mags Devlin – she lives down the road with Colm, her son – is a great supporter of your order.'

'We have missions in Africa and South America . . .' Sister Paula stopped. The story had already come to a crossroads. She could go along sidetracks about the holy founder, the work with famine victims in the 1840s . . . or take the more direct route. 'I was out on the missions in the Congo – that's now called Zaïre – from 1945 until 1960. I left half a lifetime ago.' Again the story dissected. 'I've been in South America since then but for the last nineteen years I've been at our convent in Dublin. I'm an administrator and fund-raiser.

'You probably don't remember what happened in the Congo when Independence came. I won't go into details but it was an ugly time. I was working in a coastal town called Boma, on the estuary of the Congo River.' Paula looked over at her listeners, smiled.

'Soldiers came to our hospital one night, shouting and firing off their guns. The Belgians had upped and left by then, terrified by the events, by stories of rape, torture and murder. We stayed on, hoping for the best. It is hard to leave when you've got a hospital full of patients relying on you. The sisters had had a conference and decided we should stay put. We had really not expected what happened.

'I was not afraid when the men confronted us outside the clinic entrance. I knew the leader, knew his whole family. They had been patients of mine. I had helped in the birth of three of his children. And one of them, I think, we may have seen today on the television. I know it's hard to believe, I can hardly believe I'm here telling you this either, but I can't help that. Anyway, I confronted them there, told them what they were doing was not right. They would frighten the patients, letting off their guns, threatening. But I could see that the man to whom I addressed my remarks was not as I remembered him. He seemed fierce, unmoved by what I was saying, whereas the man I remembered had been something of a stoic with a ready laugh. I decided to take a risk. I asked him to come with me away from the crazy, drugged men, into my office to talk things over. I said he owed me that. The other men nudged him to follow me with ribald comments, while my nuns told me not to be so stupid, to stay put. I don't know what they were thinking. The men could have done away with us in a second if they had wanted to. He returned the ribaldry to his men in kind and consented to go with me. I showed him into the office and tried to reason with him. I reminded him of his time in the hospital, said all the usual things about the hospital being there for the people. He seemed to accept what I was saying but then he came back at me, telling me that everything the sisters nursed had been caused by foreign presence in the first place and that it was only right we cured what we had caused. By "we" of course he meant the white people. And it was odd. He told me something that I had really not thought before, though I've often thought it since. But it was he who first planted the thought that the whole invasion of Africa and elsewhere was all of a part. We at the hospital had felt different. We stuck to our own patch. We had nothing to do with the colonial administration. It was another of the things you believed without question. The white man's burden with the Irish on the mending end. We've been landed with that function, have you noticed? Whether it's road-mending or running hospitals or schools, we've been the nation who has gone in to provide essential services peripheral to the main thrust of colonial enterprise. Anyway, I begged him to let us go, not to hurt the sisters. I was their superior and if anyone should be punished it should be me.'

Paula stopped. The story led off in two directions; one towards truth, the other to a kindly lying sunrise. She let her glass be filled by Boma, thanked her as she looked into the face whose features mirrored the mix-up of history. She decided on truth. It was time. In the face she could see the shadow of the man who had raped her with the bleak formality of a dead ritual, telling her, as he hurt her, of the wrongs committed against his father, that great stone that blocked his gall, that caused a pain which no hospital could cure.

'Your father raped me but he made his men spare the other nuns. He persuaded them that the token of vengeance was enough. His name was Bomatu, son of Lulua, and, God knows, he had reason enough to exact a worse vengeance from the whites than he did. His father, Lulua, a skilled carver, had been burnt to death and in the same fire – caused by fleeing white mercenaries – his son, Okondo, was blinded and scarred. As I said, I knew Bomatu for many years before what happened. He had always been good and generous to the sisters. The events in the Congo drove him mad.'

'What happened to him?' Boma asked.

'He was killed not very long afterwards. Before you were born, Boma.'

'You're Boma's mother!' Brid said.

Paula nodded.

'And a nun!'

'Yes.' She gestured to the bag. 'My habit's in there.'

Paula went on with her story, ignoring Brid's open mouth.

Compared to what had gone before, it was easy: she talked of her determination to keep Boma come what might; the arguments presented to her about the paramount importance of her vocation – arguments that she had at last accepted. And Boma listened. It was a good story. Better because it was true. But she was surprised to discover that it did not impinge upon her, did not move her. She was watching it, but was not engaged. She was back, aware of her separateness, the aura of unfocused dark around her vision. There were, it was true, satisfactions in the unravelling of the past, but these did not extend to any feelings of special attachment to this stranger who was her mother. She had come back for her own reasons. It was, in a way, miraculous. But Boma had experienced several miraculous occurrences since arriving at Ardfert. What pleased her, above all, were the connections, the linking up of a chain of events she had thought had broken beyond repair. Boma, Roddie, the Congo, nuns and the mixture of her, all came together. Like a mended chain or an explosion played backwards.

The lack of emotion did not worry her. Perhaps in the future some floodgate would open; some nerve-ending in her brain communicate a charge to its neighbour and set off a rush of anger or love towards Paula. But she was content to wait and see, to live in the satisfaction of the present moment, knowing that kindly spirits buzzed all about her.

'But why did you wait so long?' Brid asked.

Paula shrugged. 'I did try at first, but no-one would release any information to me. As the years passed, whenever I thought of trying – and I thought of you every day – an icy feeling of guilt and embarrassment came down on me like a black cloud. Even when Sister de Porres came up to me during the Jubilee and told me about a woman called Boma whom Matthew the taxi-driver had lifted, I might not have acted upon it. Perhaps it happening on such a significant day for me made me do it.'

'And what do you think, Boma?' Brid asked.

'I think Paula's coming is part of everything else that has been happening.' And she thought of the pictures they had seen on the television only minutes before; the waves pulsing away into the universe. She thought of the slap her face had made when it hit the surface of the ocean; a slap that had betokened the end had, in fact, biffed her back to life.

'And why? It seems to me that it was Matthew with the memory of an elephant that informed your mother.'

Boma shook her head. 'No, Brid,' she said. 'I can't believe you think it's just coincidence. After what you and I have been through! The trouble is that we've been in the middle of miracles and they've come to seem humdrum.' She saw Paula looking nonplussed. 'I think we'd better explain to Paula what's been happening around here. Then we can show her her room,' Boma said.

'I don't know . . .' Brid said. She clutched the baptismal medal under her blouse with a grip that defied outsiders to try to prise it open.

> *Loyalty is a sentiment, not a law. It rests on love, not on restraint. The government of Ireland by England rests on restraint and not on law; and since it demands no love it can evoke no loyalty.*
>
> CASEMENT'S SPEECH FROM THE DOCK, 1916

7

HAVING STARTED TO DRINK SO EARLY, CHRIS WAS READY FOR BED BY the time the traditional band took their interval. All evening he had stayed at the bar and Jimmy O'Keeffe had placed his packet of cigarettes on the counter, next to Chris. At quiet moments he would return from his bar-work to take a drag and he and Chris would resume their talk.

Tim had caught a bit of it. Chris was talking about his life in Africa and, more especially, his travels through it. At one point he nodded to Tim and said, 'Jimmy, I'd be there now but this one didn't dare.' Tim shrugged and pulled on his pint.

But, when Chris finally decided to call it a day, Tim moved along the bar and took his place on the stool that Chris had vacated. He felt its warmth. An elderly man had taken the stool he had just left. He wondered if the man was thinking the same thing.

'Chris OK?' Jimmy asked him.

'He's drunk, but apart from that he's fine.'

'I think he needs to get drunk.'

'Yes.'

'I know I would if I was in his position. Jesus, I'd never be sober.'

'He told you, did he?'

Jimmy nodded. Tim was not in the least surprised.

'He seemed anxious to talk about it.'

'Did he? That's odd.'

'He said you're from Ardfert. You've been away a while. Where's your Kerry accent?'

'Ask me another.'

'Have you family in Ardfert?'

'I've an old mother.'

'She'll be pleased to see you.'

'Ask me another.'

'What took you so long?'

'Time slips by.'

'I must write that down.'

Tim saw Jimmy about to give up on him. 'I'm sorry. It's just you're asking me questions I've been asking myself ever since we got here. We've been in touch – Mammy and I – but at a distance. I was overseas, I taught a year in Nigeria. That's where I met Chris.' He stopped, unable to go on.

'Chris has been all over.'

'Yes. A real traveller. I can't hold a candle to him. He's been pestering me to bring him to Ireland. But now he's here he'd rather be somewhere else.'

'He seems happy enough to me.'

'Good.'

'So when are you going to Ardfert?'

'When I can pluck up the courage. Tomorrow or the next day.'

'Have you seen the Tralee paper?'

Tim shook his head. 'Why?'

'There's news of Ardfert.'

Jimmy went off to serve a customer. As he was waiting for the

Guinness to settle he disappeared behind a curtain, returning with a newspaper. He handed it across to Tim with a smile.

Tim read about an apparition by Roger Casement to a priest in Ardfert.

'What do you think of that?' Jimmy asked.

'It makes me feel at home,' Tim said. 'Just like old times. Holy Ireland rides again.'

'It's not the only Casement story I've heard recently. Before you arrived on my doorstep, a man came into the bar. He got himself blind drunk and told me about what a friend had told him. This friend had been in a bar in Sligo and overheard a couple of boyos talking about a friend of theirs who had been up to some IRA business. This friend reckoned he had run up against a man who said his name was Roger Casement. He'd brought back their bomb, just presented it to them.'

'How do you mean "just presented it to them"?'

'Don't be asking me. It was just a story he heard. And I heard. Standing here like I do.'

'It's a coincidence,' Tim said.

'I wouldn't have thought anything about it if it hadn't been for the story in today's paper. So it's three coincidences, isn't it?'

'What's the third?'

'You. Chris says you're writing something on Casement.'

'No, not really. Casement comes into what I'm working on, but he's not the main subject. I'm writing about Sir Alfred Jones. He was the head of the Elder-Dempster shipping line. Casement worked for him as a young man – not very successfully. Their lives intersect at several points – sometimes quite uncannily. If it had not been for Sir Alfred Jones, I doubt we would have heard anything of Casement.'

'Why?' Jimmy asked.

'Do you really want to know?' Tim asked. 'I ask because it isn't everyone's cup of tea. You serve excellent Guinness. Don't feel you have to be polite as well.'

Jimmy seemed about to give up on Tim again. He rushed to bridge the widening divide. 'I'm sorry, Jimmy.'

'How do their lives intersect? This Jones and Casement?' he asked quietly. He was drying glasses with a tea-towel that had the Rock of Cashel on it. Another coincidence. Tim remembered wanting to buy one, but they were asking the earth.

'OK,' he said. 'Casement worked at Elder-Dempster for two years. At the Liverpool offices. In 1880–81. He was a clerk. He might have stayed there his whole working life, might have got promotion and become a pillar of the community. But for a little thing, a silly little thing.'

'What was that?'

'One day, Sir Alfred Jones called Casement into his office. He put a packet of canary-seed into his hands and told him to take it to the home of his wife on the outskirts of Liverpool. Casement refused, seeing the task as beneath him. Sir Alfred Jones fired him on the spot. It took the intercession of Casement's cousin to get him a job as purser on one of the Elder-Dempster ships, the *SS Bonny* . . . And off he went to the Congo. His life was changed.'

'Whose?'

Tim looked at Jimmy as he looked at his dimmer students. 'Casement's, of course.'

'What about Jones's?'

'It went on just as it had done. Fast track,' he said. 'Jones amassed a considerable fortune. He was one of the fathers of Liverpool's prosperity. The Elder-Dempster line controlled the whole of the West African trade. Jones established coaling stations for his ships in the Canary Islands and, while there, noticed that the cochineal industry – which had been the islands' chief product – was in decline. He also saw that the soil of the islands was fertile, but unused; the people living in great poverty. He bought up land, established the growing of bananas and later market-gardening on the islands, using his company's ships to transport the produce to the growing markets of Britain. Later on he set up The Liverpool School of Tropical Medicine to make Africa safer for adventurers.'

'So his heart was in the right place?'

'Yes, as long as charity did not get in the way of business. And usually his charity made practical business sense. But he was ruthless with anyone who threatened his business empire. And that's where he and Casement locked swords in the early nineteen-hundreds.'

'Where was Casement then?'

'Still in Africa. After a couple of trips on the Elder-Dempster ship he left to join King Leopold's Congo Free State. He worked under Stanley for several years. Then he was taken on by the Foreign Office as a Consul in Loma. He came into conflict with Sir Alfred Jones over his report on atrocities in the rubber industry. Jones, you see, was afraid that if Leopold II was offended by the report Elder-Dempster might lose its monopoly on trade to the ports of the Congo. He hired a couple of aristocrats, Lord Mountmorres and Mrs French Sheldon, paid them handsomely to go out to the Congo and write a report running counter to Casement's. This they duly did; they praised King Leopold's philanthropy to the skies, wrote at length of the happy Congolese they met on their junket. It stole some of Casement's thunder. Casement knew exactly what Jones was up to and never forgave him.'

'You're full of it, aren't you?' Jimmy said.

'I'm boring you.'

'I wouldn't say that. But I think I'm more interested in a boy from Ardfert who wanders off and is too scared to go home.'

Tim shrugged. 'What can I tell you?'

'With regards Casement, where do you stand on the Big Question?'

'Which one? There are lots of questions.'

'Was he or wasn't he?'

'Was he or wasn't he what?'

'Gay.'

'Most of the modern biographers think he was.'

'Yes, but what do you think? You and Chris are gay, aren't you?'

Tim hesitated, pointlessly. Chris had blown his cover, no doubt. 'Yes.'

'And is that why you haven't visited your mammy?'

Tim was beginning to understand how Jimmy and Chris talked so single-mindedly for so long. Jimmy was interrogative. This wasn't a conversation. It was a quiz. 'Maybe. A bit.'

'You're not happy with it, are you?'

'Look . . .'

'Well, was he?'

'I think so. Yes. It wasn't just the diaries, though the diaries have a ring of truth about them. It's more than that. In 1914 he went to New York to raise money for the Irish Brigade. There he took up with a Norwegian sailor called Adler Christensen. And for the first time in his life he was not circumspect. He was very close to cracking up and, it seems to me, he teetered on the edge of a breakdown from then until his landing in Ireland. It may have been his liaison with Adler which alerted the English government to the fact that they might have some dirty linen to produce when the time was right. Adler Christensen was flaming, by all accounts. Still, I doubt Casement cared much about his reputation by then. He must have felt lost.'

'And coming back to Ireland changed things?'

'I should think it did, yes. From his landing at Banna Strand until the moment of his death he grew in stature. In those last months when the British were baying for his blood, when erstwhile friends turned their backs, he achieved true greatness.'

'I hadn't heard about this Adler . . .'

'Christensen. He and Christensen were inseparable. People in the Fenian movement, including John Devoy the supremo in New York, warned Casement against Christensen, but Casement would not listen to them. He took Christensen to Germany.'

'That's another coincidence,' Jimmy said.

'What is?'

'Chris. I noticed his surname is Christensen.'

'Yes,' Tim said, 'his first name's . . .'

'Baker.'

'Yes. So you can see why—'

'Baker, after Baker, Oregon.'

'He's Chris to everyone.'

'It's still a coincidence,' Jimmy said.

'Do you know how many "Christensens" there are in the New York telephone directory?'

'You've got me there. But it's only the diaries that really prove it one way or the other?'

'I suppose so, but you asked me what I think. I can't prove it. But I've read enough about him to think he was. I can see myself in Casement; the travel, the running away, the failed relationships, the giving up, even something of the self-loathing and need for atonement.'

'Phew!' said Jimmy. 'I thought the Irish went abroad to *escape* all that. I have to pay the band.'

Tim had not even realized that they had stopped playing, that the jukebox had taken over.

Jimmy came back. 'I asked the boys to play *The Lonely Banna Strand* but they say they don't know it.'

'It's not the greatest song,' Tim said. 'They put back the month of

Casement's landing to May instead of April. They wanted it to rhyme with bay.'

'A bit of a pedant, aren't you?'

'A bit.'

'Sir Alfred Jones must have crowed when Sir Roger was hanged.'

'Jones was dead by then. He died in 1909.'

'Why do you think Casement accepted a knighthood?'

'He was probably flattered.'

'Yes, but it didn't sit well with his republicanism.'

'No, but it sits pretty well with his mixed motives. I don't think he was without his share of vanity. He might have hated the British for what they were doing in Ireland and in their Empire but he counted many English people among his friends. I think he compartmentalized his life. We all do it.' Tim looked at his barman's hard-to-read face. 'Well, some of us anyway. And he renounced his knighthood at the end. Then the British took it away. But it's odd. I like to call him Sir Roger Casement. Ironic that they took the title away from one of the few men who really earned it. I wouldn't call many sirs "Sir" – but I make an exception in his case.'

'Sir Antony Blunt?'

Tim could see what Jimmy O'Keeffe was getting at and was surprised that this Dingle publican was so well versed in such matters. He decided to sidestep it. 'We're back to the gay thing again,' he said. 'One thing that we as a group may – I only say *may* – be able to do is look at the way society works with a cold, dispassionate eye. We do not quite get what is going on, what makes men seek empires and armaments and all the goodies for their tribe. We know that they do but we are distanced. We understand it – it's all around us – but we don't feel it. Our priorities, the cast of our minds, are different. Perhaps our loyalties are to those ideals which we can feel. Queen and Country don't stand much of a chance. And what does family have to do with us? They throw us out . . . won't let us back in until we toe the line. But the struggles of other underdogs perhaps do reach us and demand our loyalty. So, if Sir Antony Blunt thought Communism would make the world a better place, I'd be the last to condemn him. The fact that he lived high on the hog most of his life reinforces my belief in mixed motives. Casement, however, never succumbed to all that. He never had a home, he gave most of his money away to good causes. But, above all, he had a good heart. Just that. It was in the right place. Everything else pales in comparison to that. He was a man who did his best and his best was considerable.'

'You're Irish. I can see it now,' Jimmy said.

'Sir Roger would have preened to hear that,' Tim said.

'But not Tim McCarthy?'

Tim McCarthy didn't know what to say, so smiled and shrugged.

'And now he's come back.'

'You don't believe that, do you, Jimmy?'

'You have to admit, it'd be interesting.'

'Yes, I suppose it would be,' Tim replied.

Canon Dawson came out onto the altar, placed the cruets of water and wine in the side alcove, lit the candles. He then walked down to the communion rails where the paschal candle stood. This he lit, stretching up on tiptoe to reach it with his taper.

He then looked out over the large congregation – too large to be wholesome for an early weekday mass – and called out: 'Is there anyone who will serve mass for me? The lads booked for it haven't turned up. It's getting to be a habit.'

The congregation looked at one another, seeing if any among them would stand up. Their roving looks took in Brid, Boma and Sister Paula, sitting in the third row from the front. And those who were local wondered.

Colm Devlin, who lived with his sick mother on the Ballyheige Road, stood up, genuflected and made his way towards the sacristy. The congregation continued to look around. Canon Dawson turned, and went back to put on his vestments.

Who were all those people? He had never in all his time in the parish known an ordinary morning mass to be so crowded. There were a few people he knew by sight from Tralee, including the woman reporter who had been asking questions of both Father Devenish and Miss O'Shea. But the majority of the congregation was unknown to him.

He followed Colm Devlin onto the altar and started the mass. The responses to prayers, he noticed, were only coming from a small number of the congregation.

Neither, when it came to the Communion, did many approach the altar rails to receive it. It was as if the majority were merely observers, and not participants.

When the end of mass came, Canon Dawson realized that he had gone through the whole procedure blind. Worry and misgivings had ousted prayerful concentration.

Colm went back onto the altar to put out the candles. He returned in a moment. 'Canon, I can't get the paschal candle to go out,' he said.

'What do you mean, you can't?' said the canon.

'The flame won't go out. I held the snuffer over it for the longest time, but it wouldn't snuff at all!'

'Give the snuffer to me!' said Canon Dawson. He returned to the altar. Few people seemed to have left the church. He glared out at them. He reached the paschal candle on its high holder, stretched up and placed the snuffer over the flame. Then he lowered the silver cone over the flame, held it down for a good ten seconds, then raised it again. The candle flame burnt on. He heard whisperings from the body of the church. He tried again, holding the snuffer down for so long that his arm started shaking. Then he raised it again. The candle-flame appeared. It did not recover, gasping from its lack of oxygen. It simply burnt as if nothing had happened.

Colm was standing next to him. He spoke and Canon Dawson jumped in alarm and did not hear what he had said. 'Try a good blow. I'll get a chair.'

In a minute Colm returned with a chair. 'I'm taller than you. I'll do it, Canon,' he said. He stood up on the chair and, cradling his hand behind the flame, blew hard at it. It did not even veer from the vertical, just burnt on oblivious. He tried several times but could manage nothing.

The congregation were talking among themselves, going quiet as Colm blew the flame, then continuing at greater volume when the flame failed to obey.

Canon Dawson turned to them. 'Let me remind you that you are in a church,' he said sternly. He turned to Colm. 'I'll do it,' he said. And he took Colm's place on the chair.

But Canon Dawson had no more success than Colm had had. 'Water. Fetch me a pitcher of water,' said Canon Dawson.

He poured a stream of water over the flame. The water steamed when it came into contact with the flame but did not cause it to falter for a moment. Canon Dawson kept on, determined not to accept defeat. Water from the pitcher flowed down the candle and formed pools on the floor.

When the water was exhausted, Canon Dawson once again tried to extinguish the flame by blowing. Nothing worked.

He looked out at the congregation. They looked back at him, then past him to the indestructible flame. 'Help me take the candle into the sacristy, Colm!' commanded Canon Dawson.

The canon lifted the candle from the holder, while Colm picked up the heavy holder and the two men processed with it into the sacristy. There, Canon Dawson searched around for a pair of scissors. 'We'll cut the wick.' This he did, but the flame was not affected. Then Canon Dawson inverted the candle and pushed the flame down onto the parquet floor of the sacristy. The flame burnt on.

'It's some trick,' said Canon Dawson. 'I know what's been going on and this is just one more part of it.'

'It's a miracle,' said Colm, looking up at the candle with tears in his eyes. He placed it back onto its holder reverently.

'You're a party to this, so you are. You were with Father Devenish when the Casement imitator put in an appearance. You're part of this. Don't you start talking about miracles.'

'What would you call it, Canon?' Colm asked.

'Skulduggery is what I'd call it,' Canon Dawson replied.

He could hear voices in the church, even through the firmly closed door of the sacristy. He strode back onto the altar.

'The mass is ended. I don't know what you're all waiting for. It's a weekday morning. Haven't you all got homes and jobs to go to?' he asked.

A voice came back to him from the middle of the congregation. 'Did you manage to put the candle out, Canon?'

Canon Dawson stuttered. He wanted to reply that of course he had, but his training would not let him. Instead he turned on his heel and walked off the altar to warn Colm not to tell a soul.

But Colm Devlin was not in the sacristy. While Canon Dawson had been on the altar, he had taken a small votive candle, lit it from the large paschal candle and slipped out by a side door to take the sired flame home to his sick mother.

'This is it!' said Mrs Grogan. 'This is definitely it.'

She was walking back to Ardfert with Mrs Taggart, having left knots of the congregation talking outside the church.

'Do you think so?' Mrs Taggart asked. 'I wouldn't want to jump the gun.'

'Didn't you see that candle with your own eyes, Mrs Taggart? Isn't a nod from above as good as a wink? That candle was telling us that Sir Roger is back among us.'

'But my brother-in-law – the one with the café outside Cork – he says that Sir Roger was . . . I don't like to say . . .'

'I've heard that. Of course, I've heard that. Between you and me it's probably been that which has kept Ardfert so quiet about him for so long. But don't you see, Mrs Taggart? Don't you see? Himself coming back is obviously a sign telling us that all those stories about you know what were put about by the English government to scandalize his name. That's what he's come back for; he wants us to know that he was a clean-living man after all.'

'But my brother-in-law—'

'You'd prefer to believe your brother-in-law rather than the evidence of your own eyes, would you? Sometimes, Mrs Taggart, I despair of you. I really do.'

Mrs Taggart did not like the thought that someone should despair of her. 'So you think we should change the names of our establishments?'

'I think more than that, Mrs Taggart,' Mrs Grogan replied. 'We have to change the names today. Today, Mrs Taggart. Before any of the publicans take it into their heads to become "The Roger Casement Tavern" and such like. I wouldn't put it past that one at the Eight 'til Late to have it in her head to rename her place. No, we've got to be quick. I don't want the sun to go down – what there is of it – without having that board outside St Theresa's. But, in addition to that, I think we should start displaying the cards around Ardfert. You can give over your whole window to them. You might try selling them at wholesale to the pubs and shops. Go as far as Ballyheige if you want. But we need to do more.'

'Isn't what we're doing enough?' Mrs Taggart asked.

'No, we've got to think big or we'll be caught on the hop. The big boys from Knock will descend on us like a ton of bricks bringing their own Casement products. I've got the number of a firm that will supply us with statues, medals, everything we want regarding Sir Roger. I'm going to put an order in today and get them to rush it through. I want you to go down to the sign-painters and hurry them along. Offer some extra money if you have to. Meanwhile, I'll order the extras.'

'I'm not sure . . .' said Mrs Taggart.

Mrs Grogan stopped. 'All right, Mrs Taggart, would you like me to buy you out of the whole thing? Would you?'

'I don't want to be too hasty, that's all.'

'Wake up! If you go on at your own sweet pace, there'll be nothing for us. I've seen it happen. You have to strike while the iron is hot. And, believe me, that candle flame was hot! I couldn't have thought up anything better myself.'

Mrs Taggart promised that she would get the signs and display the postcards of Roger Casement in her window. They parted at Mrs Grogan's front gate.

Colm Devlin had driven home ahead of the rest of the congregation. He held his burning votive candle in his right hand against the steering-wheel.

When he got to the car he had tried to spill some wax from the candle on to the dashboard, thinking that he could stick the candle onto it for the journey home, but no wax fell from it. Puzzled, he wondered how he was going to transport it home safely to his mother. He decided to hold on to it.

In his confusion he had forgotten to close the window of the car and only as the car picked up speed did he notice. But his hand was engaged in steering and holding the candle. A wind blew into the car but it did not affect the candle. It burnt vertically, as if surrounded by complete stillness.

He turned into his muddy farmyard, got out of the car and banged the door shut. He walked through the open door of the house, calling to his mother that he was home. He looked around, finding the candlestick they kept for when Father Devenish came to say mass. He placed the candle into it. Then, as usual, he prepared his mother her morning tea.

'Is it a special occasion, Colm?' Mags Devlin asked her son when she saw the candle next to the tea things.

'It is, I think, Mam,' he replied. 'Indeed, I am sure it is.'

'Did you bring the candle for me from church, son?' she asked. 'You'd have been better to leave it burning in front of St Anthony.'

Colm placed the tray down on his mother's bedside table. 'Do you need the commode, Mam, before we get going?' he asked, as he always did.

'Not just now,' Mags Devlin replied. 'Tell me who was at mass.'

'It was a grand congregation for a weekday, Mam. I've not seen anything like it.'

'Was Brid McCarthy there?'

'She was. Along with her brown friend – the one I've told you about – and some other biddy I've not clapped eyes on before.'

'Who else?'

Colm thought about that. He knew that he was only doing what he did every morning of his life. But today he was impatient with it, wanting to get on with the story. 'Mrs Grogan was in thick with Mrs Taggart. I've not seen them at weekday mass for years. There were lots of strangers there too. But the altar boys didn't turn up. I served for the canon.'

'I'd love a cup of tea.'

'Have you had a good night?'

Mags hadn't, but said she had.

'But I want to tell you about how we come to have this candle . . .' Colm said, and he told Mam everything that had happened. Mam forgot to ask Colm to lift the cup to her lips so that she could drink.

When he had finished his story, she looked into the candle-flame, wondering.

'This tea's gone cold. I'll get us another pot.'

'You'll make yourself late for the farm,' Mags said.

'I'll be no more than a minute.'

While Colm was downstairs seeing to the tea, Mags Devlin continued watching the candle-flame. It was odd. Those cheap candles they used burnt halfway down in the time it took to say five decades of the rosary. But the tiny steeple of this candle, the top half-inch tapering towards the wick, did not seem to have burnt down. Was Colm spinning a yarn to brighten up her day? Had he just lit it downstairs before bringing her the tea? She reached out towards the flame, her clawlike, hopelessly arthritic hands pushed painfully towards it. The agony of it made her want to cry out but she kept at it, offering up the pain for African intentions, until at last she was within an inch of the tulip-in-bud fire.

Mags Devlin gasped at the warmth of the flame, a warmth that pulsed into her hand, up her arm, and through her whole body, warming her like her electric blanket. Her fingers began to move of their own volition, unravelling like stretched strands of rope. They straightened. She felt her bowed spine relax, the knots of pain all about her body – pain that was part of routine and which no longer even had a name unless it reared up to exceptional proportions – pulsing away. Suddenly afraid, though not knowing why, she pulled her hand away from the candle flame. It followed her instructions.

Colm appeared with the fresh pot of tea. He poured his mother out a cup but, before he could put down the milk and lift the cup to her lips, she had taken it by the handle with her new hand and had done it, for the first time in years, all by herself.

There need be no hesitation to carry out the sentence if it should appear, on reflection, a sensible one. Indeed, with a view to extricating the discussion completely from a sentimental vein, I will go so far as to confess that there is a great deal to be said for hanging all public men at the age of fifty-two, though under such a regulation I should myself have perished eight years ago. Were it in force throughout Europe, the condition of the world at present would be much more prosperous.

FROM G. B. SHAW'S LETTER, '*SHALL ROGER CASEMENT HANG?*'
(REJECTED BY *THE TIMES*, PUBLISHED BY *THE MANCHESTER GUARDIAN*, 22 JULY 1916)

8

BOMA CAME INTO THE PARLOUR AND CLOSED THE DOOR AGAINST THE noise of customers. 'It's murder out there,' she told Paula.

'I've just made tea,' said Paula. 'I'll take a cup out to Brid and hold the fort for a while.'

With a sigh, Boma sat down into the chair by Stanley. 'There's not much more to sell. We've emptied the shelves. Brid's been on to the wholesalers but they say they're at full-stretch. We could have rented out your room a hundred times today. I keep telling Brid to put up a notice but she feels it's only right to tell the homeless to their faces.'

Paula looked at Boma, waiting for more. She went through to the shop.

'Here's some tea for you, Brid.'

'Why don't you try Ballyheige?' Brid was telling a Japanese. 'There might be a room there, but there's nothing here, I'm afraid. We're full up.'

The man left. 'He wanted beds for six. He's from Japanese television. We're completely out of cigarettes – even the Gold Flake's shifted – and there's only two tins of pipe-tobacco left.'

'You could close – until you get more stock,' Paula said.

'We never close,' Brid said tartly. 'Stock or no stock, it's the least we can do to provide information for the pilgrims.'

'You don't have a room for the night, do you?' asked an Englishman.

'I'm sorry, dear, I haven't,' Brid said. 'Now isn't that a shame for you after coming all that way? Have you tried Ballyheige?'

A mile down the Ballyheige Road, Colm Devlin was trying to clear away cars and sightseers in order to get his eight milk-cows across the road for their evening milking. A Garda officer, his car blocking the traffic, which backed up all the way to Ardfert, was doing his best to help him.

'Will you move that van?' shouted Colm. 'It's blocking me gate. It's cruelty to those poor beasts to keep them waiting longer.'

The van moved on and Colm made to open the gate. The cows pushed past him, aiming themselves towards the opposite gate and the milking-parlour. But a motor bike ignored the Garda officer, veered to the left and startled the cows. They made off in the Ballyheige direction. Colm followed them as fast as he could.

The Garda officer radioed for reinforcements. Colm caught up with the cattle and corralled them back to the gate. He pushed them through and slammed the gate shut. He leaned against it for a moment, wishing his mam had kept the miracle to herself.

Colm's mam, Mags, oblivious to events outside, was giving an interview to Radio Telefis Eireann. Her fee, she said, was to go straight to the missions. It would not be right for her to reap further rewards from her miracle. As she answered the interviewer's questions, she serenely knitted Colm's new pullover, marvelling at her dexterity.

'And can we see the candle?' the interviewer said.

'It'll cost you,' said Mags Devlin. 'It's all in a good cause.'

The interviewer turned off his microphone, agreed a price and Mags put aside her knitting and went upstairs, where the votive candle burnt, unconsumed and unflinching, in front of a statue of the Sacred Heart.

Mags picked up the candlestick reverently and took it back downstairs. Her every step, the slightest painfree movement, thrilled her.

The camera whirred. 'So this is it?'

'Yes,' she said. 'This is it. It's small, only a cheap candle. Colm says the big paschal candle is kept in the church under lock and key but this one did the job, so it did.'

'But how do we know you didn't just light a new candle while you were upstairs?'

Mags thought about that. 'I suppose you don't. Still, you're not going anywhere soon, are you? It's not every day I have Radio Telefis Eireann in the house, now is it? If you stay around you'll see that the candle doesn't burn down, at least it hasn't in the four days since Colm brought it to me.'

'Might I try to blow it out?'

'You can try if you like. It'll cost you, though. The mission in Kampala needs a new minibus . . . or is it a tractor?' She held up a copy of *Flaming Heart* in front of her face so the camera-eye would catch it. 'Yes, I'm right both times,' she said. 'They need a minibus *and* a tractor.'

Mags took up her knitting while the camera was turned off and negotiations proceeded with the director.

'Five hundred pounds,' said the director.

'Five hundred pounds will do for a blow. But if you want anything else – to use water or push it into sand or anything like that – well, each different sort of try will be another five hundred pounds,' said Mags. 'Don't give the money to me. Straight off to the Sisters of the Flaming Heart it can go.'

'It's risky. Way over budget,' said the director.

'But if it works we can sell it on,' said the interviewer.

'Try everything, so.'

The camera angle was set; the lights adjusted.

'Now this is the candle that cured you, Mags,' said the interviewer.

'It is. And it isn't,' Mags replied.

'How do you mean?'

'Well, you should know. The candle was the visible manifestation of an inward grace.'

The interviewer nodded. 'Now we're going to do an experiment.

I'll try to extinguish the flame.' He blew, but the flame remained deadly calm.

The interviewer inhaled, ready for another blow.

'It'll cost you!' counselled Mags.

The interviewer made a shrug and blew mightily.

The flame was unimpressed.

'Amazing! Now what we'll do is – with your permission, Mags – pour some water on the flame.' The director handed him a tumbler of water and the interviewer emptied the whole lot over the candle. It burnt on.

The interviewer looked into the camera-lens. 'I don't know what to say,' he said. He turned to Mags. 'I really don't think we need try other tests. I'm completely convinced.'

Mags knitted on. 'You might as well,' she said. 'You've paid for it.'

A bowl of damp soil was produced and placed on the coffee-table. The interviewer took the candle, turned it upside down. The flame, he noticed, was burning downwards, like a blowtorch. He plunged the candle into the soil. He left it there for ten seconds. Mags looked up from her knitting. A frown of anxiety furrowed her face. The interviewer took the candle out of the soil and gasped as the flame emerged.

Mags, the smile back on her face, returned to her knitting.

'I don't know what to say,' said the interviewer.

'You've already said that. Why not say that the African missions of the Sisters of the Flaming Heart need all the money they can collect?' said Mags. 'And if anyone wants a light from my candle they're welcome.'

'That's grand, Mags,' said the interviewer.

'Only ten pounds. The money will go to the missions.'

Colm came in. 'You can tell people to stay away. The poor cows are fed up. Ardfert'll go to the devil.'

'While the television people are here,' said Mags, 'you can show them your party-piece, Colm.'

Colm looked embarrassed.

'Go on!' She turned to the interviewer. 'It's great, so it is. Colm's been doing it ever since he was a wee lad. It always gets a laugh.' The interviewer looked at the director. 'It won't cost you anything!'

'What's it about?' asked the director.

'Shall I tell them, Colm?' Mags asked. Colm nodded. 'Well, you see, Colm gets down next to the cow and he aims the beast's udder at his mouth and squeezes a squirt of the milk in. Then he looks at me – but in this case it'll be the camera – and says . . .' Mags turned to Colm. 'Say it, Colm!'

'From cow to customer,' said Colm.

'Isn't it great?' exclaimed Mags. 'And it's all his own. He's famous for it around Ardfert, famous. And we won't charge them, will we, Colm? We'll throw it in for free.'

The interviewer smiled. 'Let's do it,' he said.

The crew packed up their equipment. Mags smoothed down Colm's grey hair, patted his cheek and sent him off to find the prettiest cow.

'This is a priority order!' shouted Mrs Grogan down the telephone to Gracefeather Piety Ltd. 'I don't care if the kilns are full of Padre Pio! I want you to get going now on casts of Roger Casement. Yes, now! To save time, you can use the Sacred Heart as your starting point. Just make sure you get the face right. Shorten the hair. The beard can stay the same. Yes. Now what you must change are the robes. Instead of the gown, I want an old-fashioned suit on him. What do you mean "how old-fashioned"? Didn't you get the snaps I faxed? Well, that old-fashioned. He can have both hands joined in front of him. "Where?" Well, where do you keep your zip fastener? There, so. Now listen carefully. I want one thousand in each size from miniature to home-shrine size. Yes, half in plaster, half wood resin. I want two hundred and fifty each of side-chapel size . . . Yes, in both plaster and resin. And five divine-size in all-weather bronze. Yes. Yes. No! We need them in a hurry! If you don't think you can do it I'll fax Living Clay in Tullamore. Oh, you can. I thought you might change your tune. Yes, delivery to The Roger Casement Fancy Goods Emporium, Ardfert, Kerry. Work round the clock! Time is what we don't have!'

Mrs Grogan rang off. She climbed over the luggage of the guests who had filled every spare inch of floorspace of The Roger Casement Hotel, slammed shut the front door and made her way through the choked streets to Mrs Taggart's.

She found her in the process of trying to shoo customers out of the shop. 'There's nothing left. I'm sorry. Look, we must close . . .'

When she had shut the door, Mrs Taggart smiled at Mrs Grogan,

'You were right, Mrs Grogan. I've sold every last one of the Casement cards. I rang to reorder at lunchtime.'

'I've just ordered the statues. They've promised the day before yesterday for delivery. And I've got candles. I went round all the churches of Tralee and bought up everything that was out. All we have to do is decorate them like miniature paschal candles, put them in those little gilt candlesticks and we can sell them for two ninety-nine. Get the women to work through the night. Pay them twenty pence a piece.'

'That's a bit high, isn't it?'

'It'll keep their noses to it.'

'I've had another idea,' said Mrs Taggart, though it was, in fact, her first. 'Why not get little models of the Roger Casement Memorial out at McKenna's Fort? They'd be great paperweights.'

'I've never seen it,' said Mrs Grogan.

'There's a company in my Fancy Goods catalogue. They'll come out and take the measurements. You need to have the inscription on it too, of course.'

'Get going, then, Mrs Taggart!'

'I will.'

And she did.

Canon Dawson was being boycotted by Father Devenish and Miss O'Shea. Not only would he not allow either of them to see the paschal candle in the sacristy storeroom, he was also refusing to even discuss the apparitions.

'I'll say this once and once only,' he had informed them at breakfast. 'If there is anything strange happening here, I think it is the work of the Devil rather than the Lord God. The candle is going to stay in the storeroom under lock and key until the bishop and his experts have had a chance to view it. I am not going to give one word of encouragement to this occurrence. Not one. And I expect you to follow my example.'

'But, Canon,' said Miss O'Shea, 'are you going to tell Mags Devlin that she's been cured by the power of the Devil?'

'If the Devil can get into the hearts and minds of the Dáil, to get them to pass those wicked laws sanctioning I don't know what kinds of immorality, then I don't see why he wouldn't be able to cure an old woman of a spot of arthritis!'

'Shame on you, Canon!' said Miss O'Shea. 'You know yourself that there is no-one in your parish more devout, more holy, than Mags. She's accepted the cross of her illness for almost two decades! How can you be so uncharitable as to think that such a thing would be the Devil's work? If you want my opinion, it's the Devil that's got into you. You don't like what has happened because it upsets your routine. You know how you want things to be just so.'

Canon Dawson, unused to being gainsaid by anyone, let alone Miss O'Shea, replied, 'I've said all I'm going to say.'

'I believe in the apparitions,' said Father Devenish. 'The church was full this morning with people who also believe it. And I had to say the usual mass and not mention that we have a miracle locked up in the sacristy storeroom. It seems wrong to me, Canon. Wrong because there are few enough miracles in the world; little enough to help faith along. And when something does come along, you lock it up. The town is filling up with pilgrims and we, who should be doing everything we can to support people in their faith, lock the doors against them.'

'But it's *Roger Casement*, Father!' replied Canon Dawson. 'What sort of faith are you trying to back up in having him come back?'

'It's true. I've never seen him as material for canonization but I've been wondering whether that hasn't been a lack of insight on my part. His work in the Congo and South America, his realization that national self-interest is at the root of so many of the evils in the world, his conversion to the cause of a free Ireland, even his so-called treachery against Britain . . . all these things point to a man who put conscience first.'

'I'll leave aside his stinking diaries,' replied Canon Dawson, 'as there is a lady present.' He picked up a book he had taken out of the permanent reserve of the Tralee library the previous day and wrapped in a brown-paper cover. 'These are the Black Diaries. There's an interesting letter, among the filth, written by Casement to accept his knighthood from the British king. Listen to this: *The Savoy, Denham, Bucks. Dear Sir Edward Grey, I find it very hard to choose the words in which to make acknowledgement of the honour done me by the King. I am much moved at the proof of confidence and appreciation of my service on the Putumayo conveyed to me by your letter, wherein you tell me that the King had been graciously pleased upon your recommendation to confer upon me the honour of knighthood. I am, indeed, grateful to you for this signal assurance of your personal esteem and support. I am very deeply sensible of the honour done to me by His Majesty. I would beg that my humble duty might be presented to His Majesty when you may do me the honour to convey to him my deep appreciation of the honour he has been so graciously pleased to confer upon me. I am, dear Sir Edward, Yours sincerely, Roger Casement.* Weasel words! The man was hopelessly compromised; an unsavoury combination of sissy, traitor and sycophant.'

Canon Dawson shut the book. 'And that's all I have to say.'

'And here's all I have to say,' shouted Miss O'Shea, watching Canon Dawson leaving the room, 'you'll get no dinner from me.'

Declan feared sleep. Ever since the incident on the Leeds-to-York motorway, sleep had never been deep enough. As soon as he drifted under, a drunken yell, a passing train or a car taking the sleeping-policeman outside his house turned into a gang of hit men banging his door down.

And, if he managed to reach unconsciousness, a vision of Roger Casement, hanged by Britain, shot by himself but refusing to lie down, came back with his sardonic smile and his warning finger. One dawn Declan woke up to find himself lying in a piss-wet bed.

Declan and Sean had returned the bomb to Pat's garage and left a note about aborted missions. Then Sean and he had parted. He had received no word from Sean since. Neither had had a word to say to one another after the incident. A shrug was their final parting.

Declan had tried to explain to friends in the organization what had happened. He passed on the message he had received from Roger Casement. They said little, but then they seldom said more. He waited to see what they would do. Looking up at the sky, over his shoulder, had become a nervous tic. He was not sure from which direction harm would come.

Declan left his job, his rooms in London, and sneaked home to West Belfast, where his mother made a fuss of him. But time was passing. Declan knew he could not stay. The way people veered away from him on the streets; the silence when he appeared in pubs; the abiding conviction that restitution was on its way.

Sitting with his mother watching TV, he saw Casement pulling Mobutu Sese Seko through the streets of Boma. It was the same man, right down to the smile and the soft, upper-crust, Irish accent. The name of the town was one more memory-hacking coincidence, bringing back to him thoughts of the woman he had sent out to deliver a gift. The IRA had been pleased with the results and the resulting mayhem to London's rail system. But Declan had been in charge of that operation. Why had he not delivered the bomb himself? Why give it to his girlfriend, the girlfriend who knew nothing about any of it? That was a black mark, a mark the York bomb was supposed to rub out. But he had failed there too. Now the IRA, he knew, were waiting and, above them, Boma.

His every waking moment, he imagined her looking down, asking, *Why?*

He asked himself the same question. *Because I'm an evil bastard*, came the reply. *I had the means – a bomb ready for priming and timing. I had the orders. And you, with your octopus arms and your own womanly timebomb waiting to smash my life to smithereens. I was fed up to the teeth with you. And I had the means. One little parcel and my life would be trouble-free. I had the one stone and the two birds right in my sights.*

Remembering his faked kindness to Boma in the days before the planned bombing; how she, distraught at his coldness since he had learnt about the baby, fell for it completely . . . could not do enough to him; hung on him; planned the future . . . while he planned the exact time to which he would set his murder-machine.

So easy it had been. He, on the nights leading up to the bombing, so tender and gentle with her. *We don't have to go all the way, you know. I wouldn't want to harm the baby.* It had been like a replay at slower speed of their first weeks together . . .

But Declan now, imagining a vengeful heaven above him, looking down at him, could not understand his old self. It was as strange, as difficult to believe in the reality of it, as belief in Holy Saints had been.

He took to going to church, sitting in the back pew of the great pile. He would watch the suspended crucifix, his eyes unblinking, until tears came from eye-strain. One day he even knelt in the queue for confession, but when his turn came he veered away, walked back up the side aisle, out into the dark and the rain.

Then Declan read the story of the paschal candle of Ardfert.

He told his mother he was going out. She was glad to see him go. He didn't like her smoking. With Declan gone, she could puff away. He put on his anorak and began walking down the street.

Keeping his shadow behind him, he continued to walk, out into the suburbs, until he had reached green fields.

The afternoon sun shone intermittently and Declan followed it south. Near Lisburn, he stopped to rest. His shoes were hurting him. Without thinking he took them off. He put his socks into them and left them sitting neatly on the verge. He walked on towards Monaghan bare-footed at the side of the penitential road.

*You are probably right about the Turks, but I am right about
the English! I wish all 'Empires' and all damnable
conspiracies against the poorer classes of mankind – generally
speaking, 'the Irish' – could be brought to book as Turkey has
been. But that does not lead me to denounce the Turk
himself, and as between the London press and its loathsome
backing of the winner, I stood for the Turk. Besides, he was
down! I knew he was beaten before it began, and when the
whoops and howls of this unseemly throng of scribblers broke
loose upon his defeated agonies I joined him – and in that
camp, the camp of the fallen, I stick.*

CASEMENT IN A LETTER TO HENRY W. NEVINSON

9

THEY HAD BEEN STAYING AT O'KEEFFE'S FOR A WEEK. IT WAS NOT
Tim's idea, though he felt he might have been quite content to stay
there until the morning they were due to depart for Britain. It would
have allowed him to avoid Ardfert and all the embarrassment.

Chris had not once brought up the idea of moving on when moving
on became, for him at any rate, a problem. They had been to see the
Gallerus Chapel near Dingle. A stone building constructed without
benefit of mortar that has stood for over a thousand years, it had been
another of the 'musts' in Chris's book. Tim, who had been taken to
see it several times with school parties and gangs of altar boys, would
have been happy to give it a miss.

It was there, while walking away from the site, that Chris began to weave and falter. He stepped into a cow-pat, stopped and said, 'There's something wrong.'

'You're standing in a cow-pat,' Tim said.

'Yes, I know. The thing is I saw it coming, tried to avoid it but walked into it just the same.'

'Story of your life,' Tim said, sensing something amiss but hoping to heal it with a crack.

'No, Tim. There's something wrong.'

Tim took Chris's arm, wondering if this would be the moment he would remember as the start of the descent. Chris shrugged it away. They continued on. He veered into Tim once or twice. 'Fresh . . .' Tim said.

But when they reached the road, with a splendid view of Valencia Island seen through mists and sun-ray to their right – a view that suddenly meant nothing – he kept veering towards Tim. He took his arm and this time Chris did not pull away. Tim led him along the road, feeling his inclination to the right, his inability to keep to a straight line.

'What do you think it is?' Tim asked him.

'One more thing.'

They ate lunch in a bar just outside Dingle. Chris seemed to have recovered himself but just as he was finishing his plate of fish and chips – Tim had already finished his and was watching him like a hungry puppy – the hand in which he was holding his fork suddenly shot up, carrying a portion of his food with it, as if his hand were attached to a string being roughly pulled by some invisible puppeteer.

'What brought that on?' Tim asked.

Chris did not reply. The colour had drained from his face. Tim tried to work out whether from shock at seeing his body out of control, or from some physical sickness. Chris sat for a long moment, looking at the half of Guinness in front of him. He seemed about to pick it up and drink from it but was afraid of what might happen. And Tim understood and *felt* for the first time how much Chris's life had become an uncertain walk along a booby-trapped road. Every step could spring a mine.

Back they went to O'Keeffe's. They had a drink at the bar but Chris did not have much to say to Jimmy. Tim made up for it, pouring great scorn on all the rumours about Roger Casement that were coming out from under the bar with Jimmy's newspapers. 'Once there's a news story, it sires others. It just goes on and on,' he said. And as he spoke he watched Chris surreptitiously. He lifted his drink to his lips with both hands. Jimmy was watching him.

'Anyway,' Tim said, 'it makes a change from the usual, I suppose.'

'There are too many stories – backed up by too many people – for them all to be lies,' said Jimmy with a smile.

'You're trying to wind me up,' Tim said.

'Impossible,' Jimmy replied, 'you've been overwound already. Anyhow, he saved the life of a Catholic taxi-driver in Derry, pushed a couple of Loyalist paramilitaries out of the car.'

'Isn't he spreading himself a bit thin?' Tim asked.

'I don't think the taxi-driver would agree with you,' Jimmy said. 'Still, he's moving around all right. Zaïre, England, Dublin, Ardfert. You missed the film on the television. That would have convinced you. It was no joking about. No vague lights. No blur. There was a man dressed in an old-fashioned suit, the spitting image of Sir Roger, bullying this Mobutu fellow along the road. It couldn't have been a fake. And then of course there's the Ardfert paschal candle.'

'What's that all about?'

Tim heard a glass smash, turned to his left and saw Chris looking down to the floor, where his glass lay in smithereens. 'I'm sorry,' he said.

'Think nothing of it,' Jimmy said, coming round the bar with his dustpan and brush, as if he had been holding the items all the time, out of sight, ready to tidy up after them.

'I think I'd better go and lie down.'

'What about the doctor? Shouldn't I call a doctor?'

'No,' Chris said.

'Are you sure? I think we should.'

'No,' he repeated, turning away from the bar.

Tim stood up, making to help him; aware of the eyes of the other drinkers. Chris held up his arms to fend him off, mouthed, *No.* Tim sat back down.

They watched him walk towards the stairs, holding on to chairs and tables for support. The other people in the place might have taken him for a drunk trying to mimic sobriety. Tim thought of the Power's man, wondered where he was, under whose kindly feathers he had found a home for the night.

Tim told Jimmy what had happened that day and he said that when Chris was ready he knew of a fine doctor near by. 'We'll see how he is in the morning,' Tim said.

Chris did not appear again that day and the following morning he was hardly able to raise himself from the bed. Tim told Jimmy and he called the doctor. Chris told the doctor everything and the doctor gave him something to make him sleep, saying that he would ring up a colleague in Dublin. He stayed and drank a cup of coffee out of Tim's breakfast pot.

He seemed an easy man and Tim answered his questions as far as he could about the course of the disease. He listed the shingles in Nigeria that had caused Chris to leave for America; the TB he had come down with there, the treatment for which had so depleted his savings; his journey to Zanzibar, where he had been as a Peace Corps volunteer in the Sixties and where he had hoped to be able to live cheaply in a warm climate but where every intestinal bug on offer had ravaged him, causing him to flee to Tim in London in order to recuperate. Yes, Tim said, Chris had a doctor at the Middlesex Hospital, but he had only been to see her twice. Chris had been fine since returning from Africa, apart from his infected eye – a result of the shingles – and the odd bout of diarrhoea, easily controlled by overdoses of Emodium.

'We're not experts at these opportunistic infections in this part of the world,' the doctor said. And Tim thought of the line past which the heathen television stations could not reach to plunder culture. *No*, he thought. *Holy Ireland exports all that.* 'Still, I'll have a chat with my colleague in Dublin. He'll maybe be able to throw some light on it. I have to confess, it baffles me.'

Tim thanked him, while a side of him could not help resenting the man's quiet, daily virtue; the way he seemed so comfortable. He could see this doctor ushering his kids into Sunday mass, accompanied by his upstanding wife. Like two solid Connemara-marble book-ends they'd be. The children kneeling between them. The sight of them would gladden the heart of the priests and the faithful; God too, perhaps.

Tim spent the rest of the day chatting to Jimmy between seeing to Chris. He seemed to be improving as the day wore on and was fit enough by the afternoon to come downstairs for a while. But that alarming tic, an extravagant gesture that seemed affected, too much to be spontaneous, kept recurring.

Some drugs arrived with the doctor the following day. They might or might not work, he said. Strong medicine, their side-effects were considerable, too long to be gone into. Chris took them for three days. He seemed to improve but showed no inclination to leave Dingle.

Each day Jimmy regaled Tim with Casement stories from Ardfert. Tim feigned indifference but a side of him longed to see his mammy's face. Knowing what he knew, he was sure she would feel her whole life had been justified; that she had chosen the true path and stuck to it. It had led her to McKenna's Fort. He, on the other hand, had been in error all along. He imagined her triumphalism. And his curiosity kept being aroused, only to disperse when the realization came that satisfying it would mean going home to face the holy music.

Then, Jimmy handed him the evening paper and Tim was looking at a picture of a smiling Mags Devlin. She had been a close friend of his mother and lived with her husband, Joseph, and her son, Colm. He had not thought of her for perhaps five years, though she had always been kind to him when he was growing up.

The story told in the newspaper was thought-provoking. Bedridden for fifteen years, a widow, looked after by her only son, she was now able to walk and her arthritic limbs worked as they had not worked for two decades. She had started knitting a pullover for Colm, she said.

'I knew this woman,' Tim told Jimmy. 'She's a neighbour of Mammy's.'

'And was she sick?'

'She was sick last time I was in Ardfert. I'd thought she was probably dead. Anyway, the disease can't have got any better.'

'It makes you think,' he said.

'Yes, it does.'

'It says the canon at Ardfert Church has locked up the paschal candle and won't let anybody see whether it's burning or not.'

'I can't say I blame him,' Tim said.

'How's himself?' Jimmy asked, looking towards the ceiling.

'He seems better. I've been trying to get him to come out for a walk to test himself but he keeps putting it off. Anyway, no sign of side-effects to the medicine.'

'Perhaps it was a small thing he had.'

'It didn't seem small at the time. You can never tell.'

'Well, look,' said Jimmy, 'you two are almost family. I'll ask Maureen to put on dinner for us tonight in the back room. We can eat away some of the profits we're making off the two of you. It's a quiet night in the bar. I'll put Liam in and take the night off. Do you think Chris will be up to it?'

'I'll ask. It's very kind of you.'

'That's what we're here for,' Jimmy said.

If Ardfert was inundated since the miracle of the paschal candle, Tralee too was feeling the effects. The town's hotels and b & bs, many a private house too, filled up with pilgrims and media people.

The people of the town welcomed the unexpected influx. Those who stood to gain at once sought about for information about Roger Casement, pumped their elderly relatives for their memories. Old people in Homes and by turf fires found themselves visited and asked about what they could recall. They willingly obliged with tales, some fanciful, some plain truth, about their memories of the long-dead hero.

Eamonn McCann still played Sir Roger Casement at the Tralee Museum. No longer rotating with Oliver Cromwell and St Brandon, he found himself under siege from both locals and blow-ins. Then, after closing time, as often as not, still wearing his Roger Casement suit, he would be whisked away by television crews to answer questions at Banna Strand, McKenna's Fort and in Tralee itself. A Japanese film crew had wanted him to stagger ashore from the ocean and then answer questions, but Eamonn drew the line at this.

After hundreds of hours shuffling around the empty museum, it came as a welcome surprise to him suddenly to be in demand. It was wonderful to be wanted, to be busy, to be listened to, to have banknotes forced into his hand as *ex gratia* payment for providing the media with information. For the first time in his life he felt he was fulfilling his vocation.

It did not take long, however, for his colleagues at the Tralee Museum to see that they were missing out on a rare opportunity to supplement their wages. Oliver Cromwell and St Brandon soon sought out suitable suits, started growing beards and mugging up on the career of Casement so that they too could act as guides. Eamonn did not mind. There was work and gold enough for all. He was the original copy, he knew, definitely the best, and the best informed.

Only one thing made Eamonn ill at ease. Everyone questioned him about the Casement diaries. Some even came prepared, with copies of the book by Singleton-Gates where sections of the diaries had been printed. When Eamonn said that the diaries had been forged a man told him that they had recently been tested and the handwriting had been found to be authentic. Eamonn, who had been hinting that he thought Casement's return was in some way designed to clear his name, began to wonder about that. He began saying that Casement's homosexuality was irrelevant or only a part, an overplayed part, of the world-balming centre of the man's life.

'I heard what you said in there. I don't call it irrelevant,' said an American reporter, who had taken Eamonn for a drink after work.

'What was that, Mr Stone? I said a lot.'

The man smiled. 'Call me Jack. You said that the homosexuality of Casement was a red herring. It may be that to you, my friend, but to a lot of people it could mean one hell of a lot. Gay people, straight people who can't stand them – among whom I'd place a fair number of the Irish Americans. Can't you see what it would mean? If Sir Roger really has come back from the grave and is performing miracles it would make him the world's first gay saint – well, the first we've heard about. And can you imagine what the Catholic Church would think?'

'I don't know,' opined Eamonn. 'To tell you the truth, Jack, I'm out of my depth. We've always been taught that the English made up the . . . the sex thing to hang Sir Roger the easier.'

'It's possible,' Jack replied. 'But was it necessary to forge so much? Wouldn't a few lines have been enough?'

'I don't know,' Eamonn said. 'You know your subject, Jack.'

'I borrowed a few books when I heard about all this. I don't think I know as much as you. Still, he was a fascinating man, a man who deserves to be better known. Don't you think he was gay? I know I do.'

'But what about the English dirty tricks?'

'I wouldn't deny that for a moment. I don't say the English weren't capable of forging the diaries, but let's assume for the sake of argument that the diaries already existed. The real crime was in releasing them when they did for their own ends – Casement's disgrace and execution. And it still goes on. The papers relating to the case are locked up in the English Home Office until 2016. They defend their own, those Brits. There's no argument. None at all. Their showing of Casement's papers was a cynical ploy to force his supporters in both Britain and the States to shut their mouths, to screw back the caps on the pens that had been going to sign the petition for Casement's reprieve.'

'Between you and me, I don't know if Roger Casement *has* come back.'

'Nobody knows that, but there has been a strange succession of events that all lead to this candle burning in Ardfert. I've been trying to get to Ardfert to see everything for myself but it's a real mob scene. Still, the people who have seen the candle say that it's miraculous. It just won't go out.'

'Which one?'

'The one in Mags Devlin's farmhouse. She's at her front gate, I hear. Every passing TV crew is invited to take "The Flaming Heart Challenge", and all the proceeds go to the missions. Nobody's seen the original. The parish priest has it under lock and key.'

'Canon Dawson's against the whole thing. I've heard that.'

Jack laughed. 'This thing isn't going to go away, Eamonn. I can tell you that. The ball's rolling. There's no telling where it's going to end.'

'It's good for the area,' Eamonn said. 'Good for me, too.'

'I was thinking,' Jack said. 'you don't know anyone in Ardfert who could help me, do you?'

'My girlfriend comes from Ardfert,' he said, wondering if she did and, if she did, if she was. 'I don't know if she can help you. What sort of things was it you wanted to know?'

'Local colour, you know,' Jack replied. 'What's her name?'

'Boma Hephernan.'

'Great! Invite . . . what's her name . . . ?'

'Boma.'

'Invite Boma to dinner. On me. Do you think she knows anything?'

Eamonn thought about that. 'She might. You never know,' he replied.

'So how long do you think you'll be staying?' Brid asked Sister Paula. Before Paula could reply, Brid had replaced the question in her head, found it cold, unlike her, felt guilt, added, 'Of course, you're welcome to stay as long as you like.'

Sister Paula caught the tone at once, weighed it and the addition, knowing that her presentiments had been correct. Brid, whatever she might say to the contrary, did not want her there, thought her an added burden. Perhaps more than that, too. 'I should get in touch with Dublin,' she replied. 'They'll be worrying.'

Boma had just left to go and meet Eamonn McCann. The day had been as busy as the previous two; the small shop full of people making purchases, enquiries, asking for accommodation. The wholesaler's lorry had had to park two hundred yards down the street in order to make its delivery to the shop, while drivers trying to push through the narrow street of Ardfert on the way to Ballyheige had started a ruckus with their horns and shouts from windows.

Paula had tried to make herself useful; carried in cups of tea, answered people's enquiries as well as she could, all the time trying to stay close to Boma, to see if their relationship – told, known, but not felt – might blossom. She did not have the least idea how this might come about. Perhaps a touch between them would set something off, unstick the glued-shut mechanism, sharpen the needle of affection and set it down on some old ballad about lost mothers and daughters.

But Boma remained a half-closed door to her. Half-open too, perhaps, but she had made no effort in the time they had been together to come closer. In fact, throughout the days following revelation, Boma had seemed to be on the run from Paula, who would set her tea down on the counter only to hear Boma, retreating to the other end of the shop or to the door to give directions, shout a 'Thanks, Paula!'

The evenings had been civil enough but neither Boma nor Brid had again mentioned anything about what Sister Paula had told them. Once having plumbed the icy depths, they had seemed content to skate along on easy, if brittle, ice.

Brid sat down by Stanley and opened the evening paper. She adjusted it to the weak rays from the pendant light and started reading it, squinting.

'You could do with a reading-lamp,' Paula said.

Brid did not look up at first. Then she saw herself not looking up and looked up. 'I've managed with the one we have for long enough. Sure, it's not worth buying one at my age.'

'It would make things so much easier for you.'

'You're may be right,' Brid observed, giving the paper a flick to stiffen it then, hearing and seeing, smoothing it with her hand to soften the abruptness of the flick.

'You don't want me here, do you?' Paula asked.

Brid saw at once that all the signs she had been giving since Paula had arrived in Ardfert had come across. She felt ashamed, though a part of her wanted to cry out, *You've finally got it, have you? You're right! For Lord's sake, go!* But instead she laid the paper aside and said, 'What makes you think that, Sister Paula?'

Paula fought for a way around the obvious. 'Well, it's a busy time for you. It can't be easy, the shop and everything. The last thing you want is another problem.' And Paula thought, *Yes, that's what I am. A problem. Nothing more. Nothing less. This has been an absurd escapade. Why could I not have left well alone?*

'I want Boma to be happy,' Brid said. 'She's had a tough time. A bit of it I know about, but there's more that I can't get to.'

'You're very close.'

'Yes, I think we are. I can't explain it. Boma was sent to me out of the blue with my medal.' Brid touched the shape of it under her blouse. 'And she's very important to me. She's like a . . . anyway, we're very close.'

'And then I come along.'

Brid laid aside her newspaper. 'Paula, I know I should be able to see you as part of everything great that's been happening. You're as much a part of the miracle as Roddie coming back with my medal, as Boma turning up, as the candle. It should all be lifting for me. It's not everyone who gets a helping of divine intervention to help faith along. And I'm having that and I'm grateful for it. But more than the knowing that there's Somebody up there who loves me, the knowing that I've been doing the right thing all these years, has been the arrival at my door of company. I know it's all been very quick but I had started to see Boma as a daughter, the daughter I never had, and then . . . well . . . you know . . .'

'Yes, I know. In a way I wish I had kept quiet and not told her anything. I very nearly didn't, you know. I almost let the moment pass.'

Brid could sense Paula's hope against hope that she would pour balm on the wound. A side of her, the exercised side, wanted to, but the strange side of Brid, a side gestated and born strong and screaming in the last few days, rose up. *Why did you, then?* the side crowed. *Wouldn't it have been enough for you to have had a look and then quietly gone back to the convent?* 'I'm sorry,' Brid said.

'No, don't be sorry. I feel a complete fool.'

'It's been so many years. So many . . .' And Brid thought of Tim, of the book she had seen and pushed into the drawer. Suddenly she knew that a part of her anger, a part unacknowledged because she had not allowed it into her head, was in fact the real source of it. 'I can see how hard it must have been for you when Boma was born. It must have been a shocking difficult decision to give her up. But so much time has passed. What can you hope to do for her now?'

Sister Paula shrugged and looked at her hands. 'I think I had better leave,' she said. 'They'll be going frantic at the convent. I'm surprised they haven't sent one of the sisters out from Tralee to see what's become of me.'

Brid, wanting to contradict, to tell Paula that these things take time, to do the decent thing, nevertheless replied from behind the shelter of her paper. 'It would be a pity, wouldn't it? After all those years given to the Lord in the convent, if you didn't endure to the end? It would be a sad thing indeed to fall away and you only a hop and a skip from the heavenly gates?'

Paula watched Brid, hidden by the confessional grille of the newspaper, not knowing what to say.

'Lord save us!' exclaimed Brid, looking up from the paper. 'Mary Coogan's gone! Just like that. It says she keeled over in the Cash and Carry. "No flowers." I'll get a mass said. God rest her. It was Mary Coogan who gave me my bath salts. She has a little shop like mine in Tralee. And she only sixty-seven! I'd have said she was at least seventy.'

> We talk'd one night of the glory days,
> When Ireland led the van,
> With scholars as thick as the stars in the sky
> And work for every man.
> 'Twill come again,' said Father Con.
> And his fertile fancy paints
> The glorious day when the sun shines on
> A new Isle of the Saints.
>
> O Father O'Callaghan,
> When will the dream come true?
> O Father O'Callaghan,
> If anyone knows, 'tis you.
> And Father O'Callaghan raised his head,
> And smiled his humoursome smile.
> 'When ev'ry man learns to rule himself
> 'Twill then be a saintly isle.'

PERCY FRENCH

10

PETER COUGHLIN TOOK HIS CAP OFF TO SALUTE THE STATUE OF ROGER
Casement as he passed it on his way to Brennan's Bar that night. He
stopped for a moment, admiring the dark silhouette of the life-size
figure, the feet planted a foot apart, his back to the night ocean and
the great world, gazing – handcuffed – over Irish horizons.

'A fine figure of a man, you were! God bless you!' said Peter Coughlin. Then he put his cap back on his head, and stepped over to the pub.

Peter was not prepared for the crowd of people in the bar. Brennan and his wife were beside themselves trying to keep ahead of the orders. Peter looked around, searching for people he knew. But if there were any regulars there they were hidden from him by the crowd of strangers, men mostly, laughing and drinking. A group had taken the side of the bar he had always considered to be his own. The television, instead of being tuned to the satellite channel and the big match from Sao Paolo, was showing Radio Telefis Eirann, the sound turned off.

'The usual, Peter?' Brennan asked.

Peter nodded. Brennan pulled his pint without another word, took his money and went off to serve some customers at the far end of the bar.

Peter Coughlin stood, a stranger in his own home-from-home, and drank his pint.

A young man occupying his usual seat at the bar, said to his companions, 'We'll walk along the beach to Banna Strand and then cut inland into Ardfert. That way we can see if we can manage to get to all the places Sir Roger was.'

'It's a long way.'

'There's no point taking the car.'

Peter Coughlin approached the group. 'You're here because of Roger Casement?' he asked them.

They exchanged glances. 'We are,' said the man in his seat. 'We've driven all the way down from Dublin.'

'You and the whole world it looks like,' Peter said.

'We wouldn't miss it,' said the man in Peter Coughlin's seat. 'Isn't it a great thing to be happening?'

'It is. If it is, that is,' replied Peter.

'It's happening all right,' said his companion. 'I'm not a great one for miracles but this one is different. Too many things happening all together to be anything else.'

'It's bloody marvellous, that's what it is!'

'He was a great patriot,' said Peter.

The men looked at one another. 'He was,' said the man with the spiky haircut.

'Do you lads have any theories about why he's come back?'

Once again, the men looked at one another. 'Because,' continued Peter, stepping into the silence with both feet, 'I think he's back to expose the wicked lies spread about him by the English.'

'Ah,' said the older man, 'you do?'

'I do. What do you think?'

There was a hesitation, a long moment of diffidence, before the man with the spiky hair said, 'We don't think so.'

'Oh, you don't? What do you think?'

'We think,' the man replied, looking towards his friends to make confession easier, 'we think that Roger Casement has come back to show us that gay can be good.'

Peter Coughlin thought about that. 'So you're saying that Roger Casement was a homosexual, are you?'

'It's obvious,' said the older man. 'You only have to read a few pages of the diaries to know.'

'It takes one to know one,' said the man with the spiky hair.

'And he's back to bring consolation to homosexuals, is he?'

'Well, we could do with a bit. It's not been easy being despised and told you're damned all these years. It's about time somebody came back from heaven to say we're not. We know it. We feel it in our bones. But it's nice to have an informed second opinion.'

Peter Coughlin saw Brennan passing by. 'Did you hear that one, Brennan? These lads are saying that Roger Casement was homosexual!'

Brennan tried to shush Peter Coughlin but it was too late. The bar went quiet. 'If you believe that, you'll believe anything!' Peter said, smiling round the bar, oblivious, looking for support. 'The moon's made of Irish butter too. Did you know that?'

But there was little enough support for Peter Coughlin. Those who might have agreed with him had already seen how the land lay in the bar. A voice from the far end of the bar shouted, 'St Roger Casement was gay. I'm gay and I've never felt better.'

Another man, invisible to Peter Coughlin, said, 'If he hadn't been gay he'd probably have settled down in the Glens of Antrim and never done any of the good he did. He's my patron saint, so he is! I've given St Paul the heave-ho!'

A cheer went up.

Peter Coughlin, seeing at last how the land lay and that it was giving way beneath both his feet, put his unfinished pint on the bar and left the pub without another word. He heard a cheer as the door banged shut.

The silhouette of the Roger Casement statue loomed across the street. Peter approached it, stood beneath the plinth for a moment, wondering where to go. His cap stayed firmly on his head. He had not frequented any other bar in Ballyheige for years. Not knowing what to do, what to think, he walked off home, forlorn.

The following morning the people of Ballyheige awoke to find the statue of Roger Casement bedecked with flowers. Bunches of daffodils and tulips lay around the plinth. On his head had been set a plaited crown of early bluebells and late primroses.

While a group of happy men from Dublin decorated Roger Casement's statue in Ballyheige, Boma was being lifted back to Ardfert by a friend of Eamonn McCann.

It had not been an altogether satisfactory evening for Boma. She had been surprised to find Eamonn waiting for her in front of the museum in company with a tall middle-aged man who had turned out to be an American reporter. This fact only emerged when the three of them were in the middle of their dinner at a fancy Tralee restaurant. At first, Boma had thought that Eamonn, uncertain about girls and the etiquette of the date, had brought a friend along with him as a kind of protection, almost as a chaperon.

And she hadn't minded that. It confirmed her impression that he was different from other men, unschooled in the ways of dating and courtship. That was really what had attracted Boma to him; that and his role in the museum as Roger Casement. It was odd how affection worked. Perhaps, after all, it was only his passing resemblance to Roddie that moved her, reminding her of the man who had saved her life on Banna Strand and then filled it with extraordinary events.

Cradling her secrets to her like a child her water-wings as she listened to Jack and Eamonn talk, she thought of Brid at home with her mother. Brid had brought down piles of old nappies from the attic, washed them and hung them out in a long semaphore line in the yard. Boma could see them through her bedroom window, flapping out the news that Brid was preparing for the birth of Roger David. And as they flapped and danced on the rope, they also said to her that she was welcome to stay. She was part of it all if she wanted to be.

Did she want to be? She was not sure. Perhaps she would only be sure when the baby arrived. But there was an easy wonder to her days at Brid's. A lightness at the realization that she was loved and cared for both by the very visible presence of Brid and the mainly unseen, but abiding, presence of Roddie.

And into this new land had come Paula, who said she was her mother. Boma still did not feel the fact but she had accepted the new presence and the stories she brought with her as one more part of the magical equation. And, having been heir to so many guilts herself, she understood Paula's. She wanted to foster this elderly nun, to bring her up happy and healthy so that she would be able to face her death in completeness, without a feeling of having left things undone.

Then, halfway through dinner, Jack said, 'Eamonn here says you know something about what's been happening.'

Boma, dragged back from her reveries, gazed out at the two men opposite. She smiled at them.

'You know, Sir Roger!' Eamonn said. Then, when Boma still did not respond, he added, 'Jack here's a reporter. From the States. He wants to know everything we can tell him.'

A waiter passed and Jack ordered another bottle of wine. As he did so, he glanced at Boma and she knew who would be paying for the meal, and why. Then, seeing Eamonn looking concerned, wanting to tell him that this was not how a decent fellow treated a woman on their first date, she laughed and, looking hard at them, locked them out with a shrug.

'But what about Mrs McCarthy?' Eamonn asked.

'Brid? She's from Ardfert. It's only natural that she should be keen on Roger Casement.'

Jack asked, 'So you haven't experienced any of these apparitions yourself?'

She looked back at him steadily. 'No, Jack. Why would Sir Roger come and visit an irreligious mother-to-be? I wouldn't mind if he did, mind you; it would make life clear, wouldn't it? It would prove that there's something out there. I'd love it to happen.'

'And what do you think about the apparitions, the candle and everything?'

'To tell you the truth, I haven't given it that much thought,' Boma lied.

Looking at them as steadily as she could, she was not able to decide whether they believed her or not. Eamonn was not concealing his disappointment very well. She knew exactly the shades of guilt he was feeling. Jack drank his wine. He offered her some more, but she refused, patting her belly to both show him she was full and remind him of her baby.

'Boma is an unusual name, isn't it?' Jack asked.

'You could say that,' she said.

Eamonn stepped in. 'It's the name of a town in Zaïre where Sir Roger once was stationed.'

'And,' continued Jack, 'the town where President Mobutu was humiliated by a man who looked very like Casement.'

Boma nodded and smiled. 'It's a coincidence,' she said. 'Life's full of them. Haven't you found that?'

'More than a coincidence, I'd say,' Jack said.

But Boma just smiled. Her resolve to stay quiet about her side of things was hardening. They had enough to be going on with, didn't they? Candles and miracles. Her side was for family only. 'What about you, Jack? Is this your first trip to Ireland?'

They saw that they were defeated. Boma listened politely to the mundane chat that garnished the pudding. Her heart was beating fast with the sweet pleasure of her secret. She wondered how Brid and Mary were managing. She wanted to be there.

Jack excused himself from coffee. She said goodbye to him and watched him at the door paying for the meal.

'I'm sorry,' she told Eamonn.

'Sorry?'

'Sorry I didn't have more to tell your friend.'

'I think seeing you would have told him everything he wanted to know.'

What did that mean? 'What do you mean?'

'Just that he knows you know more than you're letting on. Anyway, let's forget about it. I shouldn't have done that to you. It's just like me to mess things up.'

'I had thought it was going to be just the two of us.'

'It was. Honest to God. I just opened my big mouth to Jack about you and he wanted to meet you.'

'I think I was a big disappointment.'

'No, I don't think so,' he said.

'How's everything going?'

'I'm rushed off my feet. All three of us are playing Sir Roger now and it isn't enough. The problem is keeping the story straight. Liam and Will – they're the other two – are no experts on him. They got the job through the Work Opportunity Programme and bluffed their way through it. They were fine as bloody Cromwell and St Brandon. Who doesn't know about them? But they get a bit mixed up with Sir Roger. Liam makes up stuff when he gets lost. And we get people coming in who pass between us and ask me why Liam said Casement never wrote a word of the diaries when I had said he wrote them all.'

'Do you think he did?'

'I think so, yes.'

'Good,' Boma said.

'Good about the dairies being true?'

'Yes. It will help Brid.'

Eamonn laughed. 'Help Brid? I'd have thought she'd fight the idea of them being true tooth and nail!'

'What do you remember about Brid's son?'

'Tim, you mean?'

'Yes.'

Eamonn thought about that. 'Not much. I haven't seen him since we were at school.'

'Do you think he was gay?'

'You're asking the wrong person, Boma. Why do you ask?'

'Nothing,' Boma said.

'Oh, come on ! You're such a little tease, so you are!'

'Well, you must promise me you won't tell a soul. Promise!'

'I promise.'

She looked at him, wondering if she could trust him. He looked back at her, aware he was on trial. 'Well, Brid found a book that Tim left behind when he went away to England. She thought it was about the missions. She told me she was going to read it while waiting about in the shop. The book had a cover showing an almost naked Indian and a bearded white man touching the Indian's shoulder. He was wearing a sort of gown and I suppose he could have been a monk of some kind but I remember I thought at the time that there was something sexy about the look of the book. It was called *Song of the Loon*. Anyway, a few days later I asked Brid about it and she said she hadn't liked it and gave me such a look! I thought no more about it, but I came across it in the drawer in the shop. It isn't about the missions; it's a story about an Indian and a fur-trapper, and what they get up to is nobody's business!'

'And the book was Tim's, was it?'

'That's what Brid said.'

'And now she thinks Tim's gay, does she? Well, I don't remember anything like that about him. He was a bit of a loner, though. Very intelligent. It was my mammy's feeling that he was cut out to be a priest. It never came to anything, but I think his mother kept pushing him towards it. He went off to University College Dublin and then I think he got a scholarship to Oxford. He was an expert on European history. Still you probably know all that.'

'I don't. No, I don't,' Boma said. 'He hasn't been back to see Brid for years. She doesn't say much about him. I've tried but she clams up. That's not like her.'

Eamonn ordered two more coffees. The waiter said their bills had been paid but that the coffees would be extra.

'I think I can run to that,' said Eamonn.

They had gone for a walk after and Eamonn took her hand. He held it lightly, shyly, then seemed relieved when a lamppost parted them. He put the guilty hand in the pocket of his trousers.

'Fancy a drink?' he asked.

'Why not?'

They went into The Rose of Tralee Bar and Boma had a red lemonade while Eamonn ordered himself a Guinness. He waved to a friend across the bar. Martin-John. He came over and they talked and she felt out on a limb again, barged out by boys' talk. She said she ought to be getting home. Martin-John was going to Ardfert and offered her a lift.

'Shall we do it again?' Eamonn asked her as she was getting into Martin-John's car.

'Do what again?'

'You know . . .' he said.

She liked his shambling ways, the way he seemed to spend his life with one foot in his mouth, the other in a bucket. 'I enjoyed the bits with you. Just you,' she said.

'That's great!' he replied. He tripped off the kerb. Then, smiling against himself, he banged the car roof as Martin-John set off.

Martin-John stopped, wound down the window. 'What's up?' he asked.

'Nothing,' Eamonn said. 'I was just saying goodbye.'

As they approached Ardfert, Boma saw a woman with a suitcase walking along the road towards Tralee.

'Drop me here, would you?' she told Martin-John. He did so and she walked back along the road to see what her mother was up to.

Behind the blond wood of the sacristy storeroom the paschal candle burned on. Its flame lit up the statues from the Christmas crib, showed Mary with her arms outstretched to a shepherd-boy playing on a bagpipe; Joseph stood benignly surveying the wall. An ox, partly covered with a purple cloth, snoozed next to a pile of old Catholic newspapers. An old, chipped plaster statue of St Patrick watched over the beast. The Baby Jesus lay dusty in His crib, a crib He shared with a tin of furniture polish and a duster.

Quietly, Canon Dawson unlocked the door, motioning the priests from Dublin not to make any noise.

'It's still at it!' he whispered, and he lifted the burning candle off its holder, handing it to the younger priest. Then he replaced it with the one they had brought.

'It's exactly the same, is it?' Canon Dawson asked.

'Completely,' the older priest, a monsignor, replied.

'You lit it and blew it out, did you?'

'We did.'

'It's a weight off my soul, Fathers,' said Canon Dawson.

'Right,' said the monsignor. 'We'd better be off.'

Back in the sacristy the men placed the burning candle into a steel tube with a heavy screw top. They turned the lid onto it.

'Leave it with us, Canon,' the monsignor said.

Canon Dawson nodded his relief. 'What'll you do with it?'

The man looked at the tube in his companion's arm. 'I suspect that when we get back to Dublin it'll be out. Experience shows that removing an item from the place exorcizes the effect. That's how it was with the Bleeding Rock of Malin, anyway. If we're mistaken in that, of course, we'll take our investigation further. Still, you can stop worrying, Canon.'

'I hope so,' said Canon Dawson. 'It's been a terrible time.'

'You have the full backing of the hierarchy. It's not every priest who would have been so sober and vigilant in such a situation. Many might have gloried in the phenomenon and not considered the implications. And that would have caused no end of trouble for Mother Church. You know, I laughed when I heard about it all. It had all the hallmarks of the craziest things that happen in the West. But when I stopped to think about it I began to see the implications. Roger Casement back from the dead, parading as a holy saint! It's something that Mother Church doesn't need, Canon. Something we can well do without.'

The young priest was shifting about uncomfortably. 'I'm sorry, Father,' he said to him. 'That steel box must be crucifying you with its weight.'

'It's not that, Monsignor. The weight I can cope with. It's the heat that's martyring me.'

The monsignor touched the tube, felt the heat of it. 'We'd better get this under holy water as soon as we can. Come on, Father.'

They left the sacristy by the outside door and walked through the churchyard and along the road to the waiting van. The monsignor opened the back door of the van and the lid of the tank of holy water. Into this the priest dropped the tube. It hissed.

They bade farewell to Canon Dawson and drove through the quiet, car-clogged streets of the sleeping village of Ardfert. Then they turned right towards Tralee.

'Those two are late getting home,' said the monsignor, catching Boma and her mother in his headlights.

'They seem to be rowing. Drunk, I expect. What'll we do if we can't exorcize the flame?'

'Don't even think about it, Father. Still, there is some consolation either way.'

'How's that?'

'Well, if the canon's right and this is a trick of the Evil One it still proves the veracity of faith, doesn't it?'

'I don't get you.'

'Well, if the Devil exists, God exists.'

The priest opened his mouth to respond but noticed that condensation had suddenly turned his windscreen opaque. He reached for the fan switch, wiped the glass with his palm, but the condensation built up again immediately, blocking his view of the road ahead. 'The candle . . .' he began and drove straight at a bend in the road, hitting an oak tree in new leaf. The impact caused a small wave of near-boiling water from the tank at the back of the van to spill forward, to soak and scald the unconscious bodies half in and half out of the van.

'Did you hear something, Boma?' Paula asked.

'No, I didn't. Come home, Paula! I know it's difficult . . .'

But Paula continued to gaze along the road. 'The car that passed,' she said, 'I think it's crashed.'

Boma looked hard at the tail-lights of the car that had passed them, trying to make out whether the lights were retreating or were at a standstill. It was hard to tell. She took a few paces towards them. Paula caught up with her. 'It isn't moving along the road, is it?' She stared into the darkness. The red pinpricks of light stayed the same. 'No, that must have been the sound you heard. I'll run back to Ardfert, Paula. I'll phone the Gardai and an ambulance. You stay here.'

'No, Boma,' said Paula. 'You stay here and I'll go back. You mustn't rush anywhere in your state.'

'Don't disappear on me, will you?' Boma called.

The now-invisible figure of Paula waved back reassurance, though Boma could not see. She watched the tail-lights for a moment, then started walking towards them.

They were farther away than she had thought. They shone innocently enough and she began to wonder whether she would shortly arrive at an innocently parked car and have to explain a false-alarm call to the ambulance men.

'Hello?' Boma called. 'Hello? Are you all right?'

She stepped up to the passenger door, thrown open by the impact. She heard a groan. Not able to see anything, she reached out and touched wet cloth. She recoiled, thinking the wetness meant blood. Then she tried again. She heard a voice coming from the driver's side. 'An ambulance!' said the voice.

'There's one on its way!' she said, hoping that Paula would have telephoned by now. Then something made her look back into the darkness of the van. She saw a glowing rectangle of red light. It seemed to pulse brighter and brighter.

'Out of the road, Boma! Let me get at that candle!'

Boma stepped back and Roddie reached past the unconscious priest and lifted the glowing steel tube out of the car. 'But . . .' she began.

'Yes, I know. It's hot. How can I hold it? Another miracle.'

'What is it?'

'The paschal candle. These men – they're priests from Dublin – came to take it away out of Canon Dawson's sight. They think it's the work of the Devil. They're wrong there, but there's just no telling some people.'

'Is that the ambulance?' the priest asked.

Roddie placed the glowing tube down on the grass verge. 'No, Father. It isn't the ambulance. They're on their way. Be patient. Offer it up.'

'How's Monsignor Ryan?'

'He's out cold but he'll be all right. You too.' Then he turned to Boma. 'I was only here to see how you and Paula would sort things out. Did you manage to persuade her to stay?'

'I'm not sure. It's Brid.'

'Ah, yes. Brid. There was bound to be a problem there. Still, that'll all come out in the wash. Brid's got her hands full and she's got more to face. The important thing is that you and Paula sort things out. Brid'll be all right. I'll make sure she's all right.'

Boma heard the sirens from the Tralee direction. 'Did you enjoy your date with Eamonn McCann? I'm really warming to his imitation of "Sir Roger". He'll be better than the original shortly and I'll be surplus to requirements,' he said. 'Oh, yes! Before I forget. I don't want you buying any of that rubbish from Mrs Taggart's Fancy Goods Emporium. I've seen the statues she's doing of me. A terrible likeness. Why could the stupid woman not have had copies done of the statue in Ballyheige?'

And the apparition disappeared, taking the caged candle with him.

Tim left Chris in Dingle with Jimmy O'Keeffe. Though he had continued to improve, he showed no inclination to leave the friendly place he had stumbled upon.

'You go and when you find what you're looking for, come back and tell me. I'll be here.'

'While you're on those pills, you mustn't drink anything,' Tim said.

'When you decide to make a point, you really hammer it home,' Chris said. 'I'll be a good boy. You drop in on your old mother. Make everything right between you. I'd just be in the way.'

Though he would never have admitted it even to himself, Tim was relieved to be going. Promising to telephone when he got to Ardfert, he set off. Jimmy O'Keeffe and his wife Maureen joined Chris at the door of the pub to wave. He looked round as he turned the corner and saw Jimmy place his arm round Chris's shoulder, bothering him back into the house.

The car, hired in Swansea, was still on its first tank and Tim found himself resenting the wasted expense. They had paid a bonus for unlimited mileage but could easily have got away with the cheaper rate. By now, had things been different, they could have done Ardfert, and proceeded to Mayo, Sligo and Yeats country, where Chris had originally said he wanted to be.

Tim thought of his mother, of why he had let so much time slip by without visiting. He reasoned that it was not all his fault. It was not as if she had given him much encouragement. She wanted a visit when his face was ready to face the front again. He had not returned home for precisely the reasons that were building up in his head as he travelled back along the Dingle Peninsula towards Ardfert. The old secrets, the secrets between them that could not be spoken; the shame of staying in bed on a Sunday when she went out to mass; the questions about why he had not found himself the right woman, along with the promises by her friends that, were he to stay around, they would introduce him to a lovely woman from up the road . . . all the secrets that divide the generations. His mammy made him feel like a little child who has been a disappointment. A common enough problem, doubtless.

It all seemed so trivial from this perspective but even the triviality of it, weighed together with the time allowed to slip by, only increased the guilt. He tuned in the Irish-language station on the radio, trying to decipher it. There had been a time when he was a fluent Irish speaker, took a pride in his code, only known to a few members of the gang. But he'd let his knowledge rust over. Now, he only half understood the conversation. It was, he thought, about DIY.

Outside it was one of those wonderful days when mythical hero-clouds run in from the west to fight old battles. Out in the ocean, below the clouds, a black fuzz of mist showed where rain was falling.

Tralee was much busier than it had been when Chris and he had passed through it on their dash to Dingle. Tour buses, along with general traffic, clogged the streets. He decided not to take the most direct route into Ardfert but, instead, to skirt past it on a small inland road to Abbeydorney, and then come back down, via Rattoo, through Ballyheige. He knew that there would be little chance of being able to park the car in Ardfert itself, so thought he would try approaching Banna from the Ballyheige side.

Driving at last through Ballyheige, having seen that the old landscapes had come back, changed only by the addition of the odd bungalow, Tim noticed the statue of Roger Casement. No possibility of parking. A Garda officer stood in the middle of the street waving him on. But he had time to see the piles of flowers around the plinth of the statue, the crown of blue and yellow flowers around his head. Knots of people stood around as if waiting for something to happen. The bar across the road had had a new neon sign fitted, and recently too, for the workman's ladder was still up against the wall; the bar's owner looking up at it. *Roger's Place*, it read. Tim tried to think of the pub's old bar sign. Then he passed a horse-and-cart carrying it away. *Brennan's*. Yes, the times were changing, all right. The car-park down by the strand was chock-full of cars. People had pitched tents in the sand-dunes.

After an hour of stop-and-start driving he turned right towards the Strand. When he arrived there he saw how greatly changed it was, more changed than any place he had so far seen. True, the traffic contributed to this, but he was shocked by the new Banna Beach Hotel, by the bungalow-blight all about. He saw himself as a youth wandering this empty place, thinking of sex, thinking of elsewhere, thinking of sailing away for ever from the cold and the rain and the secrets. But Tim, who had ached for exile, got on with his exile elsewhere with barely a backward glance, had been counterbalanced by others who had seen this place as their ideal home – or, at any rate – holiday home.

He parked and locked the car, taking the last space in a car-park he had not ever suspected would be there. He took his shoulder-bag, the only luggage he had brought with him, and started walking over the dunes, towards the ocean. He felt like a ghost.

Cattle were grazing on the grass of the dunes. He was treated to a small electric shock as he tried to take a short cut stepping over a single wire. He deeply resented it. Then he was walking into a sheltered bowl of hog-back grass. He soldiered up the hill, covering his eyes against sand whipped up by eddies of ecscaping wind. He reached the top and the full force of the wind hit him. He wondered about going back to the car, retracing his steps all the way to the smiling safety of O'Keeffe's. He could make up a quick visit, even talk of his old mammy's home-made seed cake. Oh, he could have lied his way out of it until he even believed the lie himself. But he stepped down onto the sand and walked along it towards the place where Roger Casement had landed.

As a child he had never been sure of exactly where that was. Then the monument was erected on the far side of the dunes that was supposed to be adjacent to the exact landing-place. Today, however, he did not need to guess. A group of people, perhaps twenty of them, was standing on the ocean's edge. Tim approached them.

Two young men were filling test tubes with sand at the place, stoppering them and placing them in neat rows. A group of five women were saying the rosary on their knees, facing out towards America, while another group of men were stripping off clumsily under grey towels. As Tim approached, the first crossed himself and ran into the penitential ocean, followed by his companions. They whooped and cried out. Their white bodies in the blue ocean matched the mythic clouds against the sky. Then they joined hands in a circle and one, two, three, ducked themselves under the water. While all this was going on one young man, oblivious to the activity going on around him, picked up flat stones which he spun into the calm between the breakers, counting the bounces.

Tim did not hang about. He made his way back over the dunes to the track that led around to McKenna's Fort. Cars everywhere. A woman from one of the bungalows, washing blowing on the clothes-line behind her, had set up a tea-stand. He ordered a cup of tea from her, which she gave him in a polystyrene cup. The tea came out of the Thermos, ready-milked. He paid a pound, without argument, and a handful of cream biscuits was pressed into his hand.

'It's busy,' he said.

'Isn't it great?' she said. 'It's wonderful we've got Sir Roger back among us.'

'You're sure, are you?'

She gave him an odd look, a look he misinterpreted. 'Lots of miracles,' she said. She nodded to him. 'And you're one of them, Tim McCarthy!'

Tim tried to place her, but couldn't.

'You've forgotten me, haven't you? There goes another of the old myths. They always said that as a teacher I might not get rich but I'd be remembered by generations of children. Wrong again.'

'Miss Laverty, is it?' he said, hearing his voice Irish.

'It was. It's Mrs Healey now. I married Joey Healey who had that chicken place on the Tralee Road. We came here for a bit of peace and quiet.'

'I'm sorry I didn't know you at first. It's been a long time.'

'Have you been to see your mammy?'

'I'm on my way there now.'

'You choose your time well, don't you? The world and his wife are coming to Ardfert.'

'How is Mammy?'

'Rushed off her feet. You'll see soon enough.'

'I already know. I've had to leave my car at the other end of the Strand.'

She regarded him. 'It's been a long time, Tim,' she said.

'I know. Too long.'

'Would you do me a favour?'

'I would, of course.'

'When you come back to collect your car, could you bring me a few things from Ardfert? I'll give you a list. I'm stranded here with all the traffic. McKenna's Fort is madness.'

He felt pleased to be of use. It felt like old times. He was already seeing himself getting back into his mammy's good books by letting it slip out that he was delivering groceries to his old teacher. It wasn't much but, he reckoned, he needed all the help he could get. And if that meant letting his left hand know what his right hand was doing, well it always had anyway.

Miss Laverty – he had forgotten her married name – went off into the bungalow and returned with a list. 'I had a thought inside,' she said. 'You may find Brid's full up and can't put you up. If that happens, there's always a bed here.'

He thanked her. 'Are you in a hurry for these?'

'No great hurry, but I'll be sending out an SOS in a day or two.'

'I'll make sure to get them to you tomorrow,' he said. 'Thank you for the offer. I may take you up on it if Mammy's full up.'

She looked at him. 'It's nice to see you back. The Lost Sheep's always the one we like to see. Stop in at the church and say one for me.'

'I will,' he said.

He did not even think to stop at McKenna's Fort on his way into Ardfert. The cars, the crowds of people, the mud, were sufficient to make him walk straight past. The churchyard was crowded too, but he braved the crowds to go inside. People were kneeling all around the church. He bobbed before the altar, like a man before royalty he's not sure he approves of, went into an empty row and sat himself down. He found himself saying a prayer for Chris, then stopped himself. Then repeated it. After all, Chris wasn't dead yet.

Canon Dawson came out of the sacristy. He did not seem to have changed much. He walked to the centre of the church, genuflected and walked back up the aisle. He looked daggers at the praying people to right and left. Tim bowed his head to avoid eye-contact, knowing exactly what Canon Dawson was making of all the activity.

It took him some time to fight his way along the clogged pavements, past the Sir Roger Casement Hotel, the Roger Casement Fancy Goods Emporium, its window full to bursting with tacky souvenirs of Casement, turning left on to his street. He came to the door of his mammy's house. Two women came out. He let them pass, hesitated, said a prayer, and went inside.

Okondo's wife had found the burning paschal candle outside the family dwelling that morning. She had taken it inside to her husband. He looked up from his carving. 'Who left it here, Miriam? Did you see?' Okondo asked.

'I saw nobody,' Miriam replied.

'Such a big candle!' Okondo said. 'It will help me to work after darkness. But snuff it out for now. We do not want to waste it.'

'Perhaps one of the visitors has brought it for you,' Miriam observed, wetting her thumb and forefinger, pinching the flame to extinguish it. 'Ay!' She pulled her hand away, sucked her fingers. 'It has burnt me.'

'I am sorry,' said Okondo.

Miriam took an enamel plate and laid it over the flame. The candle-flame reared up. 'What is this, Okondo?' she asked. 'The flame will not go out.'

'Leave it here with me, Miriam. I will do it. The sun is not yet high. The candle can help me.'

Still sucking her fingers, Miriam laid the candle on a brick in the corner by Okondo. She left.

At once Okondo got up, tried to put out the flame. He had as little success as his wife had had. He sat back down. 'So, flame,' he said, 'you do not want to be sent away. You want to stay with me.'

He continued with his carving. From time to time he looked up at the burning candle. It did not seem to have burnt down at all.

In the evening the children came home from school. They saw the candle and settled down to their homework in the pool of light it threw out. Quite late, Mbunza pointed out that the candle had not lessened.

'No, son. I know that. We shall see what happens. But none of you must speak about this. Do not tell anyone.'

Then, just before he closed his eyes to sleep, he looked at the flame. It caught the face of the man he was carving out of the ebony wood. When he closed his eyes he could see the flame echoing behind his lids along with the memory of the man, whose image he was trying to record.

The following morning, the candle was still burning. It had not burnt down even a centimetre. Okondo and his family took it to themselves.

Brid looked at her son waiting his turn behind the counter. An American tourist had placed a map of Ireland on the counter and was waiting for her to direct him to a place where there might be a chance of finding accommodation.

'It's worse than the Eurovision Song Contest!' a woman in a Lourdes headscarf, holding a Battenberg cake, was telling the American.

'Abbeydorney, you could try that,' Brid said, trying to think, looking thoughtfully down at the blur of the map in front of her.

'No chance there,' said the woman. 'Try Listowel.'

'There's nothing in Listowel,' said a man behind the woman in the queue.

'Make for Limerick, so,' said Brid.

'That's one hell of a way,' said the American, doubtfully.

Brid looked up at him, smiled and thought, *Get out of my light! I've got too much to think about to be bothering with you!* and said, 'You could try Killarney.'

'We've just done Killarney,' said the American, making no move to pick up the map.

Brid took up the map and folded it, still restraining her eyes from looking over the heads of the customers to Tim.

'You could try Dingle. I think that's away from all the fuss,' Tim said.

Brid tried not to look up but could not stop herself. Tim returned her gaze, smiled.

'Hello, Mammy,' he said.

The American thanked Brid and opened his map, holding it out as if he wanted to wrap Tim in it. 'Dingle, you say? Can you show me the route?'

Tim retreated, still looking at Brid, over to the far end of the shop. She followed him with her eyes. *Why now? Why not some other time? Or no time at all? Haven't I got enough on my plate as it is?* She found the Battenberg cake in front of her and wondered how it had been made, who had ever had the spare time or inclination to think up such a queer confection. She took the money and served the next customer.

Tim was opening the door to the American, wishing him a good trip. She watched him as she weighed out wine gums, thought of the book in the drawer. He did not return to the queue, but waited, leaning against the far counter they never used, the counter where he had once played shop himself, selling little balls of soda bread, conkers and holy pictures.

When the shop had finally emptied he came over to her, smiling shyly.

'Why didn't you tell me?' she asked.

'I thought I'd make it a surprise.'

'I'm too old for all these surprises.'

'You're looking well.'

'No thanks to you. You've been the death of me.'

'I wrote. I know it's been a long time but . . . well, you know . . .'

Brid wanted to say, *So why did you? Why now? Why, when I've got my hands, my head and my heart full? Why now?* But she nodded to Tim, lifted the counter and walked through. He stepped forward a pace to kiss her but she dodged him, making across the shop to the parlour entrance. 'You'd better come through,' she said.

In the parlour sat Boma and Paula. They stopped speaking when Brid came in, followed by Tim.

'I've a visitor. This is Tim,' Brid said. A hesitation. 'My son.'

Tim nodded to Boma and Paula, went over and shook their hands

208

while Brid checked Stanley, shook the kettle. 'You need filling,' she told it.

'So you're Brid's son!' said Boma. 'You're so tall.'

'Daddy was the tall one,' Tim said. 'Are you staying here?'

'You could say that.'

Tim did not know how to proceed. He looked at the spare armchair in front of Stanley but did not even think of sitting down.

'Sit down!' Paula said. 'Have you come far?'

'No. Not today. From Dingle. Where are you from, Paula?'

'Dublin.'

'On holiday?'

She looked at Boma. 'A sort of holiday,' and Tim saw the conspiratorial smile between them, wondered about their relationship.

Brid came back into the parlour with the tea things. Boma got up to help her, took the tray.

The shop-bell sounded. Brid looked towards it, wanting to answer the summons, to take herself out of the situation. 'Don't you move!' Boma said. 'Today's special. I'll see to the shop.'

She left them, ignoring Brid's protests.

Tim watched her go, noticed her swelling pregnancy for the first time, noticed too the easy way she had, a much easier way than any bed-and-breakfast guest.

Brid saw Tim's look. 'She's a sweet soul,' she said, and looked over at Paula.

Paula smiled back.

Brid poured the tea, fetched a tin of biscuits from the dresser.

'So you're Brid's son!' Paula said.

'Yes,' Tim replied. 'I think I've turned up at a bad time.'

Paula waited for Brid to say something, but she was looking hard into the biscuit tin. 'Not at all!' she said. 'You've come back at an interesting time for Ardfert, that's for sure.'

'I've heard the stories. I had to leave the car at the far end of Banna Strand. On the walk in, some people were swimming in the sea, others were praying at the spot where Casement landed. I'd heard stories before I came, but this is amazing.'

'You're lost your Kerry accent,' Paula said.

'He has,' Brid nodded. 'And that's not all he's lost.' She handed a cup of tea to Paula, followed by the biscuit tin.

'Mammy . . .' Tim began. Then he looked over at Paula, who was looking at Brid.

'I wonder if Boma needs help in the shop,' Paula said, sensing the atmosphere.

'No,' Brid said, 'she doesn't.'

'How long are you staying?' Paula asked Tim.

'I'm not sure. I came over with a friend. He took ill and I've left him in Dingle.'

'But you'll be staying for a few days, won't you?'

Tim looked at Brid. 'I don't know . . .' Then he shrugged at Paula.

'Do you know how long this one's been away?' Brid asked.

Paula shook her head.

'Five years.'

'It's a long time,' she said, smiling at Tim, thinking of the way her own time had passed by, a day at a time, until here she was an old woman meeting her grown daughter. And now, from this perspective, she wondered how she could have let each of those days go by without performing the simple act of trying harder to get back in touch. Why had she not persisted with the social workers, pounded them with enquiries until their dogmatism wilted? 'Still, you're here now,' she said, both to Tim and Brid, and to herself. 'Brid, I think I'd better tell Tim what Boma and I are doing here.'

Brid shrugged, went back to gazing into the depths of the biscuit tin as Paula recounted everything that had happened. 'Anyway, there you have it, Tim,' Paula said. 'When I got here I found that Boma and your mammy were getting on great guns. I've been wondering why I came back, to tell you the truth. Just yesterday I tried to leave but Boma fetched me back. What I want to say is that I understand how you're feeling ill at ease, and to explain why the situation you've landed up in seems to be odd.'

Tim nodded. 'Thanks,' he said to Paula. 'It's a great story.' He looked over to Brid. 'I'm happy for you. But the rift between Mammy and me goes back a long way. It's to do with the Church and old guilts. All the old chestnuts. I've tried to talk to her about it, but I haven't managed it.'

Brid looked on stonily.

Boma appeared from behind the door. 'Brid, will you come through for a minute?' she asked.

Brid put her cup down on the tray and, without looking at either Tim or Paula, left the room for the relief of the shop.

Paula watched her go. Then she said to Tim, 'It's an old story, isn't it? Yours and mine both. I'm in mourning for the years of wickedly wasted time. I'm at an age when I should be settling down in an armchair like this one to remember the events of my life, and all the time the real event has been growing up elsewhere, waiting to come to me and present me with a huge slab of unfinished business. And the past pales into nothing. The whole of my life seems a dream and the reality of Boma and the child she'll be having soon is all there is. I'm on holiday from my convent but I actually don't know if I'll be going back, though what I will do I don't have the slightest idea.'

Tim didn't say anything. He felt fathoms out of his depth.

'You must wonder what you've landed into. I can hardly believe I'm saying all this to you. I've only known you a few minutes. But we've been in the middle of such strange events here that we've come to see them as everyday. And why would we delay in getting down to business? There is, for me anyway, so little time!'

Tim smiled wanly and shuffled uncomfortably in his seat.

11

BRID FOUND BOMA STANDING IN AN EMPTY SHOP. SHE WAS HOLDING a flat packet, wrapped up in brown paper and string.

'What's the matter, Boma? Who else has come in to moither us?' Brid asked.

'I've had Roddie in the shop.'

Brid's stern expression softened. 'You did? How was he?'

'Fine, but rushed as usual. You know how he gets. It was odd, Brid. He asked if you had a book he could borrow. He went straight to your drawer and took out that one you were reading about the missions. "This'll do," he said. "Tell Brid I took it. She'll understand." Then he gave me this.' Boma handed Brid the packet. ' "To even things out," he said.'

Brid took the packet from Boma. 'You shouldn't have let him take that book, Boma. It wasn't suitable at all. It was disgusting. Left by himself . . .' she gestured with her thumb, '. . . in there.'

'He seemed to know exactly what he wanted, Brid.'

'Well, he'll realize his mistake soon enough. The same as I did. It was full of filthy, degenerate things, Boma. I . . .' She looked at the package. 'Roddie gave you this for me?' she asked, forgetting for a moment Tim's book.

'He did. Open it, why don't you? You never know, it might sort everything out.'

'Not just yet, Boma. I can't concentrate at the moment. There's too much going on. It's all fingers and thumbs pressing in on my poor brain. Now what am I going to do about that boy?'

'If you don't know, I can't tell you, Brid. Do you remember how you were when I showed up on your doorstep? Isn't that how you always are?'

Brid scowled down at her slippers. 'You don't know a quarter of it, Boma.' She became rapt in reverie for a long moment, then turned to Boma. 'It's him turning up now that I've got my hands full. But when I was all on my ownsome, with just a couple of old biddies dropping in, I never saw even his dust. This despite letters pleading with him to pay a call. It's so typical of him, Boma. He lands in just at the wrong time. He's always had a knack for it. I was just getting used to Sister Paula – your mam – being here. Well, praying for the resignation. And now this! I've a mind to send him back to Dingle.'

Boma looked at Brid. 'I tell you what,' she said. 'I'll double up with Paula and you can put Tim in the downstairs room. I think what you need is a rest from everything. Paula and me'll look after Tim for a few hours. We'll shut the shop. How does that sound?'

'I don't know . . .' Brid said.

Boma turned the sign to 'Closed' and bolted the shop door. 'Go on, up the stairs,' she said to Brid.

Brid saw Boma looking at the packet hungrily. Boma saw her seeing her and laughed: 'You're right, I can't wait to know what's in it.'

Brid held the packet out. 'You take it, so.'

'No, Roddie left it for you. Go on. Bed.'

Boma went back into the parlour. 'Is there any tea?' she asked.

'Where's Brid?' Paula asked.

'She's gone to bed for a bit of a snooze. She's worn out.' Boma looked at Tim. 'I think that partly explains the lukewarm reception you got, Tim.'

'We've been running the poor woman ragged,' Paula said. 'I don't know how she's managed to put up with us. I've been telling Tim about us, Boma.'

'You have? I think you probably think I'm a cuckoo in the nest, Tim. But what we'll do is this: I'll move out of my room. I haven't much stuff – and it's mostly yours and your mammy's anyway. There's another bed in Paula's room.'

'Are you sure?' Tim asked. 'It might be better if I went back to Dingle.'

Boma looked at Paula. 'Everyone's been saying they ought to go. No, join the party, Tim. It's a rare old set-up you've stepped into. Your mother's a grand woman.'

'How did you meet?'

'We were introduced by an old friend of hers,' Boma said. 'I'm not sure you're ready for the details. What about you? What do you do?'

'I teach history,' Tim replied.

'So you know all about Sir Roger Casement?'

Tim did not reply, just raised his arms, wafted them about his head as if clearing away flies.

'I know,' said Boma. 'More tea?'

Tim had been greatly relieved to find Boma and her mother waiting for him in the parlour. Before he saw them he had been ready to make a bolt for it.

He knew that his mammy always took consolation from both the shop and the bed-and-breakfast blow-ins. They provided her with interest and company. But he would never have been able to imagine such a scenario. After Mammy retreated to her bed – almost as strange as anything he was to hear – Boma started telling him chapter and verse of how she had arrived at the door. It was a tale not that much dissimilar from the one the Power's man had told Chris and Tim. When she started talking about Roddie as if it was someone he should know, he let it go at first. He was, perhaps, a bit ashamed to admit his ignorance. He was, he knew well enough, already cast as the prodigal son. He did not want to appear more wicked and uncaring than he already appeared. This Roddie, he thought, must be one more person who had slipped his mind. But then Boma said that Mammy had not been able to see this Roddie and he couldn't let that pass.

'How do you mean, "she couldn't see him"?' he asked.

'Only I was able to see him. He said that was how it had to be. Don't ask me why.'

Of course, he questioned her further. Roger Casement had come back, she said. He had chosen to bring her to Mammy's because she had been kind to him. And she told him about the medal, a story he had not heard before, but which went some considerable way to explaining Mammy's devotion to Sir Roger. He wondered why she had never told him that story. But in a way he was pleased that the secrets did not go in only the one direction.

Sister Paula sat the while listening serenely as if it were all a commonplace.

'I don't believe this!' Tim said.

They looked at him as though he were a Martian. Then Boma collected herself.

'Yes,' she said. 'I keep forgetting you've only just arrived. We've grown used to it. It's become hard for us to remember how difficult it is for other people.'

He looked to Paula for help. 'Don't look at me!' she said. 'But I believe it. Every last jot and tittle. And I'll tell you why. I was a missionary in Boma, where Roger Casement was stationed. When he was shown on the video in the Congo, it was in Boma and I knew the clinic. And, of course, here I am and there have been all sorts of miraculous events taking place in Ardfert. I have absolutely no trouble at all with it. You, on the other hand, have come here cold.'

'I ought,' Tim said, 'to have been prepared. Jimmy O'Keeffe, he's our landlord in Dingle, has been filling us in on everything since we got there. To tell you the truth, it's been making it harder for me to come back.'

'Why?'

'It's so damned Irish,' he said.

'Ah . . .' Paula said.

'I mean, where would we be without our angels and our devotions and our wild Celtic beliefs in the holy well, the holy monk, the Holy Souls?'

'Where?'

'In the real world, that's where,' he said.

'Is that where you are?'

He thought about that. 'No, I don't think so. I'm stuck somewhere in between. I keep thinking of a cartoon figure doing the splits across a widening crevasse or between Fishguard and Rosslare. But I do admire the people who are realistic, who face life with a cold, a pessimistic, eye. Expecting nothing. I think that takes guts.'

'And that's what you want for Ireland?' Paula asked. 'If you take away our spiritual imagination, our mythology, you take away something precious. Maybe everything we've got.'

'That spirituality is what's kept me away from Mammy for five years and a good deal longer than that. That spirituality has cut me off from her. The easy natural love of mother for son is alloyed by her perception of me as a wicked sinner with a maggoty soul. She prays for me to return to Mother Church, just cannot accept that a fellow has his own lights, must follow his own star.'

'And where has your star brought you to?'

Tim thought about that and didn't much like what he saw. 'Mind your own business,' he said.

'I'm sorry,' she said.

'No, I'm sorry. It's a fair question. It's brought me nowhere that's worth the journey. I live with the Ghost of God, a withdrawing roar of worship. Friends think I'm Catholic. I occasionally think so too.'

'So maybe your mammy's prayers are working.'

He laughed, then stopped, seeing himself. 'Who knows? But I just feel embarrassed around here. A prodigal surrounded by good people. It's not the nicest feeling in the world.'

'No, she said. 'Still, we're all prodigals.'

He wanted to ask her what she knew about it. Then he remembered Miss Laverty and her request for groceries.

'By the way, I've promised to take some groceries to a friend of Mammy's at Banna. She's stuck there. I'll raid the shop, shall I?'

Paula looked at him oddly. 'It's your house,' she said. 'Are you walking all the way there?'

'It'll do me good,' he said.

He saw Paula smiling.

'I'll come with you,' Boma said.

'You will not,' said Paula. 'You and the baby will have a little lie-down.'

Canon Dawson returned from visiting the two priests in the Tralee hospital. They were, the sisters said, quite comfortable. The older priest, however, had been delirious through the night and kept shouting about a candle. Also, both had scalds as if a pan of boiling water had been upset over them. Could the canon think what could have caused them?

Canon Dawson couldn't.

'A lot of strange things coming out of Ardfert, so there are, Canon. The sisters are all aching to be getting over there but we've been rushed off our feet,' said Sister de Porres.

'I'd stay away if I were you, Sister.'

'We have to, Canon,' said Sister de Porres. 'There's no way round it. The events in Ardfert have attracted sick people from all over Ireland and beyond. A lot of them land on our doorstep in a bad way.'

Canon Dawson nodded and moved towards the door.

'We have one of our sisters in Ardfert at the moment. Sister Paula Lyons from Dublin. She's been there a while and the sisters are worrying about her. So maybe I'll go there to enquire about her.' She stopped. 'That'd be all right, wouldn't it, Canon?'

'Perfectly. Just stay away from all the nonsense, Sister.'

On the way back to Ardfert Canon Dawson called in at the garage where the wrecked car had been taken and asked about the tube containing the candle. The mechanic told him that nothing had been found, apart from an empty water-tank.

Back at the presbytery he telephoned the Garda, asking who had reported news of the crash.

'A lady by the name of Lyons, who gave her address as McCarthy's Bed & Breakfast,' the officer said.

His suspicions aroused, Canon Dawson decided to take the bull by the horns. He walked through Ardfert towards McCarthy's B & B, determined to find out for himself what had happened.

The crowds in the street were as bad as ever, perhaps worse. He stopped at the window of Mrs Taggart's Fancy Goods Emporium, frowned at the lines of statues on display, the rows of replica memorials, the smiling pictures of Roger Casement and, muttering to himself, carried on down the main street.

The shop door of the b & b was locked. Canon Dawson went to the summer door and knocked.

Paula answered the door.

'Good-evening,' said Canon Dawson.

'Good-evening, Father,' Paula replied.

'I'm Canon Dawson. May I come in for a moment?'

'Of course you can. Brid's in bed, I'm afraid. I'm one of her guests.'

She led the canon through the shop to the parlour. 'It's you I want to see, I think,' he said.

'Me?'

'Yes. You see . . .'

'Have a seat, Canon.'

Canon Dawson sat down in the easy chair to the left of Stanley.

'Can I get you a cup of tea? Or something stronger?'

'No, I can't stay long. Your name is Lyons. Am I correct?'

'You are.'

'And you witnessed an accident the other night on the Tralee Road?'

'Yes, I did. I was with Boma, another guest here. I telephoned the Garda. Are the poor men all right?'

'They're a bit cut about, but the sisters say they're on the mend. What I wanted to ask was, did you notice anything in the back of the van? We're missing a large stainless-steel tube.'

'No. I can't help you there, Canon. To tell you the truth it was Boma who reached the scene of the accident. But she's in bed.'

'She's still here, is she?' the canon asked.

'She is. We've a full house here, Canon. Tim, Brid's only son, came back on a visit just this afternoon.'

Canon Dawson thought for a moment. 'I remember Tim. He's back, is he? He's not darkened my door in years. He used to be a grand altar-server. Grand. Brid'll be pleased.'

'I think everything's been a bit much for her. She took to her bed a couple of hours ago. It's been a busy time for a woman her age.'

Canon Dawson nodded. 'Could I change my mind? I'd like a drink.'

Paula, flustered, wondering now whether she had the right to raid the drinks cupboard, got up to hunt around for a glass.

'On holiday, are you?' asked Canon Dawson.

'I am,' Paula said. 'There's sherry or whiskey.'

Canon Dawson looked at his watch for form's sake. 'Whiskey. Just an inch, Mrs Lyons.'

'Miss,' said Paula. She sat down opposite Canon Dawson.

'How long have you been staying in Ardfert?'

'About a week.'

'I haven't seen you at mass.'

'You haven't? I've been there most days. With Brid. I was there the day you had trouble with the paschal candle. Did you ever manage to put it out?'

'I'd prefer not to talk about it,' said Canon Dawson. 'I take a very dim view of what's been happening here.'

'Do you? You don't find it exciting?'

'I do not. It confirms my faith in the Devil, so it does. By their fruits you shall know them, Miss Lyons. And these so-called apparitions and miracles have brought all kinds of disgraceful things out of the woodwork. Did you see the *Irish Independent* today?'

'I didn't.'

'Buses full of homosexuals from every corner of Ireland and beyond are descending on the place. They've come on pilgrimage to see their very own saint! No, I was right to be sceptical, Miss Lyons.'

'But the candle cured Mags Devlin!'

'I have no further comment to make, Miss Lyons,' said Canon Dawson.

They sat uncomfortably silent for a long moment.

'The priests who were in the accident are at the Hospital of the Flaming Heart in Tralee,' said Canon Dawson at last.

'Oh, yes?'

'One of the nursing sisters mentioned a nun of her order who had gone missing. Her name was, if I am not mistaken, Sister Paula Lyons. You aren't her, are you, Miss Lyons?'

'No,' said Paula.

'No,' repeated Canon Dawson, draining his glass. 'I just thought I'd ask.'

'Why not?' Paula said, aware that for the first time in her life she had lied to a priest. What did it signify? Was she trying to get her own back for what she considered to be the wrong advice a long-gone priest had given her; trying to make apparent the sort of independence of thought that had been growing inside for decades? 'Another whiskey, Canon?' she asked.

'Just a little. That woman . . . what's-her-name . . . she's showing no sign of leaving?'

Paula was pouring the whiskey. She allowed more than intended to slide into the glass. 'Boma, you mean? No, Canon, I think she's staying put. Brid's really taken to her.'

'You know, do you, it was that woman, Boma, who started all this nonsense off, Miss Lyons?' Paula handed the canon his drink. 'Thank you, Miss Lyons. Yes, if that woman hadn't come along none of this would have got going at all. I think she's in cahoots with some locals who want to put Ardfert and Ballyheige on the pilgrimage route around Holy Ireland. You can see it all around you, Miss Lyons. The devotional objects, the postcards. They didn't just appear from nowhere, you know. All the nonsense has careful planning behind it.'

'Boma was with me when the accident happened to those two priests. They may owe their lives to her,' Paula said, with what she hoped was a hard edge in her voice.

'Oh, she was, was she? And did she phone the Garda with you? They gave me your name. They didn't mention her.'

'No,' Paula replied. 'Boma went to the van. She's pregnant, as you've probably noticed. It was too far for her to go to the telephone.'

'So while you were telephoning the Garda, this Boma was alone at the van?'

'Yes. Why do you ask, Canon?'

'It all fits, that's why. Miss Lyons, those two priests had been sent from Dublin to remove the paschal candle from my church both to get it away from all that's been happening in Ardfert and to test the flame, perhaps to exorcize it. They put the candle into a big tube – not the sort of thing that would just up and roll away from an accident – and loaded it into their van. But it has not been seen since the crash.'

'And you're trying to say that Boma took it, are you?'

'Knowing what I know about that hussy I think it's highly likely.' Canon Dawson drained his glass, laughed into it. 'Highly likely.'

'Canon,' Paula said, 'the paschal candle is a large item. If Boma had taken it, I'd have seen it. The Garda brought me to the crashed van and ran Boma and myself home. She had no candle, I can assure you of that.'

'But didn't I just say that she was in cahoots with accomplices? You wait, Miss Lyons, that candle will show up in the next day or two.'

'As in many other matters, you are wrong, Canon. That *hussy*, as you call her, by chance happens to be my daughter. Now, if you'll forgive me, I must ask you to leave.'

Canon Dawson, as unused to being spoken to in that manner as Paula was in the speaking, sat on, nonplussed.

'Either you go, or I go,' Paula said. She opened the door and saw Canon Dawson out of the summer door, slamming it hard after him.

The canon was a worried man as he walked back to the presbytery to make his own dinner. He passed the church, stopping to seek consolation from the imposing black bulk of it finely etched against the clear navy-blue sky. Then, instead of going straight into the presbytery, he decided to walk around the church, just to check. He tried all the doors. Father Devenish had locked up for the night. Then, around the back of the church, he noticed a light coming from the small window of the sacristy storeroom. He ran around to the main door of the church, unlocked it, ran into the church, switched on all the lights. He sought out the sacristy keys as he strode down the aisle, forgetting in his anxiety to genuflect, unlocked the storeroom and was confronted with the replacement paschal candle, lit, the flame burning straight in the still air. He stepped over to it, removed it from the candle-holder and blew all his pent-up rage over it. The flame burnt steadily. He tried again and again, but he knew the task was hopeless.

Mrs Grogan and Mrs Taggart were doing some stocktaking in the Roger Casement Fancy Goods Emporium. Mrs Taggart, wearing the red spectacles everyone told her had been a mistake and which she only ever wore indoors for close work, was perusing till receipts, while Mrs Grogan, like a stern warder at lock-up, was head-counting the statues of Roger Casement standing in rows around the shop.

'They're shifting nicely. Very nicely indeed, Mrs Taggart,' said Mrs Grogan, completing the count.

'We've not sold a single one of the divine size yet, Mrs Grogan.'

Mrs Grogan surveyed her partner. 'Trust you to be negative, Mrs Taggart. I ought to send you on a weekend course at the Tralee Motel. To tell you God's honest truth, Mrs Taggart, I'm surprised you ever got yourself into retail in the first place. It's no place for pessimists. Look it, we've sold almost all the souvenir size, a good chunk of the other sizes too. How much did you take today?'

'About four thousand pounds, Mrs Taggart.'

'There! You see! We're well on the way to coming out even. Everything from now on will be pure profit. I'm coining it at the hotel. And you're wrong to say you haven't sold a divine size. I'll take one off your hands. At cost price, of course.'

'There'll still be four left, though.'

'You're off again, are you? Look, Mrs Taggart, I have plans. You should know that you'd be able to trust me by now. And you can, Mrs Taggart, you can.'

'What sort of plans?'

'A procession! A procession through the streets of Ardfert, down to Banna Strand and back to where we started. We'll stop the traffic completely! We'll have a band playing all Sir Roger's favourites and a sign saying, *Sponsored by The Sir Roger Casement Fancy Goods Emporium*. And you'll see, Mrs Taggart, after the procession they'll all be in to buy their Sir Roger Casement mementos.'

'Has Canon Dawson changed his mind about the apparitions?'

Mrs Grogan scowled. 'There'll be no bringing him into this. Holy Mother Church never has anything to do with miracles until the whole thing's over and done with. They're a sceptical lot all right. We don't need to have any truck with the Church, Mrs Taggart. As usual, it's the pious laity that shows the way forward. No, this will be a do-it-yourself procession. Folks that don't like it don't have to join in. But lots will, Mrs Taggart! Lots will! You mark my words.'

'You've not been wrong before, that's true,' said Mrs Taggart.

'And I won't be wrong this time. Get your pen out, Mrs Taggart.'

Mrs Taggart did so.

'Write! Mrs Taggart!'

Mrs Taggart poised her pen over her pad.

'Saturday next. A procession . . . in honour of Sir Roger Casement . . . The Joe Burns Band . . . will lead us through Ardfert . . . to Banna Strand . . . All of Sir Roger's favourite songs and hymns . . . will be sung . . . Bring a packed lunch . . . Meet outside The Sir Roger Casement . . . Fancy Goods Emporium . . . on Ardfert's main street . . . Eleven a.m. sharp . . . Have you got that, Mrs Taggart?'

'I have.'

'Give it over to me,' said Mrs Grogan. She perused the paper. 'There's a "u" in favourite, if I'm not born yesterday. Yes, otherwise it's all right. Ten on ten, Mrs Taggart. But . . .' She looked hard at the notice. 'I wonder if it's enough? I know. At the start write in capitals, HONOUR ARDFERT'S OWN SAINT! THANK HIM FOR THE MIRACLES!'

Mrs Taggart did so.

'Now get this off to the printer. Tell him it's a rush job!'

'I will,' said Mrs Taggart. 'We need some more of those candles, too, the miniature paschal ones.'

'Are the women ready?' Mrs Grogan asked.

'Gasping,' said Mrs Taggart. 'They need the work.'

Eamonn McCann dithered in the dark outside McCarthy's Shop, wondering what to do. He had taken two pints of Guinness at the pub down the road. Without them he did not think he would have got this far. He surveyed the closed door, the darkness behind the display windows. There was no knocker, no sign of life. He went to the side door. He reached out, but his courage failed him.

Angry with himself, with this behaviour so typical of him, he retreated. He crossed the road towards the ruins of Ardfert Cathedral, stopped and lit a cigarette. He smoked it leaning on the wall, staring at the looming shapes of cross and roofless building against the black night sky.

She wouldn't think much of him, a poor impersonation of a hero. He had no idea how to please her, though he had spent his whole life trying to please everyone; juggling smiles to keep them all airborne. That had been partly why he had so readily agreed to bring Boma to talk to Jack. He had, he could see now, made Boma uncomfortable. There she was, expecting a date, and he had presented her instead with a proposition. Then, at the end, he couldn't run her home. Why would she want anything to do with him? There was a whiff of failed vocation about him. Everyone saw it straight off. His parents still expected him to end up going off for a second try. He looked through the adverts in the Catholic papers himself, hoping that one would catch his eye, would make him feel something, would spark him again. But they were all looking for young men, not shambling failures heeling forty. And shambling failures who no longer believed a word of it.

He spun his spent cigarette off into the graveyard.

He wondered why Boma filled his thoughts. He tried to stop wondering. He liked the look of her, her colour, her difference. He liked the baby growing inside her, was only dimly curious about the father. As he had always imagined a ready-made route to heaven for himself, so now the idea of taking care of a child, a child who would be his and yet not his – depending on him, yet not dependent on his own abilities to create – was attractive to him. It was where his devotion to St Joseph had brought him.

'Go and ask her out,' he told himself. 'She can only say no.'

Eamonn knocked at the summer door. He turned down the collar on his jacket, smoothed his hair down.

Brid came to the door and peered at him.

'Mrs McCarthy. Remember me?' he asked.

'I do,' said Brid. 'It's Sir Roger.'

'I'm off duty. I was wondering, is Boma in?'

'She is.'

Brid made no move to fetch Boma or let him in. He shuffled, in agony.

'It's just that me and some of the lads are at the bar down the road. They've got a fiddler in and I was wondering . . .'

'You want to take Boma, do you?'

'If she'd like. I mean, if she's not busy.'

'I'm not invited too, I suppose.'

'Well, if you'd like, Mrs McCarthy . . .'

She gave him a sideways look. 'I'll go and see,' she said.

She left him there in his agony. He waited, fully expecting that Brid would come back, shaking her head. He rummaged for a cigarette to hide his embarrassment behind.

Boma saw him there, shuffling. Her heart went out to him. He told her he was sorry to be calling without phoning.

'Thanks for thinking of me. I'll get my coat. It's just what I need.'

Inside the bar the fiddler was playing. Eamonn found them two stools in the corner, away from his friends. He fetched her a stout.

'I'm sorry about the other night.'

'It was a change for me to get out,' she said. 'I don't much, you know.'

'Yes, but that makes it worse,' he said.

'You're so tortured, so you are,' she said. 'Are you always like this?'

'Yes,' he said. 'I am. Sorry.'

'You mustn't go around apologizing all the time,' Boma said.

'No,' he said. 'A lot of people tell me that. Sorry.'

She smiled. He wondered why. 'How's business?'

'Great,' he said. 'There's never a free moment. People are full of questions. I'm still studying everything I can find about Sir Roger. I'm better at it than I was when you came in, even if I do say so myself.'

'The fiddler's good,' she said.

'Yes, he gets plenty of work.'

They clapped the man and he started into a reel, dancing around the bar as he played. A couple of men joined him, holding their pint glasses, reeling around the small space by the bar.

Eamonn contemplated his pint, then he leaned across and whispered into Boma's ear. 'I like you,' he said.

'Well, I hope you do to ask me out again,' she replied.

'Yes, but I really like you,' he said. 'Even when I'm at work I think of you. That's not like me.'

'I wonder why that is,' she said.

'You're nice.'

She nodded. 'That must be it,' she said. 'I'm also seven months gone.'

'There's . . . there's no-one, is there?'

'No husband. I had one once, but, you know . . .'

He didn't. 'That's a relief,' he said.

'Why?'

'I mean, I won't be treading on anyone's corns.'

She looked at him, trying to puzzle him out, knowing it was hopeless. 'Why do you like me?' she asked. 'I don't see much to like.'

He didn't answer at once. Then he said, 'You're different.'

She had heard that one before. She didn't need anyone to tell her that.

The bar crowd laughed and she looked up to see the fiddler dancing around and around to his own tune. And, behind him, Roddie stood. He beckoned to her.

Boma did not know what to do. She decided to pretend she had not seen him. She looked at the floor.

'Second-hand goods,' she said.

He did not know what to say.

'Listen to you!' Roddie said. 'Second-hand goods, indeed!' She looked up and he was standing in front of her, blocking out the fiddler.

Boma tried to ignore him. She smiled up at him, then concentrated on Eamonn, looking down at his half-drunk pint.

'He'll see nothing down there,' Roddie said. 'Give me a tick to get the grace together and he'll be able to see me. If he's going to make a career impersonating me, he may as well have something to go on.'

'Don't!' she said.

Eamonn looked at her as she stared off into the bar, following Roddie wide-eyed as he went to fetch a bar-stool. The fiddler saw the stool lifted and carried across the air to set itself down between Eamonn McCann and the brown woman. He stopped playing.

The rest of the bar followed his gaze.

'Do you mind if I join you?' Roddie asked, settling himself down on the stool.

'Go ahead,' said Eamonn to the stranger.

'Will you listen to your friend, Boma? Here he is having a tête-à-tête with his lady-friend and he lets a complete stranger sit down to muscle in. He's too nice for his own good, this one.'

'Why are you doing this, Roddie? The whole bar is watching!' Boma said.

Eamonn looked, noticed the silence in the bar, the way every eye was turned towards them. 'I . . .' he said. 'Can I get you a drink?'

Roddie shook his head. 'Drinks are off-limits, I'm afraid. We better hadn't give the lads over there more to worry them. In a minute or two they'll start disbelieving what they saw. I'll lay you a bet on it. Each one will be thinking it was the drink and be too embarrassed to bring it up. Better keep the tricks to one and get on with our own concerns.'

Eamonn did not understand. He looked at the bearded man. 'Don't I know you from somewhere?' he asked.

'Tell him, Boma,' Roddie said.

'You tell him,' Boma said.

'I'm Roger Casement.'

Boma stared at Eamonn to see how he would react.

'You never are,' Eamonn said.

'Let's not get into all that again, Eamonn,' Roddie said. 'For our purposes it really doesn't matter what you think. Just accept that I'm a friend of Boma's. I'm here to ask you if your intentions are honourable. I suspect they are but I need to be sure. Boma's had a bad time with men. They can be arrant ruffians. You're not like that, are you?'

It was Eamonn's turn to look hard at Boma. She looked back at him, waiting. 'I like her a lot,' he said.

'Well,' said Roddie, 'that's a start. What about your prospects?'

'That's more difficult,' he said. 'I could go back to teaching, but I really don't think it suits me. I like what I'm doing now.'

'But would it support a family?'

'Roddie!' Boma said. 'Eamonn and I hardly know each other.'

He smiled at her. 'My time is running out, Boma. I want to see you settled or at least on your way to being settled. It's partly why I came back in the first place. I hope you have understood that by now.'

Eamonn spoke up. 'If Boma does take to me, if she decides that she wants to marry me – and I can't see why she would – then I'll work hard to keep her and the baby comfortable.'

'That's what I wanted to hear,' Roddie said. He produced an envelope from his pocket. 'When you make up your mind,' he handed the envelope to Boma, 'open this. It will tell you where my wedding present is hiding. If, on the other hand, you decide against it, open it anyway. But wait until I'm out of the way.'

'How will we know that?'

'It'll be clear enough.' Roddie turned to the bar. The music had started up again, the people returning to drink and talk. 'See what I mean?' Roddie said. 'They've already forgotten a bar-stool travelling through the air without benefit of support. It's no wonder such importance is put on faith. The evidence of the senses is a fragile thing entirely.' He stood up, doffed his hat and walked away.

'Who was that?' Eamonn asked. 'He's a dead ringer for Sir Roger.'

Boma looked at the envelope. 'Sorry about that,' she said. 'He's someone who keeps an eye on me.'

'Have you known him long?'

'All my life,' Boma said, 'but we've only just met.'

My dear Bridget,

*I am writing to you through a friend, asking her to send
this letter on to you, as she will be able to find out where you
are. Your letter came to me yesterday, here in this prison cell,
and it was like a glimpse of the garden, with the wallflowers
and the Japanese cherry, to get your message.*

*First, I want to tell you that your crucifix, the medals and
the scapular came to me three weeks ago, but the letter only
yesterday. They are always with me, and please God will be as
long as I am here.*

*Remember me to so many, and thank those friends who pray
for me – and don't pay any attention to the lies. They are
compliments really, and we need not mind compliments, you
and I, Biddy dear.*

Always your friend,

Roger Casement

12

MRS HEALEY THOUGHT TIM A GREAT CHRISTIAN FOR BRINGING HER
order so promptly. She sat him down in the front room of her
bungalow and they talked while the sun settled down into the sand-
dunes.

As soon as it had disappeared from sight, Mrs Healey produced a
bottle of whiskey and, after some playing about at refusal, Tim
consented to have one.

'How did it go, Tim?' Mrs Healey asked.

'What?'

'The return of the prodigal.'

'Not too good,' he said. 'Mammy's as cold as ever. And she's otherwise engaged. I'm not getting much of a look-in.'

'It's early days,' she said.

They talked about the distant past and she produced a number of rolled school photographs, insisting that he find himself. This he did without difficulty and asked her if she knew that on one of them he appeared twice, once on the extreme left and once on the outside right.

'No, I never knew that.'

'Well,' he said, 'remember how the camera used to wander across the assembled pupils and staff? Every year one or other of us played the trick of running behind the group. I'm surprised you never knew.'

'I didn't. Still, I expect I didn't know the half of what went on. Kids keep a lot to themselves.'

'That's me. There,' he said, pointing to a tidy little boy with his hair slicked down, parted to the left.

'You've a miserable face on you,' Mrs Healey said.

'It was my policy never to smile on school photographs. But look at him. See!' He pointed to left, then right. 'He's there twice. The fellow with the hair coming down over his eyes.'

Mrs Healey looked hard. 'No, I can't tell,' she said.

She went over to the mahogany sideboard and tried to open a stuck drawer. She made the Infant of Prague on top jiggle as the drawer unstuck. She came back to the couch carrying a round magnifying glass.

'There . . . and there,' he said.

'You know, you're right. Now isn't that a case! I've never noticed before. Now I know the face. But the name escapes me.'

'It's Eamonn McCann,' Tim said. 'He was a few years behind me at school. He went off to be a White Father.'

'It is Eamonn. But you *are* out of date, Tim. He's been in Tralee ten years. He didn't have the vocation.'

'What's he been up to?'

'I think he teaches. He's a bit of a lost soul. He was at school. I'm surprised he got up to mischief like that. I would never have thought it.'

'Can I see the others?'

He pointed out – it felt like betrayal – the children who had appeared twice on each of the photographs. But she seemed to be missing the one with Tim looking miserable in stereo.

'Things got lost in the move, I expect,' Mrs Healey said.

'Where's Mr Healey?'

'Joey? He's passed away, Tim. He got us moved in here and then took to his bed. I buried him in the cathedral, just before it was forbidden.'

'I'm sorry,' he said.

'Yes,' she said. 'I only had a short hop to make between old maid and widow. But it was a sweet time while it lasted. Some don't get even that much.'

'No,' he said. He glanced out of the window at the exploding colours of twilight.

'What about you? I'm surprised you haven't been snapped up.'

'I wasn't made for marriage.'

She looked at him. 'No. Is that the cause of the trouble at home?'

He wondered what she meant. 'Partly,' he said. 'It all adds up.'

'Still, you've got good friends. In England?'

'Yes,' he said, 'very good friends.'

'Your mammy should be happy for you, so.'

He nodded, feeling like a child again. There was a moment when she looked at him and he was having a job to hold back tears.

'Let's have another,' said Mrs Healey.

He left her at eight, she asking him to come back before he left and worrying about how he was going to find his way home in the dark. He said he'd manage.

But, once out of the lights of the bungalows, it was no easy matter for him to find his way along the road. He tried to concentrate on the lights of Ardfert in the distance but managed to slip into the ditch twice. Still, what with the whiskey, he was feeling no pain, and being with Mrs Healey had lifted him. He knew he had a bolt-hole if things got too bad.

When he finally got back into Ardfert he decided to stop into a bar to top himself up. The place was different. Much larger. A turf fire burnt a touch self-consciously in the fireplace. A fiddler was playing. No-one looked twice at Tim. He took a stool at the corner of the bar, out of sight, and ordered a Guinness. When he spoke he concentrated hard on his Irish accent. He did not recognize the girl serving. She gave him a quizzical look.

He saw Boma come in with a man who looked a bit old for her. They sat down at a table by the door and the man fetched in the drinks. He wondered about joining them but thought better of it. He was not sure he could walk across the bar, in front of the fiddle-player, mimicking sobriety. And he wasn't sure he would be wanted.

The fiddler was excellent, bringing tears to his eyes. He ordered another Guinness and watched the fiddler as he danced to his own tune. He took a pull from his new pint, placed it back down on the mat and watched. Some of the lads joined the fiddler in a reel, then sat back down to applause. A man went over and put a fiver into the fiddler's cap. He stood up again at once and began playing.

Then a stool next to a table full of youngsters lifted off the ground, flew past the fiddle-player – who stopped what he was doing – and landed next to Boma and her friend. It then shuffled a bit, and was still. He saw them look at it uncertainly, then they continued talking, though Boma kept looking nervously out to the bar.

They had all seen what happened but nobody thought to do anything. The fiddler made a comment about the strength of the beer, took a swig from his pint – placed next to Tim's on the bar – winked at him, crossed his eyes and started playing again. And his music was the cue for everyone else to turn back to their business.

Tim looked at the couple by the door. They sat in silence for long moments, as if the arrival of the stool had made them meditative. Then Boma would speak, but she spoke as if the stool was her subject. He finished the drink and ordered another. When he looked again, Boma was holding an envelope. Then she put it down on the table and continued talking.

They left soon after. Tim sat on, listening to the conversation around him, the accent and cadences that had been his, but which now he was not sure he could even self-consciously mimic convincingly. And as he listened he eyed the stool.

On the way out, he ran his hands around the top of the stool. There was no sign of wires. He looked up at the ceiling of the bar, from which hung old jugs. No wires there either. It had been a good trick all right. He saluted the fiddle-player and, thinking of Chris at Blarney, put a couple of pounds in his cap.

'Now where were we?'

Tim had arrived back to find Boma alone. No sign of her friend. Paula had just turned in; Brid, she said, had gone back to bed, unhappy and silent. He had chosen not to enquire.

'I must ring Dingle to see how Chris is getting along,' he said, thinking out loud.

'Is he very sick?' she asked.

'He's on the mend,' he told her. 'I think.'

'What's the matter with him?'

'He's got AIDS. It's one thing after another.'

'You should have brought him. You never know,' she said.

'You don't believe that, do you?'

She looked at him hard, as if trying to bring his features into focus. 'After what I've told you! You can ask me that? Of course I believe it. Don't you?'

'No,' he replied, 'I don't.'

'So you think we're all liars, do you?'

He thought about that. 'No, I think you're all mistaken. It's all a great coming together of coincidences. They happen, you know. I was once waiting for a flight at Nairobi Airport and in the course of an hour I met a Ugandan who had been my student at London University. Then, on the flight, I was sitting next to a woman I'd studied with at UCD. These things come together sometimes. You just have to add the strange Irish ingredient to coincidence and you have miracles.'

'You remind me of my mum – not Paula – my other mum, Moira Hephernan. I would say things like you've just said and she – she was a great one for the miracles – would come back at me, saying, "You've got scales in front of your eyes. Go and give them a good rub." And I would rub at them until they watered while she shook her head, completely foxed that I could not see what she saw as clear as day. I made atrocious fun of her. It's odd, now I'm her and you're me, if you get me. But I can tell you about these things until I'm blue in the face. You've got to experience it for yourself.'

He nodded. 'I'm sure you're right,' he said.

Boma smiled at him. 'Brid found a book of yours in the attic.'

'There must be lots.'

'Does *Song of the Loon* mean anything to you?'

'Christ!' he said. 'Did Mammy find that? She didn't read it, did she?'

'She read enough,' Boma said.

'Christ!'

'She thought it was about the missions.'

He couldn't help laughing. 'She would!' he said. 'I should have known she'd stumble upon it. I remember when I was sorting things out, I wondered whether to throw it away but I couldn't bring myself to do it. I was given that book by an American who stayed with us. We had a bit of a fling and he said the book would cheer me up. He must have thought I needed cheering up.'

'And did it?'

'Oh, yes. It cheered me up no end. It's pretty explicit, though . . .'

'I know . . .'

'But it gave me such a lot of consolation at the time, like a love-sick girl reading Mills and Boon, I expect. I wasn't the only one. I don't know how I'd feel if I read it again. What did Mammy do with it? Burn it?'

'No, she put it in a drawer. You can't have it, though. Roddie's borrowed it. He came in this afternoon for a loan of it.'

'Boma,' he said. 'Enough's enough.' She didn't say anything. 'I think I ought to go and stay with Mrs Healey. I'm not sure I can face this.'

She twinkled. 'Don't you think it's better that she knows?'

'No, I do not. I do not!' he replied. 'Lord, it'd be better if I went now.' He searched in his pocket for the car keys, held on to them tightly, like a relic. But he was, he knew, too drunk to go anywhere.

'Well, she does,' Boma said. 'It could be why she's a bit distant. But are you sure she didn't suspect it all along?'

'Positive.'

'This is the reason for you staying away so long, is it?' she asked. 'I'd see it through, if I were you.'

He didn't say anything.

'You didn't ask why your mammy has gone off to her bed, Tim.'

'No, I didn't. I think I probably know.'

'She read the folder Roddie left.'

He suddenly remembered the stool.

'I've left it on your bed,' she said. 'You can read it before you drop off.'

'I was in the bar. You were there,' he said.

'I didn't see you.'

'No. I was hiding.'

'Why were you hiding?'

'You had company.'

'That's a friend, Eamonn McCann.'

'Boma . . .'

'You saw everything, did you?'

'Yes,' he said. 'How did you manage it?'

'That was Roddie too,' she said. 'I wish he hadn't done that.'

He shook his head in disbelief.

'Doubting Tim,' Boma said.

When he was in bed, the folder on the coverlet beside him, he remembered that he had not rung Dingle. He tiptoed back across the shop.

The sounds of fiddle and drums formed a background to Jimmy on the other end of the line.

'How's Chris?' he asked Jimmy.

'Speak to him yourself.'

The phone clattered and Chris said, 'Hello, stranger!'

'What are you doing in the bar?' he asked.

'Getting pie-eyed. How are things in Ardfert? How's your mammy?'

'Pie-eyed,' he said.

'You had a little celebration?'

'I wouldn't say that exactly. But what about you? What are you doing up?'

'I feel fine, better than I've felt in ages.'

'I'm surprised you're even up. Did you see the doctor today?'

'Yes,' Chris said. 'When are you coming back?'

'Maybe tomorrow.'

'That's no visit! Take your time,' he said. 'I wouldn't like to think that you weren't giving your mammy the benefit of a good long visit.'

'She doesn't seem to want me around.'

'I'm sure she does deep down. It'll take a day or two to get back into her good books.'

'I'll ring again tomorrow.'

'Do that. Bye.'

'Bye.'

And Chris put the telephone down too quickly for Tim's jangling sensibilities. He did not seem to be missing him in the least. Tim did not know whether to be reassured or anxious. Still, he thought, he was in good hands.

On the way back to his room he wondered to himself what his place was. He was a distraction all round. He stood still for a moment. Then he remembered the folder waiting on his bed; a treat or a final demand.

He opened it up, smelled the mildew coming off the paper, the yellow brittleness of it. He read:

And there we have it. The appeal dismissed. In truth I would be deceiving myself were I to protest that I had expected anything else. I do not protest – there seems little point – except to say that the English government could have brought me to this pass without resorting to the tactics they sank to. Far better had they kept me under military jurisdiction and raced me to the firing-squad. They could have managed it as they did with Pearse, Connolly and the others; as they managed with thousands of 'cowards' in the Army, with men who shouted, 'Enough!', who put a punch on the nose of their superior officers who had biffed them over the tops of trenches into the death-arms of German artillery. Seen from this perspective, it would have been a kindness. I might not have had my day on the stage to make my apologia but I would have died quickly, quietly, and on Irish soil, mourned by loved ones. It was not to be. Me, they had to put through the whole wretched charade of an Old Bailey trial, then to show off what they rightly perceived would be seen as my dark interior life to friend and foe alike. I had been good at friendship, had had a talent for it, I was told. And it is the greatest of all my losses, the loss of good friends.

A part of me hopes that the iniquity of the English in distributing a damning irrelevancy to blacken the character they had already plucked and dressed for the Hangman's Ball will live longer in people's memories than the supposed iniquities within. But that part wars with a gentler side, the side that wishes none harm, that hopes for forgiveness himself; a forgiveness which to work, Father Carey reminds me, needs must include my persecutors.

I was foolish, doubtless, not to destroy my diaries. I gave the wretched Blackwell, Smith and the rest an easy and infallible weapon to turn against me. Erstwhile friends fell away at the first hint that I was not all I had appeared to be. That was true enough. I was rather more. But I accept the charge of foolishness. Plead guilty to it right readily, Your Honours. But what can I tell you? Perhaps there was not enough time to be wise; to pick up after myself; to involve myself in the minutiae of sieving and burning, burnishing the good points, to make a fitting epitaph for myself. No wife to counsel caution; to mop up my peccadillos as was done with Burton and, doubtless, many another errant adventurer. Life took up my time.

Neither, I suppose, was it prudent to find my delight in the bodies of men. My vice detached me from the claims and chains of polite society, rendered me unafraid, fearless of exclusion – for it was impossible to be any farther out on that slim limb – to shout back at my paymasters, 'Aha! You think you are so civilized with your contraptions and your great mills and factories and scientific progress. But let me show you the stinking source of the rubber that rides you so smoothly along!' Not a statement, I fancy, were this ever to be read, that would be given much credence. But the idea is at the centre of my faith. Will it, I wonder, justify me, lift my soul away from the dangling husk to greet those I loved or, to my great chagrin, send me downwards, as people will have it, to burn? I, for my part, think I have burnt quite enough already.

Father Carey came to my cell today armed with a letter from Cardinal Bourne. I can only – the good cleric tells me – be received into the Catholic Church if I write a public letter expressing sorrow for any scandal I may have caused by my acts, both public or private. It is not clear what are the scandals to which the cardinal refers. Doubtless, my 'treachery' is part of it; but the other part is clearly that which the diaries revealed. My private parts, my centre! I will not do it. They want to take away my soul. Father Carey says, with a twinkle, that when the time comes Mother Church will have to let me back in. I will be baptized the night before I die under the rubric of in articulo mortis. So be it. I come in by the coal-hole. Until that hour comes, I am Catholic without benefit of clergy. No new state for me.

Joe Conrad once said I could tell some stories if I chose to. I smiled back at him across the put-me-up table in the jungle clearing, my eyes staring a mite to the right of Joe's head, where Abdou stood to attention. I told him a few stories too, stories which, I fancy, he used to good effect. But there were stories I could never have told him; stories he now knows the bare gist of and which have dried up his pen on my behalf. But I kept those stories to myself and for myself. Without them the other stories, the ones, I trust, for which I will be remembered kindly for a while, at least in the dark lands in which they were spun, would not have happened.

Father Carey knows everything. Not that I have confessed to him; nor will I until that last night comes. He has heard the stories and I would not be surprised if he has read the photographed pages, where I had wanted every last sensual sight and sound recorded for myself, for my own future delight. I wanted to know where I was, and had been. I could tell nobody; I had to tell myself. My jottings managed to keep alive for me the brief candle of my loves.

Without the joys I jotted life would have been a sad and solitary affair indeed. With them, I was able to enter and be entered by the terrors and joys of strange lives. Having lain with them it would have been impossible not to see their humanity, not to lust for the sins committed against them to be exposed, to emerge from the heart of darkness, to be paid for.

My warder knows about these pages, as, doubtless, he knows the rest. A kindly man with an Irish name – William O'Hara, if you please – though he says he is English through and through. 'Sir Roger,' he says, 'I will only take your writings to the censor if they leave your person.' And I think they will not leave me. Not this time. I shall place these last pages against my heart. Knowing my good fortune they will probably slip down into my trousers as I make the final drop.

But a sad thing it is to die with all men misunderstanding. I have said so to several of my loyal friends. They nod, thinking that I refer to the diaries and the lies in them. For I have asserted that they are lies. But were I to tell Cousin Gertrude, Conan Doyle and William Cadbury that they are true and that I cannot help but delight in their truth, would I not be testing their friendship past endurance? My exploits in Germany they could not see otherwise than treasonable. And yet they have stayed close. But to have tried them with the diaries without having the time to explain as best I can! That would be an act too dark, too dark entirely. I think, however, that they might try to understand, might try to puzzle it out. It is a puzzle all right. It sometimes seems strange even to me, the one who has lived with the knowledge from boyhood.

Time is growing short. Today a Mr Ellis came to my cell to 'measure me' for the rope. A nice enough fellow. He made me smile with his diffident manner and embarrassment while taking my dimensions with his measuring-tape. The saying of Thomas More came to mind. 'Be not afeared of your office. You send me to God.' I wondered if More had *thought it up beforehand. But I buttoned my lip, thinking I would have to think up something pretty – and pretty quick too. I asked him questions about his calling, questions which he answered plainly enough, with castdown eyes. I wanted to tell him, 'Look at me, man! The horrors you speak of are as nothing to me! I have seen men – aye, and women too – tell me of their tortures for the cause of King Rubber! I have seen the truncated tongue, the broken legs, the jarred spine from the half-hangings in the Putumayo. I have seen baskets of hands and feet and genitals. Do you really think I will flinch before your scientific explanation?'*

I shook Mr Ellis's hand and promised him that, come the day, I trusted I would not make his difficult job any more a trial than it already is. I am not sure he believes me. He has probably been the recipient of many brave words which evaporate into shaking, pulling at bindings, shufflings away from the ominous cracks in the floor as the noose is lowered; a jutting out of the chin to stop the knot passing down; a loosening and final flux of the bowels. All these things he probably expects from me too, despite my easy stance today. I can only hope that I will be able to keep to my resolve. We all have to go. Not as I will have to, true enough. Still it seems the last kindness one can do to kick off with a certain decorum. To encourage the rest.

I sleep a lot. Perhaps I am practising. Dreams come. Sometimes quite delicious dreams of bathing places by rivers, of darkness just beyond the gas-light. Of Adler too. Dear, faithless, Adler, whose final act was to offer to come over the Atlantical sea to testify against me! Even that made me laugh. Adler could make me laugh just as readily as he wound me around his little finger. He was never happier than when travelling grandly for nothing. And I was never fooled by Adler. I knew from the first night we fell over one another on Broadway that he would be trouble, if I let him. And I suppose I did let him. By then I did not have the energy to curb him. It would have been like demanding sageness from a puppy. John Devoy smelled Adler out at once, told me to watch out for him. But Devoy, though he was a lovely man, would never have understood what I saw in Adler. He had sacrificed all chance of happiness for the Irish Cause and had grown so old in his one obsession that he could not, I think, understand me. Indeed, he could not understand anyone in the whole world who was not completely obsessed with Fenianism. I think he expected it from every last member of the human race. Devoy suspected Adler. His powder, peroxide, scents and extravagant ways would have been hard even for 'Rosaleen' Devoy to have missed.

I could see his embarrassment when forced to step out between the two of us. And, I have to admit, Adler could embarrass me too. I flatter myself that Devoy did not notice the nature of our friendship. He saw everything through a lens the exact shape of Ireland — quite misted over when I began speaking of the Congo . . . failed to see it was all the same thing.

Adler Christensen was one sector of myself made visible; the self I might have been had I let my inclinations bubble up from under the khaki, moleskin, grand medals and serge. I had taken to sea as a purser from Liverpool; he had done the same from Bergen. But I had sailed south, while he had gone west. Both of us, I fancy, motivated by pique at our lowly situations ashore. In New York he fell in with an easy unconventional crowd while I was circumscribed by the trouser-presses of eager imperialists. I buried myself deep in an assumed, plumed respectability. He, having nothing much to lose, and no grand plan to consume him, lost his reputation.

I needed Adler. Adler made me gay. And I needed a good cheering-up at a time when I stood tiptoe on the precipice of treachery. The distance lent enchantment to the escapade. But I, Sir Roger Casement, had left English shores for America a well-regarded personage. A month or two later, my treachery showed scarlet on my breast. There were times when I had wanted to draw back, to accept the postponement of Home Rule that the outbreak of this war brought about, to return to England and search out a task for myself. I wanted to postpone the sacrifice, to keep friends . . . But in those first weeks in America I found myself, inch by inch, being pushed towards the precipice. Then, suddenly, one day I was over it and there was no going back. I cannot now even recall when I made that final step. A Fenian meeting at which I said the wrong thing? A letter praising the Kaiser? I did not commit my 'treasons'. I slipped into them. Then, having slipped, having stumbled over the pale by pure fluke, I had to keep going. And Adler helped. Oh, yes. Adler helped. A faithful-faithless companion nosing about me like a puppy who knows where his next meal is coming from but who also has one eye on the neighbours' dustbins down the road.

Devoy stopped Adler from coming over the ocean to do me harm. I cannot imagine what will become of him, my one shallow stab at relationship, undertaken as I warbled my swan song.

William O'Hara has come on duty to watch with me. Armed with 'John Bull', if you please! His grandfather swapped Ireland for Islington in

1849. And I know why. I once tried to question William about why his grandfather had come here. He shrugged and replied that he thought it was probably 'for employment'. Did he not know, I asked, what had occurred in Ireland in the 1840s? He searched about a bit and said that he was sorry but he didn't. Then he tried to return to his 'John Bull'.

'I'll tell you, William,' I said. 'In the eighteen-forties the population of Ireland was scythed by the potato famine. Millions fled the country to England, Australia and America. Your grandad, I fancy, would not have left had it not been for the famine. I would not have been in this Pentonville cell and you would not have been guarding me. Both our destinies were ruled by the failures of the potato so long ago.'

'Is that right, sir?' he asked, flicking his paper.

I persisted. 'William, is your grandad still living?'

'No, he fell from a ladder in the year of the Queen's Jubilee. He was cleaning windows in the Strand.'

'And he never mentioned the potato famine to you?'

'Not as I can recollect, sir.'

I was not surprised. I myself had reached the age of thirty before I learnt much of it. Odd that the presence of a time-bomb, a bomb whose presence is known to all and sundry, should be left to go unmentioned, unacknowledged. Nevertheless, it ticks away, only to explode in its own good time when it thinks it has been well and truly forgotten.

Anyway, I tried to enlighten William, while he doggedly went on reading war news in 'John Bull'. There is a battle at The Somme, apparently. I could not help noticing a very satisfactory bulge in his trousers. I spoke of the people of Mayo eating grass, the fever ships full to the gunwales with the starving en route *to America, and I wondered how I could make William O'Hara grow.*

'Is that correct, sir?' he said, when I had finished. 'Still, to my way of thinking, it was not right what you did. Not during a war. And you a knight. I mean, I know there's a lot wrong. No country's perfect. But it was still wrong what you did.'

He was looking at me, knew I was looking at his bulge. His legs snapped shut like the gates of paradise.

'Tell me what you have heard about me,' I said.

'I'm a plain man, sir,' William replied.

'What, no rumours?'

'I shouldn't even be talking to you, sir. Begging your pardon, I'd be pleased if you would let me get back to my duties.'

Having nothing left to lose and, if I was lucky, eight inches to gain, I persisted. 'Don't give me all that legalistic nonsense, William. That's not you. I can see beneath William O'Hara, the holder of a government job. The real William O'Hara has revealed himself to me already. You're not a grey bureaucrat like that Ernley Blackwell, who scratches out whole pages of my farewell letters to friends. I've seen the look you give his back as he says, "I don't think this is quite the thing, Sir Roger," and rubs out my words. In some deep recess, William, you see him as your enemy; me as your friend. Or am I wrong?'

'You're tying me in knots,' William said. 'Let me get on with my paper. And you can get on with your writings.'

I nodded sadly and did as he had requested. I noticed as I wrote that he was looking at me from time to time. Then I saw his legs move. They opened slightly . . . closed . . . opened again until they were extended as before. Paradise regained. I looked and clearly I saw a quite fantabuloso extentione. From behind his paper William must have known that I was drinking him in. But if he did the good man did not let on. Five minutes went by while I supped and salivated and remembered, he hidden behind thick funereal cloth. It jumped and throbbed. Then he shifted, coughed and placed his hand on the spot, rubbing himself.

Such ministrations were not coming as a result of anything he could be reading in Horatio Bottomley's newspaper. I knew that he knew me and knew too what I was about, what I wanted more than anything else in the whole world – more than visits from friends, more than absolution or viaticum – knew that he was doing me a last kindness. A strange brooch it was that William O'Hara offered, withdrew, offered once again from behind his paper. He might have been scratching himself. At no time did his face appear from behind the paper. He scratched, then pushed his fingers underneath to give me a better impression, then under his coconuts, pushing himself out, until the shadow of his manhood was deeply etched into my brain.

Nothing else happened, of course. Nothing else could, and I would not have wanted more. William O'Hara had – or so I choose to believe – performed the most appropriate Act of Love that any man in a condemned cell has been vouchsafed.

The governor of Pentonville came in shortly after. William stood up, neatly concealing himself with the paper. 'Sir Roger, I have been instructed to inform you that your execution will take place on August the third at nine o'clock in the morning.'

I glanced over at William O'Hara, standing to attention behind his 'John Bull'. I looked at him, avoiding the cold eyes of the governor. 'Thank you,' I said.

It is amazing how hearing the date and time of one's death pulls in the stranded mind. I have heard of people whom the doctors have given a six-month limitation on life. I am more fortunate, knowing that, unless Mr Ellis botches his job, I will be dead by 9.05 on the third of August next. I hold tight on to the medal given me by the little girl in Ardfert. It is all I have from Ireland. Her action in giving it to me when I was cold, afraid and alone, made me realize how precious such tokens are. They are, quite simply, everything. Why we are here. Writ large on the map of Africa, or small on the face of a weeping felon, her medal contains everything there is to be said about our lives on the sorrowing earth. I trust she will remember. I know I will not forget.

Time is short; so it is, I suppose, time to be memorable.

My dominating thought was to keep Ireland out of the War. England has no claim on us, Law, Morality or Right. Ireland should not sell her soul for any mess of Empire. If I die this day week, bury me in Ireland, and I shall die in the Catholic Faith for I accept it fully now. It tells me what my heart sought long – in vain. In Protestant coldness I could not find it but I saw it in the faces of the Irish. Now I know what it was I loved in them. The chivalry of Christ speaking through human eyes – and it is from that source all lovable things come, for Christ was the first Knight – and now goodbye. I write still with hope – hope that God will be with me to the end and that all my faults and failures and errors will be blotted out by the Divine Knight and the Divine Nationalist.

And if I die as I think is fated, I shall die with my sins forgiven and God's pardon on my soul and I shall die with many good and brave men.

Think of the long succession of the dead who have died for Ireland – and it is a great death. Oh! that I may support it bravely. If it be said I shed tears, remember they came not from cowardice but from sorrow – and brave men are not ashamed to weep sometimes.

I hope I shall not weep, but if I do it shall be nature's tribute wrung from me – one who never hurt a human being – and whose heart was always compassionate and pitiful for the grief of others.

The long waiting has been a cruel thing, three months and eleven days now . . .

It is a strange, strange fate, and now as I stand face to face with death I feel just as if they were going to kill a boy. For I feel like a boy – and both hands so free from blood and my heart always so compassionate and pitiful that I cannot comprehend how anyone wants to hang me . . .

It is they – not I – who are the traitors filled with a lust of blood – of hatred of their fellows.

These artificial and unnatural wars, prompted by greed of power, are the source of all misery now destroying mankind . . . I shall still hope till the Sheriff comes, and if he comes it is to prepare to go to God with calm and hope and leave all here with an infinite blessing breathed from a very finite heart . . . No man ever got so much undeserved friendship as I have found these days. The great outpouring of love and goodness on me is the greatest proof of God's love for sinful men.

God gave me into this captivity and death, and I kiss the Divine Hand that leads me to the grave . . .

Alas, so much of the story dies with me – the old, old story – yet, in spite of all, the truth and right live on in the hearts of the brave and the lowly. It is better that I die thus – on the scaffold . . .

It is a glorious death for Ireland's sake with Allen, Larkin and O'Brien, and Robert Emmett – and the men of 98 and William Orr – and for the same cause – all in the same way. Surely it is the most glorious cause in history.

Lulua! Lulua! Luluaby me!

> *Ever defeated,*
> *Yet undefeated.*

> > *Roger Casement*

Tim wasn't able to sleep much that night. He lay in bed looking up into the dark, and in the morning it seemed as if he had spent the whole night thus, his thoughts racing, engaged in endless monologues, conversations with his mammy, with Boma, with the ghost of Roger Casement.

As dawn approached through the window, he thought he could see a man sitting on the chair at the bottom of the bed, but it was only the mess of his clothes lying there.

He got up and dressed, turning the clothes that in the dark had masqueraded as Ardfert's saint into what they had been, a cover for his middle-aged bag of bones. And the bag of bones did not believe it for a moment, though every word he had read the night before smacked of the genuine. They merely added telling details to facts he had always known about the man. They fitted Casement perfectly, perhaps too perfectly, especially the friendship he had developed with his prison guard. He had been blessed in his ability to make friends. Blessed too in making friends give him what he wanted, whether it was money for his good causes or a good time. Recalling the scene where the 'John Bull'-reading guard, O'Hara, had spread his legs to show Casement the shadow of his erection seemed to exactly fit with what the diaries revealed of his voyeuristic naming of parts and their dimensions. And the decency – even the courage – of the guard to allow Casement a little of what he fancied, all struck him as true to the facts of the man that he knew. The handwriting too seemed genuine, the paper crackled and stained as if it could have come from 1916. But then, he thought, it would, wouldn't it? A forger was not going to write on Basildon Bond.

But Tim could not believe it; not any of it. The whole thing ran so completely contrary to his habit of scepticism that, though it roared its truth, a mechanism in his brain would not shift, unlock, to accept it. He felt his hand to be buried up to the wrist in the wound but he was still crying out, *Non credo!* almost desperate, almost as if he would lose something precious if he lost his on-again, off-again, neither-up-nor-down unbelief.

And another thought impinged as he read each word. *Mammy has read this.* There was cold comfort in it for her, even the honourable mention of her medal at the end could not have redressed the content which, he felt, would have her pronouncing anathema on all Sir Roger's works. He could not understand why he – genuine apparition from heaven above or imposter from over the hills – had given them to her. What was that all about? Why 'come out' to the one person who didn't want to know? Why compromise the truth that had sustained her whole life?

It was cold and clear outside. A dawn sky stained orange and red lit up the way east across Ireland. A plane flying towards Britain from North America seemed to be already in full daylight, the twin vapour trails orange-yellow, the sun glinting on the needle fuselage. There, people were waking up, raising the window blinds, drinking a miserly portion of orange-juice, worrying about customs, wanting to return to terra firma and the real world. But as far as Tim was concerned the real world was up there while, on this flat cloth of land, the most exotic other-worldly notions had come to buffet. And he had no safety-belt to fasten.

He turned right, thinking he would make for McKenna's Fort and Banna Strand. Cunningly, he would remove his car and bring it back into Ardfert before things got too busy. With his car near by he could make a quick getaway.

Some lights burnt in the houses along his route. He probably knew all the people inside those houses, though he could not at that moment think who any of them were. Neither did he very much care. The important thing, the suddenly only reason for this early-morning walk, was to retrieve the car. He would have to face Mammy at breakfast and it would be reassuring to know that he could, if things were too cold and difficult, leave with alacrity. After all, Mammy had Boma, Boma had Paula and all the interest that was busy turning Ardfert from a sleepy blink of a place into a mecca for lost, seeking souls. Perhaps he would write or phone in a week or a fortnight and resume his distant, dutiful relationship. Perhaps he would return when all the fuss was in the past and things would be different.

Lights were on in the presbytery. A couple of biddies were standing in the church porch, waiting for it to open. He walked on and turned right. Birds sang from the hedgerows. He passed a line of cars with people inside, all sleeping in untidy piles of blankets and coats.

He turned right again, and walked, where many before had walked, across the quagmire of mud to McKenna's Fort. He walked around the perimeter of it. He sat down on a fallen branch.

Often enough as a child he had come to this place; first with friends then, later, alone. He would read poetry and plot means of escape. Here he had been seduced by the American tourist staying at the b & b and had, as they say, never looked back, though the tourist had been led on by his fifteen-year-old rampant self rather than the other way round. He had given Tim exactly what he had been waiting for.

When Tim saw the man he knew immediately who he was or who he was pretending to be. He was looking at the votives left on the memorial, a tall man of late middle age with sharp features, dressed in a plain old-fashioned suit.

Tim thought to himself, *I'm not going to make the first move. I'll let him come to me.*

The man moved round the monument, his fingers nervously bothering his beard. Then, as if it was the most natural thing in the world, as if he had known him for years, he shouted over, 'Cold morning, Tim!'

'It is,' Tim said.

'How's Bridget?'

'She was fine last night.'

He nodded and walked towards him. Tim didn't move, just stared straight ahead into the mist.

'You got the papers I left with Boma, did you?'

'I did,' he said, still determined not to be impressed.

He took *Song of the Loon* out of his jacket pocket. 'Thanks for the loan of this.'

Tim took the book from the man and studied the cover. 'You're welcome,' he said.

'What did Bridget make of the papers I left her?'

'I haven't really had a chance to speak to her,' Tim said. 'I think she was probably shocked.'

The man nodded and sat down next to him on the branch. 'I enjoyed the book,' he said.

'Who are you?' Tim asked.

'Roger Casement,' he replied.

'You do a very good impersonation.'

'Is that what you think?'

'Yes,' he said, without a moment's hesitation.

The man nodded as if he had expected his reaction. 'How's your friend, the one in Dingle?'

'How did you know about him?'

'We imposters have to get our facts straight. How is he?'

'Not bad,' Tim said.

'He misses Africa. I can't say I blame him.'

Tim's conspiracy theory was spreading. He saw this man in cahoots with Jimmy O'Keeffe, with some of the regulars at the pub in Dingle.

'You're well informed,' he said.

'It's easy.'

'So why are you doing this?'

'The opportunity presented itself, Tim. I've been boiling and bubbling over things and I thought I'd come back to have a go at finishing a few of the jobs I started. I can't say it's worked. Well, perhaps I shouldn't say that. I'm happy to have been able to help Boma and bring your mammy a bit of excitement. But as far as the great world is concerned it's all been pretty hopeless thus far.'

'What's hopeless?'

'I don't know why I should tell you. You don't believe me anyway. Still, why not? I had hoped to be able to make an example of Joe Mobutu, to give him a good shake and get him to return to the straight and narrow. Then, if it had worked for him, it might have startled several other of the poor sheep back. I've done my best but it hasn't worked, I fear. Does it ever work, I wonder? The world goes from bad to worse, Tim. The institutionalized forces of evil are too much for us entirely. When I was alive we could hardly guess at the advances that were to come in your century. We had a hint about radio, but television was just a gleam in the eye of fanciful novelists. When I heard that mankind was capable of receiving pictures from all around the world I imagined an end to suffering. I thought, *Now they'll see!* My slim reports on atrocities in the Congo and the Putumayo had wrought some change, concentrated a good many minds. But what were they when placed beside the great invention of television that would bring the world's plight home to those who could help? But I was wrong there. We were all wrong. That godlike eye shows so much that everyone becomes mixed up in a great bitter soup of unknowing – taking in everything and absorbing nothing. You're all used to it by now. But I can't get used to it. I just don't know what else can be done to make you see, to make the world see, *see.*'

Tim couldn't help liking the imposter. 'I suppose you're right. We see the world as complicated. In your day it was simple. The White God in His heaven and all that. Now all we see is the knots.'

'I just don't understand how you can live with yourselves,' he said.

'We can't,' Tim said. Then he asked him again, 'Who are you?'

'I am just a little man who worked some magic tricks at the beginning of this century come back to try them out again. But they haven't worked, Tim. Still, I've told you that already. I will leave you all a sadder man, though no wiser.'

'You couldn't work a miracle for me, could you?' Tim asked.

'That depends,' he said.

'You can, I'm sure,' he said, laughing at himself. 'Everyone said it was you who cured Mags Devlin.'

'No,' he said. 'I've invested the grace I have into what I've been doing. It's exhausted.'

'I don't believe you. You could cure Chris if you wanted to. If you're the real thing, that is.'

'Ah.'

'You could! I know it!'

'I couldn't, Tim, and I'll tell you for why. Chris has already been cured. He was cured the day you met the Power's man.'

'I don't know what you mean.'

'You still don't believe me, do you?'

'I don't know.'

'You don't know. You wear your cynicism like an old Irish peasant woman her faith. Doesn't your lack of belief ever tire you out, ever tempt you to end it all? I just don't know what helps you through this charnel house of a world. You know what's wrong. All of you. Yet you do not seem to be able to find your satisfaction in helping out. Is it because of possessions? That's Joe Mobutu's problem. A poor boy under the skin who dreads going back the way he has come, who'll build a mountain of bodies to block the path back. Is that the world's problem?'

'It's part of it, I suppose,' Tim said. 'We're all rather fond of our knick-knacks.'

He nodded and looked out over the coastal plain towards the sea. 'What now?'

He shrugged. 'Not much, I fear. A turn to the ocean. A few breaths of honest Irish ozone. Maybe a paddle. Then I'm off for good.'

Tim knew he should question him, try to prove or disprove his story to his own satisfaction. But he could not think of anything to say.

'Goodbye, Tim,' he said.

'You'll remember Chris in your prayers?' Tim asked him.

The man nodded, winked and walked away down the ramparts of the fort. He disappeared behind a clump of yellow-flowering bushes.

*. . . and of the last time I saw you, and the message I gave
you. Do you remember? I know you carried it out, dear
Bridget, because I heard you did. And so farewell – and may
God's blessings rest on you and yours and be with you in your
work – and may the heartfelt thanks of one in much sorrow
and affliction of soul be part of your reward for your
affection.*

RODDIE

13

TWO DAYS LATER, CANON DAWSON DROVE OUT OF THE PRESBYTERY
on his way to the Hospital of the Flaming Heart in Tralee. He had
been asked to transport the two injured priests back to Dublin and
was happy to be going on this day especially. He had not wanted to
stay around for the procession.

'He's gone,' said Miss O'Shea, looking over her shoulder to Father
Devenish. 'You just finish your toast and we'll get on with it.'

'I don't know,' said Father Devenish.

'You knew last night,' said Miss O'Shea. 'You were a great rebel
last night – go on, finish your toast. What you weren't going to do
was nobody's business.'

'I was drunk last night.'

'Sure you were. I've not seen you drunker. But the drink can often be a clearer of blocked passages, so it can.' Then, seeing that Father Devenish was still uncertain, Miss O'Shea added, 'And don't you worry about the canon. If he gets shirty I'll tell him it was all my doing – which it is – and if he gives me the sack, sure, I'm past retirement age anyway.'

Father Devenish took out his set of keys. He contemplated them mournfully.

'Anyway, we never promised the canon that we wouldn't take out the candle. We've not been speaking to him for the best part of a week. If he gets shirty we can just say that we thought his ruling only applied to the original candle.'

Father Devenish sighed, still unconvinced, and led the way towards the sacristy storeroom.

There the second paschal candle was still burning steadily. The two gazed at it in awe for a moment. Then Father Devenish took a white cloth and, using it to glove his hands, pulled the candle out of the holder. 'Shall I try to blow it out? Just to make sure.'

Miss O'Shea nodded and, holding her breath, watched as Father Devenish inhaled and blew.

'It's a miracle,' she said. 'And miracles are for sharing.'

A few people still praying in the church watched as Father Devenish carried the candle up the aisle, followed by a smiling Miss O'Shea. They got up, genuflected, quickly followed the little procession down the road towards Ardfert.

Mrs Grogan was scowling at the divine-size statue of Roger Casement standing on the catafalque. 'Get Finbar!' she told Mrs Taggart.

'He's off seeing to the bearers, Mrs Grogan.'

'First things first, Mrs Taggart. I want some more wood wedged into the base to hold the statue steady. We don't want Sir Roger to take a tumble, now do we?'

'No, we don't,' replied Mrs Taggart, biting her lip, looking around and over the gathering crowd for a sight of Finbar. 'Look, the children from my cousin Molly's school in Limerick are arriving!'

'I hope they've brought lots of flower petals to strew about, Mrs Taggart. Now you find that Finbar. I wasn't able to get Irish Life to insure us for the procession, so we need to make sure everything's safe and sound before we start off now.'

'I'll go and see.'

Mrs Grogan brought the piles of flowers from the buckets standing in front of The Roger Casement Fancy Goods Emporium, ready for arranging around the catafalque. She smiled with satisfaction at the snake of people – Children of Mary, Catenians, Irish Legionnaires, the Mike Byrne Showband – being formed up behind the catafalque. Stewards were directing people to join the procession at the back and the people were already stretching past the ruined Ardfert Cathedral and out along the Ballyheige Road.

'Here's Finbar for you, Mrs Grogan,' said Mrs Taggart.

Mrs Grogan turned. 'Finbar! Where've you been? Don't tell me. We need the statue steadier. A couple more pieces of wood should do it.'

'It'll spoil the look of the thing,' Finbar replied. 'Sure, it's as safe as houses already.'

'So if it's as safe as houses why can I wiggle him?' Mrs Grogan pushed Sir Roger in the chest. He swayed. 'You never know what might happen, Finbar. Have you heard tell of Emotion, Finbar? Emotion is a strong thing, you know. Like an earthquake it strikes and, without warning, a whole herd of people might get carried away and try to reach out and touch Sir Roger. Now what if – I only say if – but what if the statue starts bleeding, starts weeping big tears, if the eyes wink or a smile plays around his features? What then? You never know what wildness might be unleashed. As to the look of the thing, well the whole base is going to be covered over with these flowers brought in from Dublin. Nobody's going to notice an extra piece of old wood.'

Finbar put his megaphone under his arm and searched around for his hammer.

'Give us that, you!' said Mrs Grogan, seizing the megaphone. 'Now before I start marshalling, have you got four sober boyos exactly the same size to do the carrying?'

'I have,' said Finbar, nails between his teeth.

'Now I don't want them the same size from head to toe. Their heads don't come into it at all. It's the shoulders on them I'm interested in. They must be just the same. There's nothing worse in a procession than having a statue all cock-eyed. It's just not seemly.'

'They're like four peas in a pod,' said Finbar, looking for his hammer.

Mrs Grogan caught sight of sisters from the Hospital of the Flaming Heart making their way to the back of the procession. 'You see them, Mrs Taggart?' she said, nodding towards the sisters. 'I don't know what the sick are going to be doing with themselves this morning. The entire hospital must be empty of nurses entirely!'

Mrs Taggart nodded, then frowned as she noticed two guide-dogs walking side by side with their owners. The two dogs were growling at one another, reaching over to nip. They were followed by several people in wheelchairs, some wheeling themselves, some being wheeled by helpers.

'All go to the back!' Mrs Grogan shouted through the megaphone.

The Mike Byrne Showband struck up 'The Bard of Armagh'. It continued to play even when a white cloud passed overhead, throwing the scene into shadow and then dropping a minute of heavy rain on everyone. The cloud passed and the sun came out.

'I've done the statue,' said Finbar. 'Nothing could move it now.'

'I hope not, Finbar. I hope not. Let me see.' She held Sir Roger's head and tried to rock it back and forth. It moved hardly at all. 'That should do it,' she said. 'Now get your boys together. It's five past eleven already and after me saying we'd be sharp!'

Finbar turned, looking through the crowds for the bearers. He saw coming towards him over the heads of the crowds the flaming paschal candle. Mrs Grogan saw it too. She made her way into the silence that had descended around it. 'Father! Thank you for coming! You'll be leading the procession?'

'He will,' said Miss O'Shea.

Like wind through wheat, the sight of the candle had blown back along the procession. A silence descended and everyone looked up at the small light in front of them. The band stopped playing 'Terence's Farewell to Kathleen'. They listened to the silence, then a single woman, carried away by the sight, clapped her hands once. The whole crowd at once erupted with applause.

The bearers lifted the statue and Mrs Grogan realized she had forgotten to spread the flowers around the base. This she did and then she nodded to Father Devenish to set off.

Cameramen and people with microphones ran ahead of the procession. Father Devenish quaked at the thought of Canon Dawson watching the evening news. Then someone was reaching up, lighting a votive candle from the flame he was carrying. He moved to put the candle out of reach but it was too late. 'Look it . . .' he called, looking back. But while he was distracted another couple of candles were lit from the one he carried. These small candles lit others and reproduced until a smattering of weak lights punctuated the long procession. The band played 'The Lonely Banna Strand' and those who remembered the words joined in.

Boma lit her candle from that of a nun in front. Then the nun was smiling at Paula standing beside her. Boma lit Paula's candle, then she tried to light Brid's. 'Come on, Brid,' she said.

Resentfully, Brid held out her small candle. 'I don't see the point. It's not as if they show up in broad daylight,' she said.

'Give over, Brid!' Boma said.

'I will not give over! Why should I?'

'Suit yourself!' said Boma.

'Your mother's found her old chums,' Brid said. 'They'll be wanting to get her back over the wall, I should think.'

Boma looked at Paula deep in conversation with the sisters.

'They'll have her back soon enough,' Brid continued.

'I don't know what's happening to you, Brid. You're a different woman since Paula and Tim came,' Boma said.

'And what if I am? Whose business is it save my own?'

The procession was turning onto the road to Banna Strand. A wind caught them and Boma shaded her candle. Then she took her hand away, aware that it was showing no sign of being blown out. 'Brid, our candles won't go out.'

Boma's discovery was being shared up and down the procession. A group behind started singing 'Lead Kindly Light'. A guide-dog chased a cameraman up the flanks of the procession. It caught his trouser-leg, then neatly flicked its body so that it tripped the man, sending him and his camera into the ditch.

A man waving his white cane ran up behind the dog. 'I can see!' he shouted. 'I can see! It's a grand blue day!'

Brid considered the candle in front of her. She blew a staccato exhalation at it. It did not move. Then she took the metal cross on her rosary and tried to pare it as if she were paring the eye from a potato. The wick bent and the flame fell over into the horizontal. But when the cross no longer touched it, it sprang back into the vertical. She scowled at it again.

All around her people were blowing at their small miracles. Another man ran past them towards the front and knelt by the statue of Roddie. 'I'm cured!' he shouted. Brid thought of her small baptismal medal, hidden, out of sight, unknown to the throng. She thought of her recent contentment, her sense of great events occurring all around. Her secrets that had sparked and flamed between herself and Boma before the inundation of Paula and Tim and holy candles. Now Sir Roger was loved and honoured by all and sundry. He was no longer hers alone to pray for and cherish and mind. He was public property and his miracles – if such vulgarities could be dignified with the name – had become common currency.

'We're approaching McKenna's Fort but I would ask you not to leave the procession. Saint . . . Sir Roger's statue will be placed in the centre of McKenna's Fort this evening for a vigil. Those who wish to watch and offer intentions and give thanks for favours received should go then,' boomed out Mrs Grogan.

Brid could see Paula calling to Boma. But Boma was elsewhere and Paula tried to get Brid to pass the message to her. Brid looked back at Paula stonily. Then Boma saw her mother calling her and went up to be introduced to the nuns. Brid stopped still. It was the last straw. People behind her bumped into her and she stepped out of the procession, watched it as it weaved on down the lane towards the ocean.

She waited until the whole procession had passed, then darted off the road, following the muddy track leading to the fort. She heard the singing of the faithful, the cacophony of the band, sinking below the surface of the stormy seascape of her brain, to be replaced by the twittering of skylarks.

Okondo worked all day and long into the night on his sculpture. Then, after a few hours' sleep, during which he dreamed of the face, he returned to his work.

Now that the creation was nearing completion, he ate nothing, only drinking sips of water from the gourd at his side; the same water he used to rub across the ebony wood, to cleanse it of dust, make his incisions stand out.

The sounds of life in the village continued around him. Okondo barely noticed them, so intensely wrapped up in his work was he. Miriam tried to quieten the children. If neighbours came to ask about Okondo and his absence from the fields and the village fire, she would lead them away from the thin walls of the hut before explaining that Okondo was engaged on his great work.

At night, night after night, Okondo worked to the sound of his family breathing. The unconsumed candle, a taken-for-granted part of the family's life, burnt and did not burn down, directing a golden light upon his labours.

From the memories in his fingers and his eyes Okondo chiselled the features of the man who had lifted him. Maquettes of the figure lay about the hut. These he felt from time to time while he tried to square the angle of the eyebrows, the jut of the chin, the hollows of the cheeks. He dreamed a lot and in his dreams the man came back and spoke to him and kissed his eyes. His grandfather too, his grandfather without feet, who had sat in the hut making sculptures and wooden utensils, who had, before Okondo had lost his eyes, sent him on errands, had him fill his pipe, told him tales of the man who was warrior and woman, whose heart had beaten strongly with anger and love, who had saved him from death. Day and night in dreams Lulua, Okondo's long-dead grandfather, spoke to him: *I thought while I was with you, Okondo, that it was I who owed the man everything. He had seen me bleeding in the jungle – beating my head against the trunk of a tree to make myself insensible. He took me to a hospital and helped mend me. Then he gave me money to buy the land where we live. We became friends. He saw me married and then he left our country. Without him I would not have lived my long life, would not have fathered your father or your uncle. The man saved me and so, as we say, your saviour is your flesh and blood. For without him you would not live now. He, as much as I, is the great-grandfather of your children and so it will go down the generations of our seed. But I who was saved by the man also saved him. My pitiful state after the torture of Leopold's men – the sight of my bleeding, hitting the tree with my head, crying out in my pain – became a picture in the man's head that never left him. I woke him from the sleeping sickness of his tribe.*

Okondo polished the figure with beeswax. He placed it in the corner of the hut next to the candle. Then he waited for the auspicious day to dawn when he, accompanied by his sons, would take the image into the forest to join the other ancestors.

*   *   *

Planks were laid down like a bridge over the morass of mud that the path to McKenna's Fort had become. Brid stepped gingerly onto one, shuffled and slipped. She righted herself, found herself still on the plank wondering what had happened in the spit of time between the first pace and the righting. She turned, shuffling round, and stepped off the plank the way she had come.

After surveying the tricky way forward, she decided to skirt the whole mess. She set off slowly, planning an arc through the green-sprouting field that would bring her back to the fort. She was not happy to be doing this; the farmer who owned the field and the fort had had enough to put up with in recent days without having his new crop trampled.

On reaching the halfway point of her planned route, Brid stopped. The words she had been thinking, *enough to put up with*, had slipped into her brain like a short prayer and she found she had been repeating it with each step. She looked at her wet shoes – bought in Limerick on a church trip – and felt certain she would not retrace her steps back to the road. She did not know why she thought this. She did not know where the thought had come from.

The wind blew straight in from the coast. Once or twice sounds from the procession reached her, like early-Monday bin collection heard in a daze from her bed. Perhaps now Boma would have discovered her absence, would be running forward and backward through the crowd searching for her. She quickened her pace.

The last few yards to the outcrop of the fort made further avoidance of mud a waste of time. The plank – had it been laid down by the owner of the field? – was itself two yards of mud away from her. Far too far for her to reach, and pointless too. She dithered for a moment on the edge of the foot-imprinted mud, then weighed into it. The brown mud curled around her shoes. Each pull of her foot from the mire let out a sound like the rubber drain-clearer in the kitchen at home. Muddy but still on two feet, she arrived at the fort.

He was waiting for her, though she could not see him. He had wanted to help her through the mud, to lift his friend to the place where they had so often met. But his time was nearing its end and the conditions of his furlough had stated that he was to wait at the fort for his lifting back to the Waiting Area.

He watched Brid make her way up the last slope, already tutting at the litter all about, the candle-wax and scribbled notes, the pictures and pleadings, that were stuck to his memorial. He had reached a decision; he would break one more rule and show himself to Brid.

She saw him standing among nettles in the centre of the fort.

'It's you at last,' she said, unsurprised. 'I wondered when I'd finally be granted a look-in.'

'Hello, Bridget. I'm sorry it's taken me so long. I shouldn't be showing myself to you now. You won't tell on me, so you won't?'

'Who's to tell?'

'Don't ask me. But they shouldn't have placed temptation in my way. I've never been able to resist temptation. If you had continued on with the procession, I could have left without seeing you.'

'You're leaving, are you? But you've only just come! And you've a lot to explain. Look what you've started!'

'I know,' he said sadly. 'I let all my fireworks off in the box. Everyone's been so busy panicking about the fire that they've missed the lovely colours, the rockets that explode against the blackness and squirt hope about. I should have handled things differently. But put yourself in my shoes, Bridget. You get offered a trip back, a chance to try and put things right, to put in better punctuation into the short paragraph of your life. But the world is too distracted to take you in, too bound up in its own business to see you, to believe you. I think I've spent most of my time here trying to persuade people that I'm here at all; that I'm who I say I am. I hadn't realized that people will only see what they want to see. You can box their ears as much as you like but it's like biffing cement. My small reports on dots of atrocity had more impact at the time, did more to change minds and produce reformation, than anything I've managed this time. There is, I see now, no way round it. It's as true as it ever was and I don't know why I didn't know it at the start. We must lift one another a soul at a time, a step at a time.'

Brid walked over to him. She placed her hand on his shoulder. 'You brought Boma to me,' she said.

He cheered up. 'Yes, I'm happier with that side of things. I've brought my family back together.'

'You've made my life complicated. Before Sister Paula and Tim came back I'd never been happier. I was surrounded by interest, by a new friend and the feeling that all was right with the world. My bags were packed for the off but I'd been given a taste of what was to come. But then Sister Paula comes to lay claim to Boma and Master Tim comes back and I don't want either of them here. I want you and Boma. All to myself. If I had died the day before Paula came nobody could have died happier.'

'But not now?'

Brid stepped back, wondering what Roddie was implying. 'No, I wouldn't want to go at the moment, thank you very much. There's too much to sort out. That son of mine. And the rest. Now is not the time for me to go. Not with all the uncertainty about.'

'And you're more uncertain about me and Tim than before I came, aren't you?'

'I'd rather not have known about all that. Call me a silly old woman if you like, but that's how it is. I don't like the idea that you were doing those things to those poor people – leading them astray – at the same time that you were supposed to be helping them out.'

'Can't you look at it another way, Bridget? Can't you believe that I only managed the good works I achieved because I was made that way?'

'No,' she said, 'I can't. You could have been made in that way but left the innocents alone.'

'And you won't take my word for it? You must admit that you'd be a more saintly woman if you managed to take Paula in and Tim back, and not felt irritated. Can't you accept the mix in me as you do the mix in yourself?'

'A sin's a sin,' she said.

Roddie sighed. 'Another failure. I thought if you understood me, you might understand Tim.'

'I'm too old for all that,' she said.

Roddie looked out over the flat plain towards the ocean.

'You're going, aren't you? I can tell,' she said.

'Yes. Shortly,' he replied. 'Bridget, go on praying for me, will you?'

Brid felt great relief. If Roddie still wanted her prayers it had to mean that she was going to be left behind. He was not going to take her. All through their conversation she had had the feeling that he was going to reach out and the game would be up. That's what angels and apparitions always did. Look what happened to Marcelino Pan y Vino! 'Of course I will!' she replied, feeling her two feet firmly planted on the earth and grateful for the feel, even for the cold water that had leaked into her shoes. She looked around her and saw the landscape new. Her irritation dissolved.

Roddie smiled, knowing exactly how Brid felt. 'I have one more thing to say. The start and the finish. The Congo was the best: best because there I met the man who was the start of it. He was the father of Boma's father. There is little else to say. I helped him. A small enough thing it was. You remember the story of St Christopher. He helped the little child across the river and only found when he had reached the other side that the child was Christ?'

Brid nodded. 'But the child got heavier and heavier on the way over the river because St Christopher was carrying Christ's cross too. You forgot that.'

'I did. But what I'm trying to tell you is that the man represented my epiphany. I suddenly saw in him The Victim, where evil leads. I had seen it all before, Bridget. I had been in Africa long enough to be hardened to it. I had looked at the Africans with the eyes of my European companions, eyes that I have seen facing atrocities on televisions. These dark images did not feel. Though they were close to us, they were insubstantial. Not like us. But meeting that man in the jungle that day, I suddenly saw everything. And nothing could ever be the same. All I did subsequently flowed from that meeting. He had two sons, one of whom is alive. The other son, Boma's father, was killed in the fighting following independence. He was dead before Boma was born. Perhaps you can see, then, how we are related, how it all comes round. It isn't nations and flags and borders, Bridget. They don't count. People puff them up all right. I did my bit in that direction. But now I know that they are not it. The only border is the one between good and evil, between people, and they run in knots and tangles through every inch of the planet, through every heart and every beat of our hearts and every action of every human being.'

'I don't understand . . .' she said.

'Yes, you do. You understand perfectly . . .' Roddie stopped, looked back across the field. 'Bridget, come back with me behind the tree.' He took hold of her by the arm. 'There's a man coming to the fort. I don't want him to see you just yet.'

'What?' she asked, wondering if he might want to take her after all. She let herself be led back to a place out of sight of the monument and from there looked out at the approaching figure of a man.

'That's Declan,' Roddie said. 'He's the cause of Boma's trouble, the father of her baby too.'

'What's he doing here?'

'Watch,' he said.

The man approached the monument. Brid could see how ragged and dirty he was; how he hobbled along on bare, bleeding feet. He came to the monument and knelt in front of it.

'And well you might!' Roddie said.

'I . . .' said Brid.

'That Declan is here to do penance. He has committed great sins against Boma. When he found out that Boma was pregnant with his child, your man decided to kill two birds with one stone. He sent her out to deliver a package, a gift he said, to a friend. She was to wait for a man in the centre of Hungerford Bridge and give the man the package. When she arrived on the bridge, I was there. She passed me as she went up onto the bridge and gave me money, thinking I was a beggar. I followed her and snatched the package from her. I ran away and the package exploded. I had thought that that would be the end of it, but it was just the beginning. As you know.'

'Why did he do such a thing?' Brid asked.

'Ask him yourself.'

'I'll do no such thing! I'll fetch the Gardai!'

Roddie shook his head. 'Take him home, Bridget. Wash his feet,' he said.

'What? What did you say?'

He smiled at her. 'That's the vengeance I'm after. Bring it all round, Bridget. Close the circle.'

She watched him, her brain sliced into separate continents without connection by the scythe of his last words. He took a last look around McKenna's Fort. He saw her watching him and shrugged. 'I am going, Bridget. I can't help myself. Only half my passion is spent. It feels like death again. With all men still misunderstanding. Perhaps with myself still misunderstanding. I'm sorry I was a bit of a disappointment to you. Pray for me, Bridget. And thanks again for the loan of the medal. Kiss Boma for me . . .'

She reached out to touch him. Roddie smiled, stepped quickly back a pace, as if he had stumbled over a stone, and disappeared. A skylark took off from the undergrowth near by and stepped up the sky, oblivious to Brid's cries, the dark clouds heading over, the gunfire, rape and murder, just over the circle of the horizon.

Brid walked over to the monument. She began ripping off the objects tied to it – aware all the time of the kneeling penitent near by – determined, before she did anything else, to make of it once more her own private shrine.

> *Roger Casement is in heaven.*
>
> EAMON DE VALERA

14

TIM HAD EXCUSED HIMSELF FROM THE PROCESSION.

'I knew he wouldn't want to go, Boma,' Brid said, looking him up and down, then turning away to put on her hat in front of the mirror.

'Go on!' Boma said.

Tim had shaken his head.

He hadn't mentioned anything of what had happened at the fort. He had filled in the following days with long walks, waiting for his own melting, and his mammy's too, only returning in the evenings to his hard home.

On the morning of the procession he left the house with them, saw the crowds forming up along the street and walked the other way, along the road by the cathedral and down to the remains of the Franciscan monastery.

There was no-one about. Events had shaken the small world of the snowscene of his home; the flecks had all collected around Sir Roger. Tim was left alone with the ruin.

Not so much a ruin as it had been. The monastery had been done up since his last visit; stones placed back on stones, cementing the past back together like a broken cup repaired for its sentimental value. There was information too, notices with sketch-maps detailing the original layout. Here, the monks had their refectory; there the visitors were housed.

He tried to remember how it had been before, when he was a child playing, climbing up the tower to howl rebellion down at his home town, stamping his life on the old gravestones in the nave . . . but the old form of the ruin had melted away like the first draft of a letter on a computer. Now, though still a ruin, it was halfway back up to being what it had been in the days before the strangers came. The complete ruin that he had known; had thought of as 'it', how things were, was painted over. The old ghosts replaced by new ones.

Tim found a way up into the tower, surprised that the steps were not barred. He took them carefully and came out on top of the tower with a view out past Ardfert to the ocean. The Dingle Peninsula lay blue in the distance.

He sat down there, banded his legs with his upper arms, rubbing his face with his hands, and looked out.

From his perspective it seemed as if the whole area was deserted. No procession. No circus. He thought of Chris, content in Dingle with Jimmy and Maureen. He thought of everything that had happened: a levitating bar-stool; Sir Roger's jottings; the story of Paula and Boma; his own meeting with Sir Roger. Just one of these, he felt, should have pulled him back to *something* – perhaps not the neat white and yellow rich Battenberg cake of his childhood . . . but *something*. Yet, despite it all, perhaps because of it all, he was cold, his heart unsparked and litter-bestrewn, like the dead oven of the refurbished monastery kitchen below.

In the old days, he supposed, just this view might have been enough to convince the monks of this monastery that the Godhead existed. Everything they saw was miraculous, lacked explanation. The sight that was confronting him of a land pushing out new life, the sunbeam sky, the daily course of the sun across it, the hard rock, the soft soil, the jelly-tender eyes of cows, contained its own irrefutable dogmas, sang of the busy fingers of God.

Now it droned: of clever men on television, in newspapers, explaining the phenomena – human origin and destiny to everyone's satisfaction. Mystery had had the door big-banged in its face. Perhaps he did not understand it all, but *somebody* understood it, somebody with itchy genitalia, a mortgage, a fear of death. It was all so sad, this diminution of vision, that you had to laugh. And that was good enough for us. Confronted with the stories that had come to him since his return to Ireland and Ardfert, he kept seeking about for some logical explanation. Of course, he could find none. But that was because he did not know or could not understand all the facts, had been too bone-idle to study the data. He had not sussed out the secret of the trick. He was outside the magic circle.

Tim crossed his legs and straightened his back, trying to remember the drill for emptying his mind. Perhaps, he thought, were he able to recapture the knack of concentration, clear away the distractions, the cobwebs, the butterfly thoughts, he would be able to pull aside the veil that lay between himself and acceptance or understanding. He managed ten breaths. They came out as sighs. He did not forget a thing. And the blur of the twentieth-century hangover remained.

'Help me!' he called. He repeated it like a mantra, facing west, fancying that from a distance he might appear to be an old monk on watch. Then he sensed that there was someone behind him on the tower. Another apparition would fix it. This time he would get Sir Roger to cast himself off the pinnacle.

He turned, believing he would see Roddie. There was, of course, nothing; up there no undergrowth to melt out of and into. To the east two horses cantered away across a field. He stood up and carefully trod the steep, uneven steps back down to the ground.

Tim entered the house through the unlocked shop-door. The village was deserted and he thought he would have some more time to himself. But in that he was mistaken. About to open the parlour door, he heard his mammy's voice, coming from the guest-area by the summer door.

'Declan, make sure you melt those bath cubes. They were given me by Mary Coogan, God rest her, and they take their own sweet time.'

'Mammy?' he called.

She was standing by the closed bathroom door. He could see her face change from concern to cold as he walked in.

'It's you,' she said.

'You're back early.'

'I didn't stay.'

'What are you doing?'

She did not reply, but took him by the arm, leading him into the shop. 'I know you won't believe me,' she said. 'Still, I'll tell you anyhow. We've a man in the bathroom. Sir Roger told me to take him in.'

'How do you mean, "a man"?' he asked.

' "How do you mean 'a man'?" ' she mimicked. 'A man. You know what "a man" is, don't you? I'd expect you'd know that as well as most, if not more so!'

'Mammy . . .'

'This man is a penitent,' she said. She gave Tim a hard, meaningful look and went back to the bathroom door. He followed her.

'Is everything all right in there?' she called.

There was no reply. She looked at him. 'I wonder if he's all right,' Brid said. She put her hand on the door-knob but could not bring herself to turn it. 'Maybe you should go in and check, being a man and everything.' She considered this. He could see her brain working and knew what would follow. 'On second thoughts . . .' she said. She knocked hard on the door.

The man inside grunted a reply. Brid nodded and pushed Tim out of range of temptation.

Back in the parlour he asked, 'Who is he, Mammy?'

'He's called Declan and he's walked all the way from Belfast. In his bare feet. He's a sinner all right, but he's penitent. I was talking to Sir Roger at the fort and he told me to take him in. There'll be no handing him over. Not this time.' She smiled to herself, reached up for something hidden under her blouse. Her face registered a momentary panic at not finding what she was looking for. Then she found it, smiled.

'Mammy . . .' he said.

'You could learn something from Declan,' she said.

Tim knew exactly what she was after. A side of him ached to get down on his knees with her and plead for forgiveness. A side – the stronger side – roared, *I will not!* 'Mammy . . .'

She was waiting.

Tim let her wait.

'There you are, so,' she said.

'You say Sir Roger told you to take this man in? What did he say he'd done?' he asked.

She fussed past him, back to the bathroom door. 'Have a good old soak, Declan!' she called. 'You've all the time in the world!'

Tim felt himself to be a wraith. He fiddled with the old radio, trying unsuccessfully to find Radio Four. He sat by the Stanley boiler waiting to see who would emerge from the bathroom.

A man of about thirty-five came in eventually, wearing a white dressing-gown which Tim fancied had once been his. He hobbled along, being fussed by Brid, and she directed him to the easy chair across the boiler from him. Tim nodded to the stranger.

'How you doing?' he asked.

'Better than I was.'

Brid came in, carrying an enamel bowl that Tim remembered. She had a towel and bandages under her arm. 'Give that stool over here,' she told him.

He reached for the rattan-covered stool and placed it where she had told him. She put one of Declan's feet on it. They were covered in skinned blisters and sores. His bath had not succeeded in cleaning all the dirt away. Then Brid reached for a spray-bottle of Dettox. 'This is going to sting, but it's for your own good, Declan,' she said, and sprayed the disinfectant over his foot. Declan bit his lips, then cried out. This only seemed to make Brid more determined with her trigger-finger. She soaked his foot in the stuff, then started to wipe it dry with the towel. Declan writhed. 'Won't be much longer. On this foot.' She got Tim to help her cut strips of plaster, moithering him when he couldn't get the scissors to cut cleanly, and applied them to Declan's foot.

'I'd say he needs a doctor . . .' Tim said.

Brid took no notice of him. 'Now the other one,' she said.

The shop-bell sounded. Brid took no notice. She was preparing to saturate Declan's other foot.

The door opened. 'Brid,' Boma said, 'what happened to you? Mother and I were worried sick.'

The man turn in his seat at the sound of Boma's voice. They looked at one another. For a split second a smile of welcome passed over Boma's face, only to be replaced by an expression of horror that quickly turned to rage.

'You!' she cried.

Brid chose that moment to squirt the Dettox at Declan's wounds. Unprepared, the disinfectant acted like the choke on a cold engine. Still looking askance at Boma, he moaned. His face took on an expression of terror. 'I thought . . . !' he said.

'What's he doing here?' Boma asked.

'Roddie sent him. He appeared to me,' Brid replied pacifically.

'Did Roddie tell you what he did to me?'

Brid lay the spray-bottle aside. She nodded. 'But he's sorry, Boma. Look, he walked all the way here from Belfast in his bare feet! He's a penitent.'

Declan's face was a picture of doom. He opened and closed his mouth like a beached fish.

Tim looked at Paula but she, like him, had nothing to contribute to the scene in front of them.

Boma turned on her heel and walked out of the room. Paula looked at Brid.

'He's a penitent,' Brid told her, as if it explained everything.

Tim stood, unable to understand. He heard the shop-door bang shut, its bell tinkling as it had every day that he was growing up. He followed Boma.

Outside people were milling about. He could not see where Boma had gone and walked towards the centre of the village with the crowd. He kept staring behind him, knowing that she could well have made off in the Ballyheige direction.

At last he saw her. He grasped her by the arm and she gasped with the shock of his touch.

'What?' he said.

'What? What?' Boma replied, mimicking. 'A joke. A sick joke. That's what.'

'You know Declan?'

Boma stopped stock-still. Ahead of them a beer lorry was unloading barrels onto the pavement. They dropped onto sacking with a tolling metallic sound, like a duty-free shop on a rough sea. The sight seemed to fascinate Boma. She watched the lorry intently.

People were passing. They seemed subdued, not the merry pious crowd seen earlier, on the look-out for miracles.

'Boma?' Tim asked.

She did not turn; merely watched the beer lorry. At last, still watching it, she said, 'Our candles went out.'

'Did they?' he asked her, not knowing they had had candles to light.

She addressed the beer lorry. 'We all thought we were right in the middle of something great. We got to Banna Strand and the candles all went out. Somebody said, "Sir Roger's left us," and I wanted to find out who had said it and smack her. I walked home dreading . . . dreading . . . then I get back to find . . . that horror!'

'I don't understand . . .'

She turned to him. For a moment Tim thought she was expecting him to say something, perhaps something wise. He opened and closed his mouth, but nothing came out. Boma turned away, walking over to the lorry. She climbed into the empty cab.

Tim looked up at her. Paula came and stood next to him. Boma looked straight ahead through the windscreen.

When the driver returned to the lorry, he looked at Boma as if she were an apparition. She said something to him and he started up. The lorry slowly made its way up the street in the Ballyheige direction.

Tim followed the lorry for fifty yards as it made its slow progress up the road, parting the river of pilgrims. Boma was looking out, straight ahead. But then Tim felt a hand on his arm. The touch made him jump. He turned around.

'Are you chasing the beer, the trucker, or both?' Chris asked him.

> *Roger Casement was ready and willing to die, as he said, for the cause of Irish freedom. And indeed it might be said of him that while many have died for their countries and for great causes in all ages, no man has ever in the annals of history done more than he did, by the manner of his dying, to exalt and glorify the country of his love.*
>
> EVA GORE-BOOTH

15

DEAR JIMMY:

Since I know you pant after news, were always pushing it my way when we were with you, I feel duty-bound to bring you up-to-date with everything that has happened since I phoned.

But, having said that, I know that the word wars against the word. Your poor brain is still probably spinning from everything I told you then. You can have had little notion what conundrums were going to ravel before your eyes when you took in the two refugees from the soldered-shut taps of Brannigan's B & B.

Boma did not make good her escape. During the start-and-stop drive to Ballyheige she began experiencing contractions – or whatever it is that women get when babies decide they're tired of the dark. The driver, acting with admirable presence of mind, stopped his lorry and got the Garda to take her to the hospital in Tralee where, some hours later, she was delivered of a not-quite-bouncing, but none the less viable, baby boy. He is to go by the name of Roger David . . . does it ring any bells? The hospital was, fortuitously, operated by the Sisters of the Flaming Heart and Paula, Boma's mother, informed of what was occurring, officiated at the birth.

I don't know what Sir Roger was thinking of in bringing Declan back to join the family. Boma, as I told you, had no time for him at all and, when Mammy turned up at the hospital and insisted that it was *meant* that he be there, she was met with blank looks of incomprehension. She shifted allegiances rather quickly, effectively driving Boma out of the house.

Boma would not give Declan even a look at the baby. Instead, a fellow I knew at school – name of Eamonn McCann – was very much in evidence, bonding with Roger David outside the incubator and then at the foot of Boma's bed. Eamonn has grown up to be a nice enough man, nicer than I am. Shy and retiring when out of costume. Chris and I met up with him later at the museum, where he is coining it as a 'living' Roger Casement. I was pleased to hear that Boma and Eamonn McCann have decided to tie the knot. I was also very interested to hear that Mammy has kept Declan under her wing, though she pushes him out to mass every morning and down on his knees for the rosary every night. When last heard of, he was working for Colm Devlin – the son of the more famous Mags – down the Ballyheige Road, and a very tight rein is kept on him, a rein he does not buck. From what Boma told me of her treatment at his hands, what he is going through with Mammy is probably doing him good. I, however, being of an unforgiving disposition, think he'd be better suited to a cold and uninhabited island off Connacht for the duration.

Since Chris and I got back to London, I have been tying myself in knots trying to make sense of everything that happened. I think I am reconciled to thinking that I never shall. The mystery of it all consoles me strangely. But there is still a stubborn side to me that refuses to believe any of it – though if Sir Roger grants a private boon I asked of him, perhaps I'll relent.

Do you remember the prayer in the litany we used to say – perhaps you still do say it? *From a disorderly passion for knowledge . . . O Lord, deliver us!* I used to think that the plea signified one more rather lumpen attempt by Holy Church to keep our eyes facing the front. But now I think I know what it means and when I look at the bookshelves on my study wall my finger itches to flick my Bic in the direction of those distractions.

Still, I'm a hopeless case, best left to heaven. As I write, Ulster seems to be quietening down. I would like Sir Roger to get the credit for banging heads together, though I doubt they'd be decent enough to admit it. Perhaps that is to be Declan's task in the fullness of time. Unfortunately, the people of Zaïre aren't getting any breaks. They suffer and die even more silently than when Sir Roger was alive which, I suppose, is one of the reasons he was so pissed off with all of us here – there I go again.

I was sorry to have to leave them all in the end. As it was I had to pay a sizeable supplement on the ferry ticket, as our lateness had caused the change from winter to summer rates. Chris and I stayed a couple of nights with Mrs Healey, my old teacher. Then we went off to 'do' Yeats' Country. On the way we passed Croagh Patrick – did you get the card? – and Chris commanded me to stop the car. What I thought was going to be a gentle walk around the mountain's grassy hem turned into an assault on it. We arrived at the top in the late afternoon and a lovely rare clear day it was up there, the hundreds of islands of Clew Bay green and gorgeous. I asked Chris what he thought he was doing; why, in his fragile condition, he had felt the need to exert himself like that. 'Because I had some snakes to expel,' he answered. What were you saying to him while I was away? Did that good doctor give him something?

He did not suffer any ill-effects and we drove on through Mayo to Sligo, where we spent three days touring Yeats' Country and found a b & b at a bungalow in Rathcormack, within sight of the Yeats church at Drumcliff, that rivalled yours for good fellowship. I am happy to report that he has been fine since we got back. We take it a day at a time, of course. He says he is going to go back to Zanzibar and I do not try to dissuade him. I may, if I can pluck up the courage, join him next holiday.

We called in on Ardfert on the way back to the ferry. Mammy was a mite warmer and, just as I was leaving, presented me with a small packet. She said she hoped it would bring me round. 'I know what this is,' I said. 'And I hope you know what it means,' she replied. And that was it. I am wearing it now, living in hope . . . Mammy said that Sister Paula was insisting on a transfer to the Tralee convent. I think the powers that be owe her that. To tell you the truth I thought she might leave the order altogether, but perhaps Boma does not want her on top of her, with only her daughter and young Roger David as her mission in life. And with amends to make, penitence to enact. I can understand how the prospect might have been a bit daunting.

While in Ardfert Boma sent Eamonn McCann – who does not have a car – off with us to dig around on McKenna's Fort. Roddie, she said, had left them a parting gift. We used Chris to pace ten big man's steps off into a field at a one hundred and twenty degree angle to the north-east corner of the fort. And Eamonn started digging in the field. About three feet down he came upon a small metal box. Inside, an old compass – the needle rusted stock-still to its spindle – a gun – but no bullets – and a deal of German gold coins the size of old ten-pence pieces. So now we know how Sir Roger kept himself warm on that Good Friday back in 1916 . . . or that odd few days last April.

You are handier for Ardfert than I am. I have no notion about whether the place has returned to its normal sedate self or if the Sir Roger Casement industry is going from strength to strength. I have my small statue of him on my desk, though it is not a good likeness and the paint is flaking. I should have paid extra for the one that looked like wood. I must say that I rather hope Ardfert remains a place of pilgrimage; that devotion to the man goes from strength to strength. A Sir Roger Casement International Airport would please me immensely.

Yes, I finally got round to telling Chris everything. No, he did not try to get me certified. He took a slug of his duty-free Power's and said, 'Ireland'll do that.' We left it at that.

All the best to Maureen.

God bless you, dear landlord,

Tim (Brid McCarthy's boy)